Darkness Revealed

ALEXANDRA IVY

ZEBRA BOOKS
Kensington Publishing Corp.
http://www.kensingtonbooks.com

ZEBRA BOOKS are published by

Kensington Publishing Corp.
119 West 40th Street
New York, NY 10018

All Kensington titles, imprints, and distributed lines are
available at special quantity discounts for bulk purchases for
sales promotion, premiums, fund-raising, educational, or in-
stitutional use.

Special book excerpts or customized printings can also be
created to fit specific needs. For details, write or phone the
office of the Kensington Special Sales Manager: Attn. Special Sales Department. Kensington Publishing Corp., 119
West 40th Street, New York, NY 10018. Phone: 1-800-221-
2647.

Zebra and the Z logo Reg. U.S. Pat. & TM Off.

ISBN-13: 978-1-4201-3103-1
ISBN-10: 1-4201-3103-6

First Printing: March 2009

10 9 8 7

Printed in the United States of America

Prologue

London, 1814

The ballroom was a startling blaze of color. In the flickering candlelight the satin-and-silk-draped maidens twirled in the arms of dashing gentlemen, the brilliant flare of their jewels making a rainbow of shimmering fireworks that was reflected in the mirrors that were set in the walls.

The elegant pageantry was near breathtaking, but it was not the passing spectacle that caught and held the attention of the numerous guests.

That honor belonged solely to Conde Cezar.

With the amused arrogance that belonged solely to the aristocracy, he moved through the crowd, needing only a lift of his slender hand to have them parting like the Red Sea to clear him a path, or a glance from his smoldering black eyes to send the ladies (and a few gentlemen) into a fluttering frenzy of excitement.

Much to her annoyance, Miss Anna Randal did her own share of fluttering as she caught sight of that faintly golden, exquisitely chiseled profile. Stupid, really, since gentlemen such as the Conde would never lower themselves to take notice of a poor, insignificant maiden who spent her evenings in one dark corner or another.

Such gentlemen did, however, take notice of beautiful, enticing young maidens who would boldly encourage the most hardened reprobate.

Which was the only reason that Anna forced herself to follow in the wake of his lean, elegant form as he left the ballroom and made his way up the sweeping staircase. Being a poor relation meant that she was forced to take on whatever unpleasant task happened to crop up, and on this evening, her unpleasant task included keeping a close eye upon her cousin Morgana, who was clearly fascinated by gentlemen such as the dangerous Conde Cezar.

A fascination that might very well end in scandal for the entire family.

Hurrying to keep the slender male form in sight, Anna impatiently hiked up the cheap muslin of her gown. As she had expected he turned at the top of the stairs and made his way down the corridor that led to the private chambers. Such a rake would never attend something as tedious as a ball without having a nefarious assignation arranged beforehand.

All she need do was ensure that Morgana was not the beneficiary of that nefarious part and Anna could return to her dark corner in the ballroom and watch the other maidens enjoy their evening.

Grimacing at the thought, Anna paused as her quarry slipped through a door and disappeared.

Damnation. Now what? Although she had seen nothing of Morgana, that was no assurance that she was not already hidden in the room awaiting the Conde's arrival.

Cursing her vain, self-centered cousin, who considered nothing beyond her own pleasures, Anna moved forward and carefully pushed open the heavy door. She would just take a quick peek and then . . .

A scream was wrenched from her throat as slender fingers grasped her wrist in a cold, brutal grip, jerking her into the dark room and slamming the door behind her.

Chapter 1

The reception room of the hotel on Michigan Avenue was a blaze of color. In the light of the chandelier Chicago's movers and shakers strutted about like peacocks, occasionally glancing toward the massive fountain in the center of the room where a handful of Hollywood B-list stars were posing for photographs with the guests, for an obscene fee that supposedly went to some charity or another.

The similarity to another evening was not lost on Anna as she once again hovered in a dark corner watching Conde Cezar move arrogantly through the room.

Of course, that other evening had been nearly two hundred years ago. And while she hadn't physically aged a day (which she couldn't deny saved a butt-load on plastic surgery and gym memberships), she wasn't that shy, spineless maiden who had to beg for a few crumbs from her aunt's table. That girl had died the night Conde Cezar had taken her hand and hauled her into a dark bedchamber.

And good riddance to her.

Her life might be all kinds of weird, but Anna had discovered she could take care of herself. In fact, she did a damn fine job of it. She would never go back to being that timid girl who wore shabby muslin gowns (not to mention the corset-from-hell).

That didn't, however, mean she had forgotten that fateful night.

Or Conde Cezar.

He had some explaining to do. Explaining on an epic scale.

Which was the only reason she had traveled to Chicago from her current home in Los Angeles.

Absently sipping the champagne that had been forced into her hand by one of the bare-chested waiters, Anna studied the man who had haunted her dreams.

When she had read in the paper that the Conde would be traveling from Spain to attend this charity event she had known that there was always the possibility the man would be a relative of the Conde she had known in London. The aristocracy was obsessed with sticking their offspring with their own name. As if it weren't enough they had to share DNA.

One glance was enough to guarantee it was no relative.

Mother Nature was too fickle to make such an exact duplicate of those lean, golden features, the dark, smoldering eyes, the to-die-for body . . .

And that hair.

As black as sin, it fell in a smooth river to his shoulders. Tonight he had pulled back the top layer in a gold clasp, leaving the bottom to brush the expensive fabric of his tux.

If there was a woman in the room who wasn't imagining running her fingers through that glossy mane, then Anna would eat her silver-beaded bag. Conde Cezar had only to step into a room for the estrogen to charge into hyperdrive.

A fact that was earning him more than a few I-wish-looks-could-kill glares from the Hollywood pretty boys by the fountain.

Anna muttered a curse beneath her breath. She was allowing herself to be distracted.

Okay, the man looked like some conquering conquistador. And those dark eyes held a sultry heat that could melt steel at a hundred paces. But she had already paid the price for being blinded by the luscious dark beauty.

It wasn't happening again.

Busily convincing herself that the tingles in the pit of her stomach were nothing more than expensive champagne bubbles, Anna stiffened as the unmistakable scent of apples filled the air.

Before she ever turned she knew who it would be. The only question was . . . why?

"Well, well. If it isn't Anna the Good Samaritan," Sybil Taylor drawled, her sweet smile edged with spite. "And at one of those charity events you claim are nothing more than an opportunity for the A-listers to preen for the paparazzi. I knew that holier-than-thou attitude was nothing more than a sham."

Anna didn't gag, but it was a near thing.

Despite the fact that both women lived in L.A. and they were both lawyers, they couldn't have been more opposite.

Sybil was a tall, curvaceous brunette with pale skin and large brown eyes. Anna on the other hand barely skimmed the five-foot mark and had brown hair and hazel eyes. Sybil was a corporate lawyer who possessed the morals of a . . . well, actually she didn't possess the morals of anything. She had no morals. Anna, on the other hand, worked at a free law clinic that battled corporate greed on a daily basis.

"Obviously I should have studied the guest list a bit more carefully," Anna retorted, caught off guard, but not entirely surprised by the sight of the woman. Sybil Taylor possessed a talent for rubbing elbows with the rich and famous, wherever they might be.

"Oh, I would say that you studied the guest list as closely as every other woman in the room." Sybil deliberately glanced across the room to where the Conde Cezar toyed with a heavy gold signet ring on his little finger. "Who is he?"

For a heartbeat, Anna battled the urge to slap that pale, perfect face. Almost as if she resented the woman's interest in the Conde.

Stupid, Anna. But she had already paid.

Stupid and dangerous.

"Conde Cezar," she muttered.

Sybil licked her lips that were too full to be real. Of course, there wasn't much about Sybil Taylor that was real.

"Euro trash or the real deal?" the woman demanded.

Anna shrugged. "As far as I know, the title is real enough."

"He is . . . edible." Sybil ran her hands down the little black dress that made a valiant effort to cover her considerable curves. "Married?"

"I haven't a clue."

"Hmmmm. Gucci tux, Rolex watch, Italian leather shoes." She tapped a manicured nail against too-perfect teeth. "Gay?"

Anna had to remind her heart to beat. "Most definitely not."

"Ah . . . I smell a history between the two of you. Do tell."

Against her will Anna's gaze strayed toward the tall, dark, thorn in her side.

"You couldn't begin to imagine the history we share, Sybil."

"Maybe not, but I can imagine all that dark, yummy goodness handcuffed to my bed while I have my way with him."

"Handcuffs?" Anna swallowed a nervous laugh, instinctively tightening her grip on her bag. "I always wondered how you managed to keep a man in your bed."

The dark eyes narrowed. "There hasn't been a man born who isn't desperate to have a taste of this body."

"Desperate for a taste of that overused, silicone-implanted, Botox-injected body? A man could buy an inflatable doll with less plastic than you."

"Why you . . ." The woman gave a hiss. An honest-to-God hiss. "Stay out of my way, Anna Randal, or you will be nothing more than an oily spot on the bottom of my Pradas."

Anna knew if she were a better person she would warn Sybil that Conde Cezar was something other than a wealthy, gorgeous aristocrat. That he was powerful and dangerous and something that wasn't even human.

Thankfully, even after two centuries, she was still capable of being as petty as the next woman. A smile touched her lips as she watched Sybil sashay across the room.

Cezar had felt her presence long before he'd entered the reception room. He'd known the moment she had landed at O'Hare. The awareness of her tingled and shimmered within every inch of him.

It would have been annoying as hell if it didn't feel so damn good.

Growling low in his throat at the sensations that were directly connected to Miss Anna Randal, Cezar turned his head to glare at the approaching brunette. Not surprisingly the woman turned on her heel and headed in the opposite direction.

Tonight his attention was focused entirely on the woman standing in the corner. The way the light played over the satin honey of her hair, the flecks of gold in her hazel eyes, the silver gown that displayed way too much of the slender body.

Besides, he didn't like fairies.

There was a faint movement from behind him and Cezar turned to find a tall, raven-haired vampire appearing from the shadows. A neat trick considering he was a six-foot-five Aztec warrior who was draped in a cloak and leather boots. Being the Anasso (the leader of all vampires) did have its benefits.

"Styx." Cezar gave a dip of his head, not at all surprised to find that the vampire had followed him to the hotel.

Since Cezar had arrived in Chicago along with the Commission, Styx had been hovering about him like a mother hen. It was obvious the ancient leader didn't like one of his vampires being in the control of the Oracles. He liked it even less that Cezar had refused to confess the sins that had landed him near two centuries of penance at the hands of the Commission.

"Tell me again why I am not at home in the arms of my

beautiful mate?" Styx groused, completely disregarding the fact that Cezar hadn't invited him along.

"It was your decision to call for the Oracles to travel to Chicago," he reminded the older demon.

"Yes, to make a ruling upon Salvatore's intrusion into Viper's territory, not to mention kidnapping my bride. A ruling that has been postponed indefinitely. I did not realize that they intended to take command of my lair and go into hibernation once they arrived." The fierce features hardened. Styx was still brooding on the Oracles' insistence that he leave his dark and damp caves so they could use them for their own secretive purposes. His mate, Darcy, however, seemed resigned to the large, sweeping mansion they had moved into on the edge of Chicago. "And I most certainly did not realize they would be treating one of my brothers as their minion."

"You do realize that while you may be lord and master of all vampires, the Oracles answer to no one?"

Styx muttered something beneath his breath. Something about Oracles and the pits of hell.

"You have never told me precisely how you ended up in their clutches."

"It's not a story I share with anyone."

"Not even the vampire who once rescued you from a nest of harpies?"

Cezar gave a short laugh. "I never requested to be rescued, my lord. Indeed, I was quite happy to remain in their evil clutches. At least as long as mating season lasted."

Styx rolled his eyes. "We are straying from the point."

"And what is the point?"

"Tell me why we are here." Styx glanced around the glittering throng with a hint of distaste. "As far as I can determine the guests are no more than simple humans with a few lesser demons and fey among the rabble."

"Yes." Cesar considered the guests with a narrowed gaze. "A surprising number of fey, wouldn't you say?"

"They always tend to gather when there's the scent of money in the air."

"Perhaps."

Without warning, Cezar felt a hand land on his shoulder, bringing his attention back to the increasingly frustrated vampire at his side. Obviously Styx was coming to the end of his patience with Cezar's evasions.

"Cezar, I have dared the wrath of the Oracles before. I will have you strung from the rafters unless you tell me why you are here wading through this miserable collection of lust and greed."

Cezar grimaced. For the moment Styx was merely irritated. The moment he became truly mad all sorts of bad things would happen.

The last thing he needed was a rampaging vampire scaring off his prey.

"I am charged with keeping an eye upon a potential Commission member," he grudgingly confessed.

"Potential . . ." Styx stiffened. "By the gods, a new Oracle has been discovered?"

The elder vampire's shock was understandable. Less than a dozen Oracles had been discovered in the past ten millenniums. They were the rarest, most priceless creatures to walk the earth.

"She was revealed in the prophecies nearly two hundred years ago, but the information has been kept secret among the Commission."

"Why?"

"She is very young and has yet to come into her powers. It was decided by the Commission that they would wait to approach her until she had matured and accepted her abilities."

"Ah, that I understand. A young lady coming into her powers is a painful business at times." Styx rubbed his side as if he was recalling a recent wound. "A wise man learns to be on guard at all times."

Cezar gave a lift of his brows. "I thought Darcy had been bred not to shift?"

"Shifting is only a small measure of a werewolf's powers."

"Only the Anasso would choose a werewolf as his mate."

The fierce features softened. "Actually it was not so much a choice as fate. As you will eventually discover."

"Not so long as I am in the rule of the Commission," Cezar retorted, his cold tone warning that he wouldn't be pressed.

Styx eyed him a long moment before giving a small nod. "So if this potential Commission member is not yet prepared to become an Oracle, why are you here?"

Instinctively Cezar glanced back at Anna. Unnecessary, of course. He was aware of her every movement, her every breath, her every heartbeat.

"Over the past few years there have been a number of spells that we believe were aimed in her direction."

"What sort of spells?"

"The magic was fey, but the Oracles were unable to determine more than that."

"Strange. Fey creatures rarely concern themselves with demon politics. What is their interest?"

"Who can say? For now the Commission is only concerned with keeping the woman from harm." Cezar gave a faint shrug. "When you requested their presence in Chicago they charged me with the task of luring her here so I can offer protection."

Styx scowled, making one human waiter faint and another bolt toward the nearest exit. "Fine, the girl is special. Why should you be the one forced to protect her?"

A shudder swept through Cezar. One he was careful to hide from the heightened senses of his companion.

"You doubt my abilities, my lord?"

"Don't be an ass, Cezar. There is no one who has seen you in a fight that would doubt your abilities." With the ease of two friends who had known each other for centuries, Styx glanced at the perfect line of Cezar's tux jacket. They both knew that beneath the elegance were half a dozen daggers. "I have seen you slice your way through a pack of Ipar demons without losing a step. But there are those on the Commission who possess powers that none would dare to oppose."

"Mine is not to question why, mine is but to do and die . . ."

"You will not be dying." Styx sliced through Cezar's mocking words.

Cezar shrugged. "Not even the Anasso can make such a claim."

"Actually I just did."

"You always were too noble for your own good, Styx."

"True."

Awareness feathered over Cezar's skin. Anna was headed toward a side door of the reception room.

"Go home, *amigo*. Be with your beautiful werewolf."

"A tempting offer, but I will not leave you here alone."

"I appreciate your concern, Styx." Cezar sent his master a warning glance. "But my duty now is to the Commission and they have given me orders I cannot ignore."

A cold anger burned in Styx's dark eyes before he gave a grudging nod.

"You will contact me if you have need?"

"Of course."

Anna didn't have to look at Conde Cezar to know that he was aware of her every movement. He might be speaking to the gorgeous man who looked remarkably like an Aztec chief, but her entire body shivered with the sense of his unwavering attention.

It was time to put her plan into motion.

Her hastily thrown together, fly-by-the-seat-of-her-pants, stupidest-plan-ever plan.

Anna swallowed a hysterical laugh.

So, it wasn't the best plan. It was more a click-your-heels-twice-and-pray-things-didn't-go-to-hell sort of deal, but it was all that she had for the moment. And the alternative was allowing Conde Cezar to disappear for another two centuries, leaving her plagued with questions.

She couldn't stand it.

Nearly reaching the alcove that led to a bank of elevators, Anna was halted by an arm suddenly encircling her waist and hauling her back against a steely male body.

"You haven't changed a bit, *querida*. Still as beautiful as the night I first caught sight of you." His fingers trailed a path of seduction along the bare line of her shoulder. "Although there is a great deal more on display."

An explosion of sensations rocked through Anna's body at his touch. Sensations that she hadn't felt in a long, long time.

"You obviously haven't changed either, Conde. You still don't know how to keep your hands to yourself."

"Life is barely worth living when I'm keeping my hands to myself." The cool skin of his cheek brushed hers as he whispered in her ear. "Trust me, I know."

Anna rolled her eyes. "Yeah, right."

The long, slender fingers briefly tightened on her waist before he slowly turned her to meet his dark, disturbing gaze.

"It's been a long time, Anna Randal."

"One hundred and ninety-five years." Her hand absently lifted to rub the skin that still tingled from his touch. "Not that I'm counting."

The full, sensuous lips twitched. "No, of course not."

Her chin tilted. *Jackass.* "Where have you been?"

"Did you miss me?"

"Don't flatter yourself."

"Still a little liar," he taunted. With a deliberate motion his gaze skimmed over her stiff body, lingering on the silver gauze draped over the swell of her breasts. "Would it make it easier if I confess that I've missed you? Even after one hundred and ninety-five years, I remember the precise scent of your skin, the feel of your slender body, the taste of your . . ."

"Blood?" she hissed, refusing to acknowledge the heat that stirred low in her stomach.

No, no, no. Not this time.

"But of course." There wasn't a hint of remorse on his beautiful face. "I remember that most of all. So sweet, so deliciously innocent."

"Keep your voice down," she commanded.

"Don't worry." He stepped even closer. So close that the fabric of his slacks brushed her bare legs. "The mortals can't hear me, and the fey know better than to interfere with a vampire on the hunt."

Anna gasped, her eyes wide. "Vampire. I knew it. I . . ." She pressed her hands to her heaving stomach as she glanced around the crowded room. She couldn't forget her plan. "I want to talk to you, but not here. I have a room in the hotel."

"Why, Miss Randal, are you inviting me to your room?" The dark eyes held a mocking amusement. "What sort of demon do you think I am?"

"I want to talk, nothing else."

"Of course." He smiled. That smile that made a woman's toes curl in her spike heels.

"I mean it. I . . ." She cut off her words and gave a shake of her head. "Never mind. Will you come with me?"

The dark eyes narrowed. Almost as if he sensed she was attempting to lead him away from the crowd.

"I haven't decided. You haven't given me much incentive to leave a room filled with beautiful women who are interested in sharing a lot more than conversation."

Her brows lifted. She wasn't the easy mark he remembered. She was a woman—hear her roar.

Especially if he had even a random thought of ditching her for someone else.

"I doubt they'd be so interested if they knew you are hiding a monster beneath all that handsome elegance. Push me far enough and I'll tell them."

His fingers lightly skimmed up the length of her arms. "Half the guests are monsters themselves and the other half would never believe you."

A shiver shook her entire body. How could a touch so cold send such heat through her blood?

"There are other vampires here?"

"One or two. The others are fey."

She briefly recalled his mention of fey before. "Fey?"

"Fairies, imps, a few sprites."

"This is insanity," she breathed, shaking her head as she was forced to accept one more crazy thing in her crazy existence. "And it's all your fault."

"My fault?" He lifted a brow. "I didn't create the fey and I certainly didn't invite them to this party. For all their beauty they're treacherous and cunning with a nasty sense of humor. Of course, their blood does have a certain sparkle to it. Like champagne."

She pointed a finger directly at his nose. "It's your fault that you bit me."

"I suppose I can't deny that."

"Which means you're the one responsible for screwing up my life."

"I did nothing more than take a few sips of blood and your . . ."

She slapped her hand across his mouth. "Don't you dare," she hissed, glaring at an approaching waiter. "Dammit, I'm not going to discuss this here."

He gave a soft chuckle as his fingers stroked over her shoulders. "You'll do anything to get me to your room, won't you, *querida?*"

Her breath lodged in her throat as she took a hasty step back. Damn him and his heart-stopping touches. "You really are a total ass."

"It runs in the family."

Family? Anna turned her head to regard the large, flat-out

spectacular man who scowled at them from across the room. "Is he a part of your family?"

An unreadable emotion rippled over the chiseled, faintly golden features. "You could say he's something of a father figure."

"He doesn't look like a father." Anna deliberately flashed a smile toward the stranger. "In fact, he's gorgeous. Maybe you should introduce us."

The dark eyes narrowed, his fingers grasping her arm in a firm grip.

"Actually, we were just headed to your room, don't you remember?" he growled close to her ear.

A faint smile touched Anna's mouth. Ha. He didn't like having her interested in another man. Served him right.

Her smile faded as the scent of apples filled the air.

"Anna . . . oh, Anna," a saccharine voice cooed.

"Crap," she muttered, watching Sybil bear down upon them with the force of a locomotive.

Cezar wrapped an arm around her shoulder. "A friend of yours?"

"Hardly. Sybil Taylor has been a pain in the freaking neck for the past five years. I can't turn around without stumbling over her."

Cezar stiffened, studying her with a strange curiosity. "Really? What sort of business do you have with a fairy?"

"A . . . what? No." Anna shook her head. "Sybil's a lawyer. A bottom-feeder, I'll grant you, but . . ." Her words were cut off as the Conde hauled her through the alcove and with a wave of his hand opened the elevator doors. Anna might have marveled at having an elevator when she needed one if she hadn't been struggling to stay on her feet as she was pulled into the cubical (that was as large as her L.A. apartment) and the doors were smoothly sliding shut. "Freaking hell. There's no need to drag me around like a sack of potatoes, Conde."

"I think we're past formality, *querida*. You can call me Cezar."

"Cezar." She frowned, pushing the button to her floor. "Don't you have a first name?"

"No."

"That's weird."

"Not for my people." The elevator opened and Cezar pulled her into the circular hallway that had doors to the private rooms on one side and an open view to the lobby twelve stories below on the other. "Your room?"

"This way."

Anna moved down the hall and stopped in front of her door. She already had her cardkey in the slot when she stilled, abruptly struck by another night she attempted to best Conde Cezar.

The night her entire life had changed . . .

Chapter 2

London, 1814

Anna gave a small scream as she was jerked into the dark bedchamber and the door slammed behind her.

"Do you seek something, *querida?*" A soft voice drifted on the night air. An accented voice that sent a strange shiver over her skin. "Or is it someone?"

"Conde Cezar?"

"Yes, it is I."

Anna stumbled back into the wall, cursing her damnable luck. How the devil had she managed to muck up something so simple as keeping track of her cousin?

Not only did she not know where Morgana had gone, but she had managed to get caught by the one man who disturbed her in a manner she could not entirely comprehend.

"You . . . you frightened me. I did not realize anyone was here."

"No?" A candle blazed to life, revealing the dark, impossibly handsome gentleman as he moved to stand directly before her. "Then you did not deliberately follow me here from the ballroom?"

A flush stained her cheeks, as much from his proximity as

from embarrassment. Despite nearing her six-and-twentieth birthday she had yet to have a gentleman pay her attention. And certainly none at such proximity.

It was . . .

Terrifyingly wonderful.

She sternly jerked her thoughts from such dangerous matters. "Of course not. I . . . I was searching for a maid to help mend a tear in my hem."

"So you are a liar as well as a sneak." *Without warning he planted his hands on the wall, one on each side of her head, effectively trapping her.* "Hardly attractive qualities in a young maiden. Tis no wonder you find yourself alone in dark corners while the other ladies have their pleasure in the arms of handsome suitors."

She sucked in a sharp breath, wishing she had not when her senses became clouded by his sandalwood scent.

"How dare you?"

He chuckled softly and then brazenly lowered his head to brush his cheek over hers. "Quite easily."

Dear heaven above. Anna shuddered as her entire body reacted to his touch. What was happening to her? Why did her lower stomach feel as if it were filled with butterflies? And why was her heart lurching against her ribs as if it wanted to leave her chest entirely?

"I am no liar."

His lips touched a place just below her ear. "Then admit that you followed me."

Something that might have been a whimper escaped her lips before she gathered what remained of her shattered composure.

"Fine. I followed you."

He continued to nuzzle at her throat, almost as if he was tasting of her.

"Why?"

Anna struggled to think. "Because my aunt charged me to

keep an eye upon my cousin, and when I noticed you slipping from the ballroom just moments after she claimed to be in need of the withdrawing room, I feared that the two of you had arranged a meeting." Her lids slid downward as he discovered a particularly sensitive spot. Then, realizing his hands had left the wall to tug at the ribbons on the back of her gown, she forced herself to stiffen in protest. "And for your information, I remain in the dark corners because that is what is expected of poor relations."

"Ah, so the mouse has teeth," he mocked, giving her a light nip.

Anna gripped her skirts. It was that or grip the man who was tormenting her with those tiny, relentless kisses.

"I am no mouse."

"No, you are quite right." He pulled back to study her flushed countenance, his fingers tugging at the bodice of her gown to reveal the tight corset beneath. "You, querida, are far more a shrew."

Anna was oblivious to the insult. Hardly surprising. She was alone in a bedchamber with a strange man, half naked, and while her mind was telling her to be terrified, her body was shivering as if she were wracked with fever.

For the first time in her life she was being seduced by a master. And she was helpless against the rising tide of passion.

"It is obvious that Morgana is not here," she husked. "I must return to the ballroom."

"You fear that your absence might be noted? That you might have rescued your cousin's reputation only to sacrifice your own?"

"There is no one to notice if I am missing or not."

Something dark and powerful stirred in the dark eyes. "Dangerous words," he whispered.

Anna gave a strangled cry as her gown drifted to the floor and he reached to pluck the lace cap from her head.

"My lord. Stop that."

He groaned as her hair tumbled down her back, his fingers running a restless path through the thick strands.

"Such beautiful hair when it is not being hidden under that ugly cap. The color of freshly spun honey." He pulled on her curls, drawing her head backwards so he could bury his face in the curve of her neck. "You smell of sweet figs. What do you taste of?"

"My God," she whispered as he once again wrapped his arms around her and she felt her corset being jerked off her body, followed swiftly by her thin shift. In the blink of an eye she was wearing nothing more than her stockings and heels.

"You should not have followed me, Anna. I had another who was to be my willing sacrifice, so eager to feed my needs. But you have intruded upon the game and now you must pay the penalty."

"No." Her hands lifted to push against his chest. Or at least she intended to push. It was not her fault if they instead slipped beneath his coat to stroke over the fine linen of his shirt. "Let me go, or . . ."

He nuzzled down her collarbone and over the swell of her breasts. "Or what, my beautiful prey?"

Good Lord, she could not think past the potent pleasure that was swirling and shimmering through her body. In truth, she didn't want to think past the pleasure. She wanted to drown in his touch, in the sensation of his lips suckling gently on her hard nipple, in the sandalwood scent that made her knees weak and her palms sweat.

"I . . . I swear I will scream," she muttered.

He chuckled at her absurd threat. As well he should. After all, she was ripping at his shirt to feel the perfectly smooth skin beneath.

"I do not think you will scream, *querida.*" With a smooth motion he lifted her off her feet and wrapped her legs around his waist. His dark eyes smoldered with a wicked amusement. "Not unless it happens to be in pleasure."

"Oh . . ." she breathed.

He stilled, one hand lifting to cup her face. "You are mine, Anna Randal. From this night forward you will belong to me."

Anna sucked in a terrified breath as she watched his teeth lengthen into fangs. Dear Lord he was going to . . .

Her thoughts scattered as his head lowered and she felt his fangs slide easily through her skin. There was no pain. Nothing but a heady, near overwhelming need that made her writhe against him.

"Please . . ." she moaned, her fingers stroking through his dark hair as she begged him to put her out of her misery. "Please."

"Si," he whispered, pressing her back against the wall as he positioned her and then slowly, blissfully pressed his cock deep into her aching body. With a strangled gasp he rocked his hips upward, his fingers gripping her hips so tightly she knew he would leave bruises on her fragile skin.

But that was a worry for tomorrow.

Tonight nothing mattered but the delicious invasion that was Conde Cezar.

Cezar didn't need to be a vampire to sense the tension that hummed about Anna's delicate body or to suspect that she was deliberately luring him to her hotel room for a purpose other than a bit of up-close-and-personal time.

Not that he wouldn't mind the up-close part.

It had been one hundred and ninety-five years since his body had reacted to a woman. Not since he had taken this woman's innocence and the Oracles had arrived to sweep him away from London.

Now he groaned with the effort not to reach out and touch that soft satin skin. To taste the delectable, fresh blood that flowed through her veins. To drown in that . . .

As if suddenly sensing the hunger that raged through his

body, Anna unlocked the door and swiftly stepped over the threshold. Turning to face him, she made a valiant effort to appear casual.

An effort that was ruined by the pulse fluttering like a butterfly on amphetamines at the base of her throat. Not to mention that she was clutching her silver handbag as if it held the crown jewels.

Or maybe a wooden stake.

"Are you coming in?" she demanded, then she bit her bottom lip. "Oh, do you need an invitation?"

He leaned his shoulder against the doorjamb and folded his arms over his chest.

"Not for a hotel room. I'm just the naturally cautious type."

"Aren't you immortal?"

"Immortal in the sense that I can't die of disease or old age, but a vampire can be killed."

"How?"

He laughed softly. "You can't expect me to answer that question."

"Why not?"

"That would fall under the category of being naturally cautious."

"Fine." The hazel eyes flashed with annoyance before she turned and walked toward the center of the hotel room. Then with the skill of a trained courtesan, Anna bent over to offer a stunning, gut-wrenching view of her perfect butt. "If you want to stand in the hallway all night, knock yourself out. I want to get out of these demon-spawned heels. They've been pinching my toes all night."

"Damn . . ." It was the most obvious bait that had ever been thrown in Cezar's path. She might as well have a flashing neon sign. Cezar, however, was a vampire who had been denied the pleasure of desire for nearly two centuries. He'd dare any trap, take any risk for a taste of this woman. "Now that's a temptation I can't resist," he murmured, stepping into the room and closing the door.

At the sound of the lock settling into place, Anna whirled with astonishing speed. Cezar saw the glint of silver as she lunged toward him with a pair of silver handcuffs. He could have avoided the cuffs as they snapped around his wrists. One swing of his arm could have launched her and her damnable torture devices across the room.

Instead he allowed her to believe she had managed to confine him in her devilish coils. The cuffs burned like a bitch, but they hadn't been crafted specifically to hold a vampire and there were enough other metals mixed in with the silver to mute its effect. Besides, his tolerance for silver was higher than most vampires. He could free himself if necessary. And if it made Anna feel more comfortable . . . well, he would play along.

For now.

Planting her hands on her hips, Anna regarded him with a smug smile. "Ha."

"Ha?" Cezar gave a mocking lift of his brows. "You sound like a villain in a cheesy melodrama. Do you intend to throw me onto the nearest railroad tracks while I scream for help?"

"What I intend is to get some answers that are long overdue."

"There's no need to lock me up. Granted it might be fun under the right circumstances, but surely we can sit down and have a rational conversation like normal, non-crazy people?"

"But we're not normal, are we, Cezar?"

"Speak for yourself, *querida.*" He gave a hiss as the cuffs shifted on his wrists.

She tried to remain in her Rambo mode, but Cezar didn't miss her small wince. Even two centuries hadn't managed to harden that far too tender heart.

"Does it hurt?" she demanded.

Cezar held up his wrists to reveal the blisters that were already marring his skin.

"It's burning my flesh, what do you think?"

She bit her bottom lip. "Tell me what you've done to me and I'll release you."

"Anna, I've done nothing to you."

"I know I'm not a vampire, but obviously your bite turned me into something . . ." Her words trailed away as she lifted her hand and pressed it to her neck.

The precise spot he'd taken her blood all those years ago, he realized with a flare of possessive pleasure. "Something?"

"Something weird." She glared, holding him entirely responsible for her weirdness. "Tell me what's wrong with me."

"At the risk of pointing out the obvious, there's nothing at all wrong with you, *querida*. In fact, you're nothing less than perfection." He lifted his cuffed hands. "Well, except for this handcuff fetish of yours. Next time we go with leather and whips."

"Don't lie to me, Cezar. Something happened that night." A shudder wracked her tiny body. "Everything . . . changed."

Cezar smiled at the doom in her voice. Anyone would think that discovering she was immortal was some hideous fate rather than an astonishing stroke of fortune.

"What changed?"

The gold flecks smoldered as she pointed a finger in his face. "Damn you, this isn't funny."

"Anna, I'm not teasing you," he soothed. "Tell me what happened after I left you that night."

She wrapped her arms around her waist, as if suddenly cold. "After we . . ."

"Made love?" he prompted as her words faltered.

"After we had sex," she corrected. "I fell asleep and didn't wake up until almost dawn. I had no choice but to sneak out through the window and return to my aunt's house. When I got there it . . ."

Once again her words broke off, but this time it was an ancient pain, not embarrassment, that held her in its grip.

"What, Anna?" he said softly, not bothering to try to enthrall her. As a budding Oracle she would be impervious to such mind tricks. "Tell me."

"The house had been burnt to the ground." She at last forced the words past her stiff lips. "Along with my only family trapped inside it. I was left on my own with nowhere to go and no one to turn to."

"*Dios*. How did it happen?"

"I have no idea."

He scowled at the realization that the Oracles had deliberately kept her troubles secret from him. If they had not interfered he would have sensed her need. "What did you do?"

She gave a shake of her head, her honey hair brushing over her bare shoulders and filling the air with her exquisite scent. Cezar quivered, his fangs aching for a taste. The only reason he resisted temptation was the memory of what had happened the last time he had taken blood from this woman.

He might not be the smartest vampire ever made, but he occasionally learned from his mistakes.

"I took the coward's way out." Anna's voice was bitter as she became lost in her memories. "I hid in the bushes and allowed everyone to believe that I had died along with my aunt and cousin."

"Why?"

"Because I was afraid."

"Afraid of what?" he prodded, genuinely curious. The Oracles were rarely forthcoming, and while they had revealed that this woman was born to join their ranks, they had yet to explain exactly what she was.

She couldn't be human. Her immortality proved that. And he could detect no demon blood running through her veins. Added to the fact that she didn't seem to have a clue about her powers, it left nothing but a gaping question.

A question he intended to find the answer to before she was taken by the Commission.

"I don't know." A pretty frown tugged at her brows. "It was

as if a voice was whispering in the back of my mind to flee. It seems ridiculous now, but at the time I was convinced that if I stepped from the bushes I would be dead."

Premonition? A natural ability to sense danger? Dumb, blind luck? *Dios*. The list was endless.

He met and held her gaze. "It's not ridiculous at all, Anna."

"Of course, at the time I didn't realize you had made me into some freak of nature that couldn't die."

He chuckled at her sour expression. "I didn't make you immortal, *querida*. My only means of doing so would be to turn you into a vampire, and since I can see every lovely inch of you in the mirror and you have what I can only describe as a delightful tan, it's obvious that you are still very non-vampirish."

Anna wasn't satisfied. She clearly wanted someone to blame. And that someone was Cezar. "Then you put a spell on me."

"Vampires can't cast magic."

"Then . . ."

Tired of being the scapegoat, Cezar took a step forward. They were alone in a hotel room and he didn't want to waste time being the enemy.

Not when she could be easing the vast, roaring hunger that had returned after nearly two centuries.

"Anna, your immortality has nothing to do with my bite or with any spell." His voice thickened with need. "You were born special."

"Special?" She took an instinctive step back as if sensing his dark need. "Being able to bake a soufflé that actually rises is special. Being able to sing the "Star-Spangled Banner" in key is special. Being able to pass through airport security without setting off the metal detector is special. I'm a little more than freaking special." Without warning she stiffened, her head turning toward the door. "Shit."

Cezar was on instant alert. "What is it?"

"Do you smell that?"

Cezar closed his eyes and sensed the air. It was very faint, but unmistakable. "Smoke." The word was a curse on his tongue. Vampires and fire didn't mix. "We must get out of here," he commanded, holding out his arms that were still shackled. He could free himself but he preferred to keep that little tidbit of knowledge to himself. "Anna, release me or we both will die."

She muttered a handful of curses as she reached out and slipped the key into the handcuff. They fell to the floor with a thump.

"There."

Cezar absently rubbed his blistered wrists as he allowed his powers to flow outward. His fangs lengthened as he realized that the fire was not only near, but magical in nature.

This was a deliberate attack on Anna.

"The fire is just outside the door," he warned, moving instinctively to scoop her slender body in his arms. The Oracles had charged him with protecting this woman, but even if they hadn't he would have walked through the pits of hell to keep her safe.

They had unfinished business.

Business that even now was making him hard and desperate to be inside her.

"Stop." She beat her tiny fist against his chest. As if that could possibly hurt him. "What are you doing?"

He willed the window open as he dashed across the room. "Getting us out of here. Unless you prefer to remain and sacrifice that beautiful skin to the flames?"

"The water sprinklers will put it out."

"Not this fire. It's magical, which explains why I didn't sense it the moment it was started."

"A magical fire? For God's sake . . ." Her words became a shrill scream as Cezar launched them through the window and they fell toward Michigan Avenue. With a skill only an ancient vampire could manage, he landed easily on his feet, still cradling her closely in his arms. He was rewarded with another blow to his chest. "Damn you," Anna hissed. "You scared the hell out me."

He lowered his head to speak directly in her ear. "Would you have preferred to remain to face the flames?"

She tugged at the hem of her gown, which had inched up to reveal a tiny pink thong. Cezar's erection twitched in silent tribute.

Soon, soon, soon . . .

"I would prefer that you warn me before you leap from a twelve-story building," she muttered.

He laughed, his body tingling with pleasure. *Mi dios.* It had been so long since he had felt emotions. So long since he hadn't been trapped in his cold existence.

"Next time, I promise," he husked, trailing his lips down her warm cheek.

She arched away from his touch. Her mute protest, however, couldn't disguise the passion that perfumed her skin. Ah, hormones. They were a wonderful thing.

"There won't be a next time." She reinforced her claim with yet another punch to his chest. "I don't need you or anyone else to save me."

He touched his tongue to the frantic pulse that beat at the base of her throat. "You've changed, my little shrew."

"I didn't have much choice."

His arms instinctively tightened. Damn the Oracles. They had called him away just when this vulnerable woman had needed him the most.

"No, I suppose you didn't." His touch became soothing as he stroked his lips along her collarbone, silently absorbing her intoxicating scent. It was at last the distant sound of sirens that forced Cezar to lift his head. "We need to leave here before it is discovered that you are no longer in your room."

"Wait . . ."

He ignored her protest as he bolted down the nearly empty street. It wouldn't be empty for long. Humans had a weird obsession with disasters. And a fire burning in a historic hotel filled with the elite of Chicago society would certainly qualify as a disaster.

Well, at least to some.

"Sorry, *querida*, but I don't have time to argue."

She struggled in his grasp. "Put me down."

"Not until we're away from here. Someone wants you dead and I don't intend to give them the satisfaction."

She stilled, as if startled by his blunt words. "Why?"

"Why what?"

"Why do you care if I'm alive or dead?"

He glanced down at her wary hazel eyes, a jolt of pure male possession racing through him. "I told you one hundred and ninety-five years ago that you belong to me, Anna Randal," he growled. "No one is allowed to harm you."

Chapter 3

Fury roared through Anna. Damn the arrogant vampire. She had come to Chicago with a plan. Okay, not a good plan, but one that was supposed to trap Conde Cezar and get her the answers she deserved.

Instead she very much suspected that she had once again been played by this man.

If there was a trap she was the one who had fallen for the damn lure. And for her trouble she had been nearly burned to death in her hotel room without one answer to show for it.

God, she had been a fool to ever come here.

Nothing good ever happened when Cezar strolled into her life.

He was like her own personal kryptonite.

Only cuter. With the sort of sex appeal that set her body on fire and made her think of being pressed to the nearest wall and feeling his large, hard . . .

No, Anna, no.

He was bad news.

And until he gave her a few answers there would be no hot, sweaty, delicious sex.

Stirring up the embers of her anger, Anna concentrated on the hard, male body that was carrying her with such aggravating ease. She had warned Cezar she was no longer the weak, innocent woman he had known in the past. It was time to prove her words were more than hot air.

"Stop," she commanded, forming the image of Cezar trapped in molasses. Thick, sticky, gooey molasses. "I said to stop now."

Cezar's steps began to falter, his beautiful eyes widening in shock as the air congealed and wrapped around his body, forcing him to a halt.

"*Infierno,*" he muttered, regarding her with a satisfying wariness. Ha. That would teach the arrogant ass. "I have stopped, *querida*, release the bonds."

"Do you promise to stop pushing and hauling me around whenever you want me to do something?"

"I . . ." He hissed in obvious pain. "Anna, you must release your power. My ribs are already fractured."

Her smug pleasure at having bested the vampire evaporated beneath his agonized gaze. Oh . . . shit. She had been so busy showing off that she hadn't really considered the consequences.

Just how long was it until dawn?

"I'm not sure I can," she at last confessed. "I don't exactly know how I do it."

Half expecting him to shake her senseless, or at least flash those fangs he kept so carefully hidden, Anna was caught off guard when he did no more than gaze deep into her eyes.

"Just concentrate," he murmured.

"Concentrate on what?"

"Relax your mind." His head lowered so he could whisper directly into her ear. "Shhh . . . just relax. Just let it all go. That's it, Anna."

His soft words poured through her body like warm honey, easing her fears and making her feel as if she were floating. She allowed her senses to seek out the invisible bonds, attempting to make them form in her mind. For a moment there was nothing and then, without warning, they appeared like steel bands in her imagination. Cezar gave another pained groan as they ruthlessly crushed his body. Crap. With a surge of panic she forced herself to shatter them with her thoughts.

There was a soft groan before she found herself being set roughly onto her feet. About her, the early spring breeze returned to whipping happily down the street, seemingly as delighted as Cezar to be released from her control.

Gaining her balance, Anna watched as Cezar pressed a hand to his chest.

She bit her lip. "Are you badly hurt?"

"I'll recover."

"I told you to stop."

"So you did." With a grimace Cezar lowered his hand. "Styx warned me that a woman coming into her powers is a dangerous thing. Next time I'll pay more attention to him. What did you do?"

She gave an awkward shrug. "I told you, I don't really know."

A dark brow arched. "Anna."

She met the piercing black gaze. She even managed to meet it squarely for several long, awkward moments before she blew out a resigned sigh.

Dammit, why wouldn't he let it be? She felt enough like a weirdo without confessing her *I Dream of Jeannie* routine.

"I just . . ." She gave a shake of her head. "God, it sounds so stupid when I say it out loud, but sometimes if I focus hard enough I can control the things around me."

He looked more intrigued than horrified. "What sort of things?"

She gave a wave of her hands. "The air. I can make it warmer or colder."

"Or squeeze the hell out of a vampire?"

"Bonus."

His lips twitched. "What else can you do?"

"A few months ago the drains in my condo backed up and

water was filling my basement. I freaked out when I saw the damage and suddenly the water was pouring back down the drains and the basement was completely dry."

He touched her cheek with an oddly reverent motion. "An elemental."

"Me?"

"Yes."

Her mouth went dry. "What the hell is that?"

The slender fingers slid down the line of her jaw creating all sorts of unwelcome havoc.

"I'm afraid that I'm not the one to ask for explanations. I've only heard rumors of such creatures."

She stepped back. Conde Cezar might be the most arrogant, aggravating pain in the butt she had ever met, but his touch could still turn her mind to mush.

"I'm not a creature." She sent him a telling glance. "At least not until I met you."

"Anna, the one thing I do know is that elementals are born, not created. I had nothing to do with your powers." He studied her sketpical expression before giving a shake of his head. "We can't linger here in the open."

She stubbornly stood her ground. It had been stupid to rush to Chicago and confront Cezar. She wasn't about to make it worse by happily skipping off in the dark with a self-confessed vampire.

Her bizarro talents weren't nearly dependable enough for that.

"What makes you think someone is trying to kill me?" she demanded.

"Would there be any other reason for a fire to be started outside your door?"

"It could have been an accident."

He looked at her as if her elevator couldn't possibly be going all the way to the top.

And maybe it wasn't.

"Do you truly believe that?"

"I don't know." She rubbed her aching temples. How long had it been since she had slept? Or ate? She couldn't even remember. "Christ, I've gone way past my crazy threshold. This day couldn't get any worse."

"Never tempt fate, *querida*," he warned softly. "It's a lesson that I learned at my peril."

She snorted as her gaze skimmed over his dark, knee-buckling beauty. His bronzed features were just as elegant, just as exquisitely carved as they had been two centuries ago. There wasn't even a strand of gray in the thick black hair to mar his perfection.

"You don't look as if you've suffered over the years."

Something dangerous flashed through his dark eyes. Dangerous enough to make her take a hasty step backward.

"You have no idea, sweet Anna," he said coldly. "But for now I'm more interested in discovering who's trying to kill you and why. Do you have any enemies?"

She licked her dry lips, realizing she had touched a nerve that was best left alone. What she knew about vampires might fit into a thimble, but it seemed an overall good policy not to provoke one. Not when they were standing alone on a dark street.

"I'm a lawyer who battles the world's most powerful corporations on a daily basis," she admitted. "I have an endless list of enemies."

"Any who want you dead?"

"No, of course not. That's ridiculous."

"You've lived over two centuries," he pointed out. "You were bound to piss off a few people."

Anna grimaced as she thought of the endless years she had lived in near solitude, taking menial jobs to survive, and constantly moving from one town to another to avoid notice.

"Until the past few years I've lived very quietly. It's not easy to explain why I don't age while everyone else around me grows old."

The coldness faded from the black eyes. "Yes, I'm somewhat familiar with the problem."

Oh, right. He would be. Anna briefly wondered just how old Cezar was. A few hundred years? A few thousand?

She shoved away the thought. It made her head spin. After all these years immortality still seemed like a strange, absurd dream.

"At last I decided I was tired of hiding," she continued. "If I'm going to live forever I should at least do something to make the world a better place."

The wicked amusement returned to the dark eyes. "By fighting corporations?"

"And what do you do?" she charged.

He flicked his gaze down her slender body, lingering on the plunge of her neckline. "I protect beautiful women from the things that go bump in the night."

Anna swallowed a small groan as she could tangibly feel the heat of that sinful gaze. Cezar had always been able to seduce with a mere glance. "I've told you that I don't need you to protect me."

"Well that's too bad, because that happens to be my current job."

"Job?" She frowned at his odd choice of words. "What the hell is that supposed to mean?"

He reached out to tap the end of her nose. "Precisely what I said."

She smacked his hand away. She didn't believe for a moment that he was some sort of Good Samaritan who went about protecting women. Hell, he *was* the thing that went bump in the night.

"Then consider yourself fired."

His smile was mocking. "You don't have the power to fire me. My orders come from those much more powerful than you. At least for the moment." He stilled, his head tilting back as if testing the air. Then without warning he had wrapped her in his arms and pressed them both into the shadows of the nearest doorway. Anna opened her mouth to protest only to have his hand clamp over her lips. "Ssh," he whispered close to her ear. "Someone is coming."

Belatedly Anna could hear the sound of approaching footsteps. Turning her head, she was startled to see Sybil Taylor making her way down the street, pausing at each building to peer into the windows as if she was looking for something.

Or someone.

Anna caught her breath even as Cezar whispered words in a language she didn't understand and the shadows deepened around them. In an instant they were wrapped in complete darkness.

Nice trick. It was no wonder vampires managed to remain below the radar of most people.

Cezar's attention remained firmly trained on the woman approaching them.

"Now that is intriguing," he murmured.

She pried his fingers from her mouth. "What?"

"Why would the fairy be searching for you?"

"How do you know that she's searching for me?" His arm tightened around her waist, sending a zing of pleasure through her body. She was trying hard to ignore the fact that her back was pressed firmly to his hard, perfect body. And that his sandalwood scent was making her head spin and her palms sweat. At the impatient squeeze of his arm, she realized she wasn't succeeding. She sighed and forced herself to concentrate on more important matters. Such as why she would even question the fact she was the one Sybil was searching for. It was too much a coincidence that the elegant woman would arrive in Chicago the exact day and attend the exact party for her not to be somehow involved in this current disaster. "Okay, stupid question."

"I think we should have a talk with Sybil Taylor," he murmured. "But not tonight."

It was her turn for impatience. She had always suspected there was something downright slimy about the beautiful brunette. Even before she learned Sybil was a fairy. (A fairy, for God's sake, what was up with that?) This was her opportunity to discover just what the bitch was up to.

"Why wait?" she demanded.

"For one thing I would like our conversation to be a little more private than standing on Michigan Avenue," he said, his lips brushing her ear as he spoke. "And for another, she's on her guard at the moment. If we wait and corner her, she'll be much more willing to confess her secrets."

"She won't be confessing any secrets if she manages to disappear," she pointed out as Sybil crossed the wide street and vanished from view.

"Impossible."

She tilted her head away from those disturbing lips that brushed against her ear. God, her hormones were nearly screaming with the need to turn in his arms and do something about the fierce ache that had clutched her body.

It was dangerous. Stupid. And undeniable.

She hadn't felt this potent need for one hundred and ninety-five years. Now her body wanted what it wanted. And it wanted it this minute.

Anna sucked in a deep breath, willing her heart to slow its frantic pace. "How can you be so certain you will be able to find her again?"

"No one, not even a demon, can hide from a vampire on the hunt," he arrogantly assured her, his hand stroking the line of her throat. "No one."

She turned her head to meet the dark, glittering gaze. "Is that a threat?"

"Consider it a friendly warning."

"Perhaps you should have your memory checked."

His lips twitched. "And why is that?"

"Because after one hundred and ninety-five years *I'm* the one who found *you*, not the other way around."

His smile widened. Of course. Even if Anna was too stubborn to admit it out loud, they both knew that he had deliberately lured her to Chicago.

"If it makes you feel better to think so."

She pulled away and began marching down the street. She'd had enough for one night. Enough of vampires and fairies and near-death experiences.

"Goodbye, Conde Cezar."

She'd barely taken a step when he blocked her path, his expression ruthless in the shadows.

"Where do you think you're going?"

"Back to my hotel room."

"Don't be a fool. Even assuming that it's not completely destroyed, Sybil will keep a watch on the hotel the entire night."

"Fine." She turned on her heel and began marching in the opposite direction. "Then I'll go to another hotel."

Once again she had barely taken a step and he was blocking her path, moving so swiftly she nearly rammed into him.

He crossed his arms over his chest, regarding her with lifted brows.

"And what hotel will take you in with no money, no luggage, and no shoes?"

The fact that he was right only made her want to punch him in the nose. "Look, buster, I'm tired of vampires and fairies and God knows what else that is no doubt lurking in the shadows. I just want to go to sleep and forget I was ever stupid enough to come to Chicago, let alone believe you could give me the answers I want."

He regarded her pale face for a long, silent moment. "What if I promise to make sure that you get those answers you seek?"

She narrowed her gaze. "You know more than you're saying, don't you?"

He laughed softly. "It would take the next millennium to share everything I know, *querida.*"

"Ugh."

His smile faded as he slowly held out a slender hand. "Will you trust me?"

"Never."

Something that might have been disappointment flashed through the dark eyes, but his hand never wavered.

"Will you at least allow me to take you somewhere safe for the night?"

Anna lowered her gaze to study the tips of her bare toes, grinding her teeth as she was forced to accept she had nowhere to go. Not unless she wanted to sleep in the streets.

Talk about a rock and a hard place.

"I don't seem to have much choice," she muttered, grudgingly placing her hand in his.

With a small chuckle, Cezar pulled her forward, bending his head to brush a soft kiss on her lips.

"Anna Randal, you haven't had a choice since the first night I caught sight of you."

With a soft hiss, Cezar forced himself to lift his head. *Dios.* The scent of this woman was invading him, setting his soul on fire. He ached with the need to taste her blood on his tongue, feel her warm and supple body writhing in pleasure beneath his own.

In the same moment he was nearly overwhelmed with the compulsion to take her far away from those who hunted her. To hide her in his lair and keep her safe. With his very life if necessary.

Two very dangerous obsessions that could get a vampire killed.

Damn the Oracles. They had known. They had known

precisely what his reaction would be when this woman was plunged back into his life.

With an effort, Cezar thrust aside the strange unease that flared through his heart and concentrated on Anna.

Despite her stubborn expression and the wary glitter in her beautiful hazel eyes, he could smell the fear and confusion and weariness that trembled through her body.

He needed to get her into a warm bed with a large tray of food. The sooner the better.

Grasping her hand, Cezar urged his reluctant companion down the street. She hesitated only a moment before heaving a deep sigh and falling into step beside him.

"Where are we going?"

Cezar had already considered his options. The Oracles hadn't yet given their permission to bring Anna into their presence or to reveal her own place on the Commission. And experience had taught him not to overstep his bounds, even if Anna's life was in danger. Pissing off the Oracles was never a good thing.

His only other option was Styx.

Not a bad other option.

"To a friend's house. You'll be safe there."

"How can you be so certain?"

He smiled wryly. "Trust me, there are few demons who would dare the wrath of Styx. He didn't gain his name by accident."

She flashed him a puzzled frown. "Styx?"

"It's said that he leaves a river of dead in his wake."

"Holy crap."

Cezar gave her fingers a slight squeeze. "Don't worry. His mate has trained him to keep most of the bloodshed to a minimum."

"I can't reveal the depth of my relief," she said dryly.

"You actually saw him earlier this evening."

"Ah." A tiny smile touched her lips. "The tall, gorgeous Aztec?"

Cezar's gaze narrowed, a stark sense of possession making his fangs lengthen.

"Careful, *querida*. Darcy is not only Styx's mate, she's also a werewolf who is very possessive." He tugged her close enough to his side that he could feel her heat wrap around him. "And even if she agreed to share, I wouldn't."

"A werewolf . . ." Her shock was abruptly replaced with an expression of feminine outrage. It was an expression that she had perfected to an art form over the past two centuries. "Wait, what do you mean you wouldn't share?"

He caught and held her gaze. "You know precisely what I mean."

Her steps faltered, then she tilted her chin and dredged up a glare. "You must be mental if you think you can pop in and out of my life every few centuries and claim me like some sort of booby prize."

"Booby prize?"

"Damn you, this isn't funny." She stomped her foot, only to grimace as her bare foot landed on a rock. "Ow." With yet another glare, she lifted her foot to rub it. "Can't we get a taxi?"

"I don't want anyone knowing where we've gone, especially not a human taxi driver who would reveal everything, including his ATM PIN number, under the enchantment of a fairy."

She heaved an aggravated sigh at his perfectly reasonable explanation.

"Then call your friend and have him pick us up," she demanded.

Cezar shrugged. "I don't have a cell phone."

"You're kidding me." She stared at him in disbelief. "What century do you live in?"

He was wise enough to hide his amusement this time. Although she'd lived two centuries, she was still unfamiliar with the world that she was now a part of. It would take time for her to adjust.

"My powers disrupt a few modern conveniences."

Her annoyance changed to curiosity. "Why?"

"No one has managed to discover why. There are just certain vampires who possess an aura that plays havoc with technology. There are some who can't enter a town without downing the entire electric grid. Thankfully my own disruptions are limited to cell phones and wireless internet service. Not that great a loss."

"That must make downloading your porn a tedious business," she mocked.

With a flurry of motion, Cezar had Anna pressed into the doorway of a large office building, his arms clamped around her waist and his head buried in the curve of her neck.

He'd ignored her mocking taunts because he realized she was terrified. But he'd be damned if he'd accept any slurs concerning his sexual prowess. Not when he was bloody well aching with a need to take her right there on a public street.

"Vampires have no need for such titillation," he assured her, scraping his fangs over the pulsing vein at the base of her throat before pressing his lips to the sensitive flesh. She shivered, her hands clutching at his arms as if her knees were suddenly weak. He trailed his lips down her collarbone, using his teeth and tongue to make her groan in pleasure. "Why bother with faux sex when you can always have the real thing?"

Lifting his head he claimed her lips in a kiss that revealed the dark, hungry passion that held him captive. Her lips readily parted, allowing his tongue to tangle with hers as his hands skimmed over her back with a restless need.

Anna could snap and snarl all she wanted, but she couldn't disguise the fact that she still desired him. The passion between them would never, could never, change. No matter how many centuries passed.

Drowning in pleasure, Cezar pressed her hard against his aching body, desperately wishing they were alone in a dark room with satin sheets and hours to spend in each other's arms.

His fantasy was interrupted when Anna's fingers tightened on his arms and her head arched back.

"Cezar . . . wait."

His hands gripped the back of her delicate gown, his muscles trembling with the effort to control his passions.

"I've been waiting two centuries," he muttered thickly.

"I smell apples."

He stilled, his eyes narrowed. "And?"

"And I always smell apples when Sybil Taylor is near."

His senses reached out, easily locating the fairy who was creeping down the dark street toward them.

"Damn that fairy." Reaching behind Anna he easily wrenched open the steel and glass door, thrusting Anna into the vast marble foyer as he followed close behind. "How the hell did she find us?"

He didn't give his companion time to respond as he pressed her behind one of the large potted palms and took his own position next to the door. With a low word he was wrapped in shadows, invisible even to the fairy's eyes.

Only a few minutes passed before Sybil was sniffing around the door, her expression wary as she stepped over the threshold and studied the darkness.

"Anna?" she called softly, a small crystal shimmering in her hand. "Anna, are you here?"

More than a little unhappy at having his intimate moment with Anna interrupted, Cezar flowed forward and wrapped his arms around the fairy.

"How did you follow us?" he demanded, squeezing her painfully as she attempted to struggle against his hold.

"Release me, vampire."

"Wrong answer." He pressed his fangs against her neck, hard enough to draw blood.

She gave a squeak, her struggles ending as she froze in fear. "No . . . wait."

"How did you follow us?" he repeated.

"I scried for Anna," she answered, referring to the art of crystal-gazing.

Unlike vampires, fairies were capable of small amounts of magic. But even fairies needed a part of the person they were scrying.

"With what?"

The scent of apples became nearly overwhelming as Sybil struggled to contain her fiery temper. Fairies were creatures of emotion, flitting from one to another with such speed a wise demon tended to give them a wide berth.

"I stole her hairbrush so I would have strands of her hair," she at last gritted.

"Why? What do you want from her?"

"She has a bounty on her head."

"A bounty?" Anna stepped from behind the potted plant, her face pale. "What the hell does that mean?"

"It means that someone wants you dead, *querida*," he said, instantly regretting his blunt honesty when her eyes widened in shock.

"Oh my God."

"Not dead," Sybil interrupted. "Captured."

Cezar shifted his arm so he could wrap his hand around the fairy's throat. One squeeze and she'd be dead. Not as satisfying as draining her dry, but effective.

"Who offered the bounty?"

She hesitated before muttering a vile curse beneath her breath. "The Queen of Fairies."

A chill stabbed through Cezar's heart. Dammit, he should have paid closer attention to Anna's revelation of what had happened to her aunt and cousin two centuries ago. It hadn't occurred to him that it would have any bearing on the danger she faced today.

He wasn't usually so stupid.

"What's her interest in Anna?" he rasped.

"I don't have a clue." Sybil shot a surly glare in Anna's direction. "And I don't care."

His fingers tightened. "Shall I make you care?"

She hissed in pain, holding up her hands in defeat. "Look, I don't even know if Anna is the one the queen seeks."

"Explain."

"All I know is that the word was spread that the queen would offer her priceless emeralds to any fairy who managed to locate a human who possessed the magic of the elders in their blood. When I met Anna in the courtroom I instantly sensed some sort of power. It's unstable, but very strong."

Anna grimaced at the fairy. "That's why you were always following me around?"

"Well, it wasn't for your charming personality."

Anna stepped forward, her fists clutched as if she were considering punching the woman in the nose. Cezar was swift to tug Sybil backward. Although he liked a catfight as well as the next vampire (who didn't?), he was more interested in getting to the truth before he was forced to kill the fairy.

"And the spells you cast in her direction?"

Sybil gave a jerk of surprise. "How did you know about them?"

Cezar ignored her surprise and Anna's questioning gaze. "Just answer the question."

"They were harmless for the most part," the fairy muttered. "I hoped to force her into using her powers so that I could be sure she was the one that I sought before I went to the trouble of kidnapping her."

Anna made a rude noise. "Nice."

"If your only intention was to capture Anna then why did you set the fire outside Anna's door?" he demanded.

It took another warning squeeze before Sybil was squeaking out the answer. "I assumed that you had taken her to her room for a late night snack. I couldn't risk having her drained before I could get her to the queen. I knew a fire was the one thing that would frighten you away."

Anna gave a small gasp. "Do you know how many people could have been killed by that fire?"

"What do I care about humans?" Sybil demanded in baffled tones.

It was a sentiment shared by most of the demon world. Including vampires. Oh, humans were fine enough as a convenient meal or a quickie in a dark alley, but they weren't actually considered valuable commodities. There were just so damn many of them.

Anna's expression, however, was enough to keep his mouth shut. See, he was a lot smarter than he looked.

"God, you're . . ." her words broke off as she covered her face with shaky hands. "This is ridiculous. I can't possibly be the one you're looking for."

Cezar battled the instinctive need to rush to Anna and pull her into his arms. What the hell was the matter with him? He was an ancient conquistador, a warrior, a predator. Until the Oracles had taken command of his life he had killed without mercy and took what he wanted without asking.

The world had trembled at his passing.

Now he wanted nothing more than to offer comfort to a woman because she was feeling alone and frightened.

Grimly he returned his attention to the fairy who was using his distraction for an opportunity to escape. With a low growl he lowered his head until she could feel his fangs against her neck.

"Did you reveal to the queen that you had found Anna?"

She gave a tiny squeak. "I might have sent a message that said something about bringing Her Majesty a special gift."

Cezar cursed beneath his breath. If the queen was traveling to Chicago they were in for some major trouble. She possessed a nasty temper and ancient powers she was willing to use without a care for the destruction she might cause.

He had to warn the Oracles.

But first things first.

Capable of sensing the gist of his vile Spanish curses even if she didn't understand the actual words, Anna moved forward with a worried frown.

"Cezar?"

"I must get you to Styx."

Her gaze shifted to the fairy trapped in his arms. "What are you going to do to Sybil?"

He grimaced. "She'll have to come with us. She might possess information we'll need."

Sybil resumed her struggles. "Like hell I will."

"You'll come with us or I'll kill you," he said, his voice cold enough to assure the fairy he meant every word.

"Fine, I'll come."

"I thought you might."

Chapter 4

When Cezar had told Anna that they would be staying with his vampire friend, she wasn't sure what to expect. Where did vampires live? Crypts? Sewers? The fiery pits of hell?

Turns out that vampires live in huge, elegant estates with iron gates, hidden cameras, vampire security guards, and a freaking lawn that was bigger than most third world countries.

And no doubt worth twice as much.

If Anna hadn't been so weary and hungry and downright crazed from the strange night, she might have balked at being led up the winding tree-lined drive to the sprawling Colonial mansion.

As it was she was just so happy at the thought of a warm bed and a roof over her head that she numbly returned the greetings of the towering Styx and his pretty mate, who met them in the marble foyer and after one glance at her wan face had her whisked up the curved staircase to a guest bedroom.

The room with its connecting bathroom was as large as her apartment in L.A., but she had no time to appreciate the lavender and ivory décor before she was soaking in a tub that could hold the Chicago Bears with room for a cheerleader or two.

When she had soaked herself into a prune, Anna at last pulled on a terry cloth robe conveniently left on the counter, and made her way to the wide bed. Her stomach growled as she perched on the edge of the mattress, but she found her feet reluctant to carry her from the welcome peace of the room.

Beyond the door was a plethora of creatures that most people believed were nothing more than myths. Vampires, werewolves, fairies . . .

Granted, Anna had already suspected that there were more than humans walking around. Hell, she was living proof. And over the years she had more than once considered the possibility that Cezar was a vampire.

But suspecting that Hollywood monsters might creep around in the dark was considerably different from being their houseguest.

She was still weighing the pros and cons of cowering in the bed, when the door to the room was pushed open and Styx's mate, Darcy, peeked her head inside.

"May I come in?"

Anna instinctively smiled. Darcy didn't look like a werewolf. Actually, she looked like an adorable urchin with her spiked blond hair and huge green eyes in a heart-shaped face. She also possessed one of those in-love-with-life-and-everyone-in-it personalities that made you melt on the spot.

Even the grim-faced Styx hadn't been able to conceal his absolute adoration for the woman.

"Of course."

Pushing the door wider with her foot, Darcy entered with a large tray that she set on the bed next to Anna.

"I thought you might be hungry."

Anna sucked in a heady breath of the delicious scents filling the air. "Actually, I'm starving."

"Good." With a charming lack of formality, Darcy planted herself on the bed, tucking her bare feet beneath her and staring openly at her guest. Anna hid a smile, thinking the woman looked more like a teenager than a fearsome beast in her ratty jeans and T-shirt. "I brought a fresh-fruit salad and zucchini lasagna. I'm afraid I'm a vegetarian so I didn't have any meat in the house at such short notice, but I can get whatever you want tomorrow."

Anna blinked in surprise. "But I thought . . ."

"Yes?"

Ducking her head in embarrassment, Anna took a bite of the lasagna. "Nothing."

"Please ask me whatever you want, Anna."

Anna swallowed, inwardly wondering about the etiquette of asking about a person's species.

"I just thought that Cezar said that Styx's mate was a werewolf."

"I am."

"Oh." Anna lifted her head to meet the amused green gaze. "But you don't eat meat?"

Darcy wrinkled her tiny nose. "I won't bore you with my life history, but basically I was genetically altered so that while I possess a few werewolf traits I never shift and I never feel the pangs of bloodlust." She gave a sudden chuckle. "Well, except on those occasions when my mate needs to be put in his place."

Ah, a woman after her own heart.

Anna smiled as she took another large bite of the pasta. "If he's anything like Cezar I would think that he needs to be put in his place on a daily basis."

"It does seem to be a vampire trait."

Actually Anna was quite certain that it was a man trait.

She popped a piece of watermelon in her mouth. "This is delicious."

"I can't take credit." Darcy reached out to nab a breadstick. "I lured away Viper's housekeeper, who happens to be an artist in the kitchen. She's helping me to open a new health-food store that offers prepared meals."

Anna polished off the last of the lasagna before her sticky-fingered companion could snag a bite. "If this is anything to go by it's going to be a fabulous success."

Together they demolished the fruit salad, and with a deep sigh of pleasure Anna wiped her hands and set aside the tray.

Once Anna was comfortably settled on the mound of pillows at her back, Darcy returned to gazing at her with that open curiosity.

"Cezar mentioned that you are a lawyer?"

"In L.A."

"Do you like it?"

Anna shrugged. She had chosen to enter law school only after a large corporation had purchased an entire block of low-rent apartments where she was living and happily tossed the elderly and poor onto the street so they could make a profit.

There would always be injustices in the world, but Anna was tired of sitting on the sidelines. She had decided that day it was past time to get into the game.

"I like it when I win," she admitted with a rueful smile.

"That makes sense."

There was a short silence as Darcy tilted her head and studied Anna with a strange intensity.

At last, Anna cleared her throat in discomfort. "You can ask whatever you want, Darcy," she said, repeating her guest's words.

"I was raised to believe I was human so this whole demon world is new to me," she admitted, startling Anna. "I know you're not a vampire or werewolf, but . . ."

Anna recalled Darcy mentioning that she had been genetically altered, which would explain why she hadn't realized her heritage. It made Anna feel even closer to the woman. She wasn't alone in this wild and wacky world. Darcy would understand her confusion.

"Actually, I don't know what I am," she confessed, feeling oddly relieved to unburden the secret that had kept her trapped and separated from the world for so long. It seemed that the truth really did set you free. "I hoped that Cezar could tell me."

Darcy didn't appear at all shocked. Actually she looked nothing more than curious.

"Why Cezar?"

Anna blinked at the unexpected question. "We knew each other long ago. Centuries ago. When I spotted his picture in the *L.A. Times*, which mentioned that he was in Chicago, I flew here to confront him. I thought . . ." She grimaced at her naïve assumptions. "I blamed Cezar all these years for making me different."

"Why would you blame Cezar?" Darcy wondered, then as Anna blushed at the intimate memories, she offered an impish smile. "Ah, never mind."

"I was a fool to come here." Anna gave a shake of her head. "I came here for answers, but every time that vampire makes one of his cameo appearances in my life everything goes to hell."

"You weren't a fool, Anna." Darcy reached out to lightly touch Anna's arm. "As difficult as it might be to discover the truth, anything is better than wondering and fearing that there's something wrong with you. Trust me, I know."

"Yes." Anna managed a weary smile. "You're right."

"And you can be certain that both Styx and I will do everything in our power to keep you safe."

"You're very kind."

Darcy waved aside Anna's sincere gratitude as she rose to her feet, a smile on her lips. "And you know, Cezar is rather fine even in the vampire world, where *fine* has a whole new definition. There's no reason you can't enjoy the view while you're here." She ignored Anna's startled expression as she crossed to the door. "I'll let you relax in peace and return later with something for you to sleep in. If you need anything just poke your head out the door and give a yell. I have excellent hearing."

Anna couldn't help but laugh. The woman was simply impossible not to like.

"A werewolf thing?" she teased.

"There are some good points to being special, although if you call me Cujo I won't be happy."

"Special?"

"That's what we are, Anna, don't ever believe otherwise."

Special? Hmmm. Better than freak, but still a big, fat leap from normal.

"I'll have to take your word for it."

Cezar paced Styx's private office with a restless impatience. Under normal circumstances he might have been delighted to have the opportunity to explore the rare scrolls that were carefully stored in a glass case, or the vast leather-bound tomes that lined the walls and detailed the history of vampires. Or even the stacks of petitions that were piled on the mahogany desk.

As the king of all vampires, Styx possessed the grueling burden of leadership, but he also was given access to the priceless treasures that had been collected over the millenniums.

Tonight, however, Cezar couldn't appreciate his surroundings. Instead he battled the searing need to bolt from the room and find where Anna had been taken.

Was she alone and afraid in a strange room? Had she been fed? Did she need . . .

Dios. He growled deep in his throat. The woman was driving him nuts.

Thankfully his dark broodings were interrupted as Styx entered the room and firmly shut and locked the door. Cezar was certain that the room had been soundproofed and suitably hexed to make their privacy complete.

Styx was nothing if not thorough.

"You have the fairy secured?" Cezar demanded as Styx

crossed the room to perch on the edge of the desk. Dressed all in black, the king appeared precisely as he was. A large, lethal predator who would kill without mercy.

A hard smile touched the vampire's lips. "She is in a cell that has been built specifically to dampen her magical abilities."

"There might be those who will attempt to rescue her."

"The estate is fully monitored and I left a guard at the door to the cell. Trust me, no one will get past Gunter."

Cezar offered a small bow. He had chosen wisely in coming to his leader. "Thank you, my lord."

Styx gave a wave of his hand. "You have only to ask, Cezar, and I will do whatever is in my power to assist you."

"For now my greatest request is that you protect Anna."

"Of course." Styx folded his arms over his chest. "Have you discovered who is threatening the woman?"

Cezar grimaced as he slipped off the jacket to his tux and tossed it aside. The white satin tie was given the same treatment.

"Morgana le Fay."

A shocked silence filled the room. The Queen of Fairies was shrouded in mystery to most demons. Although it was rumored she could enchant with a glance and lure even the most powerful of demons into her clutches, she so rarely left her secret lair it was impossible to know what was genuine fact and what was mere legend. She was as much mist and smoke as real woman.

"You're certain?" Styx at last demanded.

"As certain as I can be at this point." Cezar gave a furious shake of his head. "*Dios*, I have been so stupid. So blind."

"How could you have known?"

Cezar returned to his pacing, knowing that he couldn't keep secrets from Styx if he wanted his help.

"I met Anna nearly two hundred years ago in London," he grudgingly confessed, twisting the heavy signet ring on his finger. "At the time I didn't realize that she was anything more than a beautiful woman that I desired."

"What happened?"

"I seduced her."

"Hardly an unusual activity for you during those days," Styx pointed out dryly. "As I recall you seduced several London ladies."

A smile touched Cezar's lips at the memory. Ah, yes. For nearly three hundred years he had used his powers to indulge his love for women. It hadn't mattered if they were human or demon. Just so long as they were beautiful.

They had been fine years, but the insatiable desires that had once plagued him had come to an end the night he had met Anna Randal.

She had taught him that there were depths to passion he had never before experienced.

And while he had been reveling in the taste and feel of her, he had been oblivious to the evil that hunted her.

"Not like Anna," he rasped. "I sensed she was more than a mere mortal the moment I touched her, but I ignored my instincts. I wanted her and nothing was going to stop me. If I had just listened . . ."

"What?"

"She told me of her cousin Morgana, but I never considered the possibility that it could be the queen." His hands clenched at his side.

Styx pushed from the desk to cross the room and lay a heavy hand on Cezar's shoulder.

"Why should you?" he demanded. "Humans have always believed her to be nothing more than myth and legend. They readily name their daughters after the treacherous bitch even today."

Cezar smiled wryly. "I think it was more the fact that I was fully distracted at that precise moment. And, of course, there was that nasty meeting with the Oracles only moments after enjoying the delights that Anna had to offer." He shuddered at the memory of the brilliant flash of light followed by the entrance of the eight ancient Oracles. He had been lying in the bed naked and utterly sated when they arrived, their grim expressions revealing the depth of their anger. "They were not happy that I had tasted of the next Commission member."

Styx gave a lift of his brows. "They actually came to the room?"

"After they had made sure that they had put Anna into a deep sleep."

"So that's why you were forced to serve them."

It was certainly what Cezar had believed for the past two centuries. And the Oracles had done nothing to disabuse him of that belief.

But the moment that Anna had walked into that Chicago hotel, he had been drowning in his awareness of her. His every sense had been tuned to her as if she were the only woman in the whole damn world.

"I'm beginning to suspect that there was more to it than that," he muttered.

Styx regarded him with a lift of his brows. "Such as?"

"There are some things I refuse to discuss even with you, my lord."

A smile that was almost smug touched the vampire's mouth. "Ah."

Cezar frowned, fiercely refusing to consider what might be behind his friend's amusement.

It couldn't be good.

Instead he turned his mind to more important matters. "It was not just that night that Anna spoke of her cousin," he said, once again cursing his stupidity.

"What else did she say?"

"That after our night together she returned home to find it burned to the ground. She assumed her aunt and cousin died in the flames. She was no doubt right about her aunt."

"The work of Morgana?"

A sharp, biting fury raced through Cezar at the realization

that he had come so close to losing Anna. He would kill anyone who threatened her.

Even the Queen of Fairies.

"She couldn't have known that dutiful Anna was locked in a magical sleep in another house, rather than sleeping in her own bed," he bit out, his fangs fully extended. "It was the first attempt on Anna's life."

Styx gave a slow nod. "The queen must have believed her dead."

"Until Anna's powers began to surface. Once the queen sensed them she sent out word to her fairies to search for the one who possessed the blood of the ancients."

"Blood of the ancients." Styx furrowed his brows, his gaze shifting toward his vast collection of books. "I thought Morgana to be the last of the line?"

Cezar shrugged. "So did I."

"You think it is true that they're related?"

"They must be in some way."

"And now she is destined to be an Oracle." Styx returned his attention to Cezar, his dark gaze smoldering with his lethal power. "Intriguing."

"Not intriguing, dangerous," Cezar corrected. He recognized that expression on his friend's face. It usually preceded the vampire calling his brothers to battle. And while Cezar was all for the Bitch of Fairies being butchered, preferably while he watched, he needed answers first. Otherwise he couldn't be certain that the threat to Anna would die with the queen. "I don't know what Morgana le Fay wants of Anna, but I intend to find out. Once we know we can invite her to a little family reunion."

Styx slowly smiled. "I vote we make it a barbeque."

Chapter 5

The mists of Avalon were no myth.

The magical shield stretched for miles around the island, keeping it hidden from human eyes and protecting it from the intrusion of demons.

No one was allowed on the island unless they had been invited by the queen. And those foolish enough to try to slip past her barriers swiftly learned a lesson in displeasing Morgana le Fay. A lesson that few ever repeated.

Mostly because they were dead.

On this day the mists were a dark, threatening gray, reflecting the mood of Morgana as she paced the velvet carpet of her throne room.

It was a chokingly impressive room with a glass rotunda and delicate tapestries on the wall that would make a human craftsman cry with envy. Just below the rotunda was a round dais with a golden throne. And on each side of the throne stood two male fairies.

They were . . . perfect.

Perfectly matched with long blond hair that fell to their waists and features carved by the hands of an angel. Perfectly naked, to reveal their muscular forms. Perfectly trained not to reveal the least emotion without permission.

Perfectly perfect.

Morgana demanded no less.

Not that she bothered to glance in their direction. Instead she continued her pacing, the sheer white gown fluttering around her tall, slender body and her magnificent mane of red curls shimmering in the candlelight. It was not until she sensed the approaching fairy that she forced herself to return to her throne and take her seat.

She appeared calmly composed, her lovely features unreadable and her green eyes shielded by the tangled lace of her lashes. Her expression didn't change as the tall, unusually brawny man with curly black hair and blue eyes entered the chambers.

He was a stunning creature. And a magnificent lover.

A pity he had proven a disappointment.

Watching in silence she waited for the fairy to fall to his knees at her feet and press his head to the carpet.

"You sent for me, Your Majesty?"

She ignored the voice he had trained to send shivers down her spine. Her long nails, painted a deep shade of crimson, tapped on the gilt arm of her chair.

"Have you been avoiding me, Landes?" she demanded softly.

His head lifted to regard her with a wary gaze. "No, I ache to be bathed in your beauty. I tremble with the need to worship at your feet."

"Pretty, but not what I want to hear." She leaned forward. "Don't you remember, my sweet, that I was to be told the moment you made contact with Sybil?"

He paled beneath her unwavering gaze. "Y . . . yes."

"Then why have you kept me waiting?"

"There have been difficulties, my Queen."

Morgana resisted the urge to kick the man in the face. Damn the fool. She didn't want his pathetic excuses. She wanted results.

"What could possibly be difficult in such a simple task?" she demanded, the mist above the rotunda swirling in the gathering storm.

Landes cast a nervous glance upward before swallowing a lump in his throat.

"Sybil has not responded to my summons."

"You opened a portal?"

"Of course, Your Majesty, but there is something that is blocking my efforts."

"Something?"

"I don't know what it is." He lifted his hands, his expression pleading. "It's like a fog that I can't penetrate."

Dark fury raced through Morgana's blood as she slowly rose from the throne. She had devoted centuries to ending her brother's bloodline. To making sure that each and every one of her enemies lay dead on the ground.

And for a brief time, she had been certain she had succeeded. Two hundred years ago she had killed Anna Randal, the last of the damnable clan. She was at last free of her destiny.

But somehow, some way she had missed one.

There was no mistaking the growing powers she could sense. Powers that should have been erased from the world.

Her fear had returned and she had sent out word to the fairies. Two days ago she had received word from Sybil that she had found the one Morgana searched for. She had also promised to bring the woman to Avalon.

She had never arrived, and now Landes had confessed that she couldn't be contacted by portal.

Reaching down she grabbed Landes by the chin and jerked him to his feet.

"Obviously I overestimated your worth to me, Landes."

His beautiful eyes widened. "No. I will find her, I swear on my life."

With a cold smile, Morgana placed a light kiss on his lips.

"Too late, my beautiful boy. I've decided to take matters into my own hands."

Deepening the kiss, Morgana pressed her hands to Landes's bare chest, using her powers to drain the life from his large body.

He struggled for a moment before sighing softly and tumbling to the ground. Morgana indifferently stepped over his carcass and with a wave of her hand the two guards were rushing to carry the dead fairy from her throne room.

Waiting for the doors to shut behind the guards, Morgana tilted back her head and shrieked in frustration.

How dare the fates continue to taunt her?

She was a queen. A beloved leader of all fairies. She should be gracing the world with her beauty. She should be worshipped by all. Instead she was forced to hide in the mists of her land, in constant fear that her brother's final revenge was lurking just out of sight.

"Broken another one of your toys?" a reedy, female voice demanded. "How many times have I warned you about that temper?"

Whirling on her heel, Morgana watched as the shrunken old woman, with nasty tufts of gray hair stuck to her scalp and pure white eyes, shuffled into the room. The queen grimaced, disgusted by the vile smell of rotting teeth and recently slaughtered sacrifice that the woman carried with her.

Modron had taken Morgana from her crib when she was just a babe and raised her as her own. It wasn't sentiment, however, that kept Morgana from killing the disgusting creature. The woman was a powerful seer. A rare power even among fairies.

"Shut up, you old hag," she snarled, throwing herself onto her throne with a petulant frown. "I've enough troubles without listening to your tedious lectures."

The woman gave a cackling laugh, crossing to stand before the throne with remarkable ease considering she was completely blind.

"Testy."

"I'm not testy, I'm furious." Morgana waved a hand before her nose, her own scent of pomegranates filling the room to cover the hag's stench. "I've devoted a millennium to ridding myself of my brother's bloodline. I was certain Anna was the last when I roasted her in London. They should be dead. They should be wiped from the face of the earth."

Modron gave a shake of her head. "They're like roaches. They refuse to become extinct."

Morgana pounded her fist on the arm of her throne. "Not this time."

"What do you intend to do?"

"The last word I had from Sybil was from Chicago."

The hag's smile faded, thankfully hiding her rotting teeth. "You intend to travel there?"

Morgana narrowed her gaze. "We're *both* traveling there."

Modron hissed, her hands clutching at the threadbare wool gown that covered her gaunt body. "Leave Avalon? No. It's too dangerous."

Morgana leaned forward to slap the woman across the face, the blow powerful enough to send the witch sprawling on the carpet. "Perhaps you should have thought of that before you predicted my death."

Settling back in her throne, Morgana lifted her gaze toward the black mist overhead.

"I know you're out there, hiding from me like a coward, but I'm coming for you," she breathed, her hair swirling as her power flowed from her body. She couldn't see her prey, but she could sense the stirring power. "And when I find you I'm going to rip your heart from your chest."

Despite the fact that he had been given a bedchamber in a separate wing of the house from Anna, Cezar woke the moment he heard the distant scream.

With the speed only a vampire could call upon he was racing through the hallway, inwardly relieved that the house had been suitably protected against the late afternoon sun. Of course, he would expect no less from Styx.

The last of the scream was still shuddering in the air when Cezar thrust open the door. He was prepared for battle as he crossed the threshold, two daggers in his hand and a matching pair of handguns strapped to his chest despite the fact that he wore nothing but black silk boxers.

Being a guardian to the Oracles had trained him well.

A swift search of the shadowed room and attached bathroom assured him there were no enemies lurking in the corners. He crossed to the bed and found Anna still fast asleep, her beautiful face flushed as she twisted in the throes of her nightmare.

An abrupt, violent surge of relief nearly sent him to his knees as Cezar stacked his weapons on the nightstand and slid beneath the blankets to pull her shivering body into his arms. *Dios*. He had feared . . .

Hell, he couldn't even make himself consider what he had feared. Not now that he held Anna tightly in his arms, her heart beating frantically against his chest and her hands instinctively clutching at his arms.

For a moment, Cezar savored the feel of her warm body that readily curved toward his. He had waited nearly two centuries to once again feel this heady pleasure. To simply have her in his arms.

Burying his face in her soft curls he soaked in her sweet, lightly fruity scent, his hands running a soothing path up the curve of her spine.

She was wearing nothing more than a flimsy bit of silk and lace that Darcy must have loaned to her, but for the moment Cezar was more intent on easing her fear than stirring her passions.

"Ssh, Anna," he murmured over and over, his lips lightly brushing her ear.

Slowly her trembling lessened and for a blissful moment she snuggled against the hard planes of his body, as if seeking his comfort. Cezar tightened his hold, still whispering softly in her ear.

A strange peace spread through his heart and Cezar realized that if he possessed the power he might have stopped time in this precise moment. To have this woman wrapped in his arms, her slender body bathing him in heat, and the world seemingly far away.

But while he was a consummate warrior, a well-trained guardian, and a fair scholar, his skills didn't extend to time-stopping.

Anna sighed softly, her breath brushing over the bare skin of his chest, then she opened her eyes to regard him in dazed confusion.

"Cezar?"

"Si."

Her hands went from clutching him to pressing him away in alarm. "What the hell are you doing in my bed?"

His arms refused to budge. Beneath her alarm at finding him in her bed was a lingering fear. The dream had shaken her and Cezar wasn't about to leave until he'd discovered what the hell it had been about.

"You were screaming in your sleep." He settled his head on a pillow, his gaze searching her strained features. "I thought I had better wake you before the cops came to investigate."

The stunning hazel eyes darkened as the memory of the dream washed over her. "Oh."

"Tell me."

"Tell you what?"

"About the dream."

Her brows snapped together. "Why?"

He hesitated before answering. She was already freaked out

by being plunged into a world she barely knew existed. The last thing he wanted was to tip her into full-blown panic at the thought that there were demons that possessed the ability to speak, or even attack, through dreams.

"It might be important, *querida*," he at last murmured.

"What could be important about a dream?"

"I won't know unless you tell me." He studied her stubborn expression. She had her heels dug in and a petulant desire to argue with even the most reasonable request. Obviously a new tactic was in order. With a smile, he shifted to trail his lips down the line of her nose, his hands beginning an intimate inspection of the satin and lace nightgown that had been designed to entice a man's appetite. And he was definitely enticed. Enticed, beguiled, and suddenly hotter than hell. His fingers flexed in restless need, his lips brushing over hers in a silent persuasion. "Anna, I'm not leaving until you talk to me. However, I can keep myself pleasantly occupied if you prefer to wait."

Her lips parted to speak and Cezar was swift to take advantage. Deepening his kiss he thrust his tongue into the moist heat of her mouth, his erection throbbing in time to her low moans.

She tasted of fruit, as sweet and rich as a ripe fig dipped in honey. Cezar trembled as his senses roared with life, his entire body taut with the need only she could inspire.

Sucking her tongue into his mouth, Cezar was careful not to nick her with his fangs. Things were spinning out of control fast enough without the danger of his bloodlust being stirred.

His hands smoothed over her shoulders, and then fisted the satin curtain of honey hair. He growled deep in his throat. He wanted to devour her. To take her so completely that he became a part of her very soul.

The heat of her growing desire seared his skin as he untangled their mouths and trailed a line of kisses down the curve of her throat. He could smell her hunger perfume the air, feel her shivers as he thrust his arousal against her stomach.

Anna might not consciously accept that she needed him, but her response proved that nothing had changed in the past two centuries. His touch could still make her body burn with desire.

Muttering his approval, Cezar trailed his fingers through the honey hair before moving them down the length of her back. He took a delicious moment to explore the curve of her hips before inching up the silky material of her gown. His instincts urged him to rip the offending cloth from her body, but his mind warned him to keep this time together civilized. There would be plenty of nights (or days) to take her hard and fast.

Tonight it would be . . .

"Cezar." Without warning her hands went back to pressing against his chest, her head arching away from his marauding lips. "No."

He hissed in frustration, his mouth refusing to obey his will as it dipped down to capture a furled nipple that peeked through the sheer lace. *Dios*, he craved her like an addict who was in the throes of withdrawal.

"You're certain?"

She gave a strangled groan before she grasped his hair and tugged his head up to meet her glittering gaze.

"I'm not the innocent fool I was two hundred years ago."

The edge of bitterness in her voice jerked Cezar out of his sensual haze and he pulled back to regard her with a frown.

What the hell was she babbling about? That night they had spent together had been spectacular. He could still hear her cries of pleasure as he had plunged deep into her body, feel the shudder of her explosive release, taste the potent delight of her blood as it slid down his throat.

Surely to God she couldn't regret it?

"You might have been innocent, but you were never a fool," he growled, angered by her attempt to deny what they had shared.

"I let myself be seduced by a complete stranger, didn't

I?" She gave a shake of her head. "I'd call that a quality bout of stupidity."

"I'd call it destiny," he said before he could halt the revealing words.

Not surprisingly she blinked in puzzlement. "What's that supposed to mean?"

He wasn't prepared to go there. Not even in his own mind.

Time for distraction. For both of them.

"Tell me about the dream," he commanded.

Her fingers, which had unwittingly begun to stroke through the strands of his hair, pulled away with a sharp motion. "God, you never give up."

He flashed a fierce grin. "Never."

She briefly closed her eyes before heaving a deep sigh. "Fine. There was a woman."

Keeping his arms locked about her slender body, Cezar intently studied her face. Anna tended to say far more with her expression than her words.

"What did she look like?"

She gave a lift of her shoulder. "Beautiful, with red hair and green eyes."

His eyes narrowed, a chill spreading through his body. "What was she doing?"

"She was sitting on a gold throne, and there was another woman there, an old woman who was lying on a red carpet." She grimaced at the memory. "Her mouth was bleeding."

"Was she dead?"

"I don't think so."

His hands ran an absent path up her back. "Something made you scream, Anna. What was it?"

She shuddered, fear flashing through her eyes. "The woman sitting on the throne . . . she seemed to be staring straight at me . . . and then . . ."

"And then?"

"And then she said she was going to rip out my heart. I believed her."

She trembled, and pressing his hand to the back of her head, Cezar tucked her close to his body. There could be no doubt the woman in her dreams had been Morgana le Fay. And that the woman was determined to see Anna dead.

Never.

The word branded onto Cezar's heart. He would kill anything, anyone who dared to harm Anna.

"No one's going to be ripping out your heart, *querida*," he rasped, his voice raw. "That much I can promise you."

She gave a choked laugh at his arrogant pledge, but thankfully made no move to try to pull away.

"You're so certain you can protect me?"

"Yes." His lips brushed her forehead. "But beyond that, you're a dangerous woman in your own right. I still have the aching ribs to prove it."

She tilted back her head to meet his smoldering gaze, the fear fading from her eyes. "A dangerous woman, eh?"

"Absolutely."

"I like that."

He deliberately brushed his arousal against her hip. "Me too."

"I can tell," she said dryly.

"What can I say? Dangerous women are hot."

"You think every woman is hot." She frowned as he gave a sharp, humorless laugh at her ridiculous words. "What's so funny?"

One hundred and ninety-five years without a woman. Without the least stirring of desire. And now that he had at long last recovered his mojo, it only worked for a female who was determined to keep him celibate.

Yeah, he was quite the ladies' man.

"Dios," he breathed. "If you only knew."

"Knew what?"

He gave a shake of his head. "Tell me of your life,

querida," he instead prompted. "You said that you've lived quietly, but you must have done something to keep yourself occupied."

She studied his face, surrounded by the heavy fall of his black hair. "Are you really interested or are you just trying to distract me so you can stay in my bed?"

He smiled, not bothering to hide his fully extended fangs. "Both."

"There isn't much to tell."

"Humor me, *por favor.*"

She rolled her eyes at his insistence. Cezar ignored the taunting gesture. She was warm and soft in his arms, and for the moment he wanted to think about nothing but the sensation of her beating heart against his chest and the scent of her warm skin.

"I moved around a lot, which wasn't all bad since I managed to see a great deal of the world over the years," she at last confessed in a soft voice. "Venice, Amsterdam, Cairo . . . I even spent a few memorable months in Tokyo before traveling to America."

"How did you survive?"

"I took whatever job I could find. In the early days I usually worked as a maid, since it was the only respectable job open to a woman. Later I began waiting tables at cheap restaurants." She grimaced. "A job I don't recommend to anyone. Even today the smell of hot grease makes my stomach heave."

Cezar resisted the urge to skim his hands over that stomach. Or maybe he would skim his lips over that stomach. Oh . . . yes. Definitely his lips. And then he could explore down to the tiny thong and between her legs . . .

"What of men?" he abruptly demanded.

Her eyes widened. "Excuse me?"

An odd tension gripped him as he suddenly realized just how important her answer was to him.

"Did you ever marry?"

"Good God, no," she breathed in shock.

"Why not? You're an incredibly beautiful woman." He gently cupped her cheek, his thumb brushing over the fullness of her lower lip. "I don't doubt that you've had to fight the men off."

Her tongue peeked out to touch the precise spot his thumb had caressed, sending a zing of electricity through his body.

That tongue could no doubt make a vampire howl in bliss.

The mere *thought* of it was nearly enough to make him howl.

Swallowing a groan, Cezar forced himself to concentrate on her low words.

"And just how do you expect me to explain the fact that I'm some bizarre Superman clone?" she demanded.

"Don't you mean Wonder Woman?"

"That's not funny." She gave his arm a pinch. "I couldn't risk being close to anyone."

A strange pain lanced through him. "Did you want to be close to someone? Was there someone special?"

She shrugged. "Does it matter?"

"Yes." His teeth ground together. "It matters."

Their gazes tangled and for a moment Cezar feared she might refuse to answer him. Then, with a frustrated shake of her head she conceded defeat.

"No, there was no one special. I've been completely and utterly alone for . . . for what seems like forever. Are you happy?"

He was more than happy. He was fiercely pleased by the notion she hadn't given her heart to some unworthy bastard.

He was also smart enough to keep his satisfaction to himself.

Smoothing his hand down her hair, he pressed a gentle kiss to her temple. "I didn't mean to upset you, *querida.*"

She gave a snort of disbelief, her eyes narrowing. "And what about you?"

"What about me?"

"Do you have some . . ." She frowned as she struggled with the appropriate word. "Mate hanging around in a damp cave?"

A slow, wicked smile touched his lips at her grudging curiosity. "I have no mate."

"Why not?"

His lips skimmed down her cheek to nibble at the corner of her mouth. "Some things, Anna Randal, are worth waiting for."

Chapter 6

Anna's heart was lodged somewhere near her tonsils as she felt the light scrape of Cezar's fangs against the edge of her mouth.

This was insanity.

No. Waking to discover a gorgeous, heart-stopping, drool-worthy vampire in her bed was insanity.

Quivering with the need to feel the aching pleasure of his kiss was full out la-la land.

Unfortunately, her body didn't give a damn about the sanity of responding to Cezar's expert touch. It only knew that it had waited almost two hundred years to feel the cool pleasure of those fingers exploring her trembling curves and the erotic satisfaction of his fangs sliding into her flesh.

The dark, sweet craving intensified as his head bent lower, finding the tip of her straining nipple beneath the lace of her gown.

A groan caught in her throat as sharp-edged bliss shuddered through her body. His tongue was teasing the sensitive bit of flesh, flicking and stroking until her back arched in a silent plea.

Dammit, she had promised herself this wouldn't happen. There was no way in hell she was going to let this man think she was an oversexed tart who would spread her legs every time he passed through her life.

A promise easily made when Cezar had been nothing more than a painful memory. She'd convinced herself that it had been her innocence that made her so susceptible to the delicious vampire. After all, she had spent two centuries resisting the various men (some of them downright edible) who had desired to lure her to their beds. She was older, wiser, and capable of controlling her desires.

Ha.

She was going up in flames as his fingers coasted down the back of her thighs, tugging up the gown with a determination that was unmistakable. Even worse, the soft words he muttered beneath his breath as his lips searched out her other nipple were drugging her mind, making her forget precisely why she was supposed to be saying no.

He had to be casting a spell over her, she fuzzily told herself. That was why her fingers were digging into his arms until she was drawing blood, and why her core was so hot and wet that she thought she might come at the slightest touch.

Otherwise it would mean . . . .

A sudden pounding on the door interrupted the terrifying thought.

"Cezar." A male voice floated through the air, making Cezar lift his head with a blast of dark curses.

"Si?" he bit out.

"Sorry to intrude, but we have a situation." Styx's commanding voice carried through the door with remarkable ease.

There was another string of curses as Cezar grudgingly released his hold on Anna and surged from the bed.

"I'll return in a moment," he muttered, heading for the door.

Following in his wake, Anna reached for the robe that Darcy had kindly loaned her and, shoving her hands into the sleeves, silently assured herself that the shivers that wracked her body were nothing more than relief.

Only they didn't feel like relief.

They felt like gut-wrenching frustration that was settling in for a good long stay.

"Wait, Cezar." She forced herself to reach out and lay her hand on his arm. "If this concerns me then I want to be involved."

Coming to a halt he turned to stab her with an impatient gaze. No. Not impatient. Frustrated. The same expression that was tightening her own features.

She didn't doubt if she glanced down she would discover he was still hard and aching to be inside her.

With an effort she squashed the urge to confirm her theory and instead concentrated on holding that burning gaze.

"Querida . . ." he began, only to give a startled blink when she pointed a finger directly in his face.

"I mean it," she gritted. "The days when I was forced to beg on my knees for a bit of food and shelter are long over. These days I take care of myself. I won't give that up."

Something flashed through his dark eyes. Something that might have been disappointment? Pain? Wounded pride?

"You refuse my assistance?" he demanded softly.

She ignored the odd prick of regret. She couldn't have hurt him. The man was arrogant, and aggravating, and utterly impervious to anything remotely resembling human emotions. Except for desire. Hell, hadn't he seduced her and then abandoned her for nearly two centuries?

Still, she found her voice softening despite her best intentions. "Of course not, I'm not stupid. I don't even know what I'm up against." She gave an awkward shrug, tugging the belt of her robe tighter. "But, accepting your assistance is considerably different from being ordered around and kept in the dark. We're either partners or I'm leaving."

A tense silence filled the room. It was obvious that Cezar's arrogant need to be in charge was grimly warring with the knowledge that she wasn't jerking him around. She fully intended to walk if he didn't agree.

Expecting an angry response, Anna was caught off guard when his lips at last twitched with a wicked amusement.

"Partners, eh?" he murmured, his hand reaching up to trail through the tangled strands of her hair.

Her eyes narrowed with a wary uncertainty. This all seemed waaaay too easy.

"I'm not kidding, Cezar. I'd rather be dead than back to feeling like a beggar."

His gaze deliberately skimmed down to the deep vee of her robe. "You know, I wouldn't mind doing a little begging if you would . . ."

Reaching up, Anna slapped a hand over his mouth. His low voice was a nearly tangible caress that flowed over her sensitive skin, bringing with it thoughts of pushing him back onto the bed and crawling on top of him.

They were both nearly naked. It would only take a few tugs and . . .

Focus, Anna. Focus.

"Do we have a deal?" she rasped, gritting her teeth at the knowing expression on his face.

He could sense the desire that still pounded through her, but strangely he didn't try to take advantage. Instead he gave a small shrug. "I'll try." He abruptly lifted his hand as her lips parted. "Hear me out, Anna. I've been alive a long time."

"How long?" Anna demanded, unable to halt the question. She'd had a lot of time to think and brood over this man. Her curiosity went way beyond casual.

"Over five hundred years."

She studied the bronzed, breathtaking beauty of his face. "Were you a conquistador?"

His brows lifted at her words. "When I awoke after the transformation I wore the uniform of a conquistador."

"You don't remember?"

"We have no memories of a life before becoming a vampire." His lips twisted in a wry smile. "A good thing, actually."

His confession startled her. How odd to simply have your life erased. Surely they must be curious as to who and what they had been before?

"Why is that a good thing?"

He nodded his head toward the door. "Because my king is an Aztec."

"Ah." A grudging smile touched her lips. "Yeah, I suppose that could be trouble."

His hand shifted to grasp her chin between his thumb and finger, his gaze shimmering with his restless energy. Despite Hollywood's depiction of vampires, they weren't walking corpses. Their skin might be cool to the touch, and their hearts might not beat, but they possessed a frenetic power that surrounded them like a force field. In truth, being close to Cezar was like being next to an electrical charge.

"My point is, that I have a tendency to act first and think later," Cezar said with a grimace. "Trust me, I've learned to regret the habit, but it hasn't changed who I am. I can't promise you I won't . . ."

"Be a pain in the ass?" she finished sweetly.

He gave her chin a pinch. "Something like that."

There was another rap on the door. "Cezar?"

Ignoring the distinct edge of irritation in his king's voice, Cezar stepped close enough to shock her with the force of his nearly bare body.

"A minute," he rasped, his eyes glittering as he stared down at Anna's pale face. Without warning he leaned down and captured her lips in a rough, demanding kiss. Anna gave a soft moan of pleasure, but before she could even begin to respond, his head lifted and he was regarding her with an intensity that made her breath catch in her throat. "You will never be a poor relation again, Anna Randal," he whispered. "You were born to rule the world."

She gave a small jerk at his outlandish words. Or maybe it was just a delayed reaction to his scorching kiss.

Holy crap, her lips would be tingling for a month.

"What did you say?"

He smiled mysteriously, but didn't bother to answer her question.

Of course not. She could threaten and demand all she wanted, but the whole partner thing would be at his freaking convenience.

Turning, Cezar pulled open the door, revealing the towering vampire who waited in the hall with a grim impatience.

"My lord, you have news?" he demanded.

Anna resisted the urge to back away from the leather-clad giant who turned to stab her with a searching gaze. Yikes. He looked quite capable of sacrificing her on the spot.

"What of the female?"

Anna's quaking knees stiffened. Female? *Female?*

The oversized vampire was lucky she didn't have full use of her powers. He would look mighty funny plastered to the ceiling or tumbling down the hall like a soccer ball.

Perhaps sensing her flare of annoyance, Cezar reached out to grasp her hand, giving her fingers a little squeeze.

"She insists on knowing whatever information you have."

A heavy, chiseled brow arched, but rather than the argument she was expecting the demon merely offered a smile. A smile that might have been more reassuring if it hadn't included a pair of lethal fangs that could bite through a tank.

"Very well." His unnerving attention switched back to Cezar. "The fairy is dead."

"Sybil?" Anna breathed in shock.

Styx gave a short nod, his long braid threaded with turquoise beads swinging across his back. "Yes."

"Good God."

Cezar's face revealed no shock. Instead it was a hard mask of granite that sent a chill down her spine.

"How did it happen?" he demanded in flat tones, his body coiled with anger. "You said her cell was protected."

A matching anger briefly touched Styx's eyes. He seemed like the sort of man who disliked it when things didn't go as he planned.

"It was, and I don't have a clue as to how she died. She has no visible wounds, and Gunter swears that no one entered or left the cell. She's simply dead." Styx reached up to touch a medallion that hung around his neck. "I've called for Levet to come and examine the body once night has fully fallen."

"Levet?" Cezar scowled at the other man. "*Dios*, why?"

"He can sense magic that we cannot," Styx said.

Anna struggled to keep track of the conversation. Inside she was a quivering mess. Sybil was dead. Granted there'd been more than a few times she would have willingly choked the life from the annoying bitch. And the knowledge she would never again have to look over her shoulder and discover the woman lurking in the shadows offered a sick sort of relief, but . . . dead? And while she was protected in this house where Anna had been sleeping like a baby?

The thought was enough to give her the heebie-jeebies.

With a shiver she crossed her arms over her stomach and tried to look brave. Dammit. She was the one who was demanding to be a partner in this nasty business.

I am woman hear me roar, she chided herself, *not oh-my-God I'm going to toss my cookies.*

"Who is Levet?" she forced herself to demand.

Despite her best efforts there must have been something in her voice that warned Cezar she was strolling near the edge.

His concerned gaze skimmed over her faintly green face before he tugged her to his side and slipped an arm around her shoulders.

"He's a gargoyle," he grudgingly confessed.

"Ah." She couldn't halt the short, wild laugh. "Of course."

Cezar's thumb rubbed the taut line of her throat, his touch magically easing back the panic that had threatened to boil to the surface.

"Don't worry," he soothed. "He's the runt of the litter and the only frightening thing about him is his warped sense of humor."

Styx regarded Cezar's movements with a narrowed gaze. Almost as if he was startled by the vampire's protective intimacy. Which was laughable. Anna knew firsthand that Conde Cezar made a habit of exchanging his women on a nightly basis. She had been one of the exchangees.

With an odd smile the giant vampire gave a dip of his head. "I will leave you to prepare."

"Good idea," Cezar murmured, shutting the door in the face of his king and crowding her against the wall before she knew what was happening. "Should we hit the shower first?"

A shower? Naked skin. Warm water. Silky soap. Hot, steamy . . .

The image of the two of them entwined as water poured over them was so vivid, Anna was forced to close her eyes and suck in a deep breath.

"Absolutely not," she muttered, already feeling hot and steamy as he deliberately leaned into her body, his head lowering so he could bury his face in her hair.

"Why?" He nipped at her earlobe. "You can wash my back and I'll wash yours. We're partners, remember?"

Her eyes rolled to the back of her head as his hands stroked up her sides and then boldly cupped the heavy fullness of her breasts.

Right. *Now*, they were partners. When he wanted to get up close and personal.

Well, she was going to . . . she was going to nip this in the . . . his thumbs teased the tips of her nipples and Anna moaned.

What the hell was she going to do?

Something besides melt into a puddle at his feet, surely?

The thumbs did another gut-wrenching brushing motion and Anna knew she was about to drown in his potent passion.

Holy crap.

"The only shower you're getting is going to be a cold one in your own room," she managed to rasp.

He laughed, his fangs deliberately scraping against her neck. "Harsh."

"Cezar, stop that."

"Why?" His tongue replaced his fangs in his campaign to send her up in flames. "I can smell your desire."

"You're going to be smelling my fist if you don't stop."

He laughed. "So violent, *querida*. First handcuffs and now threats. You used to prefer your lovemaking far more gentle."

Lovemaking?

No.

This was sex. Raw, animal sex.

Something she had sworn off two hundred years ago.

With a desperate wrench she was pushing him away and trying to collect her senses. A minute passed, and then five more, her rasping breaths the only sound in the room until she was at last able to meet Cezar's glittering gaze.

"Go away, Cezar."

The dark eyes flashed as he stepped toward her, his fingers cupping her cheek. "Someday, *querida*." His head bent to steal a kiss that was edged with desperation. "Someday very, very soon."

Anna felt better after a long, icy shower that helped to ease the sexual tension and washed away Cezar's sandalwood scent.

She felt even better when she returned to the Olympic-sized bedroom to find her suitcase on the bed. She didn't know how the miracle had occurred, and she didn't care. It was just a relief to pull on her own faded jeans and a pale yellow short-sleeved knit shirt.

Slipping on a pair of flip-flops, she paused long enough to pull her damp hair into a scrunchie and headed out the door.

As she moved down the wood-paneled hallway and hit the curved marble staircase, she briefly considered that her casual clothes didn't fit the sprawling mansion. Although she had lived simply over the past two centuries, she had spent enough time among the London aristocracy when she was young to recognize that the marble statues came straight from a Grecian temple and that the oil paintings that hung on the oak paneling were genuine masterpieces.

She paused at the bottom step and then gave a shrug as she went in search of her hostess. She was done trying to fit into places she didn't belong. Done trying to please others.

Besides, Darcy had been just as casual. The sort of casual that came from the soul, not from her clothes. Maybe werewolves were a little more go-with-the-flow than vampires, she wryly told herself.

Hearing sounds from the back of the house, Anna managed to negotiate the labyrinth of hallways to at last enter a beautiful kitchen that was filled with stainless steel appliances and pots of fresh herbs set on the window sills.

It was also filled with a peculiar creature that stood barely three feet tall with gray skin and strange bumps all over his knobby body. Even more odd, he possessed a long tail and a pair of wings that were startlingly beautiful.

"Oh." Coming to a halt on the black and white ceramic tiles, Anna sucked in a shocked breath. Maybe roaming around a house filled with demons wasn't such a good idea. Her gaze shifted to Darcy, who was seated at a cherrywood table. "I'm sorry. Am I interrupting?"

"God, no," the woman breathed, rising from her chair to cross the room. This morning she was wearing another pair of jeans with a well-worn sweatshirt that nearly swamped her tiny body. Her blond hair was carelessly spiked and her face free of makeup and yet she glowed with beauty.

It was no wonder the big, scary Styx melted whenever he glanced in her direction.

Anna was about to relax when the . . . thing scuttled across the floor in Darcy's wake, one clawed hand holding up a piece of cardboard that had a large E drawn on it.

"What are you doing?" the creature demanded, his voice thick with an astonishing French accent as he waved the cardboard in the air. "We have not finished the game. You must tell me how many of the vowels you wish to purchase."

Darcy reached out to pat the thing on its head. Right between its stunted horns.

"We'll finish later."

"Later?" There was a spat of French curses. "My audition could be any day. There is no later."

"Of course there is," Darcy soothed with remarkable patience. Just as if she were humoring a petulant child. "I've told you, Levet, it's Bob Barker who retired, and I might add, has already been replaced, not Vanna White."

Anna blinked. This was Levet? This was the gargoyle that was supposed to sense magic?

Cezar had said he was the runt, but . . . jeez. She really did have to stop watching horror flicks. Vampires, werewolves, fairies, gargoyles. So far they hadn't got anything right.

"Ah, this Vanna White is a human, is she not? She could drop dead at any moment," Levet protested, then without warning he was moving to stand directly in front of Anna. He pointed a claw up toward her face. "You there. You're a human. Aren't you afraid that you might just drop dead one day?"

"Well, I . . ." Anna cleared her throat.

She had no idea what to say, especially after the gargoyle leaned forward and blatantly began sniffing her leg.

"No, not human," he murmured, his gray eyes lifting to regard her with what Anna hoped was curiosity and not hunger.

"Good grief," Darcy muttered, sending Anna a rueful smile. "Anna, this is Levet. Levet, Anna Randal."

Anna remained speechless as the creature circled around her, sniffing at her jeans and occasionally poking her with a stubby claw.

"What are you?" he demanded as he came to a halt in front of her, his hands planted on his hips, his long tail twitching in frustration.

"Umm, Darcy?" Anna whispered, caught between disbelief and a startling urge to laugh.

"Levet, please stop sniffing my guest," Darcy commanded. "It's not polite."

The gargoyle made a rude noise. "You said that scratching my privates in public wasn't polite. Now I cannot even sniff the guests? You are such a buzz-kiss."

Darcy rolled her eyes. "Buzz-kill, Levet. The word is buzz-kill."

"Whatever." Levet returned his attention to Anna. "You smell like a fairy, but . . ."

"A fairy?" Anna took a startled step backward. She would know if she was a fairy. Wouldn't she? "I don't think so."

"Who were your parents?" Levet demanded.

"I don't know. I was raised in an orphanage until my aunt took me in."

"So one of them *could* have been a fairy?"

"I . . . suppose."

Levet tapped his foot, clearly not satisfied with her grudging concession. "There is something else. Something I can't put my toe upon."

"Finger, Levet," Darcy corrected wearily.

Levet ignored the werewolf as he moved forward, intent on discovering the mystery of Anna's heritage.

"Take a step closer to her, gargoyle, and I'll have you mounted on my wall," a cold male voice warned from the doorway.

Anna had no need to turn. Her skin was already prickling with awareness and her heart jolting into overdrive.

It couldn't be anyone but Cezar.

Foolishly undaunted, the gargoyle stuck out his tongue and astonishingly sent the looming vampire a raspberry.

"I hear that's the only way you can mount these days . . ." His strange words had barely left his lips when Cezar was across the floor with the point of a dagger pressed to his throat. "Eek."

"You have any other charming revelations to make, gargoyle?" Cezar growled.

"Ah, no." The wings fluttered at a frantic pace. "Not a one."

"Good choice."

With fluid speed Cezar straightened, the dagger tucked away so swiftly that Anna couldn't follow the motion.

Not that she was paying attention to the dagger.

She was far too busy reminding herself of the need to breathe as her gaze traveled over the loose white shirt that was half unbuttoned, revealing a generous amount of his smooth chest, and the black jeans that clung to his butt with a tasty perfection. His dark hair was damp, the top layer pulled back with a strip of leather and the rest falling about his broad shoulders.

The elegant, sophisticated gentleman had been transformed into a dark, lean predator. A hunter who was poised and ready to attack.

Strolling into the kitchen, Styx glanced around with a narrowed gaze, easily sensing the tension in the room.

"Damn, have I been missing the fun?" he demanded, instinctively moving to stand beside Darcy in a protective manner.

The tiny blonde flashed him a smile. "Cezar was just about to make a shish kebab out of Levet."

The large vampire's lips twitched. "Maybe you should wait until after he's inspected the cell," he told Cezar. "I'd hate to finally have the pleasure of toasting him over an open fire just when he might have a bit of use."

"Ha, ha, ha. You are a million chuckles," Levet muttered, waddling toward the door. "Where is this cell? I have better things to do than go around playing Christopher Columbus."

Anna glanced toward Darcy. "Christopher Columbus?"

Darcy laughed. "I think he means Colombo."

"Ah."

Styx and Darcy fell into step behind the retreating gargoyle. Anna followed behind them, not surprised when Cezar appeared at her side and took her hand in a firm grip.

He wasn't the bring-up-the-rear sort of vampire.

"Did he trouble you?" he demanded in a low voice.

She lifted her head to meet his searching gaze. "Who?"

"The gargoyle."

"Not at all." Anna hid a smile. She didn't need special powers to know that Levet annoyed the hell out of Cezar. "I think he's . . ."

"An obnoxious pain in the neck who should have been made into a pair of shoes and matching handbag eons ago?"

"I can hear you," Levet called out.

"I know," Cezar muttered.

"I think he's cute," Anna said.

"Cute?" Cezar glanced at her as if he feared she'd taken a blow to the head. Perhaps several. "That . . . sad embarrassment for a demon?"

"I'm French, Cezar," Levet said smugly. "Females always find me cute. It is both a blessing and a curse."

Cezar muttered beneath his breath, "I'll give him a curse."

Anna chuckled as they turned from the main hallway and Styx took the lead. He halted at what appeared to be a plain piece of paneling, his large hand stroking over the wood. A hidden door sprang open and with a backward glance toward Cezar, he led them down the dark, narrow staircase.

A dark chill wrapped around Anna as they climbed steadily

downward, the eerie silence making her clutch at Cezar's hand, even as a small voice in the back of her mind warned that he was probably the most dangerous thing lurking in the shadows.

Down and down they went, occasionally halting to unlock another set of doors before continuing. It was only when Anna was certain they must be in the deepest bowels of the earth that the stairs came to an end and they stepped into what appeared to be the intersection of several tunnels.

Torches set into the dirt walls offered a wavering light, giving a hint of the vastness of the underground cavern.

"Holy crap . . ." Anna breathed, her eyes wide as Styx tugged one of the torches from the wall and headed down a dark tunnel to the left. "I thought the upstairs was huge."

Cezar's thumb absently stroked over her knuckles as they moved through the flickering shadows, no doubt sensing her growing feeling of unreality.

"A vampire always makes sure he has a few escape tunnels in his lair," he whispered close to her ear.

Anna sucked in a deep breath of his sandalwood scent, oddly comforted by his presence. As much as this vampire aggravated her, she knew she would be a nervous wreck without him at her side.

"A few?" She gave a shake of her head as they walked through the tunnel, an occasional steel door set in the walls. "The entire city of Chicago could evacuate to Mexico in these."

Cezar flashed a wry smile, but before he could respond Styx halted before one of the steel doors that was guarded by a tall, blond-haired . . . well, Goth was the first thought that popped into Anna's mind. Not the Goth of today, but the ancient Germans who'd battled the Roman Empire.

Tall and muscular with dark blond hair spilling down his nearly naked body, the vampire looked like he had been carved from sheer granite. And he was a vampire, she silently acknowledged. Even standing several feet away, she could feel that electric buzz filling the air.

Of course, the fact that he was heart-stopping, knee-melting gorgeous was clue enough.

Styx spoke with the vampire in a strange language. Then, with a faint nod, he pushed open the door to the cell.

"This is it." He pointed toward the gargoyle. "Levet, come."

The gargoyle tossed his stunted arms in the air, but he wasn't stupid enough to ignore the stark command. Shuffling forward, he stomped past the looming vampires, his tail twitching in annoyance.

"You do know that I'm not a dog?" he muttered, his voice lowering to sound remarkably like Styx. "*Come, Levet. Sit, Levet. Roll over, Levet.*"

Without warning Cezar was moving forward, reaching out to grasp the tiny demon by one horn. He lifted the gargoyle until they were eye to eye and even Anna shivered at the expression on the dark, beautiful face.

"This is no time for your peculiar sense of humor, gargoyle. You will shut your mouth and do your thing or you will answer to me. Is that clear?"

Levet gave a tiny squeak. "Ah . . . very clear. Clear as crystal. Clear as . . ."

His words trailed away as Cezar lowered him back to the ground and he was able to scurry into the cell with his tail between his legs.

Styx and Darcy entered behind the demon, but as Anna moved to follow them, she felt a restraining hand on her shoulder.

"Anna, there is no need for you to go in there."

Anna swallowed her snappish retort. As much as she longed to blame Cezar for this craziness that was now her life, she had to concede that it wasn't entirely fair.

Whatever had happened between them in the past, there

was no mistaking that he had done everything in his power to
protect her over the past twenty-four hours.

Whether it was out of a desire to crawl back into her bed or
out of genuine concern still remained a question.

"I've seen death before, Cezar," she said in a quiet voice.
"And I need . . . I need to see if I can help Levet. I need to *do*
something, not just wait around for that woman to rip out
my heart."

His brows snapped together. "That was just a dream . . ."

She pressed a finger to his lips. "Cezar, partners don't lie
to one another. We both know that wasn't just another dream."

Chapter 7

Cezar growled deep in his throat. He'd never been good at compromise. Especially when it came to females.

He saw, he took, he conquered.

End of story.

Now he was forced to battle his natural instincts as Anna regarded him with those huge, hazel eyes that could melt the damn Arctic. *Dios.* Global warming had nothing on this woman.

He wanted to toss her over his shoulder and return her to that soft bed where he could distract her with his fierce, driving hunger. He wanted her soft and willing beneath his body, a satisfied smile curving her lips as he thrust her to a mindless orgasm.

Instead he could do nothing more than jerk her close to his body, his head lowering to claim her lips in a frustrated kiss.

"You do know you're going to drive me stark, raving mad?" he whispered against her mouth, demanding another hungry kiss before lifting his head. "Let's get this over with."

She appeared momentarily dazed, her hands lifting to touch her lips. Then, with a shake of her head, she was tilting her chin and forcing her feet to carry her into the cell.

Cezar was a half step behind her.

Unlike the dirt tunnels, the cell was lined with heavy lead

that was etched with scrolling symbols that looked faintly like hieroglyphics. The room had been hexed by an imp to dampen any magic.

In the corner of the small cell was a cot where the once beautiful Sybil Taylor rested in silent peace.

Ignoring the gargoyle who was circling the cell, his eyes closed as he used his senses to detect any lingering spells. Anna moved to stare down at the fairy.

"She looks so peaceful," she breathed. "Almost like she's sleeping."

Cezar moved to her side with a faint grimace. "I can't detect magic, but I do know the scent of death."

"*Oui*, she's dead," Levet offered.

"The question is how?" Cezar growled.

Levet opened his eyes, a faintly puzzled expression on his ugly face. "I smell . . . pomegranates."

"Pomegranates?" Anna lifted her head, her face pale and her eyes dark with a strange, powerful emotion. "Sybil always smelled of apples."

Levet's wings gave a small flutter. "Fey magic. I don't know how, but whoever did this was very powerful."

"It was the woman from my dream," Anna said slowly, licking her dry lips. "I smelled pomegranates when she looked at me."

"What dream?" Styx demanded from the doorway.

There was a short, tense silence as every eye turned toward Anna. Cezar paused, inwardly cursing. This was *not* how he wanted to tell Anna what he suspected.

"It was a dream of Morgana," Cezar at last said, his tone flat and his gaze on Anna's fragile features.

"Morgana le Fay?" Styx demanded.

Cezar gave a reluctant nod as Anna's eyes widened and her mouth parted in shock.

"Morgana-freaking-le-Fay?" she demanded, her voice edged with growing panic. "The sister of King Arthur?

Knights? Dragons? Round tables?" She gave a wild shake of her head. "No. Way."

Moving slow enough that Anna could track his movements, Cezar reached out to take her hands in his. Her skin was cold and clammy, revealing the depth of her shock.

"Give us a moment," he commanded, gently pulling Anna away from the dead body and urging her into a wooden chair set in the corner.

Once the cell was cleared of demons, he squatted in front of Anna and gave her hands a squeeze.

"Anna," he said softly. "*Querida*, please look at me."

An eternity seemed to pass before the long sweep of her lashes slowly lifted to reveal her dazed, frighteningly vulnerable eyes.

"Are you going to tell me that I've been Punk'd?" she said, her voice so thick it made his heart contract in pain.

He gave a shake of his head. "Punk'd?"

"You know, reveal that this is all some huge joke?"

He lifted her fingers to his lips. "I can tell you that if that's what you want."

She sucked in a deep, shuddering breath. "No, I want the truth. Tell me about this . . . Morgana le Fay."

"She's the Queen of the Fairies, although little is known of her. Since Arthur's death she has hidden in her fortress upon Avalon." He kept his voice cool, indifferent. It was that or growl with fury at the mere mention of the fairy queen.

"If Morgana is really after me, what does she want?" She shuddered. "Besides my heart."

"I don't know yet." He paused and then cursed beneath his breath. Hell, he might as well get it over with. "I think you might be related to her."

She jerked as if he had physically struck her. "Related to Morgana le Fay?"

"*Si*."

"God." She gave a short, humorless laugh. "Over the years

I came up with a number of wacky explanations of why I was so different, but this was never one of them."

"You preferred to believe that I was responsible?"

"Yeah." A faint heat brushed her too pale skin. "I suppose I did."

"And now?" he prompted.

"Now I don't know what to think."

Hardly a rousing vote of confidence. More like a grudging, gun-to-the-temple sort of vote.

"Anna, I would never hurt you. That night . . ." He bit off his impatient words as he realized that now was not the time.

"What?"

With a smooth motion he rose to his feet and began pacing the cell. Suddenly it seemed way too small. And way too filled with Anna's sweet, fruity scent.

"There's more," he said abruptly. "I think that Morgana was the 'cousin' you lived with in London. I believe she burned down your townhouse, killing your aunt and assuming that she killed you as well."

"No." She rose to her feet, shaking her head. "That's not possible. My cousin didn't look anything like the woman in my dreams."

"Morgana would be capable of a powerful glamour. She could have altered her appearance so that the human eye would see only what she desired."

She wrapped her arms around her waist, shivering as if the room were ice cold. "But not a demon?"

"I could have seen through her magic, although she obviously took great care not to allow me to catch sight of her," he admitted. "You said yourself that first night she had disappeared only moments before I entered the room."

"That's true, but . . ."

Cezar rushed forward as she swayed and nearly pitched face first onto the ground. With a tenderness he didn't even know he possessed, he was carefully urging her back into the chair.

"Here." His hands tightened on her shoulders as she struggled to rise. "No, *querida*, just sit for a minute. Breathe." He watched as she drew in a shaky breath. "Again."

In time the greenish tint left her cheeks and she was lifting her head to meet his concerned gaze. "Sorry."

"For what?"

"For acting like a pansy after my big speech about wanting to be Xena Warrior Princess."

His hands absently stroked over her shoulders, not at all certain how to ease the shivers that still shook her body.

Dammit. He didn't like seeing her so shaken. It made him want to . . . kill something.

Preferably something of the fairy variety.

"I don't know any Xena, but I suspect that even a warrior princess would be a little shaky in your position," he murmured.

"You mean, if she discovered she possessed a murderous cousin who tried to burn her to death in her own bed and now is on the hunt for her heart?"

"Anna, I can't be certain that it was Morgana who burned your house." His hands tightened on her shoulders. "But I think we should at least consider the possibility."

"Yes. Yes, you're right." She lifted her hands to rub her temples. "I need . . . I need to think."

"There will be time for that later."

"Actually there won't be." She lowered her hands and glanced at the watch strapped to her wrist. "I have a flight to L.A. that leaves in less than six hours."

"No."

Cezar cursed his abrupt response as her eyes narrowed and her expression hardened. After five centuries of dealing with females of every race and persuasion, he should have learned that the one way to make them dig in their heels was to give them a direct command.

"What did you say?" she demanded.

Cezar paused, considering his words with care. It was time for a little damage control. He would prefer not to be forced to hold her against her will.

There were lots of women who found being chained to a bed as sexy as hell, but unfortunately Anna wasn't one of them.

"Anna, you must remain here," he said, his voice soft. "At least you will be safe."

She deliberately glanced toward the dead Sybil. "Not so safe."

"Then I will take you . . ."

"No, Cezar." She wrapped her arms around herself, as if to try and hide her shivers. "I can't spend the rest of eternity in hiding, or constantly on the run."

"It won't be for an eternity."

"You think Morgana le Fay is going to forget about me?" she demanded. "Or maybe she'll suddenly have a Dr. Phil moment and decide it isn't really nice to go around killing her family?"

Cezar curled his hands in frustration. He couldn't reveal her destiny with the Oracles. Nor the fact that once she became a member of the Commission no demon, no matter how desperate, would dare risk the wrath of the Oracles in an attempt to harm her.

"Your powers will continue to grow every day," he said, his hand reaching out to lightly stroke her hair. "Soon enough you will be able to protect yourself. Until then you need to remain with those who can keep you hidden from Morgana."

She rolled her eyes at his perfect logic. "You mean I need to remain with you?"

He stepped closer to her enticing heat, his fingers finding the curve of her cheek.

"Would that be such a terrible thing?"

Her lashes fluttered as she struggled not to respond to his soothing touch. "My life is in California. I have an apartment, a job, people who are depending on me. I can't just disappear."

"You won't have a life if you take on Morgana before

you're ready." He took another step closer. Because of her powers he couldn't compel her with his mind, but he had other weapons. His fingers drifted downward, his thumb stroking the fullness of her lower lip. "You're not a fool, *querida*. Stay here and accept the help that we are willing to offer you."

She stared into his eyes for a long, silent moment. Cezar smugly assumed that he had managed to bewitch her with his touch. It wouldn't be the first time a woman had been speechless beneath the power of his seduction.

Then, a shrewd glitter entered the hazel eyes and she reached up to grasp his teasing fingers in a firm grip.

"There's something else, isn't there?"

"Something else?"

"You aren't trying to protect me out of the goodness of your heart. There's something you're not telling me."

The plain, wooden house that was stuck in the middle of acres of farmland was as different from Avalon as it was possible to be.

The house was old and cramped, with furniture that had long ago grown shabby from use. There were a few cross-stitched pictures on the white walls and gingham curtains on the windows, but nothing could disguise the dampness that was slowly rotting the wood, or the infestation of mice that had taken over the attic. There was also an annoying scent of spearmint that permeated the air, as if the old lady that Morgana had buried in the back garden was addicted to chewing gum.

In fact, the only positive things about the dump were that it was well secluded and far enough from Chicago that Morgana could continue her search without being sensed by others.

Lying on the bed in the upstairs bedroom, Morgana attempted to ignore the heavy dust and damp mold that filled the air. For the moment she was far too weary to improve her surroundings. By the gods, she was too weary to even brush aside the heavy quilt that Modron had spread over her naked body.

Her powers were elemental, not those of the fey, and conjuring a portal that was large enough not only for herself but the old hag as well had drained her completely. It would take days to recover her full strength.

Of course, even with only a portion of her powers, she was still capable of killing most things.

Sipping the warm tea with honey that helped to ease her lingering pain, Morgana watched as Modron shuffled into the room.

The seer's tufts of hair were matted to her skull and she was wearing one of the shapeless dresses that had belonged to the old woman who had called the farmhouse her own—well, at least until Morgana had drained her pathetic life.

Not even the bath that Morgana had insisted the hag take could make her anything less than disgusting.

"The demon is arriving," the woman rasped, her blind eyes trained directly on Morgana.

"Good. Bring him to me here."

Modron raised a gnarled hand. "You are still too weak. You should wait."

Morgana hissed at the chiding words. The hag had been bitching and moaning since Morgana had summoned the Adar demon.

"I gave you a command, hag," she snapped. "Bring the hunter to me."

The seer remained grimly poised in the doorway, her ugly face hard with displeasure.

"We wouldn't need the Adar if you hadn't killed the fairy."

Morgana tossed the mug of tea at the aggravating witch. It splintered against the door as Modron easily sidestepped the missile, her cackling laugh echoing through the room.

Morgana hadn't been happy when her spell had revealed that Sybil was being held in a hexed room. There was no way to trace her and no way to retrieve her without exposing Morgana to unacceptable risk. There had been no choice but to kill the fairy.

"I told you, you stupid bitch, I couldn't risk having her reveal my interest in the human."

"You don't even know if it was the one you seek who captured Sybil."

"It doesn't matter now, does it?"

"Oh aye." The hag gave a shake of her head, the strands of gray hair floating eerily about her wrinkled face. "And now you have nothing more than a corpse you can't question and can't find."

Morgana settled back against the pillows, refusing to be goaded. She had to regain her strength. Until then she was far too vulnerable.

"I have something better than that. If Sybil was captured by the one who holds my brother's tainted blood, then her body will lead me straight to where I need to go." A dull chime sounded through the house, warning that something had crossed the barrier she had placed around the yard. Morgana narrowed her gaze with warning. "Go greet the Adar and keep a decent tongue in your mouth. Otherwise I might just allow the demon to take his price out of your flesh."

With a grimace Modron turned and made her way down the stairs. An Adar demon demanded the blood of the one who requested its services.

That and a rather large amount of gold.

A handful of minutes passed as Morgana carefully smoothed her expression and lowered the quilt to expose one creamy shoulder and a hint of one breast.

Of all her powers, her exquisite beauty was the most potent.

There was no sound before the Adar appeared in the

doorway, his movements so carefully controlled that not even the layers of dust on the wood floors were stirred.

He appeared human at first glance. A small, delicate child with the face of an angel and a curly mop of golden hair. His skin was pale, nearly white, and his slight body was covered in a pair of jeans and a sweatshirt.

His eyes, however, revealed his heritage. Too large for his urchin face they were slanted and consumed with an inky blackness. There were also the unmistakable fangs that flashed when he offered a faint smile.

"Mistress."

Morgana lifted a beckoning hand. "Come closer, Adar."

"No offense, Mistress, but I would rather stay here," he purred.

"I don't need to use my hands to kill you."

He shrugged as he leaned against the doorjamb. "True, but I prefer the view from here."

The air shimmered with heat. "You play a dangerous game with me."

His smile widened, revealing his bottom fangs as well. An angel with a serious bite.

"Is there any other kind of game?" he said, his voice far too deep for his delicate form.

"Enough." Realizing the demon was impervious to her potent sex appeal, Morgana impatiently tugged the quilt higher. His opportunity had passed and it was time for business. "I have need of your services."

"You know my price?"

"There is very little I do not know, Adar."

The black eyes studied her with wary suspicion. He sensed a queen wouldn't be pleased to open her vein for him.

"And you are willing to pay?"

Morgana shrugged. No sense telling him that she had every intention of killing him once he had managed to locate her prey. Demons were a little touchy about such things.

"You would not be here if I was not," she said smoothly.

He paused a long moment, his fierce desire to taste the blood of a queen warring with his fear that this was some sort of trap.

At last it was his bloodlust that overcame his good sense. The dark eyes flared with need and he offered a deep bow to seal the bargain.

"I will need something of my prey," he said as he straightened. "Something that carries their scent."

Morgana pointed to the expensive leather suitcases set in the corner. She had sent Modron to discover where Sybil had stayed during her time in Chicago the moment they had arrived. Retrieving her luggage had been a simple matter.

"Take what you need."

The demon ripped the bag open, shuffling through the explosion of designer clothes before plucking a silk scarf from the mess. His face was intent as he pressed the scarf to his nose.

"A fairy."

"She was last seen . . ."

"That is not necessary." He dared to interrupt, a small smirk on his lips.

It was fortunate that Morgana's powers were strained. Otherwise she might have killed him on the spot. Then she would have had the bother of summoning another.

"Do not be overconfident, demon," she warned, her voice filling the air with a thick heat. "The woman is being held in a room protected by a powerful spell."

Unaware of how close he had been to death, the Adar headed back toward the door.

"Magic cannot hide her from me."

"Adar."

He paused at her commanding tone. "Yes?"

"Track the woman to where she is hidden, but do not try to approach. Once you have the location you will return to me with the information."

Darkness swirled in his unnerving eyes, as if he were eager

to be on the hunt. "I won't charge you extra for bringing the fairy to you."

The heat in the air thickened until the demon was struggling to breathe.

"You'll do exactly as I say or you will discover just how painful my displeasure can be."

He touched his throat, as if it might ease his discomfort. "Actually, I think I've already discovered."

With a wave of her hand the power lessened. "Go."

"Yes, Mistress."

Anna stood directly before Cezar as she waited for his answer. She might not know jack squat about the demon world, but she was perfectly capable of sensing when someone was hiding something from her. She was a lawyer, after all.

And Cezar was definitely hiding something.

It was simply too much a coincidence to think he would make a public appearance that was bound to lure her to Chicago, just when her life could be in jeopardy. And even if she were willing to stretch her imagination and assume that it was all one big fluke, why would he make such an effort to protect her? It wasn't as if she meant anything to him. He'd proved that two hundred years ago.

While vampires might be many things, she wasn't idiotic enough to believe there was even an ounce of Good Samaritan in their unbeating hearts.

She planted her hands on her hips and grimly ignored the sheer beauty of the man standing before her. The lingering feel of his touch was distraction enough.

"Cezar, what are you hiding?"

The bronzed, heart-rending features were smooth, unreadable. "I have told you all I know of Morgana and her threat to you."

Which was a nice sidestep.

"Cezar . . ." Intent on grilling him until he was forced to confess the truth or gag her, Anna was abruptly distracted as a soft glow filled the room. Turning her head she realized that the glow was coming from Sybil. Her stomach churned as she watched the strange aura flicker and dance over the dead body. "Good God."

Cezar was on guard instantly, his eyes darting about the room as he searched for the threat.

"What is it?"

"Sybil." Anna instinctively backed against a wall. If the dead fairy so much as twitched, she was out of there. "She's glowing."

"I see nothing." Cezar studied her horrified expression for a heartbeat before he was flowing toward the open door. "Levet."

"Oui?" Entering the cell, the tiny gargoyle instantly turned his attention to the glowing body. "Ew . . ."

"What is it?" Cezar demanded.

"An Adar demon." The gray eyes briefly flickered toward Anna before landing on Cezar. "He's tracking her."

Cezar muttered a curse, his dark expression not doing a damn thing to relieve Anna's growing fear.

"What's an Adar demon?" she demanded.

"Very bad news," Cezar muttered, turning back toward the door. "Styx."

The warrior appeared in the doorway. "What?"

Cezar leaned close enough that they could speak in undertones, only an occasional word reaching Anna's straining ears. Styx muttered something about caves and Commissions and hiding, only to be firmly vetoed by Cezar. Then the word Viper was bandied back and forth. At last Cezar placed his hand on the larger vampire's shoulder and gave a short nod.

Reaching out, Styx captured the arm of the gargoyle and they disappeared from the room. Cezar headed directly for Anna.

"We must leave." His expression was commanding, hard. "Now."

Anna's instincts screamed in agreement, but she forced herself to ignore the hand that he held out.

She desired the vampire (okay, maybe it was more than mere desire, maybe it was lust on an epic scale) and she was even discovering that she actually enjoyed his company (when he wasn't being an annoying ass) but that inner voice continued to urge caution.

He had proven over the past hours that he was determined to keep her alive, but the question was . . . for what purpose?

The alternative to death was not always preferable.

"I'm not going anywhere until you tell me what the hell is going on," she said, her voice grim with warning. "Why is Sybil glowing?"

She could feel his frustration wash over her in a blast of icy energy. He clearly wasn't in the mood to offer a reasonable explanation. He was more in the mood to toss out orders and have them obeyed.

Or maybe knock her on the head and drag her out by her hair.

"Once Adars have the scent of their prey they are capable of casting a spell that will lead them straight to their quarry."

Oh. That didn't sound good.

"Then why not just move . . ." She winced as she glanced toward Sybil. "The body?"

"Because the scent of her will linger. The Adar will know that Sybil was held here for some hours."

She shivered, struggling to understand what was happening. "Why would the demon be searching for Sybil?"

With a low hiss Cezar began pacing the cell. Like a panther in a cage that was too small.

"They're what humans would call bounty hunters."

"Bounty hunters?"

He turned his head to stab her with a dark, smoldering

gaze. "The Adar has been hired by someone to find Sybil and nothing will halt him until he has found his prey."

"Hired by Morgana," she said, her voice thick.

"That would be my guess." He deliberately held her gaze. "And very soon she will know just where to find you."

She squeezed her eyes shut. "God."

"We have to go."

"Where?" She forced herself to open her eyes. It was way past the point that she could pretend all of this was some horrible nightmare. "If that demon is after me . . ."

"So far he is only tracking Sybil, but we must be swift. We can't take the risk that he has already contacted Morgana."

"What of Styx and Darcy?" She frowned, belatedly realizing that more than her own life might be threatened by the demon. "Will they be in danger?"

Cezar shook his head, stepping toward her. "Styx is the Anasso, the King. If there is need he can call in the entire vampire nation."

She managed a strained smile. "Handy."

Another step and he was close enough to brush the back of his fingers down her cheek.

"Besides, Darcy would kill anything that threatened him."

Anna widened her eyes. "Darcy? Sweet, tiny, vegetarian Darcy?"

He gave a low laugh. "She might possess the soul of an angel, but her heart is all werewolf."

Chapter 8

Standing at the mouth of the tunnel, Cezar was wrapped in shadows, his gaze trained on the woman who was restlessly pacing the dirt floor.

It had been less than ten minutes since they had realized she was being hunted, but in that short time Styx had gathered his servants to search the grounds for the Adar, Darcy had brought Anna's possessions to take with her, and Levet was busy conjuring some spell that would supposedly destroy any scent that Anna might leave behind.

Cezar wanted to be far away from the estate when that particular spell went off. Levet was well-known for creating large-scale disasters when he attempted magic.

Just beyond the tunnel was a narrow path that circled the back of the large estate. Styx had promised he would send a vampire to pick them up, but so far there was nothing to be heard but the sound of the distant frogs and Anna's soft, nervous footsteps.

He had attempted to give her a sense of privacy as she struggled to collect her shaken courage. If he had learned nothing else in their short time together, it was that she hated for him to see her vulnerable.

At last, however, he was forced to give in to his screaming

instincts. He could tangibly feel her bewildered fear. It cloaked around him, stirring a fierce need to do . . . something.

Something that involved his fangs and blood and death.

Unfortunately, there was nothing nearby that needed killing—well, unless he counted the annoying gargoyle.

With a low growl he moved to stand directly before Anna, bringing her to a halt by lightly placing his hands on her shoulders. A frown touched his brows as he felt her tremble.

"You're shivering," he said, his voice soft enough it wouldn't carry. "Are you cold?"

She stood stiff beneath his touch, perhaps afraid that if she relented an inch she might shatter.

"I'm fine."

"The air is damp. Do you have a sweater in your bag?"

She took a step backward, dislodging his hands. "Cezar, if I'm cold I'll simply warm the air around me." Her eyes abruptly widened. "Did you just hiss at me?"

Cezar folded his arms over his chest as a sharp anger surged through him.

Dios. The woman took stubbornness to a whole new level.

"I'm weary of you treating me like the enemy, *querida*," he said coldly. "I have done nothing but try to protect you since we have met again."

Her gaze briefly flickered, as if he managed to strike a nerve. Then, with a forced determination she lifted her chin. "Well I haven't forgotten our first little rendezvous, Cezar."

Heat arced through him as the memory of pressing this woman to the wall and entering her with a long, delicious stroke rose to mind with a vivid clarity. "You think I have?" he husked.

"You forgot me the moment you walked out the door," she accused. "I was just another easy lay. Oh no, wait, it was more than that. I was dinner as well, wasn't I?" She sucked in a shaky breath. "God, I felt so used."

Cezar swallowed his angry words, suddenly struck by a startling realization.

It was nothing new to have a woman holding a grudge against him. Hell, during his earlier years he had been slapped, stabbed, and nearly staked by furious ex-lovers. But, it seemed a little excessive for any woman to still be nursing such a raw, passionate sense of betrayal for two centuries.

Unless . . .

Unless she still cared.

His anger eased and with care not to startle her, he once against stepped close. Close enough that the scent of honeyed figs filled his senses.

Christ, had there ever been a more erotic aroma?

"I didn't leave you, Anna," he said. "At least not willingly."

"Don't insult my intelligence with one of your practiced lines about doing it for my own good or intending to call on me later . . ."

"I am not giving you some practiced line," he denied, his hands framing her face, his gaze holding hers with grim determination. His sins were no doubt legendary, but he had never intentionally attempted to harm this woman. Never her. "While you slept in my arms I was visited by the Commission."

She frowned. "The Commission?"

"They are the . . ." He grimaced, struggling for the words that would easily translate the purpose of the Oracles. "I suppose you could say they're the Supreme Court of the demon world. Those who dole out justice and punishments."

Not surprisingly her frown only deepened. Demon politics brought a frown to a lot of people's faces.

"What did they want with you?"

He smoothed his expression to an unreadable mask. He could get them both killed if he didn't take care.

The Commission had little patience and no forgiveness for those who broke their rules.

"I'm not allowed to speak of the Oracles or what they desired of me. Not unless I have a sudden death wish."

She made a sound deep in her throat. "That's convenient."

"It's anything but convenient." His hands tightened on her face. "Unfortunately, it's the truth."

Perhaps sensing he wouldn't budge on this subject, she turned to her next grievance.

"Why didn't you wake me before you left?"

"The Oracles had rendered you unconscious; it was not my place to interfere."

"Unconscious?" He could feel the sudden heat bloom beneath her skin. "Ha. I knew it. God, I couldn't believe I fell asleep in that room." The hazel eyes sparked with anger. "Dammit, what right did they have?"

"You will discover they feel they have every right," he said dryly, his thumbs stroking her warm skin. His body instantly reacted to the sensation, keenly recalling that satin skin pressed against his own as he moved deep inside her. "And look at it this way, if they hadn't interfered you would have been in your own bed the night your house burned to the ground. They saved your life." A tiny smile tugged at his lips. "Actually, if you think about it, I was ultimately responsible for keeping you alive and well."

She rolled her eyes. "Oh, please."

His smile faded. He bent until his forehead rested against hers, the soft brush of her breath warming his lips.

"Anna, I didn't abandon you that night. In fact, there's a very good chance that if we hadn't been interrupted we would still be in that bed." Her mouth parted to argue, but Cezar had a sweeter means of keeping those lips occupied. Closing the space between them, he captured them in a soft, yearning kiss. It was a bare touching of their lips, but it was enough to send an explosion of hunger ravaging through his body. *Too long, too long, too long*. The desperate words echoed through his head as he used his thumbs to open her lips so that his tongue could slip into her moist heat. This was not the place or time for such intimacy, but his need for this woman was straining his self-control to the breaking point. "*Dios*, I will never tire of the taste of you. So sweet."

Her hands fluttered before at last landing on his chest, the heat of her palms searing easily through Cezar's shirt.

"Wait," she breathed, her husky voice revealing that she was far from indifferent to his touch. He shifted to nuzzle the tender spot just below her ear. She gave a shaky sigh before she was determinedly arching from his touch. "Cezar, wait."

He growled, his body twitching at her abrupt retreat. He could taste the desire that ran through her body. Why was she so damned determined to deny it?

"I've told you that I was forced to leave, that I would never have gone willingly."

"But you haven't explained why you came back."

He eased away, his aching lust replaced by a sudden wariness. As much as he desired this woman, he wouldn't risk allowing her to discover more than the Oracles had allowed him to reveal.

They were more dangerous than Morgana le Fay on her most evil day.

"What do you mean?" He kept his voice light.

Her eyes narrowed. "You deliberately lured me to Chicago. I want to know why."

With a timing that was straight from the gods, Cezar heard the distant sound of an engine. Turning away from her far too intelligent gaze, he moved back to the mouth of the tunnel.

"Our ride has arrived," he murmured.

He heard her low, impatient sound, but with grudging steps she moved to join him, peering through the branches that hid the tunnel from prying eyes.

"How do you know it's our ride?" she demanded, her gaze searching the darkness that shrouded the wooded area.

"This road is part of Styx's estate. Any traffic must be

admitted through the front gates." He smiled wryly as he recognized the soft, yet powerful purr of the approaching car. "Besides, only Viper would choose a Rolls-Royce Phantom for a rescue mission."

"Who's Viper?"

"A brother."

"You mean a vampire?"

"Yes." He lifted his brows. "Is that a problem?"

"Not so long as he understands I'm not dinner."

The vision of another vampire wrapping his arms around this woman while his fangs sank deep into her flesh seared briefly through Cezar's mind before he grimly forced it away. His control was precarious at best right now and thoughts like that were custom designed to make him feral.

"You don't have to worry. Viper won't so much as lay a finger on you."

Something in his voice had her regarding him with a searching gaze. "How can you be so certain?"

"For one thing he is already mated, and for another, I would kill him."

He didn't miss her soft gasp. "Even though he's your brother?"

There was no hesitation. "Yes."

A silence descended as she absorbed his stark words. Then, sucking in a deep breath, she deftly turned the conversation to safer waters.

"Where is he taking us?"

Cezar watched as the Rolls slid to a smooth halt directly before the tunnel. Reaching out, he knocked aside the branches, searching with his senses to make sure that nothing lurked in the darkness.

"Viper has a number of establishments spread throughout Chicago, most of them possessing more security than the Pentagon."

"Enough security to keep out Morgana le Fay?" she demanded with a shiver.

Taking her hand, Cezar led Anna toward the waiting car, debating whether to offer comfort or truth.

At last he settled on truth.

She possessed a pesky aversion to lies, even when they were for her own good.

"I'm not certain." He shrugged. "It will at least give us time to consider our options."

"What options . . ." Her words came to a halt at the same time as her feet. For a moment, Cezar thought that they must be under attack. Then, with a grimace, he realized her wide gaze was trained on the silver-haired vampire that was uncurling from the car. Damn. He should have prepared the poor woman. There had never been a female who hadn't gone a bit breathless at the sight of the magnificent demon. "Holy cow. He's . . . he's . . ."

"Taken," Cezar growled, unable to control the need to lean down to steal a kiss that was pure possession. Only when he felt her melt against him did he at last lift his head and regard the vampire he had called friend for centuries. "Viper, thank you for coming."

Viper gave a small bow, his long silver hair glowing in the moonlight and his perfect features softened by the shadows.

"You have only to ask," he said, his dark gaze shifting toward the silent woman at Cezar's side. "And this is Anna?"

Cezar nodded. "Anna Randal."

Viper allowed his gaze to stroke over the speechless woman at Cezar's side.

"She's beautiful."

"Yes, she is." Cezar's voice was cold as he slipped a jealous arm around her shoulders. Even knowing his friend was well and truly mated couldn't halt his instinctive need to mark Anna as his own. "I think we should go, before the Adar catches our scent."

A small, knowing smile twitched at Viper's lips. "Of course."

Cezar waited for the vampire to slide behind the wheel before he bundled Anna into the backseat and settled himself next to her, his arms tugging her close. Within moments they were speeding out of the estate and heading toward the south of the city.

Leaving the elegant neighborhood behind at a speed that would curl Jeff Gordon's hair, Viper glanced briefly over his shoulder.

"I don't mean to pry, Cezar, but if I'm to find the best place to stash your companion then I need to know what I'm hiding her from."

"Morgana le Fay."

Viper's attention returned to the road as he squealed around a corner, choosing the narrow side streets that were empty of traffic.

"Anna's a fairy?" he demanded, a faint hint of surprise in his voice.

Like any vampire he was accustomed to his senses giving him precise details of the living creatures that surrounded him. Most vampires could even read the souls of others, always presuming the creature possessed a soul.

"We're still searching for her heritage, although we suspect there's a connection between the two," he said carefully, shielding his mind so that the vampire wouldn't suspect there was more to his interest in Anna than the obvious desire that was impossible to hide. He couldn't risk Viper suspecting any connection to the Commission.

A beat passed before Viper flashed another curious glance over his shoulder.

"You suspect that she possesses the blood of the ancients?"

"She does command the powers of an elemental."

"Truly?" A hint of respect entered Viper's voice. "A rare talent and one that suggests she's more a warrior than a mere fairy."

"Hey." Finding her voice despite her obvious fright at traveling at light-speed through the dark streets, Anna elbowed Cezar in the side. "I'm right here, you know."

Viper gave a low, husky chuckle. "Forgive us, Anna Randal. We have been friends for many centuries and have often enjoyed long debates over the mysteries that life offers."

Cezar made a rude noise. "Some might call them arguments."

Viper narrowly dodged an oncoming car. "Philosophy does tend to be a heated subject."

Cezar glanced toward Anna, who was staring at him with an odd expression. "He once threw a priceless Fabergé egg at my head."

"I knew it couldn't damage that thick skull," Viper retorted.

Anna gave a shake of her head, as if clearing it of cobwebs. "You're interested in philosophy?"

Cezar reached up to tug on a honey curl that had strayed from her ponytail.

"Despite your belief that I'm a shallow, womanizing lech, I do have interests outside the bedroom."

Viper laughed. "Oh yes, Cezar once had interests that spanned every room in the house."

"Oh, really?" Anna drawled, flashing Cezar a dangerous glare.

"Of course now he's been all but neut . . ."

"Shut up, Viper," Cezar growled.

Viper gave a soft curse. "She doesn't know?"

"Know what?" Anna demanded.

Cezar allowed his power to fill the car, making the nearby streetlamps shatter from the pulse of energy.

"Was there a part of *shut up* that wasn't clear?"

Anna stiffened at his side, her tiny features hard with suspicion. In that moment Viper was lucky that Cezar possessed an aversion to killing his brothers.

Not that he was averse to a good ass-kicking.

"I knew there was something you were hiding from me," she hissed.

His arms tightened around her taut body, catching and holding her wary gaze.

"This has nothing to do with you, Anna, I swear," he said softly, grudgingly turning his head toward the window as Viper made another sharp turn. They were driving down a ramp to an underground parking lot. Although he couldn't sense the spells that were wrapped around the building to repulse humans, he knew they would be in place. What he did sense, however, was the nearly overwhelming scent of vampires, blood, and fairies. A combination that could only mean one place in Chicago. *"Dios,"* he breathed in shock. "What the hell are you doing, Viper? This place is filled with fairies."

Skidding to a halt directly in front of the bank of elevators, Viper switched off the car's engine.

"Precisely."

"The point is to keep Anna away from Morgana and her subjects."

Viper flashed a smile that would have sent a chill down the stoutest spine.

"Trust me."

"Great," Cezar muttered, reluctantly sliding from the car and taking Anna's hand as she joined him.

She glanced around the lot, her brows lifting as she noted the dozens of gleaming cars that only the Fortune 500 could afford.

"What is this place?"

"The Viper Nest," Viper said with a smug smile.

Her gaze turned to Cezar. "A blood bar," he grudgingly revealed.

"Again I ask, what is this place?" she muttered.

Viper shrugged. "Fairies, like humans, can become addicted to a vampire's bite. My little establishment provides the service they desire."

Her face paled. "Addicted?"

Cezar cursed beneath his breath. Why couldn't Viper be one of those silent, brooding sort of vampires? The kind who preferred to keep his lips shut.

He gave Anna's fingers a small squeeze. "You are far too stub . . . strong-willed to ever become addicted."

Viper gave a sharp burst of laughter. "You at least learn fast, Cezar."

Anna sucked in a deep breath, ignoring the smell of exhaust and oil as she watched the tall, silver-haired vampire pull a small keycard from his pocket and insert it into the card reader next to the elevator.

Demon or not, he truly was a stunning creature. Like a Raphael angel. Of course, no angel had such dark, wicked eyes or a smile that could make a woman think of black satin sheets and flickering candles.

Strangely, however, he didn't stir her senses. Not like another dark-eyed vampire whose lightest touch could make her heart quiver and skip and sometimes come to a complete halt.

Her gaze shifted back to Cezar, her mind a tangled mass of confusion.

On the one hand was her annoyance at the sheer number of things he continued to keep hidden from her (not the least of which was the fact she might have become addicted to his bite) and on the other hand was the grudging acceptance that, for the moment, she depended upon him.

And of course, there was that whole *he didn't abandon her like a piece of trash* newsflash that she still had to wade through.

Belatedly realizing that both vampires were regarding her as she stared at Cezar like a mindless idiot, Anna wrenched her gaze toward the open elevator and allowed Cezar to lead her into the dark-paneled lift.

With a whisper of sound the doors closed and they were

whisked to the top floor. Anna shivered. The elevator was as large as some apartments, but being enclosed with two powerful vampires made her skin prickle and the hair on the nape of her neck stand upright.

Even more disturbing was that in the sheen of the silver doors she could see nothing but her own reflection. As if she was eerily alone.

God, she had come to Chicago to find answers and instead . . .

She swallowed the hysterical urge to laugh.

Instead she had well and truly fallen down Alice's rabbit hole.

The doors slid open and her wacky thoughts were shattered by the sight of the long hallway lined with glass walls. Behind the glass were elegantly appointed rooms, all of them different. One looked like something out of Versailles, all gilt and delicate furnishings, the next was a jungle theme with towering plants and zebra-striped couches, the next a tawdry Los Vegas hotel room.

All incredibly beautiful, but what caught and held her eye was what was within those beautiful rooms.

Vampires. Male or female, tall or short, slender or muscular, they all shimmered with that sexual potency and unearthly beauty that marked them as clearly as if they wore nametags.

"So what happens?" she demanded as they headed down the hall, her eyes flitting from one glass room to another. Inside the vampires lounged on sofas, flaunting their perfect bodies or else . . .

A sudden heat touched her cheeks as she realized that some of the rooms held couples. Naked, entwined, groaning couples.

And drinking blood was not all that the vampires were doing.

She cleared her throat, her eyes trained firmly on Viper's velvet-clad back as they moved deeper into the building.

"Fairies come here to get bitten?" she asked, hoping to distract herself from those writhing bodies. God, she was hot and bothered enough just being next to Cezar. The last thing she needed was up close and personal displays of what she was denying herself.

Viper gave a low, husky laugh, as if he knew exactly what was going through her fevered brain.

"There are a variety of entertainments offered."

Cezar didn't laugh. Instead, he wrapped his arm around her shoulders and tugged her close. His sandalwood scent made her heart pound, but his touch offered a comfort she couldn't yet explain.

"You haven't told me how you intend to hide Anna among her enemies," Cezar demanded of his friend.

Viper waved a hand toward the glass rooms. "I discovered after opening this little business that while fairies are wealthy customers, they are far too volatile to have dozens of them under one roof without causing some sort of chaos." He gave a shake of his head. "I was spending more money repairing the damage from their drunken brawls than I was making. I was finally forced to have the walls lined with lead."

"Lead?" Anna demanded in confusion.

"It dampens the power of fairies."

Strange. She cautiously concentrated on her own elusive powers. They swirled through her like bubbles of champagne that were just waiting for the cork to be popped. They certainly didn't seem lessened by the lead.

Easily reading her mind, Cezar gave her shoulder a squeeze. "The lead won't affect you," he murmured, his gaze switching to Viper. "And it won't stop Morgana."

They arrived at two double doors that blocked the hallway. Viper once again used his keycard to open the lock.

"Not if she arrives on my doorstep, but I thought the purpose was to try to keep Anna hidden," the silver-haired vampire said, opening one of the doors and allowing them to pass into a vast apartment. "What better place than an establishment that is already filled with fairies?"

Cezar frowned before giving a reluctant shrug. "I suppose it's the last place she'd look."

Anna struggled not to gape at the splendor that surrounded her. Styx's house was grand, but this place was Trump territory. The floors were white marble, the walls built with alcoves to hold the numerous Greek statues, and the ceilings molded and highlighted with gilt. The furniture was covered in a dark red satin that perfectly matched the drapes at the far end of the room.

Wow. Obviously blood and sex were worth a pretty penny.

She forced her attention back to Cezar. Not a particularly difficult task. There was a part of her that would be happy to sit and gawk at that lean bronzed face for an eternity.

"What about that . . . Adar thing?" she demanded. "Can he find me here?"

Cezar's beautiful features hardened. "We must trust that Styx managed to rid us of the demon before he caught your scent."

Anna grimaced. It wasn't that she doubted Styx's skill. Even as a non-vampire she had sensed the thunderous power he possessed. Still, it would have been a bit more comforting if she knew that the hunter was out of action.

Easily sensing her unease, Cezar reached out to run a cool finger down her cheek, his dark eyes mesmerizing. A portion of her tension eased, swept away by the sheer force of his presence.

Nothing would harm me so long as he was near, a small voice whispered in the back of her mind.

Chapter 9

Anna lost track of how long they stood there simply staring into one another's eyes, but at last Viper cleared his throat, his dark eyes shimmering at their unwitting display of intimacy.

"These are my private rooms. You won't be disturbed here," he promised. "If you have need of me, you only need to press five on the phone. It's a direct line to my office."

Cezar's gaze never wavered from her face. "Thank you, *amigo*."

It was the sound of the door closing with a soft click that finally brought Anna out of her odd trance.

Of course it still took several moments before she could convince her brain to obey the command to turn away from that hypnotizing gaze.

Her body knew what it wanted. It wanted to stay close to Cezar.

Really, really close to Cezar.

Naked, sweaty close.

Her mind, however, was not nearly so clear on what it wanted.

It was enough to make any woman of unknown origin and species a bit crabby. Rubbing her suddenly chilled arms, she glanced around the palatial living room.

"Do all vampires live in such lavish style?" she demanded.

She heard his soft hiss of frustration stir the air, but when he answered his voice was as smooth and dark as chocolate.

"Most, although for centuries Styx preferred the damp caves south of the city. He would probably still be there if . . ."

She turned back as his words abruptly broke off. "If what?"

"If Viper hadn't demanded the Anasso needed something a bit more grand," he continued easily.

Her hands landed on her hips. Damn. Did he think she was stupid?

"Another lie, Cezar?" she rasped. "You're just chock-full of them, aren't you?"

With an impatient motion, Cezar reached up to tug the strap of leather from his hair. The dark curtain fell about his lean, beautiful face like a river of ebony. Oh . . . damn. She'd never seen a more beautiful sight.

Thankfully unaware that her heart had lodged somewhere in her throat and her stomach was a quivering mass of awareness, Cezar shoved his fingers through the silky strands.

"Anna, there are simply things that I can't tell you," he at last admitted, an edge in his voice.

"Why? Because then you'd have to kill me?"

"Because someone else would."

She blinked at his blunt words. Was this a sort of bad joke?

"Right."

Without warning he was standing directly before her, his hands cradling her face.

"You're new to the demon world, or you wouldn't for a moment question my word."

She had to force herself to remember to breathe as his thumbs stroked her cheeks in a soft caress. Ah yes, this was what her body wanted. Needed. His touch. His scent filling her with sandalwood heat.

"What's that supposed to mean?" she struggled to demand.

"It means that while many of us appear human, we're not. We don't live by the same set of morals and rules as humans and we don't hesitate to kill when we feel it necessary."

She searched his expression, finding no hint of apology in his dark, finely chiseled features.

"That's a big comfort."

"I'm sorry, *querida*. I don't mean to frighten you, but you have to understand that there are dangers beyond Morgana le Fay." His hands tightened on her face. "I will do everything in my power to protect you, even if that includes hiding the truth when necessary."

She struggled to think of an argument. Some reason to insist that he put all his cards on the table so she didn't feel as if she were walking blindfolded through a minefield.

But if he was right . . .

If the truth really *could* kill her, well then, maybe she should rethink the whole *tell me what I want to know right now or I'll break your nose* thing.

Just maybe stumbling around in the dark wasn't quite so bad.

Before she could come to any conclusion there was a sharp knock on the door and with that low growl that she was beginning to recognize as annoyance (oh, and sometimes God-that-feels-good), Cezar turned and crossed the tiled floor.

He opened the door just far enough to slip through, conducting a low-voiced conversation with a person on the other side before stepping back into the room and closing the door.

"Your bag," he murmured, holding out the leather suitcase until she moved forward to take it. Almost as if he didn't trust himself to come closer. "If you want there's a hot tub in the bathroom. I'll order you dinner while you soak. What do you prefer?"

Although food was the last thing Anna desired, she knew

that she should try to eat something. Being weak from lack of sustenance seemed like a bad idea.

"Do they have food here?"

"Viper has a full kitchen staff to serve the fairies."

Setting down the suitcase Anna was struck by a sudden thought. "And what about you? Are you going to . . . eat?"

The dark eyes flared with a raw, pulsing hunger that struck Anna with the force of a blow.

"Are you offering?" His voice deepened, his fangs glistening in the light of the chandelier.

Anna took an instinctive step backward. Not because she was horrified by his words, but because she wasn't. She wasn't even frightened. Instead, her entire body tingled with a sensation that could only be . . . excitement.

And desire.

Desire that raged like a sudden inferno.

Dear God, she remembered the feel of those fangs sliding through her flesh. The feel of him sucking her blood as her body convulsed with such bliss she had thought she had surely died and gone to paradise.

"Anna?" With that fluid speed he was standing so close she could feel the brush of his cool power. His dark eyes held a compelling heat as he stroked light fingers up the bare skin of her arm. "Will you allow me to drink from you?"

"No," she said, more to end her erotic thoughts than in response to his question.

His jaw tightened before he shuttered his expression and stepped backward.

"Then I'll have to find my blood elsewhere."

Anna reacted without thought. One moment she was listening to the words leaving his mouth and the next her powers were stirring and Cezar was thrust back against the door.

Hard.

"You ass," she hissed.

With a frown, Cezar pushed his hair from his face and glared at her flushed face. "What the hell was that for?"

She pointed a finger in his direction. "You're going to those fairies, aren't you? You're going to suck their blood and . . ."

Astonishingly, his expression eased and a tiny smile touched his lips. "And?"

She turned away. She didn't know what was written in her expression, but she was certain she didn't want Cezar reading it.

"I saw what was going on in those rooms," she muttered, her unstable powers once again threatening to burst out of her at the mere thought of Cezar climbing into one of those glass rooms with a beautiful fairy. A fairy who would no doubt be happy to offer up a hell of a lot more than just blood.

"What would it matter, *querida*? You've made it clear that you no longer want me as your lover." When she didn't respond, he unpeeled himself from the door and crossed to grasp her shoulders. With a relentless tug he forced her to turn and meet his narrowed gaze. "Anna? Why are you so angry?"

"I'm not angry."

"You just cycloned me into the door," he said dryly. "If you're capable of calling on your powers then your emotions must be . . . aroused." Aroused? God, she was burning as if a fever was running through her body. "Could it be that you're jealous, my little shrew?" he demanded.

Well, duh. Of course she was jealous. Card-carrying, board-certified, over the top jealous.

Despite all the anger she had harbored and nurtured over the years for Conde Cezar, there had been a part of her that had thought of him as her own.

He was her first lover. Hell, he was her one and only lover. He was also her first known exposure to the world beyond her mundane human existence. At least her first exposure that she actually knew about. (She had never suspected her cousin Morgana was anything more than a bitch.) And heaven knew that he had managed to haunt her over the past two centuries.

It was no wonder that she was feeling a little possessive.

All right, so she was feeling massively possessive.

"I thought we were supposed to be avoiding fairies?"

"Their powers are limited in this building." He slowly smiled, his fingers running a path up her throat. "You didn't answer my question, *querida*. Are you jealous?"

"I . . ." She was forced to halt and clear her throat. "I'm going to find that hot tub."

The dark eyes smoldered. "The hot tub can wait. I can't."

His head swooped down and before she could guess his intent he was kissing her with the sort of impatient, forceful hunger that had tormented her for the past two centuries.

This was no soft seduction, no pleading, no tentative foreplay.

Just a stark demand that made her knees quiver and her head swim.

Oh . . . yes. God, yes.

Delicious sensations flooded through her, so intense that they nearly sent her to her knees.

Wrapping his arms around her, Cezar jerked her against his body, his tongue plunging into her mouth and his fangs pressed against her lips. Anna gave a small sound between a gasp and a moan, her hands lifting to clutch at his arms.

Some small voice in the back of her mind tried to warn her that she should remember why this was a bad idea. Why she was supposed to be saying no.

The small voice, however, was no competition for the blaze of heat that spread through her body and pooled in the pit of her stomach.

Her lashes slid downward as his lips eased and strayed over her flushed face, his tongue tracing a moist trail down the line of her jaw.

"You taste of figs dipped in honey," he whispered.

"Figs?"

"Plump." He gave her ear a small nip. "Ripe." He scraped his fangs down the curve of her neck. "Sweet figs."

She moaned as his tongue touched the pulse pounding at the base of her throat. "Cezar, we shouldn't . . ."

"We should," he interrupted in a harsh voice, easily hauling her backward until she was pressed to the wall. "We really, really should."

Flashbacks to the last time she had been pinned to the wall by this man flared through her mind. It should have cooled the fever that burned like a white-hot blaze. It should have warned her that she was about to walk down the same path that had led to disaster.

Instead all she could remember was the feel of his hands skimming over her skin and the dark pleasure of his bite.

Her head hit the wall as her neck lost the ability to hold it upright, her hands ripping open the silk shirt so she could find the smooth, hairless skin beneath. There might be a bazillion reasons why this was a terrible idea, but at the moment all that mattered was the *one* reason it was a great idea.

Her body ached for this.

Ached with a force that overwhelmed everything.

His hands skimmed down her waist, dipping beneath her shirt so that they could trace a devastating path back up to cup her breasts. Her skin quivered beneath his light touch, her breath coming out as a small explosion as his thumbs stroked over her tight nipples.

"Tell me you like this, Anna," he rasped, his hands impatiently tugging the shirt over her head before ripping aside the lacy bra. "Tell me that it feels good."

Her nails bit into his shoulders. "Yes," she moaned. "It feels so good."

He muttered something low, his head moving downward so he could capture a nipple between his teeth, teasing it mercilessly with his tongue. Anna gasped at the explosion of sensations.

Dear God. No matter how vivid her memories and dreams, nothing could compare to the actual feel of him.

Continuing his assault on her breasts, Cezar allowed his hands to skim lower, swiftly undoing the zipper of her jeans and lowering them so she could kick them off her legs (along with her flip flops) and out of the way. Her panties followed the same path.

His cold fingers left a trail of fire as they explored the skin of her inner thighs. He gave her nipple a last nuzzle, then lifted his head and buried his face in her neck.

"If you're going to say no, *querida*, it must be soon," he husked, his body trembling as his fangs rubbed over the thick vein in her neck. "My hunger for you is too great to toy with."

No?

Not a chance in hell.

She could already feel the tension building deep within. Could almost taste the blessed relief that lurked just out of reach.

"Don't stop," she panted, her hands fumbling with the stiff zipper of his jeans. "Don't you dare stop."

He growled, stepping back so he could shed his clothing. His movements were so swift that Anna could barely follow the striptease. A pity since she could have spent hours enjoying the sight of all that smooth, bronzed skin stretched over rippling muscles. A body that was meant to be savored with hours of seductive worship.

Hell, she barely caught a glimpse of the large, perfect erection before he was once again pressed against her.

Of course it wasn't all bad, she discovered. Gazing was all well and good, but there were other senses. Senses that were rejoicing in the feel of his hard shaft brushing against her lower stomach, in the spicy scent of him seeping into her skin, and the taste of his lips as they captured hers in a rough, demanding kiss.

Her arms encircled his waist, stroking up the smooth perfect skin of his back.

Cezar shuddered, his growl rumbling through the air.

"You have tortured me for so long," he whispered, his fingers once again stroking her inner thigh until he at last reached the wet slit between her legs. "Night after night I've hungered for you, aching to have you in my arms . . . to taste of your blood."

Anna tilted her head back, silently urging him to take what he desired.

His finger dipped into her body, his thumb finding the source of her deepest pleasure. Slowly the finger stroked deeper and deeper, making Anna arch toward him as the gathering storm threatened to burst.

She sucked in short gasps of air, needing more. Needing him inside her when the explosion hit.

"Cezar, please," she moaned softly, her hands grasping his hips.

"What, *querida?* What do you need from me?"

She was way past coherent thought, let alone actual articulation, so instead she grasped his hair and shoved his face against her neck.

"Please."

He quivered, his hunger so intense she could feel the waves of it searing over her skin.

"*Dios*, I want to taste you," he said, his voice oddly strained.

"Then do it," she commanded, her leg shifting to wrap around his, opening herself to his penetration in a blatant motion.

Cezar hissed.

There was a part of him that knew there would be hell to pay for this delicious encounter. Anna might be overcome with lust at the moment, but the minute sanity returned she would remember all the reasons she had kept him at a distance and then she would find a hundred ways to punish him.

Probably a hundred and one.

And of course, there was always the possibility the Oracles would decide to torture him for this taste of paradise. It'd happened before.

Thankfully, that small, rational part of him was no match for the hunger that was roaring through him.

He had been a warrior his entire life. A hunter that took what was offered and damn the consequences (at least until the Oracles had nailed his ass to the wall). And what he wanted was Anna Randal.

Now.

Forcing away what little conscience he possessed, Cezar opened his mouth and with one smooth strike he buried his fangs deep into her neck.

Anna jerked and then moaned, her nails digging deep into his flesh. The tiny pain only increased his pleasure as the sweet, potent taste of her blood slid down his throat.

Drowning in the pleasure, Cezar continued to suck, his hands smoothing down the back of her legs to part them and then, with one powerful motion, lifted her off her feet. Quick to understand, Anna readily wrapped her legs around his waist.

Cezar pulled back to meet her eyes as he slowly, steadily slid her onto his erection.

A shout was wrenched from both their throats when he was at last buried as far as he could go, her moist flesh pulsing around him in the most intimate caress imaginable.

For a moment Cezar held perfectly still, simply absorbing the sensation of being one with this woman. He was man enough to have missed sex over the years. To have rued the impotency that the Oracles had inflicted.

But right now he knew that any sex he might have indulged in with other women, even the most skilled lover, would have been nothing more than a shallow imitation of this. A worth-less release that would have left him empty.

This was what he had longed for. The only thing that could truly touch his cold heart.

Anna wrapped her arms around his shoulders and Cezar's illusion of control shattered. The smell, the heat, the taste, the very essence of her was flooding through his body and he wasn't going to be able to make this last near long enough.

Pressing her against the wall, he plunged his fangs back into her neck as he drank deep of her blood, his hips pump-ing in a steady rhythm.

"Cezar," she cried softly, her head lowering and her teeth sinking into his shoulder.

The feel of her bite, even if her teeth didn't pierce his skin, was enough to send a jolt of shock through Cezar's body. *Dios*. Nothing had felt so good before.

Withdrawing his fangs before he drank too deeply, he tilted his head back and roared as he felt her climax clench around his arousal, clenching and stroking him over the edge.

Sweet ecstasy spread through his body, prolonging the vi-olent orgasm. He muttered soft words beneath his breath as he slowed his thrusts. Words of soft pleasure, and pledges to protect her for all eternity.

When he was at last capable of clearing his thoughts he gently carried his beautiful lover into the bathroom and set her in the hot tub. His fingers trailed over her face, covered in a light sheen of perspiration.

He waited for her to speak, or at least lift her lashes to meet his gaze. When she kept them stubbornly lowered, he gave a low chuckle and climbed into the tub with her.

"Anna, you will have to look at me eventually," he mur-mured, his arms wrapping about her to pull her close. "At least tell me that you're okay."

Her lashes lifted, but her gaze drifted over the bathroom rather than meeting his eyes. Not that he could entirely blame her. With Viper's usual over-the-top style, the room was an explosion of ivory and gilt, with flying cupids painted across the ceiling.

At last her gaze halted on the marble statues that were set in alcoves and carved to represent entwined couples in various stages of intimacy.

They were exquisite works of art that were realistic enough to bring a slight blush to her cheeks.

"Why wouldn't I be?" she at last muttered.

He ran his fingers through her tangled hair, sensing her muscles ease as the hot water bubbled around them.

"You might feel weak for a few hours. I did, after all, take your blood. When I call for your food I will ask that they send you orange juice as well."

"I don't feel weak."

"Good." Dipping his head, he brushed his lips over her temple. The taste of figs and warm delicious woman instantly stirred his senses, hardening him with a speed that was shocking even for him. Of course, he had just filled himself with one of the most powerful essences that a vampire could hope to taste. He would be buzzing for hours. "Although, it's not really surprising. You have the blood of ancients coursing through your body."

Her hazel gaze turned toward him, a hint of puzzlement in the golden green depths.

"What does that mean?"

He trailed the back of his fingers down her cheek. "Your blood is more potent than the average human. You're capable of losing far more without being affected, and perhaps more importantly, I need only take a small amount to satisfy my needs."

"So you're . . . satisfied?"

Cezar choked as he tried to swallow his burst of laughter. Couldn't she feel his sated pleasure? It filled the entire room.

Then he realized that she was thinking of her ridiculous

assumption that he would join the other vampires in the building to relieve his hunger with the waiting fairies.

Hell, he would rather wait another two hundred years than soil himself with anyone but Anna Randal.

"Utterly, blissfully, completely satisfied," he murmured, his fingers touching the tiny puncture marks on her neck. The sight of them made something deep inside him growl with possessive approval. This was how she was supposed to look. Tousled, well-loved, and carrying his mark for all to see. "Although I'm a vampire, so I'm always ready for another round of satisfaction whenever you want." The hazel eyes briefly darkened with an answering heat before she abruptly ducked her head to allow her heavy honey hair to form a curtain between them. A sudden chill marred his sense of absolute peace. "Anna?"

"What?"

"Do you regret what happened between us?"

There was the sort of silence that could never be good. "I suppose not."

"Hardly a ringing endorsement," he said harshly, trying to squelch his flare of anger. *Dios*, what they had just shared had been earth-shattering. It was the sort of thing that could tremble through universes and alter destiny. And she *supposed* she didn't regret it? "In fact, I'm not sure I've ever been so damned by such faint praise."

She attempted to scoot away from him. "What do you want?"

His arms tightened, keeping her firmly anchored to his side. "A bit of honesty would be nice."

"Fine." Her head lifted and she stabbed him with a glittering gaze. "The truth is that a part of me thinks that I should regret what happened, but the rest is utterly, blissfully, completely satisfied. Happy now?"

A slow, wicked smile curved his lips. "I'm getting there."

She blew out a disgruntled sigh. "You don't have to look so smug."

Cezar allowed his fingers to drift beneath the bubbling water, his mind already filled with images of Anna straddling him as she rode him into bliss.

"I would look a lot more smug if you would . . ."

Before Cezar could finish his delicious suggestion, his head was slammed into the edge of the hot tub. His eyes squeezed shut as darkness surrounded him and then the sound of a familiar, rasping voice echoed through his mind.

Chapter 10

Anna felt as if she were floating.

Okay, she actually was floating in the deep, deliciously warm
water. But it was more than that. It was as if her entire body had
become a boneless mass of sated pleasure.

It was a sensation she hadn't felt for two centuries and while
she hadn't lied to Cezar when she said that she should regret
what had just happened between them, she just couldn't stir up
the least hint of remorse.

God . . . it had been fantastic.

The feel of him moving deep inside her at the same time he
was taking her blood was an experience that went way beyond
mere sex.

They had been connected so deeply that it had been as if
they had been as one. Two halves that were only complete when
they were together.

A terrifying thought.

But not as terrifying as the sight of the powerful vampire suddenly bowing backwards, his head smacking against the edge
of the hot tub and his eyes squeezing shut as if he were in acute
pain.

"Cezar?" She gripped his beautiful face in her hands, her
heart halting in fear. Was he under some kind of attack? Some

vampire thing that she couldn't see or sense? Or could he be sick? "Dear God . . . Cezar." She crawled onto his lap, her powers swirling through the room. Not that she noticed the heavy statues that tumbled and shattered beneath the force, or the pictures that crashed to the floor. Her attention was focused on Cezar as his face contorted with a flare of agony. "What's wrong?"

After what seemed to be an eternity, Cezar slowly relaxed, his eyes fluttering open to regard her with a blank gaze.

"Anna?"

"Yes. Are you hurt? Do you need Viper?"

He lifted a hand to touch the back of his head, the dark eyes clearing as he surfaced from the strange power that had held him in thrall.

"Nothing more than a cracked skull and a raging frustration," he muttered, his dark gaze skimming down her naked body still straddling his waist. "Typical of the Oracles."

She stiffened, a very bad feeling replacing her fear. "The Oracles?"

"*Si.*" He grimaced, his hand shifting to push the damp strands of his hair from his face. "They have yet to catch on to the whole cell phone thing. Not that I could use one even if they did."

Despite the heat of the water, Anna felt chilled as she slid off his lap and wrapped her arms around her waist.

"What did they say?"

His expression became shuttered. "I must leave you for a short time."

"Leave me?"

"I hope I won't be gone long, but . . ."

Anna surged to her feet, her stomach clenched with a sense of sick dread.

"Oh no, Conde Cezar, not again," she hissed.

With a far more elegant motion, Cezar was standing directly

before her, appearing like some god rising from the water as his bronzed skin glowed in the dim light.

"Anna, I must leave," he said darkly. "When the Oracles call, no demon can ignore their commands. Not unless they're in a hurry to be planted in their grave."

She stepped back, until her legs hit the edge of the tub. She was furious, but the temptation to reach out and stroke that perfect bronze skin was nearly overwhelming.

"Oracles." She gave a short, bitter laugh. "Jeez. At least think of a new excuse to dump me. God, I'm such an idiot. You're the master of hit-and-run sex and still I let you . . ."

"God dammit, Anna, this is not some scheme to try to sneak away." He easily closed the space between them, his hands reaching out to grasp her shoulders in a near painful grip. "If there were any way I could tell the Oracles to go to hell and stay here with you I would. And I swear on my very life that the moment I am free I will return to you here."

"Like you did last time?"

He jerked as if she had slapped him, then without warning his hands lowered and he was sliding the heavy signet ring from his finger.

"Here."

She frowned as he pressed the ring into her palm and closed her fingers tightly around it.

"What are you doing?"

"That ring has been upon my finger since I first awakened as a vampire. It's an intimate part of me."

"I still don't understand."

"You possess the blood of the ancients, elemental magic." He peered deep into her eyes, his power tingling over her skin with a cool breeze. "With this ring you could find me no matter where I might be in the world. Just as Sybil was capable of following you. It would even call to me between dimensions."

She frowned, glancing down at the heavy gold ring with its strange scrolling.

"How?"

"I have no talent for magic, but I know you possess the skills." His finger slipped beneath her chin and tilted her face up to meet his stark expression. "Anna, I will return to you, I swear it."

Instead of replying, Anna stepped out of the water and reached for one of the terry cloth robes that were placed neatly on a shelf. Tugging it on, she at last turned to regard him with a suspicious frown.

Deep inside, she knew innately that he wasn't lying. She could physically sense the sincerity etched across his heart. But she had had two hundred years to build up a healthy distrust of this man. One bout of mind-blowing sex wasn't going to erase that.

Maybe if they could have two or three bouts . . .

She abruptly thrust the distracting thought away.

"What do these Oracles want of you? And why now?"

"Who knows?" His expression hardened. "They rarely feel the need to explain their actions."

"Are they very powerful?"

An odd, mysterious smile touched his lips. A smile that said he knew something she didn't. "The most powerful of all demons."

Powerful? She was suddenly struck with a brilliant thought. "Then maybe they could help me."

Stepping from the tub, Cezar swiftly dried his smooth skin. "I will request their assistance, but don't get your hopes up. The Oracles only interfere when they believe it their duty."

The brief hope sputtered and died. "Convenient," she retorted dryly.

The dark eyes flashed. "There's nothing about the Commission that is convenient."

She followed as Cezar returned to the obscenely large living room and watched as he tugged on his jeans and white shirt. For a moment she couldn't concentrate on anything but the sight of the reverse strip-tease, shocked to discover it was as erotic as watching the clothes being taken off. Maybe the realization that he was commando beneath those tight black jeans had something to do with it.

Wondering how the room had suddenly become so hot, Anna cleared her throat and struggled to think of something beyond that hard male body.

"You said that the Oracles came for you that first night we were together."

Tying his hair back with a leather thong, he gave a short nod. *"Si."*

"Do you . . . are you one of them?"

His lips twisted in a strange, annoying smile. "I don't have the power to become an Oracle, I'm merely a servant."

She snorted at the ridiculous words. "*You* a servant?"

"I didn't say I was a very good one." Tugging on his boots, Cezar crossed to lightly touch the puncture marks on her neck. A strange thrill of pleasure raced through her. "Anna, I must go. If they are forced to call for me again I will be suffering for days."

For a moment she tried to hold on to her suspicion. Maybe because it was her last line of defense against the potent obsession with this vampire that threatened to consume her. Then, heaving a deep sigh, she gave a nod. "Go."

"I'll have dinner sent to you." He brushed a tender kiss over her lips before lifting his head and regarding her with a worried gaze. "Don't leave these rooms. And if you need something there will be a guard at the door. If you scream she will come running."

"She?"

"This place reeks of blood and sex. I'm not going to take any chances."

With a last kiss that was far less tender and a lot more frustrated than the first, Cezar turned to walk toward the door. He had stepped over the threshold when she called out softly.

"Cezar."

He paused. "What?"

"Be careful."

Morgana glared down at the pretty demon that lay dead at her feet. The Adar had returned as commanded and then received his rightful reward.

Rightful as far as she was concerned.

Any low-blood demon who was stupid enough to believe he was worthy to taste the flesh of a queen deserved to die.

She had at least made it swift, if extraordinarily painful.

"Vampires?" She kicked the lifeless body. "What a waste of my time."

Modron shuffled forward, her stench filling the small bedroom.

"The Adar seemed very certain that the lair hiding Sybil belonged to a vampire. A very powerful vampire who had more than one of his brethren in his company." Her white eyes held an eerie glow in the dark room. "And we both know that Adars are never wrong."

Morgana reached down and with an ease that was shocking for her slender, nearly delicate body, she lifted the Adar with one hand and tossed him through the window.

"Damn his rotten soul," she hissed, watching as his body broke through the panes of glass. She wished the Adar wasn't already dead. She firmly believed in killing the messenger when she didn't like the news. "If it is vampires, why would they interfere in this? They care about nothing but their own kind."

"How should I know?"

Morgana turned and slapped the hag across her ugly face. She was *not* in a good mood.

"Damn your disgusting hide, you're a seer, aren't you?"

Modron turned to spit blood on the floor, her wrinkled face filled with mocking amusement.

"My visions aren't cable TV you can turn off and on with a remote. They come when they come." She grimaced. "Besides, they never work on the undead. They're a void to all mystics."

Morgana cursed. She'd never liked vampires. Oh, they made extraordinary lovers, and no one could deny they were the most beautiful demons to walk the earth. But they were stubborn and unpredictable and far too domineering for her taste. Worse, they refused to bow to her will as was only proper for a queen.

"Fine, then I'll take care of this myself."

"You intend to confront the vampires?"

"Of course not, you idiot," Morgana rasped, shaking back the sleeves of her silk robe. "Not even my powers could overcome an entire pack of the walking dead."

"Then what do you intend to do?"

"If I can't follow my prey then it seems I shall have to bring my prey to me. Hand me my dagger."

Modron raised a gnarled finger. "No. You're too weak . . ."

Morgana offered another slap across the face, this one hard enough to send the old woman flying into the wall.

"Worthless hag," she seethed, crossing to the dresser where she had placed her most precious treasures. Choosing a dagger that had once belonged to a powerful sorcerer, and a wooden bowl, Morgana made her way to the bed and sat cross-legged on the bed.

Closing her eyes, she ignored Modron's low moans, as she breathed in deeply and allowed her power to flow through her body.

Morgana had managed to touch the mind of her prey when she had still been in Avalon. It had been nothing more than a brief brush while her enemy was locked in a deep sleep, but it had been enough to reveal that the old blood ran strong in the stranger.

Too strong.

She didn't dare wait to destroy the power that threatened her.

Morgana lifted the dagger and with one smooth motion she had cut a shallow wound into her inner arm. Stretching out her arm, she made sure that the steady drops of blood landed in the wooden bowl.

The air stirred, thickening with the magic that ran through her veins. She tilted back her head, chanting in low tones:

Blood calls to blood.
Hearts beat as one.
Ancient shadows stir and seek
Find what is hidden and reveal.

The scent of pomegranates and dark magic filled Morgana as she peered into the blood that was pooling in the bottom of the bowl.

She sensed Modron as she limped to stand at the side of the bed. "Your Majesty?"

Swaying side to side, Morgana abruptly stiffened as she reached into the darkness and discovered the faint echo of her own blood.

"Yes, I sense the power," she murmured. "Not fully formed, but pulsing beneath the surface."

"Do you see a face?"

"No." She tested the barrier that held her from fully claiming the mind she sought. "A female, but her face remains hidden."

"Is she shielded?"

"It's her own power that shrouds her in darkness, but she can't keep me out completely. I already established contact during her dream." Morgana trembled as she concentrated on the tenuous connection, using her centuries of skill to enthrall her prey. It was far more difficult than it should have been. "Come to me, my lovely one. Follow the sound of my voice and discover the destiny that awaits you."

"You're losing too much blood," Modron hissed.

Morgana ignored the warning as well as the weakness that was attempting to claim her body.

"Come to me." She whispered the powerful command over the miles. "Come."

Cezar's mood was dark as he returned to the Viper's Nest. Not unusual after a confrontation with the Oracles.

After the tedious journey to the caves, he had endured a fierce grilling on everything he had discovered concerning Anna, as well as the death of Sybil and his belief that Morgana was the threat they had sensed.

On the plus side, they hadn't struck him dead for having dared to drink of Anna's blood, he acknowledged as he entered the building and made his way to the upper floors. They hadn't even mentioned the fact that he was covered in the scent and taste of her.

Of course, they had also refused to provide him any assistance in keeping her safe. Just a bleak warning that if anything happened to her, he would be held personally responsible.

As if he wouldn't welcome a stake through his heart if Anna was harmed.

Jackasses.

Weary from the journey and the approaching dawn, Cezar struggled to smooth his features and ease his tension. He didn't want Anna worried when he joined her.

At least, no more worried than she already was.

The elevator doors slid open and Cezar blinked in surprise at the sight of Viper standing directly in front of him. Instantly alarmed, he reached out to haul the silver-haired vampire forward, his expression stark with fear.

"What is it?" he demanded. "Has something . . ."

Viper gave a soft laugh, managing to rescue his velvet shirt from Cezar's death grip.

"Everything is well," he assured Cezar. "At last check your Anna was fast asleep. Did you meet with the Oracles?"

Cezar wearily rubbed the muscles of his neck. "Yes."

Viper's elegant features hardened with distaste. Like Styx, the ancient vampire deeply resented the Oracles' hold over a fellow brother. And of course, there wasn't a vampire that walked the earth who didn't have authority issues.

"I suppose it would be a waste of time to ask what plot they have brewing?"

Cezar assumed a bland expression. "They're here to rule on the werewolf king, as Styx requested."

Viper narrowed his midnight eyes. "Something that should have taken less than a few hours to complete."

"The Commission works at its own pace."

"And are not to be questioned?"

Cezar arched a brow. "Not if you value your skin."

With a grimace, Viper took Cezar's arm and pulled him into a corner as the elevator opened to spill out a dozen drunken fairies.

"Did you at least request their assistance for your Anna?" Viper demanded in a voice low enough only another vampire could pick it up.

The lights flickered at Cezar's blast of anger. Although not as ancient as either Styx or Viper, his powers were swiftly growing beyond those of all but a handful of vampires.

"They refuse to intercede." He gave a disgusted shake of his head. "They claim her destiny must unfold without their direct involvement."

"Meaning they don't intend to get their own hands dirty."

"Something like that."

Viper leaned against the wall, his intricately braided hair gleaming silver in the dim light. "Do you know, I have the strangest feeling that Anna's arrival in Chicago at the same time the Commission is visiting is more than a coincidence," he murmured.

Cezar regarded his friend with a blatant warning etched on his face. He had spent enough time with the Oracles to know that they didn't screw around when it came to ridding themselves of unwanted curiosity.

"Speculations like that can get a vampire killed, *amigo*. As thickheaded as you might be in your philosophy of the origins of demons, I wouldn't like to see you left to roast in the sun."

"I wouldn't particularly like to see that either," Viper said dryly. "Still, it truly pisses me off that those Oracles hold you like a dog on their leash and then refuse to grant you the one thing you desire."

Just a day ago Cezar would have readily agreed with Viper's dark mutterings. He'd been virtually imprisoned by the Commission, with the added insult of being forced into celibacy (an insult that could get people killed). Now, however, he couldn't manage to stir even the faintest sense of regret for the grim years.

"Actually, the Commission is responsible for giving me precisely what I desire," he said, his gaze instinctively turning toward the doors at the end of the long hallway. "Now, I must discover how the hell I'm going to keep her alive."

Viper lifted his brows, but he was wise enough not to press the issue.

"You should know that Styx called."

"And?"

"The Adar managed to slip away before he could kill it."

Cezar cursed. Couldn't one damn thing go right? "Did Levet catch its scent?"

"No. It never entered the estate."

"Morgana must have commanded it to return to her when he found Sybil's location." He imagined his hands around the Queen of Fairies' throat as he choked the life from her.

"That would be my guess," Viper murmured. "Which means that she also knows that Sybil was in the hands of vampires."

"And it won't be a great leap to suspect that her prey was

there with us." Spinning about, Cezar smacked his fist into the wall with enough force to make the floor shake. Thankfully the reinforced lead kept the damage to a minimum. "I'm commanded to protect Anna, but given no direction of how I'm supposed to do it. Morgana has shrouded herself in such mystery I don't have a damn clue what powers she possesses or if she has any weaknesses."

Viper watched him in silence, waiting until Cezar had managed to regain his composure before placing a comforting hand on his shoulder.

A wise move considering vampires were known to bite first and think later when they were upset.

"I might know someone who could help."

Cezar struggled to contain the emotions that pounded through his body. It had been so long since he had felt anything beyond frustration that it was far more difficult than it should be.

"Who?"

Viper paused. "First allow me to contact him. He rarely meets with others."

"He's a vampire?"

"Yes." Viper's expression remained closed, as if he were hiding something. "He's a dedicated scholar who has collected the legends and fables of every demon to walk the earth."

Cezar's brows snapped together. "Dammit, Viper, I can't keep Anna safe with legends and fables. Not unless Morgana can be killed by a fairy tale."

Viper held up a slender hand. "Among his books is a vast collection of forgotten histories. Many are so obscure that not even Styx has seen them. It could be that he has information on Morgana that has been forgotten over the centuries."

A great big hell of a maybe.

Cezar kept the thought to himself. Viper was trying to help. "I suppose it's worth a try," he said wearily. "It's not as if I have any other brilliant ideas."

A hint of concern touched Viper's elegant features. "Don't be so hard on yourself, my friend. You're doing everything . . ."

The words of comfort came to a dramatic halt as there was an explosion of air and the doors at the end of the hallway shattered, sending a bombardment of deadly shards through the air.

Cezar knocked Viper to the ground as the wooden splinters flew over their heads.

"By the gods, what was that?" Viper breathed.

Cezar flowed to his feet as the last of the splinters lodged into the wall, his gaze trained on the ragged opening into Viper's private rooms.

"Anna."

Viper cautiously rose to his feet, his pale skin a distinct shade of white at being nearly skewered.

"You told me she possessed the powers of an elemental, but you said nothing of being able to rip apart my club as if it was made of cardboard."

A nasty chill inched down Cezar's spine as he watched Anna walk toward them wearing nothing more than the short, terry cloth robe, her hair floating as the air swirled around her. There was something wrong.

"Her powers are still untutored and only emerge when she is in the grip of a strong emotion," he muttered, studying Anna's blank face and the lifeless hazel eyes. It was almost as if she were completely unaware of her surroundings. Certainly there was no recognition on her beautiful face as she approached. "She has little control of them."

"So you're saying she's a loaded bomb with no off-switch?"

Cezar grimaced, knowing his friend wasn't far off the mark. "I don't think she would intentionally hurt anyone."

"And unintentionally?" Viper stiffened as Anna came closer, his own power beginning to fill the hallway.

Cezar didn't blame him. Already the force of the wind was stinging his face. Still, a growl sounded deep in his chest. If push came to shove he was quite willing to battle Viper should he threaten Anna.

"I don't know what the hell is going on, *amigo*, but I need you to stand aside and let me handle this."

"Cezar, her power . . ."

"That's not a request," he hissed, his gaze flickering toward his companion in a silent warning.

Viper's expression tightened, but with a small nod he melted into the shadows, no doubt hurrying off to call for his guards. Whatever his seeming agreement there was no way he would allow Anna to harm any of his vampires.

Including Cezar.

Which meant he had only a few moments before all hell broke loose.

Chapter 11

Standing directly before the open elevator doors, Cezar ignored the wind that whipped around him, and braced for Anna's approach.

"Anna? Anna, can you hear me?" There was no response. Not even a flicker of her dull, unseeing eyes. Not until she lifted her hand and pointed it in his direction. "Anna." Her name was wrenched from his lips as the blast hit him and he was tossed away from the elevator and into a wall.

Glass shattered and screams filled the air as he struggled back to his feet, indifferent to the deep gashes that marred his skin. Impatiently wiping away the blood that flowed from his forehead and dripped into his eyes, Cezar watched as Anna stepped into the elevator.

"No." Launching himself forward, he was too late.

Smoothly the elevator doors slid shut, cutting off the violent winds and leaving behind a trail of destruction and an eerie stillness.

There were shouts and screams behind him, but Cezar barely heard them. Nothing mattered but getting to Anna. Reaching the elevator doors, he ignored the buttons and simply punched his fist through the metal. Sticking his fingers into the hole he'd made, he gathered his strength and pulled the elevator doors apart.

There was a piercing screech as the doors reluctantly parted to reveal the empty shaft. Without hesitation, Cezar leaped onto the descending elevator, landing lightly on his feet and instantly reaching to rip open the trap door.

Anna stood in the center of the elevator, never even glancing up. She didn't need to. The blast of wind knocked Cezar on his ass even as the elevator jerked to a halt and she was stepping out of the compartment.

Dammit, he had to stop her before she reached the streets. If he didn't then Viper would.

Dropping through the open trap door, Cezar darted out of the elevator and entered the underground parking garage. He hissed softly as he watched Anna walk through the shadows, her power tossing expensive cars out of her path as if they were no more than twigs.

Dios.

Now he understood the Commission's belief that this woman was born to be an Oracle. Even untutored, her power was an awesome sight to behold.

Unfortunately, it was also a pain in the ass. At least in this moment.

Cezar was accustomed to his own (not insubstantial) strength enforcing his will. Now he not only had to find some means of halting a woman who could crush him with a thought, but one he couldn't hurt, no matter what the circumstance.

Perfecto.

Following in her destructive wake, Cezar resisted the urge to physically try to halt her steady retreat. Instead he closed his eyes and concentrated on his psychic skills. She was too strong-willed for enthrallment, but if he could reach her mind then perhaps he could help to break whatever spell held her captive.

Using his senses to keep from stumbling over the rubble

left in Anna's path, Cezar closed his mind to all but thoughts of the woman before him. The fact that he held her blood within him made matters far easier, giving him a bond that went deeper than a mere sexual connection.

Or at least it should have been easier.

As they neared the ramp that would lead to the streets of Chicago, Cezar found his thoughts ramming into a steel wall.

Someone was already in there. Someone who smelled of pomegranates and who was determined to keep him out.

A trickle of panic wormed through his heart. Already he could sense the heavy approach of dawn. If Anna made it to the streets he would be unable to follow her for long. Always presuming that Viper wasn't already out there waiting with his guards.

He had to get into her mind. And he had to do it *now*.

Clenching his teeth, Cezar gathered his will. There was no way to do this subtly. He would have to crash through and simply pray that Anna wasn't hurt.

Focusing once again, he sidestepped subtle and went straight for one swift, brutal thrust.

Pain shot through him as he crashed into the thick barrier, nearly going to his knees as he battled not to be thrust out. For a moment the intruder was laid bare to her senses, revealing her greed, her conceit, and her ugly lust for power. More importantly, she revealed her identity. Morgana le Fay. Then, Anna stumbled as well, falling to her knees and clutching her head in her hands.

Reaching her side, he stretched out his hand to touch her face. The intimate contact strengthened his powers, allowing him to at last breach the power that held her captive, shattering it with enough force to send him sprawling backward and to make Anna cry out in pain.

"Anna?" With a shake of his head to clear the lingering shards of agony, Cezar crawled forward, not trusting his legs to hold him as he gathered a trembling Anna into his arms.

Just for a moment she stiffened in fear, then her beautiful eyes cleared and she gasped in a deep breath of air.

"Cezar?"

"I'm here." He gently pushed her hair from her face. Her hazel eyes painfully attempted to focus on his face. Then they widened in horror at the cuts that had yet to heal. "Oh God, Cezar."

"Sssh." He touched a finger to her lips. "It's okay."

"I hurt you."

He savored the feel of her in his arms, his body trembling with relief. For a moment there he truly feared he might not be capable of breaking Morgana's hold on this woman.

"Nothing that won't heal."

Her hand lifted in a weak motion so her fingers could touch the gash on his forehead.

"I'm sorry, I couldn't stop it. It was like I was possessed or something. A part of me realized what was going on, but I couldn't stop myself. I had to . . ." She broke off with a shake of her head.

"Had to what?" he prompted.

Her brow furrowed as she struggled to remember. "I had to get somewhere. This voice kept calling to me and I had to follow it."

"Morgana," he said bleakly.

"Are you certain?"

"I glimpsed into her mind while she held you captive."

Her tiny body stiffened in his arms. "She possessed me?"

"In a way."

The air around her began to heat. Whether out of anger or panic was hard to determine.

"Damn her."

He brushed his lips over her curls. "You're safe, Anna."

"Yeah, but for how long?" she demanded, her voice unsteady. "If she can take control of my mind then there's nothing to stop her from making me go to her whenever she wants."

It was a thought that Cezar refused to contemplate. He had every intention of putting an end to Morgana before she could strike again.

"I'm here to stop her."

Regret flared deep in her eyes. "At what price? I could have killed you."

Cezar shrugged. It was true enough. The woman possessed enough power to destroy just about anything that stood in her path. The knowledge, however, didn't frighten him.

In fact, it was a relief.

Whatever happened to him, Anna would soon be able to protect herself.

"I'm not so easily put in my grave, as many have learned to their regret," he said with a wry smile. "Besides, you can learn to keep shields in place so she is incapable of intruding."

She made a choked noise deep in her throat. "Can I learn to shield in the next five minutes?"

"There will be no attacks for awhile."

"How can you be so certain?"

His finger absently traced the outline of her lips. "I'm not precisely certain, but I do know that when I broke through to your mind it shattered Morgana's hold on you, and not in a pleasant way. I could hear her screams before the connection was severed."

The hazel eyes darkened. "Good. I hope she has a freaking headache from hell."

Cezar chuckled, his head abruptly lifting as he sensed the rapid approach of vampires.

"No, Viper, it's over," he growled, his arms tightening around Anna until she gave a squeak of protest.

Sliding from the shadows, Viper regarded them with open concern. "Is she harmed?"

Anna pushed herself to a sitting position, as if she disliked appearing vulnerable before his brothers.

"Apart from a raging headache and a weird taste of pomegranates in my mouth, I suppose I'm fine," she said, not giving Cezar time to reply.

Viper's lips twitched as he turned his dark gaze to Cezar. "And you?"

"I'm fine."

Surging to his feet, Cezar helped Anna stand, keeping an arm around her waist as he sensed her give a sudden shudder.

"Holy crap," she breathed, her gaze surveying the tumble of cars, more than one of them destroyed beyond repair. "Did I do that?"

"*Si.*"

Her already pale skin turned a sickly shade of ash. "I'm sorry. I didn't mean to."

Viper dismissed her apology with a wave of his hand, a hint of respect in his expression as he studied Anna's delicate body. A vampire was always swift to appreciate power. And even more swift to consider the best means to use that power for their own benefit. "It doesn't matter. The owners will be compensated. I will speak with them now."

Viper disappeared as he wrapped himself in shadows, leaving Cezar alone with the trembling Anna.

Unlike the vampires, she didn't seem to see the glorious wonder of her abilities. In fact, she seemed more terrified by what she had accomplished than she had by Morgana's hold on her.

For long, silent minutes she simply studied the impressive destruction, her breath coming in shallow gasps.

"This is horrible," she at last muttered. "I could have killed someone. I could have killed *everyone.*"

"Anna . . ."

"I don't want these powers," she interrupted, her eyes flashing. "They're dangerous."

"Powers are always dangerous." Ignoring the stiffness of her body, Cezar pulled her close and touched his lips to her temple. "That's why we must discover some means to control them."

She shook her head. "Can't you just make them go away?"

Cezar absorbed her heat, allowing himself to drown in the feel and scent of her. He had come way too close to losing her.

"They're a part of you. They flow through your blood," he said softly. "Besides, I wouldn't take them away even if I could. Those powers might very well save your life."

"Or take away yours."

"I've told you, I'm very difficult to kill." Without giving her time to argue, Cezar swept Anna off her feet and cradled her against his chest. "Dawn is coming, I must return to our rooms."

She frowned, but by some miracle she didn't struggle against his hold. Actually, she buried herself closer to his chest, as if unwittingly seeking the comfort he was so eager to offer.

"Are you sure Viper will let me stay?" she muttered.

Cezar chuckled as he headed for the nearby stairs. He was still aching from his last elevator ride. "Viper has had his clubs destroyed by rampaging hellhounds, hexed by angry imps, and on one memorable occasion set on fire by one of Levet's misdirected spells," he assured her. "You don't even rate in the top hundred of spectacular mishaps."

A faint smile touched her lips. "Thank you."

"There's one thing though."

"What's that?"

He easily moved up the stairwell, Anna so feather-light in his arms she seemed almost ethereal. A strange sensation considering she had just finished trashing a dozen cars.

"I don't think I have to worry about any of my brothers troubling you while we stay here."

"Why not?"

He smiled down at her puzzled expression. "You just scared the hell out of them."

Anna had been certain that she wouldn't sleep a wink. Not after her stunning imitation of the Incredible Hulk.

It wasn't every day that a woman had her mind seized by a homicidal fairy and forced to rip her way through a determined vampire and several high-end automobiles. That sort of thing was bound to keep a person walking the floors.

But despite her eventful night (or perhaps because of it) she was barely able to keep her eyes open as Cezar carried her to the elegant apartment, avoiding the shattered mess of the once solid doors, and tenderly tucked her into bed.

The fear and confusion that pounded through her poor, abused brain was no match for the beckoning darkness. Her troubles would be waiting for her when she woke up (damn the luck). It would be nothing short of a blessing to enjoy a few hours of oblivion.

Allowing herself to slip away, Anna fell into a deep, dreamless sleep. A sleep that remained undisturbed for nearly ten hours as her body and mind struggled to recover from the strain of using so much power.

It was at last the sensation of fingers at her neck that brought her out of her coma-like state.

Waking with a sense of confusion, Anna's first thought was that she was completely naked beneath the heavy ivory comforter. A shocking discovery considering she wasn't the sort of woman to sleep in the buff even when she was alone. The next thought was that those fingers that had woken her were still tickling the back of her neck.

Slender, cool fingers that she would recognize even if she were dead.

Wrenching open her eyes, she discovered Cezar leaning

over her, his chest deliciously bare and his dark hair framing his lean face like a curtain of black satin.

Wow. Wow. Wow.

This was how a woman liked to wake up.

A mouth-watering, drop-dead gorgeous, gloriously naked vampire hovering over her with a heart-stopping smile and wickedness in his dark eyes.

His hands smoothed down her chest and she glanced down to realize that he had placed his signet ring on a gold chain and clasped it around her neck. The gesture was not lost on Anna despite her ignorance of the demon world.

This ring was obviously more than just a piece of jewelry. It held an importance to him, and more importantly, it revealed a level of trust she was not entirely certain she deserved.

"How do you feel?" he demanded, his voice deep and gravelly, as if he'd just awakened.

Her sluggish blood started zinging through her body as those clever fingers drifted over the curve of her breasts, his touch light, but skilled enough to make her entire body tingle with excitement.

"The way your hands are wandering I think you could answer that question better than I can," she said, her voice already thickening with desire.

His fangs lengthened as he lowered his head and buried his face in her neck. "You feel spectacular. So delicate and yet curved in all the right places." He pressed close enough to her body to reveal it wasn't just his bloodlust that was aroused. The thick hardness of his erection brushed against her hip as he nibbled the sensitive skin at the base of her throat, his fingers finding the tips of her breasts. He chuckled at her soft gasp of pleasure. "And warm. So deliciously warm."

Her lashes fluttered downward as her breath rasped loudly through the air. His tongue was teasing the racing pulse at the base of her neck, his leg shifting to part hers with an unmistakable intent. All too soon she would be beyond thought. At least any thought that was rational.

"Cezar?"

"Mmmm?" He nipped lightly at her skin, one hand skimming down her quivering stomach.

"Shouldn't we be worried about Morgana?"

He planted a path of searing kisses down her collarbone. "There's nothing we can do about Morgana right this moment except try to forget about her."

Her hips arched off the bed as his fingers slid between her legs and found the moist readiness awaiting him.

"And I suppose you have a plan to accomplish that?" she panted.

"I have my ways," he murmured before his mouth closed around a straining nipple. Anna's hands lifted to grasp his shoulders, an explosion of pleasure rocking through her body. She had encountered hundreds, even thousands, of men over the years, and yet not one of them had managed to stir her interest. Certainly none of them had made her long for their touch. She groaned softly, sucking in a deep breath as his fingers slid deep inside her. Cezar lightly scraped his fangs over the sensitive skin of her breast. "*Dios*. I have never desired a woman as I desire you."

"Never?" She forced her lashes to lift, meeting his smoldering black gaze. Despite the heat pounding through her body, she wasn't so far gone as to believe complete nonsense. After all, she was hardly the sort of experienced woman he was accustomed to enjoying. "You'll forgive me if I find that hard to believe."

His expression became unexpectedly harsh. "It's the truth, Anna. Since I first touched you . . ."

"What?" she prompted as his words trailed away.

There was a tense silence before he gave an abrupt shake of his head.

"There's been no other woman."

Anna gave a tiny jerk, her hands shifting to frame his beautiful face.

"What did you say?"

The dark eyes flashed with an unreadable emotion. "I haven't been intimate with a woman for two centuries. Not until last night."

This potent, sexual creature remaining celibate for two centuries? Not freaking likely.

"Is this a joke?" she demanded.

His lips twisted. "No man, demon or otherwise, would ever joke about something like that."

"But . . . why?"

The long tangle of his lashes lowered to hide his eyes. "I wanted to blame the Oracles, but now I'm afraid the answer is not nearly so convenient."

Anna frowned. "Is that supposed to make sense?"

He gave a shake of his head, his lashes lifting to reveal a simmering intent in the dark eyes.

"Maybe this will."

Swooping his head downward, he claimed her lips in a fierce, relentless kiss. She moaned as his tongue slipped into her mouth, his finger moving between her legs in a steady rhythm.

Her body was swiftly melting beneath the hungry onslaught, but her mind was still reeling from his astonishing confession.

Turning her head from his marauding lips, she tried to catch her breath, succeeding only in filling her senses with Cezar's spicy, erotic scent.

"Cezar?" He ignored her as he nuzzled her cheek, the curve of her ear, and down the line of her throat. Anna shivered in ecstasy. "Cezar, are you trying to distract me?"

He teased her nipple with the tip of his tongue, his thumb finding that tiny nub of pleasure between her legs.

"Am I succeeding?"

"Oh," she moaned, her legs parting as her heels dug into the mattress. Holy crap, he was more than succeeding. He was a few strokes away from a complete, total victory.

He gave her nipple a last lick before trailing a line of heart-stopping kisses down her stomach, pausing to tease her belly button.

"How about this?" he husked.

She twisted her head on the pillow, no longer able to recall what had been so important. In this moment all that mattered was the molten heat that was pooling in the pit of her stomach.

His lips continued downward, nipping gently at her hip and then stroking a blazing path to her inner thigh. Anna's eyes glazed over and her entire body trembled with anticipation.

"Cezar."

Slowly he angled his head so he could meet her gaze, his eyes glowing like polished ebony.

"Don't ever doubt how much I want you, Anna Randal. You are a part of me."

As the soft words left his mouth his fangs struck, sliding smoothly through her skin into the vein that ran through her inner thigh.

Anna gasped, her hands tangling in the sheets as she felt his first tugs. Oh . . . God. A thundering wave of pleasure crashed through her, ravaging her senses and clenching her body with a climax that tore a scream from her lips.

It happened so fast that her head was still spinning when she felt Cezar shift over her and with one stroke he was deep inside her. Instinctively her hands lifted to clutch at his shoulders, her lips parting to accept his devouring kiss.

The tiny tremors were still wracking her body as he rocked his hips with a slow, steady rhythm, his smooth chest rubbing over her tender breasts. Impossibly, she felt her hunger stirring again as she arched her back to meet his devastating thrusts.

Then again, maybe it wasn't such a surprise.

She'd waited two centuries for another taste of passion. What woman wouldn't be a little greedy now that she had this glorious vampire back in her bed?

Allowing her thoughts to drift away, Anna gave in to pure sensation, the feel of him moving inside her, the scent of his skin, the lingering taste of his lips on hers. She groaned in bliss, her gaze locked on the beautiful warrior's face poised above her.

It was worth the wait.

Chapter 12

It was nearly two hours later when Cezar at last sprawled across the bed and tucked Anna close to his side. He had never felt so warm and utterly sated in his very long life.

A sensation that could be easily explained by having just enjoyed the rich, powerful blood that flowed through Anna's veins, but Cezar wasn't entirely convinced.

The contentment that filled him wasn't that of a power rush. Or even just a wild, intense bout of sex. This contentment went deep. The sort of contentment that could last for an eternity.

Which was enough to send clanging alarms racing through his mind.

Thankfully the blissful feel of Anna cuddling next to him was enough to stifle the urge to explore the dangerous feelings. As long as she was safe in his arms, then he didn't give a damn about anything else.

A smile that held an edge of smugness curved his lips as Anna allowed her fingers to trail lightly over his chest, drawing aimless circles that sent a shudder of pleasure through his body.

Soon the tray of food he called for would arrive and it would be time to rise and prepare for the coming nightfall.

Until then he simply desired to soak in the peaceful pleasure that shimmered between them.

As the silence stretched, Anna at last tilted back her head, her gaze searching his content expression.

"You said that after you were . . . transformed, or whatever you call it, into a vampire, that you awoke in the uniform of a conquistador, but that you have no memory of being a human?" she demanded.

Cezar blinked, startled by her question. It certainly wasn't what he'd been expecting.

Then he realized he should have been.

Anna was not the sort to give herself lightly to a man. Hell, she'd had no other lover but him.

It was only natural that she would need to know something about the creature she had put her trust in.

"I remember nothing."

"That's strange, isn't it?"

"Not really." He allowed his fingers to trail through the strands of her hair. "A vampire must first drain the blood of a human, and then before the human takes his last breath, he must make his victim taste of his own blood. That's how the demon is transferred."

Her brows lifted. "You mean you have to kill them."

"Si," Cezar admitted without apology. He was what he was. There was no changing that. "It's my belief, although Viper would argue with me, that the demon can't take command of the body until the soul has departed."

"And the memories go with the soul?"

"Of course. They are a part of the very essence that was once human."

It was obvious that she battled against her natural instinct to be disgusted by his calm explanation. A common reaction. There were few who could understand the compulsions that drove a vampire.

"Then the demon is left with an empty body to fill?" she demanded.

"In a manner of speaking."

"Did you ever . . ."

"Ever?"

"Ever transform someone?"

He smiled faintly at her reluctance to ask the question that was clearly troubling her.

"*Si*. I've sired others. Even vampires feel the urge to procreate."

She shivered, her beautiful eyes darkening. "So you have children?"

Cezar felt an ancient pain tremble through him. Unlike many of his brethren he had never turned a human and left them to fend for themselves. A habit that had nearly been the end of vampires.

Instead he had taken them as clan members and did his best to make sure they possessed the skills necessary to take their place in the demon world.

Unfortunately, his tutoring hadn't been enough to save them from the savage vampire wars that had once spread across Europe. Or even from their own stupidity.

"It isn't quite the same," he said softly, regret in his voice. "And no, none of those that I sired has survived. The last was staked by his lover shortly before I met you."

She lifted her head, her expression shocked. Cezar hid a small smile. *Dios*. In some ways this woman remained heartrendingly naïve.

"By his lover?"

He gave a small shrug. "Vampires can be as foolish in love as anyone else."

She pondered the notion a moment before a faint smile curved her lips. "And obviously you don't have a prejudice against other species."

He allowed his gaze to deliberately roam over her gloriously naked body.

"Obviously not."

She gave his arm a small pinch. "I mean that Styx chose a werewolf as a mate, which I assume is something like a wife."

Mate. A strange quiver rushed through his body. One he was determined to ignore. Nothing could match a vampire when it came to ignoring things he didn't want to acknowledge.

"It's far more than just a wife," he said softly, "but yes, vampires often seek their mates among other demons. Viper's mate, Shay, is a Shalott, which is one of the few demons capable of besting a vampire, and Dante is mated to a goddess."

"A goddess?" She gave a short, disbelieving laugh. "You've got to be kidding?"

"Not at all." Cezar tugged one of her honey curls. "Abby is a Chalice that carries within her a spirit that is worshipped by many, and feared by even more."

"Do you worship her?"

"No. Vampires don't worship the Phoenix, although I'm intelligent enough not to piss her off. Dante is a brave vampire to live with a woman who carries such power within her." A wicked smile touched his lips as he studied her delicate features. "Of course, many would consider me brave to dare being so close to you."

She gave a soft snort. "I'm far from a goddess."

Cezar hid his smile. As a member of the Commission, Anna would be revered by vampires and demons throughout the world.

Her word would quite literally be law.

"Perhaps not so far from a goddess as you believe," he murmured. Then, as she frowned in confusion, he brushed a kiss over her lips and reluctantly slipped from the bed. "As much as I hate to end this lovely interlude, your dinner will soon be here. We must make our plans for the night."

"Plans?" Sitting in the center of the mussed bed, Anna reached for the robe and pulled it around her naked body. Cezar stifled the urge to reach out and tug it back off. As much as it might be a sin to ever cover such beauty, he wasn't about to risk having the dinner tray arrive while Anna was still naked. Viper might not be entirely happy if Cezar was forced to kill one of his servants. "You have plans?"

His lips twitched at her obvious disbelief. "They're still a work in progress."

"Ah." She slid off the bed and moved to stand directly before him. "Meaning that you don't have jack crap?"

He tapped the end of her nose. "Get dressed, little shrew. I must speak with Viper."

Locking herself in the bathroom, Anna indulged in a quick shower before pulling on her one clean pair of jeans and a heavy sweatshirt. After her recent demolition derby in the parking garage, she had no desire to play around with her powers. Not even to warm the air around her.

Pulling back her hair and securing it with a scrunchie, she brushed her teeth and returned to the bedroom to find a tray filled with eggs, French toast, bacon, and a muffin drenched with butter and honey. At first glance it appeared to be enough food to feed an army, but once she began eating she discovered herself unable to stop.

It could be the fact that her meals had been few and far between since arriving in Chicago, or that the use of her powers had increased her appetite, or it could be quite simply that Viper's chef possessed the touch of an artist.

Whatever the case, she made swift work of the mounds of food, not setting aside the tray until it was empty. Only then did she pour a mug of coffee and allow the caffeine to stir her blood.

Walking toward the windows on the far wall she twitched aside the heavy curtains to watch the sun slip over the horizon. Three stories below her the street was narrow and already cloaked in shadows. Night was creeping across

Chicago and soon she would be forced to decide what she was going to do.

Which truly was a hell of a question.

She'd always considered herself an intelligent, fairly resourceful woman. After all, she'd managed to survive for two centuries completely alone. Nothing to thumb her nose at.

But during all those years she never had to face something like Morgana le Fay. She hadn't even known there *was* anything like Morgana le Fay. How the hell was she supposed to protect herself when she didn't have a clue what might be thrown at her next? It wasn't like she had a *Dummies Guide to Battling Demons.*

Leaning her head against the chilly pane of glass, Anna remained lost in her dark thoughts until a subtle movement caught her gaze.

Instantly on alert, she stiffened, her gaze searching the shadows across the street. It didn't take long to spot the tall, redhaired man standing in a recessed doorway across the street. Holy crap. It wouldn't take long to spot the man anywhere.

Large and muscular, he wore a stunning pair of lime-green spandex pants and a sparkly T-shirt so tight that it looked painted across his rippling chest. And his hair . . . even in the darkness it held a fiery glow and fell well past his waist in thick waves.

Definitely the sort to stand out in a crowd, let alone near an empty street.

It could be nothing, she tried to reassure herself. This was a nightclub and the man could simply be waiting for night to fully fall and the vampires to arrive for a little fairy goodness.

It could be, but Anna couldn't ignore the prickles of warning that raced over her skin. There was a frozen watchfulness about the stranger, the sense of a predator on the scent of his prey.

God, what if she was the prey?

Instinctively she stepped back, her hand pressed to her

racing heart. As she moved, a pair of strong, familiar arms encircled her waist from behind, bringing with them a sense of reassurance that only Cezar could offer.

"Anna, what is it?" he whispered close to her ear. "I can sense your fear."

She pointed a finger toward the window. "There's something down there watching the building."

His arms tightened. "An imp."

Imp?

She blinked in shock. She thought that imps were tiny little creatures that danced about causing mischief. Not towering oafs who looked as if they could crush her with one hand.

"Are imps different than fairies?" she rasped.

"They are distant cousins, although they rarely admit the connection. They've been at war for centuries over which race is superior to the other."

Bad for them, but maybe good for her.

"So they wouldn't be in the command of Morgana?"

His arms tightened. "If she called upon the imps they would have to respond."

"Great." Her brief flare of hope faded and she turned in his arms to meet his worried gaze. "How could they know I'm here?"

His brows drew together as he swiftly considered the various possibilities. "One of the fairies must have realized that the wreckage in the garage wasn't due to the troll that Viper claimed had gotten loose, and contacted the queen."

"Troll?"

He shrugged. "There're few other things that could cause such damage. And many establishments keep one or two around to deal with troublesome customers."

Anna shivered. God, she didn't even want to imagine what one of those might look like. "Remind me not to cause trouble at a demon bar."

"We must leave."

Anna was more than ready to leave before the imp decided he was tired of just watching, but she wanted to be assured that they had some kind of plan.

Something beyond running through the dark streets with a pack of imps nipping at her heels.

"And go where?"

"First I need to find somewhere you will be safe."

"And what about you?"

"Viper has a friend who might possess information that will help us discover more about Morgana le Fay."

She frowned, sensing that he wasn't entirely happy with their proposed destinations.

"What kind of information?"

"I don't know for sure." A grimace touched the lean, bronzed features. "I hope he might have a book that includes the history of Morgana before she retreated to Avalon."

"You think that could help us?" she demanded in confusion. She enjoyed books as well as the next person (perhaps even more than most), but right now it seemed like a big gun or maybe even a flamethrower would be a little more helpful.

"It might reveal why she has remained hidden there. If there is something she's afraid of, it might help us."

It took a moment before realization at last hit. "Ah. The enemy of my enemy is my friend?"

His dark eyes held a hint of regret. "I know it's not much . . ."

She placed a finger on his lips. This man had done everything possible to keep her safe. She wouldn't allow him to feel guilt because things weren't running as smoothly as either of them might want.

That blame lay firmly on Morgana le Fay's shoulders.

"How are we going to get anywhere if the building is being watched?"

His grim expression eased as he arched a dark brow. "Surely you haven't forgotten that a vampire owns this building?"

"No, but . . . oh. Tunnels?"

"Of course." His head tilted, his eyes abruptly narrowing. *"Dios."*

"What is it?"

"It sounds as if the imps have grown tired of simply watching. No doubt Morgana has promised them a reward for your capture."

Anna's stomach clenched with dread. "Or my death."

"Never," he hissed, grabbing her hand and dragging her out of the bedroom. "This way."

Cezar led Anna through the large living room and out the doors that had so recently been repaired. Once in the hall he paused to allow his senses to flow outward, swallowing his curse as he realized that the imps were already in the building and heading up the elevator.

"The stairs," he muttered, pulling Anna behind him as he turned and darted down a small corridor. His instinct was to toss her over his shoulder so he could use his superior speed to reach the tunnels, but caution warned him that if they were attacked he would need his hands free.

It was a caution that served him well as he neared the door that led to the stairs. Even as his hand reached toward the knob the door flew open and three imps charged through the opening.

He had a brief glimpse of the ever-youthful features and pale golden hair before they were upon him. Pushing Anna behind him, he prepared to meet the onslaught. He didn't doubt that he could easily dispatch the imps. They were far better at hexes and charms than actual fighting. But, they were an obstacle he didn't need right now.

Already braced, he didn't budge when the first imp rammed straight into him. Closing his arms around the slender form he kept himself firmly between the attackers and Anna. With a squeeze he crushed the imp in his arms. He heard the crack of the imp's spine and was dropping the screaming demon even as the second hit him from the side.

This time the force threw Cezar against the wall. His hand shot out to grasp the imp, but moving with an agile speed, the golden-haired demon darted away to grab Anna's arm.

A savage fury rippled through him and his growl filled the hallway with a lethal warning. The imp had time to glance toward him in sudden fear before Cezar launched forward, his arms clamping around the imp and his fangs burying deep into the slender neck.

It was a quick kill, but not quick enough to prevent the final imp from throwing himself into the fray.

Cezar staggered as the imp hit him from behind, but his hold on the demon in his arms never faltered. He sucked with swift efficiency, sensing the demon's heart flutter as death ruthlessly approached.

There was a blow from behind and Cezar felt the cool thrust of a steel blade slide through his side, striking his rib with a jarring pain. Refusing to be distracted, he continued to drain the imp. The wound was far from fatal, and if stabbing him kept the attacker busy, then so be it.

Anna, unfortunately, wasn't nearly so indifferent to the sight of a wild-eyed imp plunging a knife into his flesh.

With a muttered curse, she held out her hand and the wind began to swirl. All too aware of what was coming next, Cezar tossed the now dead imp aside and fell to the ground. He'd already been on the receiving end of Anna's power. He was happy to give this one a miss.

Of course, he didn't mind enjoying the show, and turning his head to the side, he watched as the imp came to an unnatural halt, his green eyes widening as he struggled to breathe.

For a moment the demon attempted to break free of the invisible bonds that held him, his fingers clenching and unclenching and the veins of his neck popping. Cezar knew firsthand that escape was impossible, especially for a creature that actually needed to breathe. Those bands she created might be nothing more than air, but they might as well be made of pure steel.

It took a few moments, but soon enough the imp slumped against the unseen bonds that held him and with a ragged sigh Anna closed her eyes as she struggled to release the power surging through the hallway. Cezar was careful to remain utterly still, not wanting to distract her. She could bring down the entire building if she lost control at this point.

Her pale features grimaced, as if she were in pain, then with a loud gasp, she fell to her knees. Cezar ignored the imp who tumbled unconscious to the ground as he rushed to Anna's side. Bending down, he pulled her into his arms.

"Anna?" He tilted her chin up so he could peer into her dazed eyes. "Are you okay?"

"Yeah." She shook her head as if to clear it, pushing herself to her feet. "What about you?" She reached out to touch the blood that stained his silk shirt, biting her bottom lip at the deep wound that marred his side.

Taking her hand, Cezar lifted her fingers to his lips. "I'll heal, although I would appreciate you not mentioning this little incident to Viper. He would never let me live it down if he discovered I allowed myself to be wounded by a mere imp."

"An imp with a knife," she reminded him.

Cezar smiled. "It wouldn't matter if he'd been carrying a missile launcher. A vampire has a reputation to uphold."

She managed a weak smile before hissing softly as her gaze caught sight of the imp lying lifeless on the ground.

"Dammit, I swore I was done doing crap like that. Is he . . . ?"

"He's just unconscious."

Relief rippled over her face. "Thank God."

Cezar frowned. Although he would prefer that Anna not use her powers until she learned enough control that she didn't endanger herself, he didn't want her hesitating out of fear she might hurt someone.

"Anna."

She glanced up, revealing the shadows that lurked deep in her eyes. "What?"

Cezar swallowed his words and reached to take her hand. Now was not the time to remind her that Morgana le Fay was playing for keeps and that she might be forced to kill more than once.

Time enough for that when they were away from the damned imps.

"Let's get out of here."

There was no argument from Anna as she fell into step beside him. They bypassed the two imps that Cezar had dispatched and moved through the door to the stairs. In the distance he could sense imps moving through the building, but none of them was close enough to trouble them.

At least not yet.

They took the stairs two at a time, pausing as they hit the ground level and encountered the heavy lead door blocking their exit. Cezar reached for the keycard he had slipped into the pocket of his jeans and slid it into the lock.

With a click the door opened, revealing the nearly empty parking lot. It was still too early for most vampires or customers to arrive, and the damaged cars had already been towed for repair.

Pausing in the shadows of the doorway, Cezar studied the oddly peaceful lot. Imps weren't known for their battle tactics. Hell, for the most part the demons were successful shopkeepers and bankers, not warriors. The glitter of gold was far preferable to the dangers of wading into battle. Even if the battle offered the opportunity to kill a fairy or two.

But even an imp should have enough brains to leave someone to guard the exits.

"What's wrong?" Anna whispered at his side.

His gaze continued to scan the shadows. "The entrance to the tunnel is on the other side of the lot."

"Then why are we waiting?"

"This has to be a trap."

There was a faint scrape before the tall, crimson-haired imp who'd earlier been watching the building stepped from behind a cement column.

"So it's true that vampires do think with something besides their fangs on occasion," the intruder drawled, his emerald eyes sparkling with mocking amusement.

Cezar growled, furious that his senses had failed to pick up the threat.

"Imp."

"No, not just *imp*," the tall demon corrected, his hands held behind his back as he gave a proud toss of his head. "I am Troy, the Prince of Imps. No need to bow, although you can grovel if you wish."

Cezar knew what he wanted to do with the oversized imp, and bowing or groveling definitely wasn't involved.

"How did you mask your scent?" he demanded.

The mocking smile widened to reveal his too-white teeth. "I just told you, I am a prince. My powers are far greater than the average imp."

Cezar took a step forward. "We're about to find out just how great those powers are."

Troy's smile never faltered as he pulled a hand from behind his back to reveal a small crossbow already loaded with a wooden arrow.

"Unless your intent is to share some of that nummy vampire goodness, which I am quite willing to enjoy, I suggest that you stay precisely where you are," he warned.

Cezar narrowed his gaze, stepping in front of Anna. "You better start praying to whatever god you serve that you don't miss your target, imp."

Troy shrugged. "I never miss my target, Cezar, but I didn't come here to kill you."

Cezar frowned, wondering how the hell the demon knew his

name. "That might be a little more convincing if the building wasn't being overrun by homicidal imps."

The pale, perfect features hardened with fury. "When the queen calls I must respond, but that doesn't mean I can't tweak her nose when the opportunity arrives."

Cezar stilled. So, the rumors of the bad blood between fairies and imps weren't an exaggeration. This prince was not a bit happy with his queen.

That didn't mean, however, that Troy wouldn't kill them if there were some advantage to be gained. Imps had few morals and would sell their own mothers if they could make a profit.

"Tweak her nose?" Cezar demanded, keeping a close eye on the arrow pointed directly at his heart.

Troy gave an offended sniff. "I don't like being given orders. Especially not by Morgana le Fay." His eyes narrowed as he peered over Cezar's shoulder at the silent Anna. "Are you the one responsible for bringing her to Chicago?"

Cezar growled low in his throat, not giving Anna time to respond. "You even glance in her direction again and you'll be Troy, the dead Prince of Imps."

"You're not mated. What do you care?" The emerald eyes that held centuries of knowledge studied Cezar before his lips twisted in a wry smile. "I'll be damned. Why is it that every time I finally find a decent screw they're always taken?"

Cezar lifted a hand, not about to discuss his strange, unpredictable emotions toward Anna with a damned imp. Prince or not.

"Tell me what you want, imp."

Troy studied him for another long moment before he unexpectedly lowered the bow and strolled forward.

"As I said, I can't ignore the queen's command to send my minions into battle, but she can't force me to play the game entirely by her rules." Troy buffed his nails on his skintight T-shirt, his expression smug. "I'm here to make sure that you and your little sweet pea get out of here alive."

His little sweet pea gave a small snort of disbelief as she moved to stand at his side. She was beginning to learn that in the demon world, if something *seemed* too good to be true it really, really *was* too good.

"Why would you help?" Cezar demanded, not bothering to hide his suspicion. "You wouldn't risk your life if there wasn't something in it for you. Something beyond tweaking Morgana's nose."

Troy flashed his white teeth. "That's true enough. I'm doing this as a favor to a friend."

"What friend?"

"The Chalice."

Cezar slowly allowed his coiled muscles to ease. He might not have to kill the imp after all.

A pity.

"Abby sent you?"

"I contacted her when Morgana called for the imps to attack the Viper Nest. I thought she might be interested considering that her mate is a clan brother to Viper, and I was right."

"And what do you get out of this?"

"She's promised me a favor if I manage to get you out of here."

"A favor?" Cezar briefly wondered just how unhappy Dante was to know his mate had been bargaining with an imp. And if he intended to take that unhappiness out on Cezar. "What kind of favor?"

"I haven't decided yet," the imp purred. "I like knowing a goddess is in my debt."

"I can imagine," Cezar said dryly.

Stifling a yawn, Troy glanced toward the door. "So, are we done with the chitchat so we can get the hell out of here, or would you rather hang around until my clueless infantry manages to stumble across us?"

Chapter 13

Anna decided that being a demon must be a good gig.

Contrary to Hollywood's ridiculous insistence on portraying them as creepy, brimstone breathing, eternally damned creatures who hid in damp graveyards, they lived a hell of a lot better than the majority of humans.

What wasn't to like about eternal life, cool powers, and a lush lifestyle that included a seemingly endless supply of elegant cars and gargantuan houses?

Crawling out of Troy's sleek Lamborghini Murcielago after a hair-raising ride through the busy Chicago streets, Anna gaped at the lavish mansion that seemed to consume an obscene amount of space.

Jeez.

She'd always thought fat-cat corporate executives lived the good life. Now she had to accept that not even the fattest corporate cat could keep up with these Joneses.

Which was a good thing, she decided.

The lush excess didn't really bother her as much when it came to demons. She happened to like them a lot more than the CEOs she'd met. Well, except for the demons who kept trying to kill her.

She didn't like them.

"Anna?"

The soft female voice had Anna abruptly turning to watch the dark-haired woman with stunning blue eyes, and a tall, wickedly handsome vampire with long raven hair and gold hoop earrings, cross the drive toward her.

In some ways the vampire reminded Anna of Cezar. There was the same hint of arrogant confidence etched on his perfect features and the same sensual promise smoldering in his eyes. The same elegant saunter that revealed he knew all too well that he was irresistible to women.

"Yes?"

"I'm Abby, and this is Dante." The woman held out her hand in greeting. "Welcome to our home."

Despite the lavish house, Abby was dressed in casual jeans and T-shirt, and her smile was warm.

Anna shook the slender hand, her own expression rueful. "Thank you, but you might not be so welcoming once you get to know me. I seem to bring disaster wherever I go lately."

Abby and Dante shared a glance that was filled with the sort of intimate amusement that only truly happy couples ever shared.

"Dante and I wouldn't know what to do with ourselves if we weren't in the middle of some disaster or another. And I can at least promise you that only the most desperate demon will try to enter this estate." She wrinkled her nose. "They usually try to avoid me like the plague."

Anna gave a tiny jerk. "Oh, I forgot you're a goddess. Am I supposed to kneel or something?"

"Only if you want to piss me off," Abby said with a laugh, reaching out to take Anna's hand. "Come on, I'm in the mood for a stiff drink, what about you?"

Strong arms encircled her waist from behind, the familiar scent of Cezar cloaking about her as he buried his head in the curve of her neck.

"I wouldn't mind a sip or two, myself," he murmured, his

lips feathering over her skin and sending a rash of awareness through her.

"Cezar." Anna stepped away, her face flaming as Dante tilted back his head to laugh at his friend's antics. "Stop that."

The dark-haired goddess rolled her eyes. "Vampires."

Cezar's smile faded as his gaze rested on Anna's face. "Can I have a word alone with Anna?"

"Sure." The goddess heaved a sigh, turning to glance toward the red-haired imp who leaned casually against his quarter-of-a-million-dollar car. "I suppose I should speak with Troy."

Cezar grimaced, his gaze briefly flicking toward Dante before returning to Abby.

"We are in your debt, Abby."

She reached out to lightly touch Cezar's arm. "There is no debt among family."

Abby turned to walk toward Troy, her steps slowing as Dante instantly moved to her side, his arm wrapping protectively about her shoulders.

Anna smiled, a small prick of envy entering her heart at the sight of their obvious devotion.

Over the long, lonely years she had almost managed to convince herself that love was an illusion. Watching from afar it seemed like most couples, no matter how devoted, ended up as indifferent acquaintances at best or outright enemies at worst.

Now, however, she was beginning to suspect that she had denied the truth of love because it was easier than bearing the knowledge she was missing out on the greatest gift in life.

With a slow shake of her head, she turned to discover Cezar watching her with an intent expression.

"You know, you're very lucky to have such wonderful friends," she said softly.

"*Si.*" He ran his fingers through his long hair, wincing as if his side was still tender. "Few vampires are so fortunate to have such devoted brothers, but Styx is working hard to overcome our feral natures, which have caused endless clan wars throughout the centuries."

"A vampire Gandhi?" she demanded, finding it hard to picture the big, scary man as some sort of kindly pacifist.

Obviously Cezar found it a little difficult himself as he gave a small chuckle.

"Don't ever say that to his face," he warned. "For all his love for peace he does have a reputation to maintain. It's fear of being hauled before our Anasso that keeps most vampires in line."

"More of a speak-softly-and-carry-a-big-stick kind of guy?"

"A very big stick."

Anna grimaced. "I'll keep that in mind."

There was a short silence. At last Cezar reached out to lightly touch her cheek.

"Anna, I hate to do this, but I must leave you . . ."

Without thought she reached up to capture his caressing finger in a tight grip.

"No."

His brows lifted, a speculative gleam entering the dark eyes at her vehement tone. "No?"

Belatedly realizing she had revealed just how desperately she wanted him at her side, Anna dropped her hand and sucked in a deep breath.

"You're still injured," she lamely added. "You need to rest."

A satisfied glint remained in the dark eyes, a knowledge that she had come to depend on his presence.

"I must find out how we can stop Morgana, *querida,*" he said gently. "So far it's been nothing more than luck that has kept you alive. I won't risk stumbling around in the dark anymore."

Ah. It didn't take her lawyer skills to decipher where he was headed.

"You're going to the historian?"

"*Si.*"

She reached out and grasped his arm. "Then I'll go with you."

"That's impossible."

"Why?"

"Jagr has been a recluse for centuries. He allows no one into his lair unless he has specifically agreed to meet with them." Cezar grimaced. "Viper could barely convince him to see me. And it's only with the promise I would come alone and never return that he even conceded that much."

Holy crap. She'd met some peculiar scholars over the years, but this one seemed to take the cake.

"He sounds dangerous."

"Not dangerous, just eccentric." He covered her fingers with his own, the cool touch sending a jolt up the length of her arm. "I'll be fine."

She licked her lips. "And what about me? What if Morgana takes control of my mind again?"

He shifted closer, his expression somber. "I've asked Dante to call for Levet."

"The gargoyle?"

"He possesses some magical abilities. He should be able to train you to shield your mind from Morgana."

A shiver raced through her body that had nothing to do with the chilled wind. "I don't like this."

Bending his head, Cezar brushed his lips over her forehead. "*Querida*, I promise I will return soon. Until then you will be safe with Abby."

It was the edge of concern in his voice that at last stiffened her sagging spine. Dammit. Hadn't she told herself she wasn't going to be that weak, clinging orphan ever again? Especially in front of Conde Cezar.

She was old enough (God, was she old enough) to stand on her own.

With an effort, she tilted her chin and squared her shoulders. Inwardly she might be a mess, but outwardly she had on her stiff upper lip.

She'd been raised British. She could do it with the best of them.

"When is Levet coming?"

Cezar's features tightened. He really, really didn't like the cute little gargoyle.

"Too soon for my taste." He gave her another too-brief kiss before stepping back. "In fact I should be leaving before he arrives. One of these days I'm going to choke the life from that annoying little bastard. I'll return before dawn."

He turned, and within two steps had completely disappeared into the shadows.

Left on her own, Anna struggled against the cold sense of loneliness that washed through her like a tidal wave.

Crap. Crap. Crap.

She was in big trouble.

And it had nothing to do with Morgana-freaking-le-Fay.

Cezar studied the abandoned warehouse with a suspicious gaze. It didn't look like the lair of a scholar. Hell, even the most fledgling vampires were able to enthrall mortals and acquire enough money to live in comfort.

Of course, this Jagr sounded like he took the solitary nature of vampires to the extreme.

Perhaps he preferred such an unwelcoming lair precisely because he wanted to be unwelcoming.

On the point of creeping forward, Cezar abruptly reached behind his back and pulled out his hidden daggers. In one smooth movement he turned to meet the vampire who slid from the shadows of a rusting dumpster.

The stranger was large, nearly as large as Styx, with pale skin, golden blond hair that he wore in a long braid down his back, and pale blue eyes that shimmered in the moonlight. It wasn't his size, however, that made Cezar lift his brows. Or even the ancient robe that would attract precisely the sort of attention that most vampires tried to avoid.

It was the remote, distant expression on the starkly beautiful features.

Instinctively his fingers tightened on the dagger.

The vampire had the look of death.

Death he was willing to deal out without conscience or hesitation.

"You are Cezar?" he demanded, his voice a low rumble, as if he rarely used it.

"Si." Cezar lifted a brow. "I'll go out on a limb and assume you're Jagr?"

The blond head dipped in a formal acknowledgment. "I am."

"You have my thanks for allowing me to search your library."

The blue eyes became downright frosty. "I do this because I am in debt to Viper."

Ah, so that was it.

"You and nearly every other demon in Chicago," he muttered dryly. "Al Capone was a lightweight in comparison to Viper."

A hint of disdain touched the stark features. "It is not a monetary debt. Come."

Charming.

Cezar grimaced as he followed the tall form into the shadows of the warehouse. It wasn't unusual for vampires to resent allowing another demon into their lairs. They were territorial creatures. But the animosity that smoldered in the air was stirring his own natural instincts to assert his authority.

A dangerous combination that could lead to all sorts of bad things.

Reminding himself that Anna was depending on him, Cezar resisted the urge to ram his dagger in the center of that broad back. Instead he concentrated on avoiding the piles of rotting trash as he waited for Jagr to tug open a hidden trap door in the floor and reluctantly followed the vampire down the narrow steps into the damp tunnel beneath.

"You know, if you wanted atmosphere there are several lovely sweatshops to choose from," he muttered.

Jagr never halted his swift pace. "I agreed to allow you to view my library, not to bandy lame jokes, Cezar."

The dagger twitched in his hand. "Are you naturally this surly or is it something you work at?"

The blond head briefly turned. "I'm working at it now."

Cezar's steps faltered before he gave a short laugh. "Fair enough."

He allowed the silence to go undisturbed as Jagr halted before a heavy steel door blocking the tunnel. Several moments passed before the door at last swung open and they were headed down another tunnel that ended in yet another door.

Cezar gave a silent shake of his head. Even for a vampire this Jagr took his security to an extreme.

There was another wait as Jagr dealt with the numerous locks and hexes, then as the second door swung open he stepped aside and waved Cezar into the room ahead of him.

On full guard, Cezar stepped over the threshold, ready for anything that might leap out of the dark. Jagr was obviously capable of any number of nasty surprises.

When there were no fangs sinking into his throat or claws ripping open his flesh, he slowly lowered his dagger. In that same moment, Jagr clicked the switch and the long, steel-lined room was flooded with light.

Cezar's eyes widened, a flare of envy racing through him at the long rows of shelves that were filled with hundreds of leather-bound books.

"Dios." He stepped forward, wishing that he had days, not hours to explore the shelves. Viper hadn't been exaggerating when he said this Jagr was a historian. "This is astonishing."

Indifferent to Cezar's pleasure, the vampire swept past him and pointed toward a distant shelf.

"The books that I've collected on Morgana are there."

"Do you have any that specifically deal with her retreat to Avalon?"

"A few, although most were written by fairies and are

nothing more than the usual gibberish of poems and legends." The blue eyes flashed with distaste. "They have little sense of history."

"Great."

On the point of moving forward, Cezar was brought to an abrupt halt as Jagr appeared directly before him, an unmistakable warning etched onto his pale features. "You may remain in this vault for as long as you need, but do not try to leave on your own. I will escort you out when you are done."

Cezar narrowed his gaze, refusing to back away. "You don't have the books hexed, do you?"

"There are many that would cause harm to the unwary, but not those concerning Morgana."

"You're a little paranoid, aren't you?"

"I've learned the hard way to be paranoid."

"Haven't we all?"

In the blink of an eye, Jagr had Cezar pressed against the steel wall, his fangs extended in anger.

"Some more than others."

Cezar flashed his own fangs. "Do you have a point?"

The blue eyes were chips of ice. "Not all of us have been pampered pets for the Oracles."

"Pampered?" The lights flickered as Cezar used his powers to thrust the large vampire away. There was a pained grunt and then a hiss of frustration as Cezar used his thoughts to keep Jagr pinned against the shelf. Damn the churlish recluse. Did he think he was the only one who ever had a glimpse of hell? "For your information, I've spent two centuries as a slave for the simple transgression of taking the blood of the wrong woman. I've been isolated, sometimes left alone in my barren room for years on end with nothing to occupy me but books and a Pectos demon who was mute. I've been forced to battle demons who sought to kill me for no other reason than their hatred for the Commission. I have been forced to kill brothers in the name of justice. I have been forced to remain a eunuch, kept away from the one woman I could still desire . . ."

His words were cut short as Jagr lifted his hands and with one smooth motion wrenched open his robe to reveal the deep scars that crisscrossed his chest and down his flat stomach.

Cezar hissed at the sight. For a vampire to carry such visible wounds meant that he had first been tortured and then starved for months, maybe even years, so he couldn't regenerate.

It was the worst punishment a vampire could endure.

Worse than death itself.

"Save your tragic sob story for someone who cares, Cezar," the vampire growled, pushing himself from the shelf as Cezar released his powers. "Finish what you came for swiftly. My patience is limited."

Cezar frowned as he watched the vampire stalk through the rows of books to the door at the back of the room.

Maybe he should have a little talk with Styx.

Jagr seemed just a shade too close to Hannibal Lecter territory for his peace of mind.

When Anna had dreamed of her future it had always been simple. In her early years it had included a husband and family and a house that could offer her security. A place to truly belong.

As the years passed she had given up the idea of husband and family. She'd even given up on a true home. It was impossible to remain in one place when she didn't age.

Instead she had become increasingly focused on the injustices in the world.

If she couldn't have security then she could at least have purpose. If she could make some small difference then surely her life would be worthwhile?

In all of her various visions, however, not one of them had included sitting cross-legged on a bed that was owned by a vampire and a goddess, while a miniature gargoyle tried to teach her how to shield her mind from Morgana le Fay.

Life was funny.

No, actually life was a freaking nuthouse.

Trying to ignore the small, leathery hands that were pressed to her face, Anna desperately attempted to concentrate on the lesson he was teaching her. Not an easy task when she could hear the flap of gossamer wings and the scent of granite was thick in the air.

There wasn't anything that wasn't weird about this whole situation.

"What's that?" Levet at last demanded.

"You said to think of a fence."

Levet clicked his tongue. "Not a white picket fence that couldn't keep out a bunny. You must concentrate."

Anna's eyes opened so she could glare at the ugly, bumpy face so close to hers.

"I am."

Sitting back, Levet crossed his arms over his chest, his expression one of disdain.

"No, you're thinking about Mr. Tall, Dark and Dead. Your mushy brain is so filled with him it's making me nauseous."

Anna's cheeks flooded with color. She wasn't accustomed to having someone in her head, rooting around through her thoughts. It was . . . embarrassing.

"I'm worried about him," she muttered, not entirely lying. She *was* worried. But, the truth of the matter was that Cezar would've been filling her thoughts regardless of whether or not he was in danger.

When he was near it was easy to thrust away everything but the power of his presence. When he was gone, however, it was much easier to allow all her doubts and fears to come rushing back.

Fears that he would disappear as swiftly and completely as he had two hundred years ago. Fears that he was merely toying with her. Fears that he was using her for some mysterious reason.

"He's a vampire," Levet said with a roll of his eyes. "He'll be fine. They always are. Trust me, I know."

Anna tilted her head to the side. For all his sardonic wit, she liked this tiny gargoyle. And more than that, she trusted him.

He was perhaps the only one she could truly talk to about this crazy world she had been thrown into.

"You know a lot of vampires?"

"More than I want," he said wryly.

"You don't like them?"

"They're arrogant bastards."

Anna laughed at the blunt words. "So I noticed."

"And what's up with them always getting the girl?" Levet groused. "Oh sure, they're tall and they have those cool fangs. And I suppose a few aren't entirely repulsive, but look at me." His wings gave a delicate flutter. "What woman in her right mind wouldn't think that I'm three feet of delicious goodness?"

"Umm . . ."

Blithely ignoring her hedging, Levet ran a loving hand over one stunted horn.

"Not to mention the fact I also happen to be a powerful sorcerer."

Anna hid her smile. "Yes, I can see where you would be quite a catch."

Levet sniffed in annoyance. "And yet a vampire has only to enter a room and suddenly I'm minced eggplant."

"Minced . . . ?" Anna gave a shake of her head. Levet's English was nothing if not creative. "Never mind. Do vampires do a lot of . . . dating?"

"That depends on what vampire you're talking about. If they're mated then they are completely monogamous. Of course, they have no choice. But before they are mated . . ."

"Before they're mated they're what?"

"Hounds." The gargoyle shook his head. "Complete, utter hounds."

She bit her bottom lip. Cezar had claimed that he hadn't wanted another woman since they had first met all those years ago. And certainly he made her feel as if she were some sort of cherished treasure. Still, a true womanizer was skilled in making a woman believe she was special, wasn't he?

At least until the moment came for him to move on to his next victim.

"Oh," she breathed softly.

"Anna?" Levet leaned forward with a frown. "Is something wrong?"

She gave a shake of her head. What did it matter if Cezar was bound to disappear from her life again? It wasn't as if . . .

With a flare of panic she refused to allow the rest of the thought to form.

She had enough troubles on her plate for the moment.

Good God, did she have enough troubles.

"Nothing," she said firmly.

Levet frowned, but obviously realizing she had no intention of baring her heart, he nodded. "Then let's try to shield again."

Anna grimaced. So far all she'd managed to accomplish was one big, throbbing headache. "Not fences."

"Fine. Close your eyes and picture yourself walking down a long corridor."

Closing her eyes, Anna sternly forced her wayward thoughts to picture a long, narrow hallway. When she was certain it wasn't about to fade into oblivion, she sucked in a deep breath. "There."

Levet's hands cupped her face. "*Bon.* Now with every few steps imagine that you are closing a door behind you. No, a steel door. *Oui, oui.* Very good."

Tossing herself completely into the illusion she was creating, Anna walked down the brightly lit hallway, forcing herself to create a new door every few steps.

It seemed so very real. Almost tangible.

So real, in fact, that it took a moment of listening to the strange knocking on the door behind her before panic actually set in.

"Levet?"

"What?"

"Is there supposed to be someone knocking on the door?"

There was a flurry of French curses as Levet's fingers tightened on her face. "Concentrate, *ma petite*. Do not let them in." Without warning Levet's hands fell from her face and he was sucking in a sharp breath. "Oops."

"Oops?" Anna kept her eyes scrunched shut, her head throbbing as she frantically pictured the steel door. "The door is shut tight. What's oops?"

"That."

Not at all sure it was a good idea, Anna slowly opened her eyes, her head turning to follow Levet's wide gaze.

Oh no. It most certainly wasn't a good idea.

What the hell was that strange shimmer floating in the air near the window? It looked almost like a mirror that wasn't entirely formed. Or maybe it was a wavering tunnel of light.

"Holy crap," she breathed, her heart lodged in her throat. "What is it?"

Levet hopped off the bed, his tail twitching in agitation. "A portal."

"Portal?"

"A door between time and space."

Oh, of course.

Shaking her head, Anna forced herself to simply accept Levet's explanation. She'd seen too much over the past few days to be shocked by a bit of warp-speed travel.

"Why is it here?"

"Obviously your visitor decided if they couldn't reach your mind they would call in person."

She slid off the bed, her body knotted with tension. There

was only one person who would be trying to force their way into her mind.

"This isn't good."

"It's rude, is what it is. You do not just make a portal in the middle of someone's bedroom without permission. What if we were . . . you know." Levet lifted his brows at Anna's sharp, disbelieving glare. "Don't look me like that, it's entirely possible."

She blew out a sigh. "Levet, let's just concentrate on what's coming."

His tail twitched, his hand reaching up to grab hers. "I think we both know what's coming."

True enough.

Already the scent of pomegranates was filling the air, the fruity scent making Anna's skin crawl with fear.

"We have to get out of here," she whispered, but her feet seemed frozen to the ground. "Levet . . ."

The gargoyle grunted, his expression dark. "I can't move either."

Anna strained against the invisible bonds as the portal widened to reveal a tall, red-haired woman dressed in a long gossamer gown, a stunning emerald necklace around her neck.

The image was fuzzy, but there was no mistaking those perfect features or pure emerald eyes.

The woman from her dreams.

No, not dreams. Nightmares.

"Damn," she breathed, her fingers tightening on Levet's fingers. The woman wasn't actually in the room, but she was a hell of a lot closer than Anna wanted her to be.

"Danteeeeeeee!" Levet screeched, his voice bouncing through the room with an eerie echo.

The woman gave a throaty laugh, but to Anna's horrified gaze it appeared that the pale, perfect face held a hint of strain. As if holding the portal was not as easy a task as she wanted them to believe.

"The vampire can't hear you, gargoyle. Nor can the Phoenix. You are all alone."

"Morgana." Anna wasn't even aware she spoke the name aloud until the emerald gaze swung in her direction and widened in shock.

"You." Morgana shook her head, her expression one of utter disbelief. It might have been funny if Anna wasn't scared out of her mind. "Anna Randal. No. It cannot be. I killed you."

Chapter 14

So. This was the woman who had been responsible for the fire that had killed her aunt and nearly brought an end to her own life.

The . . . bitch.

Anna tilted her chin, her body trembling with something more than fear.

"Yeah, well, you missed," she said, knowing it was lame, but it was the best she could do under the circumstances. What she wanted to do was get her hands around that perfect neck.

The emerald eyes narrowed in fury. "How did you survive the fire? The spell I used should have killed you."

"I have a few powers of my own." And a healthy dose of blind luck.

Morgana hissed, the fruity scent so powerful that it was making Anna's stomach queasy. Or maybe that was just the terror.

"I should have killed you the moment I suspected who you were."

"Why didn't you?"

Morgana's image became sharper, clearer. As if the portal's reception was being fine-tuned.

"I had to be sure. I had to know that you were the one with the powers I had sensed before I risked exposing my presence."

"Exposing your presence?" Anna shivered with the age-old pain. "You mean burning a townhouse to the ground and killing an innocent woman in the process? Tell me, was Aunt Jane even related to me?"

"Of course not," Morgana scoffed. "She was just a foolish old woman with a mind that was pathetically easy to control."

God. How had she ever lived beneath the same roof with this woman and not sensed the evil that marred her soul?

"And what of my real parents?" she gritted, her hands squeezing poor Levet's fingers until he gave a small squeak. "Did you kill them?"

Morgana laughed, her slender fingers lifting to stroke through the fiery curls.

"I killed a vast number of your relatives. I can only suppose that among them were your parents."

"Ummm . . . Anna," Levet whispered.

Ignoring the gargoyle, Anna glared at the woman who was determined to see her dead.

"Why? Why are you trying to kill me?"

"Anna. *Sacrebleu*, woman," Levet snapped, jerking on her arm until she could no longer ignore him. "We are about to be pulled into the portal."

Too late, Anna realized that the shimmering glow was indeed growing, the outer tentacles reaching across the room to where she stood.

"Crap." She vainly struggled against the power that held her motionless. "How do I stop it?"

Morgana held out a slender hand, a smug smile curving her lips. "You cannot, my sweet. Soon we will be done with this tedious game."

"Levet?" Anna rasped.

The gargoyle shot her a desperate glance. "Now would be a good time for those powers of yours."

Morgana laughed. "She cannot best me. I am a queen. My powers are without limit."

Anna could feel the strange ripples of energy brushing her face. Damn. This was bad. Really, really bad.

"Don't you have a spell or something?"

"*Oui*, but . . ."

"But what?"

"They are not always so predictable."

"Perfect."

The gray eyes were round with fear as the demon gave her fingers a painful squeeze.

"Do it now, Anna."

Do it? Do what?

Anna squeezed her eyes shut. A part of her warned she was as likely to bring the roof down on their heads as to save them, but with that strange energy beginning to surround her, she knew that she had to do something.

Anything.

Releasing the doors in her mind, Anna focused on the blood rushing through her veins. In that blood was the magic that was growing stronger with every passing day.

So strong that she wasn't at all certain what was going to happen.

Reluctantly opening her eyes, Anna met the triumphant emerald gaze of Morgana le Fay and allowed the building power to explode around her.

Cezar was returning to Dante's mansion when he felt Anna's distress.

He had wasted hours among the books, searching for any hint of Morgana's weakness. Hours that revealed nothing more than one obscure poem that only confirmed what he'd already suspected.

At last it was the approaching dawn that had driven him

from the tunnels and back onto the streets of Chicago. He said a terse good-bye to the hovering Jagr and tracked his way toward the north of the city.

He was still blocks away when he felt the first surge of fear race through him.

It had taken him a moment to actually realize that it was Anna's feelings he was experiencing. As a vampire he could read the souls of those standing close to him, and even their emotions if they were strong enough.

But this was different. This was far more personal. Far more intense.

It was almost as if they were . . . mated.

He didn't have time to worry about the dangerous sensations flowing through his body. Not when the fear that he sensed reached the level of terror, then disappeared with a shocking wrench.

Anna.

With blinding speed he consumed the last few blocks and burst into the massive house, the door swinging open with enough force to rattle the pictures on the walls.

"Anna?" he bellowed, heading for the stairs, when Dante abruptly appeared before him. Coming to a halt, Cezar glared at his friend. "Where is she?"

Something that might have been sorrow touched the lean features. "Cezar."

"Dammit, Dante." Cezar reached out to grab the vampire by his shoulders, giving him a violent shake. "Tell me where she is."

"We don't know," Dante muttered.

He gave the man another shake, a cold dread forming in the pit of his stomach.

"That's not good enough," he rasped.

Abby appeared at his side, her hand reaching up to lightly touch his arm. Under normal circumstances that light touch would have been enough to send him bolting away. The spirit within Abby had a nasty habit of setting demons on fire.

Now he didn't even flinch.

"Cezar, I know you're upset," she murmured.

"Upset?" he growled, glaring into her brilliant blue eyes. "I'm way past upset."

Her expression remained calm even as the lights flickered and more than one bulb burst beneath his surge of power.

Obviously she was accustomed to dealing with angry vampires.

"I know, but if we're going to find Anna and Levet then we can't fight among ourselves," she pointed out softly.

Cezar hissed. He was wise enough to know that Abby was right. If Anna was in danger then he needed all the help he could gather to rescue her.

But at the moment, he didn't want to be wise.

He wanted to tear the city apart brick by brick until he had Anna in his arms.

Backing from her touch in case he did something truly stupid, he held himself with a rigid restraint.

"Tell me what you know."

Glancing briefly toward Dante, Abby sucked in a deep breath. "Anna and Levet went to her rooms to discover a means of shielding her mind. They had been in there less than half an hour when I brought a tray to them and discovered they had disappeared."

"You heard nothing?"

"Nothing."

"What about the room? Was it . . ."

As his voice cracked, Dante clapped a steadying hand on his shoulder. "There were no signs of a struggle. No blood. But there is something you should see for yourself."

Cezar grudgingly allowed himself to be led up the stairs. *Dios*. His entire body trembled with the fierce need to be on the hunt. Anna was out there . . . somewhere. And no matter how great her powers, she needed him.

Stepping into the room that Anna had stayed in so briefly,

Cezar came to an abrupt halt as her sweet scent invaded his senses.

Closing his eyes he allowed the lingering essence to seep into his body.

"Cezar?" Dante murmured softly.

With a shake of his head, Cezar forced himself to move further into the large room decorated in shades of yellow. His gaze skimmed the canopied bed and French armoire, noting that everything seemed to be in order.

If there had been a fight here then it had been a tidy one.

It was as he was moving to check the window that he was struck by the too familiar odor.

"Pomegranates," he snarled. "Morgana."

"That was our guess," Abby breathed softly, kneeling beside a scorched mark that stained the ivory carpet. "This was not here before."

Cezar frowned. "Magic?"

"Yes, although I don't know enough to say for certain what sort," Abby confessed.

"It had to be a portal," Dante gritted, his silver eyes flashing with fury. He didn't like magic any better than Cezar. "There is no other means for Morgana to get past my security."

"Morgana has Anna." Cezar's cold dread was replaced by a raging fury.

The Queen of Fairies had to die.

She had to die now.

Turning on his heel, Cezar blindly stalked out of the room, heading down the stairs and entering the foyer before Dante could leap in front of him and bring him to a sharp halt.

"Cezar, wait," the vampire snapped, his muscles trembling with the effort of restraining the furious Cezar. "You can't just charge out without knowing where you're going. It will be dawn soon."

Cezar shook his head. Mixed with the fury was a raw, pounding pain that made him want to howl.

"I can't stay here."

Dante refused to ease his grip. "At least wait until Viper and Styx arrive. We can't do anything until we know how to find Morgana." The silver eyes narrowed. "Did you discover anything among Jagr's books?"

Knowing he would have to distract Dante if he was ever to get out of the mansion, Cezar dug into his pocket and handed over the scrap of paper that he used to copy the original text.

"Nothing more than a vague poem that refers to Morgana's retreat to Avalon."

Releasing his hold on Cezar, Dante smoothed the paper and read out loud.

From the ashes of her brother's grave
Shall emerge the means of her demise.
In ancient blood will powers stir
Arthur's revenge once more to rise.

The vampire gave a snort at the gibberish. "What the hell is that supposed to mean?"

"It means that Morgana is determined to kill every last descendent of Arthur," Cezar growled, darting past Dante and charging toward the door. "And next on her list is Anna."

He was a step away when the door was thrown open and Styx stepped over the threshold.

For an odd moment time seemed to stand still as the ancient vampire studied Cezar's bleak features.

Then, with one fluid motion, Styx raised his hand and Cezar found himself flying across the foyer to blast through the wall and into a marble column in the next room with enough force to rattle the house.

After that everything thing went blessedly black.

*   *   *

That was it, Anna decided, as she lay flat on her back in what she could only assume was some farmer's field. That was the very, very last time she was using her freaking powers.

All she had wanted to do was free herself and Levet from Morgana's portal. It wasn't as if she'd even allowed more than a trickle of her power to escape.

But the moment the stirring wind had touched the portal things had exploded.

Really and truly exploded.

As in flashing stars, mind-numbing concussion, flying debris (well actually, she and Levet were the debris), and landing with a bone-jarring thud.

The only plus side was there wasn't a damn portal in sight and the sickening scent of pomegranates had been replaced by the scent of recently plowed dirt and fresh air.

Feeling as if she'd been beaten with a baseball bat, Anna struggled to sit upright, swiveling her head as she frantically searched for Levet.

At last her gaze landed on his tiny form only a few feet away. He was standing, but his wings were drooping and he was anxiously inspecting his long tail as if he feared it had been damaged.

Hell, he was lucky he still had a tail.

Portal travel was worse than braving the Chicago L during rush hour.

"Are you okay?" she managed to rasp, batting the clumps of dirt from her jeans. She didn't even try to smooth her hair, which felt as if it was standing on end.

Levet dropped his tail, his ugly little face scrunched into a grimace as he peered through the shadows that shrouded the surrounding countryside.

"I am fine, but where the hell are we?"

"I . . ." Anna gave a helpless shake of her head. There was nothing to see other than the fields and a few abandoned buildings clustered near a dirt road. In the distant sky there was a faint glow, as if the lights of a city were being reflected, but there was no way to know what city.

They could be a handful of miles from Chicago, or they could be in the middle of Kansas.

Or hell, maybe that had just exploded their way to Oz.

"I don't have a clue," she muttered.

"Don't panic." The gargoyle began pacing in a tight circle, his poor, battered wings flapping in tempo. "We will somehow get out of this mess. Just do not panic."

"Okay."

"We have to think clearly. We have to . . ." Pace, pace, pace. "We have to think and not panic. That is the most important thing."

"Not to panic."

"Right. Do not panic."

Anna cleared her throat. "Levet."

Coming to a halt the gargoyle regarded her with a wild glitter in his eyes. *"Oui?"*

"I'm not the one panicking."

"Okay." He lifted his stunted hands. "Good point."

Waiting until Levet had managed to calm his fluttering, Anna took a step forward.

"I don't suppose you have a cell phone on you?"

Levet managed an offended sniff at the perfectly reasonable question. What was it with demons and technology?

"I am a gargoyle. I do not need such foolish devices."

"Can you contact someone with your magic?"

"Of course."

Her heart turned over in relief. "Thank God. You have to let Cezar know that . . ."

"Wait, Anna," Levet interrupted, wrinkling his tiny snout. "I am not certain that would be such a good idea."

Anna counted to ten. They were stuck in the middle of

God-knew-where, and he didn't want to contact anyone to come and get them? "Why not?"

"I communicate with portals."

Her hope died a swift, painful death.

"Oh." Anna grimaced. "Yeah, I think we should avoid portals for a while."

"My thought exactly."

Anna lifted her hand to lightly touch the signet ring that dangled on the chain around her neck. Cezar had promised that she could find him anywhere with the ring, but unfortunately it didn't include an intercom system. Even if it did, she wasn't about to stir up her dangerous powers for any reason. The next time she might toss herself to Mars instead of the middle of nowhere.

Glancing around the vast emptiness, Anna heaved a sigh. She had spent enough time over the years living in various places around the Midwest to realize that they were probably miles from the nearest town. "Then it looks like we need to find a friendly farmer who will let us use his phone."

"Ummm . . ." Levet rubbed one of his horns. "Actually I need to find a place to hide."

"Can Morgana find us?"

He shrugged, glancing toward the pinkish glow on the edge of the horizon.

"I don't know, but the sun will soon rise."

"Will it harm you?"

"I am a gargoyle, Anna," he said, as if she were particularly dimwitted. "When the rays of the sun touch my skin I will turn to my statue form."

"Ah." Feeling like an idiot, Anna once again surveyed their surroundings, finding nothing but the dilapidated house and barn. "What about that barn?" she suggested.

The gossamer wings gave a sharp flap. "A barn? Do I look like a cow?"

"Fine." She slapped her hands on her hips. "Then you find a place."

Turning a full circle, Levet muttered beneath his breath. "I suppose the barn will have to do."

"Then let's go."

Together they stumbled across the rough field, Anna's aching body protesting each step. Being blasted out of a portal was obviously something to be avoided.

Tripping over a loose clump of soil, Anna moaned as she forced herself upright.

Yeah, definitely to be avoided.

Levet's small hand reached up to tug on her sweatshirt. "Anna, we must hurry."

With a weary smile, she grabbed his cold fingers in her hand and tugged him through a gap in the sagging fence. From there it was a battle with the horseweed and blackberry brambles that had taken over the yard.

At last they managed to reach the door of the barn that was thankfully intact, and pulling it open she led the weary gargoyle across the dusty floor into the shadows of the far corner.

The barn was nearly empty. There were a few rusting farm implements scattered about the floor, and a pile of old newspapers that were being slowly nibbled to bits by mice. Whoever had once called this remote farm home had long ago left for greener pastures.

"Here," she murmured, pushing aside a forgotten bale of hay to tuck him into a narrow stall.

The gargoyle would at least be hidden from casual sight, although if someone actually searched the barn he would be easily spotted.

Where were all those freaking vampire tunnels when you needed them?

On the point of finding her own hiding place, Anna was halted when Levet grasped the sleeve of her sweatshirt.

"Anna."

"Yes?"

"Once the sun rises I will not be able to help you. If something comes you must run." Loosening his grip he reached for a stray nail that had been left in the stall and scratched through the dirt. "This is Darcy's number. Call her as soon as you can find a phone."

Her brows snapped together. "I won't leave you, Levet."

"You must. Nothing can hurt me while I am in statue form."

Anna blinked. That seemed like a handy little trick to have up his sleeve.

Especially if Morgana decided for an encore performance. "Nothing at all?"

Without answering, Levet glanced toward the narrow window that was blooming with a pale pink wash of dawn.

"Anna, I am sorry."

She stumbled backward as the tiny body began to glow and then hardened into unrelenting stone before her very eyes.

"Damn."

Maybe she should be used to the strange and the wacky. God knew that there had been enough of it over the past few days. Hell, there'd been enough of it over the past two centuries.

But the sight of the gargoyle altering from a living being to a chunk of granite was above and beyond what she was prepared to watch.

Bolting out of the stall, she paused to shove the hay bale across the opening before moving across the barn and climbing the narrow stairs to the hayloft.

The beams were low enough that it was easier to crawl on her hands and knees than to risk whacking her head, and thankfully the loft was empty of everything but a few stray wisps of straw. Taking care to test the warped boards before putting her full weight on them, she inched her way to the back of the loft and pushed open the small door that offered a view of the surrounding countryside.

From here she should be able to keep watch for anyone approaching. Friend or foe.

What the crap she intended to do if something attacked the barn was an entirely different matter.

Chapter 15

Anna knew at once she was in one of those dreams that wasn't really a dream.

For one thing, she didn't remember ever falling asleep. One minute she had been keeping a vigilant watch out for the bad guys and the next she was tumbling through a black void that seemed to devour her.

Besides, her sense of awareness was too clear, her surroundings too crisp and vivid for the regular run-of-the-mill nightmare.

Glancing down to make sure that the bizarro world included clothes, she was relieved to discover she was covered in a long green gown with an embroidered tunic that fell nearly to her knees. She looked like she had just stepped out of a medieval painting, but she was too happy not to be stark naked to care.

Of course, the ridiculous dress seemed to fit the strange place.

With a shiver she took in the crumbling ruins of the ancient castle that surrounded her. It was nothing more than a shell of worn, gray stones that were covered in mold, along with empty windows that revealed that the castle was perched on the edge of a cliff with some unknown sea crashing against the rocky shore.

With her heart beating with the same force as the distant waves, Anna slowly turned about, searching through the odd, silvery mist for the familiar form of Morgana.

For long moments there was nothing to see. She might have been completely alone in the isolated, peaceful ruin. Even better there wasn't the faintest whiff of pomegranates to mar the salt-scented breeze.

Then, as her eyes widened in fear, a large, silver and black wolf appeared in an arched doorway, regarding her with an unnervingly intelligent green gaze.

"Oh . . ." She took a hasty step backward, her hand pressed to her heart. The wolf halted, as if realizing it had startled her—which might have been a lot more comforting if a strange glow hadn't started to shimmer around the large animal—and in a blink of an eye it took on a misty, ethereal shape of a man. "Crap."

"Do not fear, I mean you no harm," a deep voice rumbled from within the mist.

Anna shook her head. Despite the vague impression of a large, very male figure in heavy armor, it was impossible to make out any actual features. Almost as if the mist battled against holding a steady shape.

That, of course, didn't mean the . . . thing wasn't dangerous. With her current streak of luck, she could almost count on it.

"I seem to be hearing that a lot lately," she muttered. "Usually right before someone tries to hurt me."

The mist stirred and Anna had the impression that the stranger had lifted his hands to remove his helmet. It was nothing more than a feeling. Just like the feeling that the man possessed craggy, worn features and a long mane of silver-peppered black hair.

"I sensed Morgana leaving Avalon and moving through the world," he said, ignoring her comment. "That is what has brought me here."

She took another step backward. "You know Morgana?"

His short, bitter laugh echoed through the empty room. "Intimately."

"Then that whole claim of not meaning to hurt me was just a big lie?" she rasped.

"No, Anna Randal." His hand lifted in what she assumed was a gesture of peace. "I am here to offer you what little protection that I can."

"Why?" she demanded suspiciously. "Why would you want to protect me?"

"You are blood of my blood."

Blood of my blood?

A strange surge of excitement raced through her, only to be swiftly squashed. Jeez. How pathetic was it to be excited by the thought that she might have found a long lost part of her family?

He was a blob of mist, for Christ's sake.

"You mean that we're related?" she demanded, her tone deliberately indifferent.

"We are more than mere relatives." The mist stirred, as if in reaction to some strong emotion. "You are the culmination of centuries of hope and sacrifice. You are my ultimate weapon of justice."

"Weapon of justice?" She shivered as a sudden chill lodged in the pit of her stomach at the ominous words. "I don't think I like the sound of that."

"Morgana must pay for her sins."

"Sins against you?"

"I am but one of her victims, just as you are." The mist neared, bringing with it the smell of warm, rich sage. "There have been an endless number of victims over the years. And should she ever be truly liberated from her citadel in Avalon . . ."

She frowned as his words trailed away. "What?"

The man hissed, shaking his head. Or at least she thought that he shook his head.

"The world will be bathed in her perversions," he said, his

voice vibrating with a fierce command. "You cannot allow such a fate."

"Me? What am I supposed to do?"

"You possess the power to destroy Morgana."

"Oh, no." She gave a wild shake of her head. The ghost, or shade, or whatever the hell he was, was clearly off his nut. If Anna ever fell into Morgana's hands she didn't doubt the woman would bitch-slap her from one end of Chicago to the other. "I don't. I really, really don't."

"You have proven otherwise by simply being alive. Morgana has gone to great lengths to be rid of you."

Her laugh held a world of bitterness. "Good God, all I've done is cause one disaster after another. It's a wonder that I haven't managed to kill myself and everyone around me. And for your information, the only reason I'm still alive is because of Cezar, not because of any power I might possess."

The mist seemed to still. "The vampire."

Anna blinked in shock. "You know him?"

"I see much, even here."

"Ah."

Anna wasn't sure if she should be pleased or creeped out. It was nice to think someone might be watching over her. On the other hand, the last thing she wanted was a mystical peeping tom. She cleared her throat.

"You underestimate yourself, Anna Randal." His voice softened. "You are bred to be a champion. Your destiny is greater than even I could have imagined for you."

Anna planted her hands on her hips. Dammit. She was tired of people referring to her destiny as if they all knew something she didn't. And she didn't like the thought that people were depending on her to accomplish some wondrous goal when she felt like she was drowning in the mess that was her life.

"Right now my destiny is being trapped in a filthy barn with an incapacitated gargoyle and no clue of where I am or how to protect either of us," she gritted. "Hardly a champion."

"You possess the power," he stubbornly repeated. "You merely lack the ability to command your gifts."

You think? Anna thought dryly, recalling the painful battle she had just waged with the portal.

"If you're some sort of relative, why don't you teach me?" she challenged.

Once again she sensed the shake of his head. "Forgive me, Anna, but my time here is limited."

"Exactly where is here?"

A tangible sadness filled the room. "It was once my home. Now I suppose it is my tomb."

Anna bit her lip. "I'm sorry."

"I have accepted my fate."

His voice was flat, but Anna suspected that he was a long way from accepting fate. He blamed Morgana for whatever had happened to him, and he intended to see her punished. Obviously using her as the weapon. Great. "Will you tell me who you are?"

The mist shifted, and Anna could have sworn that she felt the light stroke of a finger down her cheek.

"You know who I am, Anna."

"Are you Arthur?" she husked, startled by the flood of warmth that rushed through her heart. "As in roundtables and Camelot?"

"I am Arthur, and your very distant grandfather." The misty hand stroked down her arm and then she felt a sudden weight in the palm of her hand. "This is for you."

Startled, Anna nearly dropped the heavy silver necklace, which held an emerald that was large enough to make Liz Taylor drool.

"What is it?" she breathed.

"A pendant that was given to me by a great sorcerer. It will allow you to focus your powers."

She slowly lifted her gaze. "I don't suppose it has an owner's manual that comes with it?"

The mist moved back, halting near the arched doorway. "It was crafted to respond to the ancient magic that flows in your blood."

With shaking fingers, she stroked the flawless jewel, mesmerized by the purity of its green fire. "Did I inherit my powers from you?"

"Yes."

"But they didn't stop Morgana?"

His soft sigh rippled through the air. "Treachery, not power, was my destruction, Anna Randal. You have a mind that seeks justice, but do not allow your compassionate heart to lead you to my fate."

"But . . ." She hastily swallowed her words as the mist swirled and then once again she was staring into the unnerving eyes of the large wolf. "Damn."

Cezar hissed as the clinging darkness ebbed away and the wave of pain rushed in to replace it.

His entire body felt as if it had been run over by a truck (a fully loaded cement truck), but it was the lingering ache at the back of his head that warned him that his poor skull had absorbed most of the damage.

Hardly surprising. He'd flown completely through the foyer wall before taking out a marble column. Only the fact that he was a vampire had kept him from being laid out in the nearest morgue.

Instead he seemed to be lying on a narrow sofa with a strong pair of hands pressed against his chest to hold him still.

"He's waking," Dante murmured, close enough to reveal he was the one holding him captive.

"Damn, Styx, I thought you had killed him," Viper murmured from nearby.

"Not to mention putting a hole through my wall," Dante groused.

"Would any lesser blow have kept him from running into the dawn?" Styx demanded. "Besides, I recall being chained in a cell when the two of you decided I was a danger to myself."

Cezar forced open his eyes, discovering Dante perched on the sofa next to him and Styx and Viper bending over him with concerned expressions.

Not that Styx's was nearly concerned enough, Cezar thought as he sent the ancient demon a jaundiced glare. "Then why the hell didn't you hit them instead of me? I didn't chain you in a cell."

A hint of amusement touched Styx's dark eyes as he shoved a glass into Cezar's hand. "Here."

With an effort, Cezar managed to shove himself to a sitting position and take a deep drink of the blood. It would speed his healing and help him recover his strength.

Something he was in desperate need of.

Polishing off the blood, he set aside the glass and frowned at the gathered vampires.

"Anna. Have you heard . . ."

"No, Cezar, there's been nothing," Dante said, his tone edged with sympathy. "I'm sorry."

Cezar didn't want pity. He wanted Anna in his arms.

"I have called for the clans to gather," Styx assured him. "We shall find Anna."

"I can't wait." With a surge of power he was off the sofa, sending his friends stumbling backward. He could sense that night had fallen and nothing was going to keep him from going in search of his woman. "I have to do something."

Dante and Viper looked ready to attack and hold him down by force if necessary, but before Cezar could prove the dangers of screwing with him when he was in this mood, Styx lifted a commanding hand.

"Leave us," he growled to Dante and Viper.

The two vampires grudgingly calmed, then with a bow

toward their leader they filed from the small anteroom that Cezar assumed was near the foyer. It was one of those extra, useless rooms that mansions always seemed to possess.

Squaring his shoulders, Cezar glared at the looming vampire. No one could match Styx's sheer power, but he was bloody well willing to give it his best shot. "You are my Anasso, Styx, but you can't stop me," he said, his voice filled with a lethal promise. "I am bound by the Oracles to protect Anna."

Styx moved to lean casually against the wall, his towering leather-bound form close enough to the door to make sure that Cezar would have to go through him to escape.

Not a pleasant prospect.

"And that is the only reason you risk your life to find her?" he demanded.

Cezar stiffened. He didn't want to discuss his fierce connection to Anna. It was too intimate, too raw, to share with anyone.

But he knew that expression on Styx's harsh face. The older vampire wasn't about to allow Cezar to rush into the night until he'd had his say.

"You know it is not," Cezar at last growled.

Styx gave a slow nod, his dark eyes troubled. "Cezar, even if Anna survives Morgana, she is destined to become an Oracle."

Cezar gave an impatient wave of his hand. Dammit, he knew Anna's fate better than anyone. Better than Anna herself.

"Do you have a point?"

"The point is that you are destined to lose her whether it's to Morgana or the Commission."

"The Commission doesn't have plans to execute Anna."

"No, but they will claim her as one of their own," Styx pointed out gently. "Cezar, they took you captive for merely daring to take her blood. Do you truly believe they will allow you to mate her?"

The aching need to make Anna irrevocably his own pounded through Cezar with enough force to make his knees tremble. His every instinct screamed that the sweet, delicate woman belonged to him.

Solely, completely, and eternally.

No one, not even the Commission could alter that absolute truth.

"Once Anna is a full member of the Commission she will be able to make her own decisions," he growled.

"Do any of them take a mate?"

Cezar jerked as an unexpected pain lashed through him. *Dios*. Was Styx a closet sadist? Was he deliberately attempting to drive him mad?

"Enough, Styx." Cezar shoved his fingers through his hair, pacing the small space with a rising sense of claustrophobia. He wanted to be out of here. He needed to be searching for Anna, not dwelling on a future that held the potential to be as bleak as his past. "There's been no talk of mating."

"But it is what you desire," Styx prodded.

"Desire?" Cezar laughed with a bitter flare of humor. "Is there ever a choice?"

"Perhaps not, but I do not want to see you forced to suffer more than you already have. It is not too late to put some distance between the two of you and . . ."

"You're wrong, Styx. It's far too late," he interrupted, his voice rough. "Two hundred years too late."

There was a tap on the door before the tall, blond vampire that was a member of Styx's Ravens (death-dealing bodyguards) stepped into the room.

"Forgive me, my lord."

Styx straightened, his expression dark at the interruption. "What is it?"

"Your wife has arrived."

"Darcy?" His eyes narrowed. "Send her in." The vampire bowed and backed out of the door, swiftly replaced by the pretty werewolf that had firmly captured the King of Vampires. "What is it, my love?"

"Levet contacted me. He's with Anna."

Cezar didn't even realize he was moving until he was standing in front of Darcy, his hands gripping her fingers.

"Where is she? Is she harmed? Take me to her."

Styx bristled at Cezar's rough grasp, but a glance from Darcy was enough to make him take a step back.

"Levet wasn't certain of their location, but I sensed that it's outside of Chicago in an old barn west of here," she said, her gaze steady and filled with determination. "He said that Anna is unharmed, but he's unable to wake her. He fears she might be in some sort of trance."

Cezar hissed, the cold dread he had been battling since he felt Anna's distress threatening to overwhelm him.

"What happened to them?"

Darcy gave a shake of her head. "He only said that Morgana attempted to trap them in a portal and that Anna used her powers to release them. He could not talk for long, he feared that Morgana could trace his voice."

Styx reached out to lay a hand on Cezar's shoulder, as if sensing the raw pain that held his heart in a vise.

"Darcy, can you track Anna?" he demanded.

"If we get close enough." She gave Cezar's fingers a gentle squeeze. "Shay is here as well. Between the two of us we will find them."

Cezar was already on his way to the door. "Then let's go."

Anna was dreaming. This time a regular, old-fashioned, nonlethal sort of dream.

Well, maybe not entirely old-fashioned. It did include a demon. One handsome, wickedly delicious demon who was doing all sorts of wonderful things with his hands and lips and tongue . . . oh yes, definitely his tongue.

"Anna. Anna," he whispered, his voice oddly high and edged with a French accent.

French accent?

Crap.

The delightful vision of Cezar began to slip away and with a sigh of regret, Anna wrenched open her heavy lids to discover Levet bent over her with a worried expression.

"*Mon dieu*, you scared me," he breathed, his warm breath brushing her cheek. "I couldn't wake you. Did you hit your head?"

Scooting to a sitting position, Anna grabbed her head as it throbbed with disapproval at her sudden movement. "It feels like it." For a moment she simply concentrated on the unpleasant ache in her forehead, then, slowly realizing that a part of the pain was something digging into her skin, she lowered her hand to study the magnificent emerald hung on an ancient silver chain that lay in her palm. "Crap."

"*Sacrebleu*." Levet gave a nervous flap of his wings, his eyes wide. "Where did you get that?"

Oh, it was just a little thing handed to me by my multi-great grandfather, who happens to be King Arthur, and oh yeah, he's dead and haunting some ancient ruin.

She choked back the hysterical urge to laugh. "Would you believe from a dream?"

"A dream?" Levet rose to his feet, his hands waving above his head. "Oh, perfect. My dreams give me nothing more than a dry mouth and a stiff neck and your dreams give you priceless baubles. Life is so unfair."

Anna rolled her eyes, and then wished she hadn't when a sharp pain shot through her head.

She had a priceless gem, but it might as well be just another chunk of rock if she didn't learn how to use it to control her powers.

"I couldn't agree with you more." She absently brushed the bits of straw from her jeans, her brows snapping together as she belatedly realized that night had fallen while she slept. God, she'd been out for hours. "What time is it?"

"Shortly after dusk." The gargoyle paused, wrinkling his snout. "I have managed to contact Darcy."

Sheer relief rushed through Anna. An annoying sensation considering she wanted to be the sort of woman who could always take care of herself.

Still, there it was.

The calvary was on its way and she was happy as hell about it.

"How? You said it was too dangerous to use a portal."

"I couldn't wake you, so I took a risk." The gossamer wings drooped as Levet glanced toward the small door. "I hope it doesn't come back and bite us."

"Will they be able to find us?"

Levet shrugged. "We have a werewolf and a Shalott searching for us, not to mention an entire pack of vampires. It might take a while, but they'll find us."

"Meanwhile we also have a pack of homicidal fairies searching for us," she said dryly. "Maybe we should find a better hiding place."

"I scouted while I was on the hunt." Levet patted his belly, as if he were pleased with his hunt. Anna didn't allow herself to consider what a gargoyle might eat. She liked Levet and didn't want the image of him crunching on little kitties to ruin their friendship. "There is nothing but farmhouses and one small town for miles. We are as safe here as anywhere."

Anna sighed. "That's not massively reassuring."

"I know."

A silence descended as they both considered all the horrible things that could happen before help could arrive. At last, Anna gathered her erratic courage and reached out to lightly touch the gargoyle's hand.

"Levet."

"Oui?"

"You could fly away from here."

The gray eyes widened. "No."

"Listen to me," she urged. "You could fly to Chicago and bring Cezar directly to the barn. Surely that would be faster than having them searching all over the state for us?" She grimaced. "Even assuming that we're still in Illinois."

"We are, although Chicago is some distance away."

"Then go, Levet." She shifted until she was kneeling before him. The poor gargoyle had already suffered enough because of her. "You can save both of us."

"I will not." As Anna's lips parted he pointed a stubby finger directly in her face. "No. Not another word."

Sitting back on her heels, Anna heaved a deep sigh. What was it with demons?

"Are all demons trained to be stubborn or is it something that just comes naturally?" she groused.

"It is all natural, of course." He waggled his brows. "Just like my beauty."

Anna couldn't help but laugh. "I see."

Obviously pleased he had managed to bring a smile to her face, Levet stepped to one side and pointed to a plate that was filled with fried chicken, mashed potatoes, and what smelled like freshly baked biscuits. Her eyes widened even as her stomach rumbled with appreciation.

"I brought you food."

She shifted her gaze to the beaming gargoyle. "Where did you get this?"

"Does it matter?"

"You stole it, didn't you?"

His expression was one of absolute innocence. "I might have borrowed it from a nearby kitchen."

She lifted her brows. "Borrowed?"

"Trust me, I just saved some overweight farmer from an

early heart attack. I was doing him a favor." He gave a snort of disgust. "Besides, unlike vampires I can't really pass as a human. Can you imagine me strolling into a restaurant and ordering take-out?"

Anna thrust aside her faint guilt at having stolen some poor farmer's dinner and reached for the plate. Levet had not only kept guard over her while she slept, but he had gone to the effort to make sure she was fed.

A warmth filled her heart. It was a strange, wonderful feeling to have others in her life that actually cared about her.

It had been so long.

"Thank you, Levet, it was very thoughtful of you," she whispered softly, ducking her head to dig into the small feast in an effort to hide her expression.

Easily sensing her tightly wound emotions, Levet settled close to her side, his wings brushing her back in a comforting motion.

"Ah well, I am French. I know how to make a lady happy."

Continuing to eat, Anna shot her companion a swift glance. "Are there a lot of gargoyles in France?"

"Europe is littered with them." Levet made a rude noise. "Thankfully few of them are willing to leave their Guilds to come to America."

"Guilds?"

"It is our clan, or family if you prefer."

Anna struggled with the image of a family of gargoyles sitting around watching TV and eating popcorn.

Wow.

"You don't have a Guild here?"

Levet shifted, his hands clenched. "I am not allowed in any Guilds. Gargoyles have little sympathy for those who are . . . different."

Anna abruptly set aside her plate, a wave of painful compassion washing through her.

She knew all about not fitting in.

Anywhere.

"Yeah," she muttered. "Neither do humans."

The gray eyes lost their hard glitter. "So we are both without a Guild."

"Yes, it would seem we are."

"It is not pleasant to be alone." He tilted his head to one side. "But, I have found Shay who has taken me into her family. Perhaps Cezar will offer you a place as well."

Anna's breath tangled in her throat. Oh . . . God. She couldn't allow herself to think of an eternity with Cezar. Or the thought of being surrounded by those who thought of her as family.

Not after she had devoted so many years to accepting that she would always be alone.

Hope was the most dangerous thing in the world.

"Levet . . ." Anna abruptly stiffened, alarm bells ringing through her mind as she caught the unmistakable scent of apples. "Do you smell that?"

Levet gave a nervous nod. "*Oui*. Fairies."

"Shit."

Chapter 16

Anna squeezed her eyes shut, ridiculously praying that the scent would simply disappear. She'd had a bellyful of fairies. In fact, if she never had to deal with another fairy or imp or deranged queen again in her life, she would be a happy, happy woman.

Of course the scent didn't disappear.

It spread to fill the entire barn.

Hell, why should her luck turn now?

Wrenching open her eyes at the sound of footsteps, Anna met Levet's worried gaze and with a grimace stretched out on the grimy boards and began wiggling her way to the edge of the loft.

"There is no use in hiding, Anna Randal," a soft, female voice called out just as Anna reached her destination. "I know you are here."

Peeking over the edge of the loft, Anna sucked in a sharp breath, her fear replaced with sharp, horrified disbelief as she caught sight of the dark-haired woman who stood in the center of the barn.

She knew that perfect pale skin and the dark, mocking eyes. And that scent . . . apples.

"Oh my God," she husked, her entire body trembling. "Sybil? But you're . . ."

"Dead?" the woman taunted, her perfectly manicured hand reaching up to pat her perfectly styled hair.

Anna blinked. And then she blinked again. The woman didn't look like she had just crawled from her grave. There wasn't so much as a speck of dirt on her pressed khakis and knit shirt. Surely there should be some sign of her recent demise?

This had to be a trick.

It had to be.

"She is dead," Anna rasped.

The woman's grating laugh echoed through the barn. "Do you fear she might have come back from the grave? That she intends to haunt you for killing her?"

"I didn't kill her."

The dark eyes flashed with pure hatred. "Oh, Morgana might have struck the deadly blow, but it was because of you that she was trapped in that cell and unable to defend herself. You are responsible for her death. Now it's time for you to pay."

Stuck in a sense of unreality, Anna remained frozen in place rather than running for life and limb.

Stupid. Stupid. Stupid.

"Who are you?"

"I am Clara, Sybil's sister." Her lips twisted as understanding dawned in Anna's eyes. A twin. Of course. "She called to me as she was dying. She pleaded for me to seek revenge from those responsible. And that is exactly what I intend to do."

Anna's stomach rolled at the memory of Sybil lying on the cot, stone-cold dead. She felt horrible that the fairy had died.

But not horrible enough to allow herself to be killed in retribution.

With an effort, she forced herself to a kneeling position and glared down at the woman who was the most recent threat in a very long line.

"How did you find me?"

"Actually, I have Morgana to thank for this golden opportunity."

She heard the sudden flap of Levet's wings. It echoed the rapid flutter of her heart.

"She knows I'm here?"

"Not specifically here, although she knows that you managed to escape from her portal to somewhere between her rotting farmhouse and Chicago. She called for her faithful subjects to go in search of you, but unlike the rest of the fairies I had a secret weapon."

Secret weapon?

What was she, the Pentagon?

"And what's that?"

"I once saw you in a courtroom in L.A. when I was visiting Sybil. I will never forget your face . . . or your scent," she replied, her smile smug. "I knew that if I came across your trail I could find you. Of course, I wasted far too much time beginning my search so close to Chicago. I never dreamed you would nearly be upon Morgana's doorstep."

Anna's heart gave another unpleasant flutter. Just how close was Morgana?

Doorstep didn't sound good.

Shoving aside the nasty thought to worry about later, Anna concentrated on the fairy below.

"So you found me." She narrowed her gaze. "Now what?"

Clara smiled with cold amusement. "Ah, a woman who likes to cut to the chase. I don't know whether to be impressed or laugh at your stupidity."

"I know which," Levet muttered at her side.

Flashing the gargoyle a warning frown, Anna returned her attention to Clara.

"Tell me what you intend to do."

Clara crooked a mocking finger. "Why don't you come down and we can discuss the situation like two reasonable adults?"

Levet snorted. "It's a trick."

"You think?" Anna said dryly, leaning over the edge of the loft. "Thanks, but I'm comfortable where I am. Just tell me what you want."

The perfect features twisted with a perverse fury. "What I want is to watch you die."

"Nice," Anna muttered with a shiver.

"But first I intend to make Morgana pay dearly to have you turned over to her."

"Ha." Levet moved to stand at Anna's side. "You intend to bargain with the Queen of Bitches? Why don't you just start digging your own grave now?"

"Oh, she will negotiate. She's desperate to get her hands on Anna Randal."

"Why?" Anna abruptly demanded. "Why does she want me dead?"

"You don't know?" Clara laughed. "How perfect. You should go to your death still wondering why you're dying. Just as Sybil did."

"She doesn't know, Anna." Levet leaned forward and directed a raspberry in Clara's direction. "She's nothing but a peon. Dirt beneath Morgana's feet."

The pale features flushed with fury as she lifted a slender hand in Levet's direction.

"You slimy little reptile . . ."

Anna felt a tingle of power before Levet was launched backward and his tiny body lay unnervingly still against the floorboards of the loft.

"Levet." Crawling toward his unmoving form, Anna desperately attempted to waken her friend. "Levet. Oh my God."

There was no response, and a combination of fear and absolute fury pounded through her. Spinning on her knees she moved back to the edge of the loft, launching herself over the side to land on the dirt floor. She was beyond caring about her own danger. This woman had hurt one of her friends. One of the first friends she'd had in nearly two centuries. The evil fairy was going to be very, very sorry she had messed with Anna Randal.

"You . . . hideous, horrible . . . demon. You want a fight, you got it."

Something that might have been fear replaced the smug assurance in Clara's dark eyes. Holding up her hands, she took a step backward.

"I only stunned the beast," she rasped. "Stay back or I'll kill you."

"No you won't," Anna mocked, unconsciously gripping the priceless emerald in her clenched fist. "You want to barter me, remember? You have dreams of riches dancing through your head."

"I'm not Sybil, I won't sacrifice my life for wealth."

The air heated as Anna's fury spilled from her tense body. "Tell me why Morgana wants me dead."

With suddenly wide eyes the fairy took another few steps backward. "I . . . don't . . ."

"Tell me," Anna snapped, her hair beginning to dance in the rising wind.

"All I know is that Modron had a vision of you," Clara squeaked.

"Modron?"

"Morgana's seer."

Seer? What the hell was that?

"What was the vision?" she asked instead, not in the mood to be distracted.

Clara licked her lips. "That an heir of Arthur would rise from the darkness and condemn Morgana to hell."

"A lovely thought, but why does she think I'm the heir destined to send her to hell?"

"You possess the blood of the ancients."

"And?"

The dark gaze briefly flicked toward the nearby door before returning to Anna's grim face.

"And she has devoted her life to killing off Arthur's line. It doesn't matter if you're truly the Destined One or not, she can't let you live."

Anna's heart clenched with a sharp, poignant pain. So much death. So much loneliness because of a stupid vision.

"She slaughtered my entire family," Anna muttered, unable to conceive that anyone, queen or not, could be so evil.

"Yes, if I were you I would . . ." Without warning, Clara launched herself forward, clearly sensing Anna's distraction. Anna barely had time to gasp before the woman had plunged a knife into her stomach, sending her flying backwards.

Scrambling back to her feet, Anna ignored the blood flowing down her body and swiftly ducked as Clara threw another punch.

"Damn you," Anna muttered.

"You are the one who will be damned if you don't get on your knees and do exactly as I say."

Wrenching the knife from her gut, Anna gritted her teeth as a strange buzzing rushed through her body.

"Are you mental?" she rasped, forcing herself to concentrate on remaining upright. Damn, the blood still flowed from her deep wound, defying her usual ability to heal herself.

"No, I'm very, very clever," Clara warned. "That knife was hexed, and unless you allow me to remove the curse you will die."

Well . . . crap.

She didn't know anything about hexed knives or curses, but she did know if she allowed this woman to gain the upper hand she would soon be Morgana's plaything.

She'd rather die in this barn than allow that to happen.

Sensing another attack, Anna threw out her hand, as much to shove the woman away as to harm her. Her powers, however, had other ideas. As her palm connected with Clara's arm the woman shrieked and the stench of burning flesh filled the barn.

Anna grimaced, but there was no time to feel guilt as Clara hit her with an unseen force that felt like a sledgehammer to her chest. She grunted in pain, fairly certain that the damn fairy had just broken her rib. Another blow hit her forehead and more blood began to flow.

She struck out, blinded by the blood and only managing to skim the woman's cheek as the fairy jerked backward.

"Stop this or you'll die," the woman hissed. "Only I can break the curse."

"I'll risk it," Anna managed to mutter before being launched backward by an unseen strike to her chest.

"Allow me to bind you and I promise I won't hurt you anymore."

Riiiight.

Anna pushed herself upright. "You'll just hand me over for Morgana to kill."

"If you're the Destined One then you'll kill her," Clara taunted, her powerful fist connecting with Anna's chin.

Dammit, she was being pummeled like a punching bag. If she didn't start fighting back she'd soon be dead.

Ignoring the pain that flared through her body, Anna forced herself to focus on the heat that swirled around her. She wasn't certain she could control the wind enough to keep it from knocking the barn down on top of them. If Levet still lived she couldn't risk hurting him even more.

Besides, her smoldering fury demanded something more than a breeze.

A red haze shimmered before her eyes, her mind so consumed with the power she was building that she barely noticed the blows that Clara continued to strike against her. Not even when Clara launched forward and scratched her nails down her neck.

"Stop, you bitch," Clara hissed.

"This will stop . . . now." Grasping the fairy's arms in a tight grip, Anna allowed the pent-up heat to charge the air around them.

At first she could feel nothing but the prickling of her own skin and Clara's frantic attempt to free herself. The heat almost seemed to be waiting for some direction.

Or maybe some mystical, magical word that she didn't have a clue about.

Wouldn't that just be perfect?

Panic began to rise, but before it could fully take on a full-throttle status, the glint of the emerald, which she now had pressed to Clara's arm, caught her attention.

With a strange, hypnotic pulse that light began to fill the barn with an eerie green glow. Clara gasped, her gaze shifting to the gem that would make any fairy green with envy.

It wasn't envy, however, that twisted her beautiful features. Instead it was a stark, disbelieving fear.

"No . . . please, no."

Her plea might have swayed Anna. She didn't possess a vicious enough heart to enjoy inflicting pain on others. But the choice of stopping was taken out of her hands as the emerald flared and without warning a fierce explosion rocked the barn.

Anna felt herself being launched backward, a searing pain racing through her blood. Then, with a crack that resounded through her brain, her head hit the far wall and she fell heavily to the dirt floor.

"Anna . . . Anna." A tiny hand touched her hair and Anna managed to lift her heavy lashes enough to find Levet's face swimming before her dazed eyes.

"Levet?"

"*Oui*. Do not move."

Move? God. The last thing in the world she intended to do was force her weary, aching body to so much as twitch.

"Did we win?"

A smile touched the truly ugly face, even as her consciousness began to fade.

"Booyah."

The ridiculous word was the last thing she heard as a welcome void reached up to swallow her.

The Hummer was a perfect choice to race over the rough back roads of Illinois. It was spacious enough to hold four vampires, a Shalott demon, and a werewolf, and sturdy enough to survive Viper's zealous attempts to cross the state in a new record time. Cezar, however, chafed at being confined.

He wanted to be running through the dark, using his skills to track the woman who called to him even when she wasn't near.

Unfortunately, Styx had been right when he pointed out that his strength would only last so long. And that when he did find Anna it would be quicker to rush her back to the safety of Chicago in a car rather than having to carry her.

Wisely left undisturbed in the backseat of the Hummer, Cezar growled as Viper slowed to a crawl, allowing Darcy and Shay an opportunity to take deep breaths of air. Cezar logically understood that his friends were just trying to help, but his logic wasn't in control at the moment.

Every futile delay was like having a silver stake thrust through him.

Grinding his teeth in an effort to hold back his frustration, Cezar suddenly stiffened. There was no scent, no sound, no tangible sign that Anna was near.

But he knew.

He knew with absolute certainty.

"Stop," he growled, shoving open the back door. "Stop the car."

"What is it, Cezar?" Styx demanded.

"I feel her. I feel Anna." A shudder shook his body. "She's been hurt."

"Cezar . . . dammit." Dante reached to halt him, but Cezar was already throwing himself out of the moving vehicle and flowing through the darkness with blinding speed.

They would be able to follow his trail, but he couldn't wait for them. Not when his every instinct was screaming that Anna was slipping away from him.

The recently plowed ground was no impediment as he streaked through the night, the faint scent of apples only spurring him onward.

A fairy had passed this way.

Recently.

Leaping over the sagging fence, Cezar headed toward the distant barn. As he neared, the smell of apples became mixed with the scent of Anna's blood. A cold fury washed through him.

Whoever had dared to harm Anna was about to die.

Not bothering to try to hide his rapid approach, Cezar threw out his powers to blast open the rotting door and charged into the shadows of the barn.

"Anna," he bellowed, nearly drowning in the cold terror that filled his body.

"We're in here," Levet called from a distant corner.

In a blink of an eye, he was kneeling at Anna's side, his hand gently stroking her battered face.

"*Dios*. Anna." With a rapid inspection he realized that she was gravely injured. The deep wounds on her face and neck were losing far too much blood. And a rib had been shattered, puncturing her lung. Why wasn't she healing? "What happened to her?" he rasped.

"There was a fairy." Levet shuddered. "She looked just like Sybil and she stabbed Anna with a hexed knife."

Cezar hissed, his fangs elongated and ready to kill. "Where did she go?"

Levet gave another shudder and glanced around the barn. "Everywhere. She . . . exploded. I really think we should get

Anna out of here before she wakes up. She's not going to like what she did with that beautiful bauble."

With a frown, Cezar noted the emerald clutched in Anna's bloody fingers.

"Where did it come from?"

"Would you believe a dream?"

"A . . ." Cezar gave a shake of his head. It didn't matter. Nothing mattered but the sight of Anna's battered and nearly broken body. He leaned down to press his lips to her forehead. "Never mind."

"You can fuss over her later, Cezar," Levet said, his voice high and edged with fear. "Right now we need to get out of here."

"She's too weak to move." Cezar closed his eyes and battled the rising panic. "We're losing her."

Levet sharply snapped his wings, his tail twitching. "Do something. Give her your blood. That should break the curse."

Cezar hissed, his lethal glare making the gargoyle wisely stumble backwards.

Damn the annoying gargoyle. He, better than anyone, knew that his blood would save Anna. But sharing his blood with this woman wasn't without complications.

Complications that would bind him to her for all time.

"It's not so simple," he muttered.

"Why?" Levet demanded, then sucked in a deep breath as realization hit. "Oh."

Oh, indeed.

To share his blood with this woman wasn't just an act of mercy. His entire body hummed in preparation of being mated, and the moment his blood hit her lips, he would be bound for eternity with Anna Randal.

It was a step he was willing to take.

No, a step he was *eager* to take.

And regardless of whether he was ever physically mated

to Anna, he already knew that there would never be another for him.

She was his destined mate.

But there was a part of him that rebelled at the thought of taking her as a mate while she lay unconscious. It was a sacred event, after all. A once in an eternity event. And the sort of thing that should never be done without the full consent of a partner.

Especially not a partner who was so prickly and independent she might very well kick his ass when she discovered what had happened.

"Cezar . . ." Surging through the door, Styx slowed as he neared Anna, his expression somber. "Damn. She lives, but barely."

"Si."

Kneeling beside Cezar, Styx placed a hand on his shoulder. "Will you heal her?"

"You know what will happen," Cezar said in rough tones.

There was a moment of silence before Styx reached a hand toward Anna.

"Then I will . . ." His words broke off sharply as Cezar was on his feet and had the King of Vampires pinned to the wall. "Shit, Cezar."

Balancing on the balls of his feet, Cezar leaned in close enough to be nose to nose with the dangerous vampire.

"Do not touch her again," he rasped.

Styx narrowed his gaze. "Then do what you have to do."

Cezar trembled, the violent urge to punish this demon for touching Anna a tangible pulse in the air. At last it was Levet who pulled him away from the brink of disaster.

"Cezar, she is fading."

Muttering curses beneath his breath, Cezar quickly turned and bent next to Anna. Levet was right. The flutter of her heart warned that she was swiftly reaching the point of no return.

There was no choice.

He could accept Anna's fury.

He couldn't accept her death.

Lifting his wrist to his mouth, Cezar scored a deep groove with his fang. Instantly the blood began to flow, and leaning over Anna he pressed the wound to her lips.

For long moments nothing happened.

Cezar could sense the blood filling her mouth and dripping down the back of her throat, but she was too weak to swallow. Reaching out his free hand he gently stroked her throat, silently willing her to take what she needed.

"She's not getting better," Levet muttered, wringing his hands and being a general nuisance as he scattered the dust and bits of straw with his rapidly beating wings.

"Not now, Levet," he growled.

"But . . ."

"Not now."

The gargoyle retreated to mutter dire predictions in a corner as Styx kneeled close to Cezar's side. Cezar didn't notice. His entire concentration was focused on Anna as he willed her to take the sustenance that he offered.

"Come on, *querida,*" he softly urged. "Let me help you."

More minutes passed, but Cezar didn't waver in urging the blood down Anna's throat.

At last a hint of color began to replace the ashen pallor of her skin, and her breathing deepened. Styx reached past him to touch the pulse at the base of her neck.

"She will recover," he said, his expression one of satisfaction. "I think we can safely take her back to Chicago."

Cezar nodded, unable to speak as he slowly lifted Anna's hand to study the red, intricate tattoo that was scrolled beneath the skin of her inner arm.

Anna was saved and he was mated.

The deed was done.

And for the first time in five hundred years he felt utterly, completely at peace.

* * *

Anna woke with a sense of déjà vu.

Good God. She'd been knocked unconscious . . . again.

How many times had that happened in the past few days?

Certainly more than it had happened in the past two hundred years combined. And she was freaking sure that it was a trend that needed to be nipped in the bud.

Keeping her eyes closed, she carefully cleared her mind of the ridiculous ramblings. She needed to determine where she was. And more importantly, just how much danger she might be in.

Astonishingly, it took less than a heartbeat to realize that Cezar was near.

She wasn't sure how she knew. There was no sound, no scent, no indication that she wasn't completely alone in the darkness. It was just an unshakable certainty.

Allowing her lashes to lift, Anna turned her head on the pillow to discover the faint outline of a man standing near the door.

"Cezar?"

"I'm here." A candle flickered to life as Cezar swiftly moved to the bed and settled next to her on the mattress. "No, don't move," he commanded, his hand pressing against her shoulder as she struggled to sit up.

Not bothering to fight against the inevitable, Anna settled back against the pillows and glanced about the bare room that held nothing more than the bed and a large armoire in the corner. The walls were paneled, and there was an Oriental carpet on the floor, but there were no windows and nothing to relieve the stark simplicity.

Not exactly the swank sort of crib she expected from vampires.

"Where are we?"

"We are in the tunnels beneath Viper's house. It was the safest place I could think to bring you."

Anna smiled wryly. She didn't think that there was a tunnel

deep enough to keep her from the wrath of Morgana. Still, she couldn't deny that she was relieved to be away from the dusty, remote barn.

And the crazed fairy who had nearly killed her.

Abruptly she stiffened. "What about Clara? Did you capture her?"

Cezar gave a lift of his brow, appearing every inch the conquistador in his black Chino pants and white, silky shirt that was unbuttoned to reveal the muscles of his broad chest. The top of his hair was pulled back and braided with a leather strip, emphasizing the chiseled perfection of his features.

Yow . . . it was almost worth being knocked senseless to wake to such a yummy sight.

"Clara?" he demanded, his eyes darkening as if aware of the excitement that was beginning to zing through her body.

"Sybil's twin." Anna shuddered, her pleasure replaced by distaste at the memory of the horrid fairy. "She tracked me down and threatened to hand me over to Morgana. Well, after she made a tidy fortune off me."

"She wasn't there when I arrived."

Anna narrowed her gaze at the unmistakable sense that he wasn't being entirely honest.

"You're hiding something from me," she accused.

He hesitated before giving a restless shrug. "She's dead."

Anna's breath tangled painfully in her throat. She remembered holding onto Clara as the emerald had pulsed with its strange power. Then there had been an explosion and everything had gone black.

"I killed her, didn't I?" she husked.

Cezar gave a slow nod. *"Si."*

"It was the emerald." Anna glanced down at her hand, relieved to discover that she no longer clutched the priceless gem. She didn't care where it was as long as it was no longer touching her. "I thought it was supposed to control my powers, but instead it only made things worse."

"No, Anna." The dark eyes flashed with a fierce emotion. "You're alive."

"But . . ."

"That's all that matters," he growled, pulling the offensive emerald from his pocket. "Levet said this came from a dream?"

She shuddered, pressing herself away from the delicate green glow. "No, it couldn't have been a dream, it was far too real."

"What happened?"

Anna unconsciously clutched the blanket that covered her, that aching sense of loss tugging at her heart.

"I was in a ruined castle and there was a man there." She sucked in a deep breath as her voice threatened to crack. "He claimed he was a relative. My grandfather of sorts. He also said that he wanted Morgana punished."

With that uncanny ability to read her emotions, Cezar wisely didn't pry into the disturbing vision. She wasn't prepared to discuss the bittersweet feeling of at last meeting a relative, only to have him be nothing more than a fleeting apparition.

"And the spirit gave you this?"

Spirit? Yes. She liked the sound of that. Much better than crazed hallucination, or creepy phantom.

"He claimed it would help me to focus my powers."

His lips twisted in a wry smile. "I would certainly say that it accomplished that."

"God." Anna lifted her hands to cover her face, guilt spearing through her. "I killed that woman. It's awful."

"You saved yourself and you saved Levet." Grasping her wrists, Cezar tugged her hands down so that she was forced to meet his glittering gaze. "Don't forget that, *querida*."

"Levet," she breathed, another wave of guilt assaulting her as she realized she hadn't even asked about the poor gargoyle. "How is he?"

Cezar grimaced. "In considerably better shape than you, I promise."

"Thank God." Anna gave a shake of her head. "She knocked him out and then she stabbed me with a knife that she said was hexed so I couldn't heal." Her eyes abruptly widened as she recalled the gaping wound in her stomach. Instinctively she reached beneath the covers, discovering she was attired in nothing more than a T-shirt and her underwear, and more importantly, that her stomach was smooth and perfectly healed. "How . . . how did you save me?"

There was nothing to read on the dark, beautiful face, but Anna easily sensed the sharp wariness that suddenly raced through him.

"I gave you my blood."

"Oh." Anna scooted up on the pillows, her gaze searching his guarded expression. "It broke the curse?"

"*Si.*"

Okay. Something was definitely up.

Folding her arms over her chest, she cocked her head to one side. "There's something that you're hiding, I can actually feel your tension. What aren't you telling me, Cezar?"

His brows drew together before his lips twisted. "*Dios.* I hadn't considered this side effect. It will take me a while to become accustomed."

Side effect? That didn't sound good.

"Cezar?"

He briefly closed his eyes before meeting her worried gaze. "You were dying, *querida*. I couldn't bear to lose you. I had to do something."

"I'm glad you did," she said softly, not at all certain why he was so disturbed by the fact he had saved her life. "Despite my numerous years, I'm no more eager to die than anyone else."

"The only means to save you was to give you my blood."

She gave an impatient click of her tongue. What was this

ridiculous obsession about giving her blood? Did he truly think she'd rather die than to drink the blood of a vampire?

"And?"

"And . . . when you took my essence inside you it bonded me to you."

She stilled in confusion. "What do you mean, bonded?"

He captured and held her gaze. "I am your mate."

Chapter 17

Although Cezar had prepared himself for Anna's shocked reaction, his heart still clenched with regret as she surged out of bed and began pacing the cramped room with obvious distress.

"I . . . I can't believe this," she muttered.

Dios. Would she ever forgive him?

Rising to his feet he crossed the room and grasped her shoulders to halt her jerky steps.

"Anna, listen to me," he urged. "This changes nothing for you."

"Nothing?" Her beautiful hazel eyes widened. "Being mated may mean nothing to you . . ."

"Nothing?" He gave a short, bitter laugh. "No, *querida*. I have waited for what seems an eternity to at last claim you as my own. To know that I am forever bound to you fills me with a joy that I have never known before. My life is complete."

Her features slowly softened as his fierce words sank in. "But . . ." Her words cut off with a gasp as she at last caught sight of the scrolling that marked her inner arm from her wrist to the bend of her elbow. "Oh my God. My arm."

"That is the proof of my bonding," he hastily assured her. "It won't harm you."

She blinked, looking stunned.

The sort of look to be expected from a young woman who awoke to discover herself bonded to a vampire.

"Is it permanent?"

He struggled to hide the tidal wave of smug contentment at the knowledge that nothing could alter the fact he was forever bound as her mate. He was supposed to be sympathetic, not smirking with satisfaction.

"Utterly and completely permanent," he said, unable to halt the instinct to shift his hand and stroke his fingers down her cheek.

"But you just said that it changed nothing."

"What I meant was that you are not bound to me." His thumb brushed the corner of her mouth. "The ceremony has not been completed. Until you accept me as your mate and allow me to take your blood you're still . . ."

"Unattached?"

Cezar smiled, grimly refusing to reveal the jagged flare of pain that raced through him. The dark ache beneath his contentment was something that he'd have to become accustomed to.

"*Si.*"

She lowered her thick lashes, almost as if she were trying to hide her inner emotions.

"We both know that's not true," she said, her voice so low that he wouldn't have heard the words if he hadn't been a vampire.

"What?"

"I've been very much attached for the past two centuries."

A bolt of lightning shot through Cezar as he tugged her chin upward and studied her rueful expression.

"Anna?"

Her eyes narrowed, a dangerous glitter stirring to life in the hazel eyes.

"Don't try to act surprised," she accused him. "You've

known since I followed you to Chicago that I never managed to forget you."

Amazement at her blunt confession swiftly altered to something far more wicked. When he'd first brought Anna to this secluded room, he had felt nothing but concern as he had stripped off her clothing and tucked her beneath the covers. Then there had been the unpleasant task of revealing that he had mated her while she lay unconscious.

Now, however, his body refused to be denied any longer.

He didn't know why she wasn't ready to kill him for mating her against her will. Or why she was actually admitting that she didn't hate him. All he knew was that they were alone in the bedroom and for the moment they were safe.

And most wonderful of all, she was already half naked.

What more could a hungry vampire desire?

Cupping her cheek, he allowed his free hand to drift lightly down her arm.

"I did suspect that there was more than a desire for answers that prompted your swift arrival," he husked. "You, however, accused me of being arrogant."

"You are."

He laughed softly, bending his head to run his lips down the curve of her neck. "True enough."

Her hands reached out to grasp his arms, as if her knees were suddenly weak. "But unfortunately, you were quite right," she whispered, her neck arching in silent invitation.

Cezar shuddered, his body aching with the need to sink his teeth deep in her flesh and taste of her blood.

Dios, he hungered for her.

Attempting to avoid temptation, Cezar turned his attention to stroking his lips over every inch of her face.

"Why unfortunately?" he demanded, lingering a moment on the sensitive hollow beneath her ear.

She gave a tiny gasp, her nails digging through his shirt. "Because I was supposed to be able to get my answers and return to L.A. with you at last buried in the past where you belonged."

"Never the past," he rasped, scooping her into his arms and heading for the bed. "Our futures are forever entwined."

Laying her down on the mattress, Cezar stilled as her hand lifted to gently touch his cheek.

"Forever? You promise?"

His heart squeezed at the vulnerability in her eyes. Like him she had been isolated and alone for too long. She no longer trusted that fate would not snatch away any chance for happiness.

"I will do everything in my power to keep you close to me, *querida,*" he rasped, joining her on the bed and pulling her into his arms. He wanted to swear that he would never let her go. That the mating would ensure they would never be parted again. But so long as the Oracles considered her one of their own, he couldn't make such promises. "You are, and always will be, my mate."

His words seemed to comfort her and the hazel eyes flashed with something that might have been pleasure as she reached up to wrap her arms around his neck.

"Does that mean you have to do everything I say?"

He gave the lobe of her ear a punishing nip. "I specifically said mate, not slave."

She deliberately allowed her fingers to trail down his back. "A pity. I think you might enjoy obeying me on occasion."

Cezar lifted his head to meet the sensuous gaze. His entire body hardened in reaction, the coldness that had held him captive since becoming a vampire melting beneath the heat of her searing hazel eyes.

"On occasion, eh?" he demanded, his voice already thick with need. "What sort of occasion?"

Her smile was slow and exquisitely wicked. "Like this occasion."

His already hard erection gave a painful throb. *Dios.* He

might be a five-century-old vampire, but this woman had the power to make him feel as if every touch, every searing sensation, was something that he had never, ever experienced before.

And perhaps it was.

Anna was his destined mate.

The one woman who was so intimately entwined with him that her slightest emotion, the very beat of her heart, was echoed in him.

Certainly he could feel her desire like a wave of longing that crashed through him with shocking force.

He groaned as he lowered his head to bury his face in her hair, filling himself with her delectable scent.

"I'm yours to command, *querida*," he murmured.

Just for a moment she hesitated, and he smiled as he realized she was battling a flare of nerves. So far he had always taken control of their lovemaking. Now, she struggled to gather the courage to take matters in her own hands.

To take *him* into her hands.

He swallowed a low groan at the mere thought.

"Very well," she at last managed to husk. "Roll on your back."

Cezar readily followed her command, rolling until he was flat on his back. Anna paused another moment, then with a bold motion she sat up and before he could guess her intent, she was straddling his hips and gazing down at him with a tiny smile.

Cezar hissed, grasping the covers to prevent himself from jerking her downward and bringing a swift, explosive conclusion to the game.

If she was in the mood to play, then by God, they would play. And play. And play. And play.

Even if it killed him.

Easily feeling the tremors that shook his body, she held up a warning finger.

"Lie still."

Cezar gritted his teeth, his fingers nearly ripping through the mattress as she calmly grabbed the edge of her tiny T-shirt and yanked it over her head. He didn't need the candlelight to appreciate the beautiful thrust of her breasts or the smooth curve of her waist, or the ivory perfection of her skin.

"Dios . . ." he groaned, his hips thrusting upward to rub his erection against the thin strip of satin that was all that covered her moist core. "You're so bloody beautiful."

"You once thought me a wallflower and a . . . shrew, wasn't it?" she demanded, her hands shifting to his shirt and making swift work of his buttons.

He struggled to think as her fingers explored his bared chest, circling his nipples before heading ever lower. It was the sweetest torture he had ever endured.

"I wanted you from the moment you entered that room, Anna Randal," he growled, his hands shifting to run up her bare thighs. "You might be a shrew, but you're *my* shrew."

She chuckled softly as she slowly leaned forward and pressed her lips to his. "I watched you from the shadows, you know. You were so handsome, so exciting." She gave his lower lip a teasing nip. "So far above me." Her tongue trailed down his jaw, wrenching a groan from his throat. "And now I have you beneath me."

He arched his back as a surge of pleasure raced through him. "You can keep me here as long as you want."

"As long as I want?" Her lips skimmed down his throat, her hair spilling over his chest, the tips of her breasts brushing his skin. "That's a rather dangerous offer."

"Not nearly so dangerous as teasing a vampire," he growled, his hands skimming up so he could rip off the delicate underwear.

"Behave yourself." She nipped at his stomach. "You're supposed to be lying still."

He hissed as her hands began tugging at the zipper of his pants. "I may be undead, but I'm not made of stone, *querida.*"

Tugging his pants down, Anna was forced to pause to yank off his shoes before she could complete her task. Once she had him bare she straddled his legs and began crawling back up his body, her gaze squarely on his straining erection.

"You may not be made of stone, but there're some parts of you that are as hard as a rock."

His arousal twitched, silently pleading for her touch, even as he ruthlessly sought to control the passion that was swiftly raging out of control.

The fire that burned inside him threatened to turn him to ash on the spot.

"*Dios*, Anna, I can't take much more."

She slowly smiled, clearly pleased with her power over him. "Patience, Conde Cezar."

Patience? Patience?

He could write a book on patience.

But after two centuries of wanting and longing for this woman, patience was not top on his list of priorities.

"Patience is highly overrated, Anna Randal," he groaned.

That wicked smile curved her lips. "Maybe I can change your mind."

On the point of assuring her that nothing could change his mind, not in this moment, Cezar gave a strangled shout and nearly shot off the bed as Anna shifted upward and took his straining shaft into her mouth.

He could die in this moment and be a happy vampire, he decided as she used her tongue to make his torture complete.

Oh, so, so, so happy.

His hips lifted off the bed as she enthusiastically explored every quivering inch of him, seeming to take special delight in tearing moans and groans from his raw throat.

At last Cezar could bear no more. One more lick and the entire game would be over.

Reaching down he grasped her arms and jerked her to sprawl on top of him. She sighed as her legs fell on either side of his hips, her slick core pressed to his erection and her hair draping around him like a river of honey silk.

Dios. Until this moment he hadn't truly believed that there could be a paradise on earth.

"Anna, we can practice my patience skills later, I need to be inside you," he groaned, his fingers skimming up her inner thighs to stroke through her moist heat.

"I . . . yes," she breathed, bending down to kiss him with such tenderness that Cezar shuddered with bliss.

This woman—this wonderful, precious woman was his.

And he would give his life to keep her safe.

Stroking and teasing until she was at last pleading for release, Cezar gripped her hips and with one smooth thrust he entered her.

With his lips, he caught her moan of satisfaction, careful to keep his fangs from grazing her fragile flesh. The last thing he needed was to accidentally take her blood in the heat of the moment.

Lifting his hips from the bed, Cezar angled himself even deeper, the pleasure so intense that he had to pause a moment to simply allow himself to absorb the exquisite sensation.

"Cezar," Anna groaned, her fingers tangled in his hair.

He hissed. "Am I hurting you?"

"God, no. It's . . ."

"It's what?" he demanded.

"I can sense everything you're feeling." She pulled back, her hazel eyes glowing in the pale light. "It's as if you're a part of me."

"I am." He shifted his hands to frame her face as he began to stroke in and out of her in a determined rhythm. "You hold my heart, my very soul in your hands, *querida.*"

"Cezar."

Her head once again lowered and their lips tangled as Cezar continued to thrust deep inside her, his entire body humming with a joy that he had never dreamed existed.

* * *

Wow.

Anna decided that the word pretty much summed up what had just occurred between her and Cezar.

Well, maybe super duper wow.

Struggling to catch her breath, she snuggled next to the gorgeous vampire on the bed, feeling amazingly at peace considering in the past few hours she'd been ripped through a portal, nearly killed by an angry fairy, and woken up mated to a vampire.

Of course, it really was on par with how her days seemed to go lately.

No, that wasn't quite true, she thought with a tiny smile. Everything had changed.

With a sense of wonderment she opened herself to her awareness of Cezar's feelings. She was aware of his sated satisfaction, his pleasure in holding her in his arms, his restless anger that she was still in danger, and an odd fear that she was to be taken away from him.

It was beautiful and baffling and most of all . . . extraordinary.

She would never, ever be alone again.

For the rest of eternity, no matter what happened, Cezar would be a part of her.

Unaware that Cezar was closely watching the various expressions flit over her face, she gave a startled blink when he stroked a finger over her lips.

"I'm not sure I trust that smile, *querida,*" he said, his voice a pleasant rumble as she rested her head on his chest. "What are you thinking?"

She paused, then, tilting back her head, she met his curious gaze. "Tell me about the rest of the mating ceremony."

His expression was instantly wary. "Anna?"

"You said it wasn't completed," she prompted, her eyes

narrowing as she easily sensed he was guarding his emotions. "What else does it take?"

His fingers traced a path through her hair. "It would first take your willing desire to become my mate. You would have to be committed without reservation and without fear."

She smiled wryly. Just a few days ago she would have been convinced that no one could enter a relationship without at least a few reservations. After all, there was nothing more terrifying than opening your life and heart to another.

Now, however, she knew that she was prepared to leap headfirst, without a parachute or safety net, with this man.

No, not man. Vampire.

"And then?"

His dark eyes flickered, as if in pain. "And then I would take your blood."

"That's it?"

He forced a smile to his stiff lips. "I suppose you could dance naked around the bed or sing, 'I'm bringing sexy back,' if you want." His arms tightened around her, his head bending so he could plant tiny kisses over her cheek. "In fact, we don't even have to be mated for you to do that."

Anna instantly reacted to the cool touch of his lips. Okay, maybe it was more than reacted. The merest caress was enough to make her pant with desire.

And drool. There was definitely drool involved.

Still, her newfound sensitivity to his emotions warned her that this was as much about distraction as it was about passion.

"Cezar."

His lips drifted down the length of her nose. "Hmmm?"

"Why haven't you asked me to finish the ceremony?"

With a low groan, Cezar rested his forehead on hers. "Anna, this is not the time to be making a decision that will affect you for an eternity. You have enough on your mind at the moment."

"You mean my homicidal great, great, great aunt and her band of fruitcake fairies?"

He lifted his head to offer a wry smile. "They were first on the list."

She paused, then gave a firm shake of her head. "No."

"They're not?"

"That's not what's bothering you," she clarified. "It's something else."

Without warning he pulled away and slipped from the bed to regard her with a somber expression.

"Stop, Anna," he husked.

Holding the blanket over her naked body, she sat up in the bed. Unlike Cezar she wasn't yet comfortable with flashing her more private parts.

You couldn't live through the Victorian age and not be somewhat affected.

"Why?" she demanded.

"It's dangerous."

She narrowed her eyes and concentrated, only to discover that Cezar had retreated deep inside himself. A place she couldn't reach.

"Dammit." Anna crossed her arms over her chest, glaring at the vampire who hovered over her. Okay, maybe it was more of a leer. After all, he was standing there stark naked, his hair tousled, and looking good enough to eat. Literally. "When are you going to tell me the truth?"

"When I'm allowed." He lifted a slender hand to halt her angry retort. "I'm sorry, *querida*, but that is simply how it has to be."

"Forever?"

"No, not forever."

She heaved a deep sigh, wondering how her simple, boring life had suddenly become so complicated.

"This mysterious fate thing is really starting to wear on my nerves," she muttered.

His stark expression eased at her petulant tone and a tiny smile tugged at his lips.

"Never fear, Anna Randal, all will be revealed in tim..."

Without thought she plucked a pillow from the bed and tossed it at his head. "Now you're just trying to piss me off." She watched as he easily sidestepped her fluffy missile, his dark eyes regarding her with a strange intensity. "What are you looking at?"

"You." With a coiled elegance he moved to perch on the bed, his finger brushing a strand of hair from her cheek. "You've changed from those days in London."

"Changed how?"

"You have much more . . ." He struggled for the proper word. "Confidence in yourself."

Anna smiled, unable to halt her flare of pride. She *had* changed. Or maybe she had simply grown into who she was intended to be.

In either case, it had taken several decades and a lot of work to accomplish.

"I've learned that I can stand on my own," she said, her voice filled with satisfaction. "It's an important lesson for every woman."

His expression tightened. "I wish you hadn't been forced to learn it. If I had been allowed to stay with you . . ."

She hastily pressed her fingers to his lips. She didn't want to recall how many years she devoted to trying to make this man her enemy. It had been ridiculous, even childish, and she couldn't deny a sense of guilt that she had been so selfish that she had never considered he might be battling his own demons.

Well, she assumed the Oracles were demons.

Instead she turned the conversation to a few of the less explosive questions that had niggled at her over the years. "You know, you've never told me why you were in London that year."

His brows lifted, but with a smooth motion he shifted so he could pull her back into his arms and rested his cheek on the top of her head. "Viper requested that I join him in England. At that time Dante was being held prisoner by a coven of witches and he hoped that I could help him research a means to release him from his chains."

"That's awful." She briefly wondered why any witch would want to hold a vampire captive. It seemed kind of like having a tiger by the tail. Never a good idea. "Did you help?"

Cezar grimaced. "No, all I managed to do was to become a captive myself."

"To the Oracles?"

His lips brushed her hair. "And to you."

Her heart gave a pleasant flop. Did all vampires know just what to say to make a woman all warm and tingly?

"What were you doing before you came to London?" she demanded, knowing her deep curiosity would take years, or perhaps centuries, to be satisfied.

She felt him shrug. "I was a part of the Spanish court. Every so often I enjoy dabbling in politics and royal intrigues."

His tone was casual, but Anna gave a sudden blink. Damn, she'd never thought about how easy it would be for vampires to alter the course of the human world.

How many times had they . . .

No, she didn't want to think about it. Not now.

"So you truly are a Conde?" she asked instead.

"I was given the title some centuries ago for a small service to the king."

She wrinkled her nose. She suspected that small service was another thing she didn't want to dwell on.

"Wasn't it a little awkward when you didn't age over the years?"

"I rarely remained more than a few years, and when I would return it was easy to convince others that I was a son of the previous Conde."

It sounded way too easy and she tilted back her head to meet the dark gaze.

"You used mind tricks on them, didn't you?"

"When necessary."

Had she been just another human, she might have been offended by the ease with which he used his powers to manipulate them. After all, it wasn't precisely nice. But her own years of being forced to hide and lie to protect herself had given her an appreciation of how difficult it was for an immortal to live in a world dominated by mortals.

"What did you do when you weren't at court?"

"I spent time with various vampires and on occasion I was called to war between clans, but usually I retreated to my lair in the Alps to enjoy the books and works of art I had collected over the years."

That sounded . . . perfect.

An isolated lair, a huge library, beautiful artwork, and Cezar all to herself.

"You liked being alone?" she demanded.

"At times, but I always knew that something was missing." His fingers brushed her cheek. "A part of myself."

A blush touched her cheeks as she studied the bronzed, elegant features. "Did you ever take women to your lair?"

He seemed startled by her question. "A vampire never shares his most private lair with another. Not until he mates." His roaming fingers outlined her lips. "Someday I hope to take you there."

Anna pulled away, regarding him with a sudden flare of hope. "Why can't we go now? Maybe if we hide there long enough Morgana will forget about what that stupid seer predicted. I mean, prophecies are never accurate. Not unless you count a bunch of mumbo-jumbo that is so vague it could mean anything."

His dark eyes narrowed. "How do you know of the prophecy?"

She did her own bit of eye-narrowing. "How do you know?" she charged back.

"It was written in one of Jagr's books."

"Oh."

He grasped her chin. "Anna?"

"Clara the Fairy spilled the beans."

"What did she say?" he demanded. "Tell me exactly."

Anna heaved a rough sigh. The sooner she could put Clara and her horrid death from her mind the better.

"She said that some seer had claimed that an heir of Arthur would climb or appear or something from the darkness and condemn Morgana to hell."

Cezar gave a slow nod. "And she believes you're the heir?"

Anna made a rude noise. "It doesn't matter to her if I am or not, she's made it a mission to kill all of Arthur's heirs just to be on the safe side."

A lethal fury flashed through his eyes before he made an effort to smother his instinctive reaction. Anna didn't doubt her mate would rip the limbs right off the Queen of Fairies if he could get his hands on her.

Not the most pleasant image.

"Anna, she will not stop this madness until we have managed to defeat her," he rasped.

She heaved a rueful sigh as the dream of disappearing into Cezar's remote lair was shattered. He was right, of course. If she'd learned nothing else over the past few days, it was that her lunatic aunt was nothing if not freaking persistent.

"Did you happen to pick up a clue in Jagr's books as to how we're supposed to do that? Some secret Kryptonite that will steal her powers or turn her into a frog?"

His expression remained somber. "No, but you did."

She frowned. "What do you mean?"

"It's you, Anna," he said, his tone flat. But Anna could easily feel the frustration smoldering deep inside him. He wanted to keep her safely tucked away while he battled her dragon (or rather her psychotic aunt), and the knowledge that he didn't possess the ability was like a raw wound. "You're the only one who can kill her."

She smiled wryly. "A family thing, huh?"

Pained regret twisted his features. "I'm sorry, *querida*, if I could do this task for you . . ."

She once again silenced him with a finger to his lips. There was no way in hell she was going to cower behind anyone, not even Cezar. And she certainly wasn't going to allow him to carry around a load of unnecessary guilt.

"No, this is my battle and I should fight it," she said firmly. "Actually, I *need* to fight it."

He frowned. "Why?"

"If you were being hunted by a crazed member of your clan would you hide away while I went to slay them?"

His frown deepened. "Of course not."

"Then why should I feel any differently?"

His lips thinned. "You haven't trained for battle, Anna, I have."

"I've trained for the courtroom, which I can personally assure you, is as nasty and treacherous as any battlefield."

The vampire wasn't amused. "The judge doesn't demand that you use your powers to kill anyone."

Anna couldn't hide her flinch. Dammit. This was the downside to having someone capable of reading her like an open book.

"If you want me to admit that I don't relish the thought of killing anyone, including my evil Aunt Morgana, then fine, I admit it. But I've already proven that I'm willing to kill if necessary."

"Not without cost," he said harshly.

Her brows drew together. "It should never be without cost. To take another's life . . . even someone horrible . . . it should demand regret and even pain." She sucked in a deep breath. "I don't believe in revenge, Cezar, but I do believe in justice. My aunt has slaughtered my entire family, and who knows who else, and if I'm the one who must hold her accountable, then that's what I'll do."

He studied her a long moment, a strange expression on his face. "I begin to understand why fate has chosen you, Anna Randal."

Chapter 18

Cezar watched the puzzlement fill Anna's eyes at his soft words. Not surprising. Despite her hard-earned confidence in her abilities, she was still remarkably oblivious to just how truly special she was.

The Oracles, however, were very much aware that her talents were more than her ability to control the elements, or even the ancient destiny that coursed through her blood. Her true power was her unwavering integrity.

This was not a woman who would be swayed by power or anger or fear. She would do what she felt was right in her heart.

He had chosen well, he acknowledged with a flare of pride.

"Is that another one of those mysterious comments that you have no intention of explaining?" she demanded with an edge in her voice.

Cezar smiled wryly. "I think we should move on to more pressing matters."

"Such as Morgana le Fay?"

"Si." His arm tightened around her. *Dios.* He would give his life if he could keep her out of this battle. As her mate it was his sacred duty to protect her and keep her from harm. But, while his instincts screamed to send her far from Chicago so

he could hunt Morgana, logic dictated that his martyrdom would achieve nothing more than leaving Anna alone to face the Fairy Queen. He couldn't kill Morgana le Fay. All he could do was stand at Anna's side and do everthing in his power to see that she succeeded in defeating the bitch. "Morgana le Fay—and how the hell are we going to find her?"

"Oh." Without warning she struggled from his tight grip and turned around on the bed to face him.

"What?" he demanded.

"I remember something." Her forehead creased. "Something Clara said."

"About Morgana?"

She gave a slow nod. "She was babbling about how she tracked me, and then she said that it took so long because the barn was nearly on Morgana's doorstep."

Cezar clenched his hands at the startling revelation. He knew he should be happy. If Morgana was within striking distance then this madness might soon be at an end and Anna would be safe. But happiness wasn't what flooded through him. Instead it was a sharp horror at the mere thought that Anna would soon be forced to face the woman determined to kill her.

With an effort he unclenched his stiff jaws and pushed aside the fear.

"We must tell Styx."

"Now?" With a small smile, Anna leaned forward, boldly pressing her lips to his chest. Cezar hissed at the feel of her soft caress and the magical scent that wrapped around him. "Right . . ." Her lips trailed downward. "Exactly . . ." She nipped the taut skin of his stomach. "Now?"

Cezar tangled his fingers in her hair as he squeezed his eyes shut in sheer bliss.

"Maybe we could wait a minute or two," he rasped.

"Or three," she muttered before taking him into her mouth and ending all coherent thought.

* * *

Morgana was seated in her bedroom having her long hair brushed by her current lover, a lovely fairy with long blond hair and blue eyes, when Modron staggered into the room and fell to her knees.

Ash screeched in alarm as the hag's eyes glowed with an eerie white light, but Morgana was swiftly on her feet and shoving aside her squeamish companion.

It had been centuries since the last time, but she recognized when her seer was in the grips of a vision.

"What is it, Modron?" she demanded. "What do you see?"

"Green fire," the woman moaned, wrapping her arms around herself as she rocked back and forth. "Bathed in green fire."

"Green fire?" Morgana frowned. "Is it a magical fire?"

"Green fire is everywhere."

"Yes, you've said that, you annoying twit. What does it mean?"

Modron moaned, shaking her head. "Fire . . . it burns. It burns."

A cold fear pierced Morgana's heart. Striding forward she slapped the hag across her ugly cheek.

"Damn you, what is it?"

The glowing white eyes turned toward her, sightless and yet filled with some awful knowledge.

"Arthur," Modron rasped, her gnarled finger pointing directly at Morgana. "He comes. He comes for you."

Ash gasped in fear, but Morgana's face twisted in fury at the mention of her brother.

There was nothing more certain to stir her ready temper than the mention of Arthur.

"Impossible," she hissed.

Modron shook her head. "Not impossible. Even now he stirs, his weapon cutting through air like an arrow toward its target. The end is coming."

With an infuriated motion, Morgana backhanded the seer with enough force to send the woman flying into the wall. When she bounced onto the floor she was dead.

At the sound of the disturbance the door to the bedroom was thrust open and two male fairies rushed in, waving their ridiculous guns as if they could be some sort of help.

"Get her out of here." Morgana pointed toward the bundle of rags in the middle of the floor. "Now."

With fearful glances in her direction, the two minions scuttled to grab the lifeless Modron and tugged her from the room. Morgana waited until they had crossed the threshold before she slammed the door shut with her powers.

Damn Modron. The stupid woman had no one to blame but herself for making Morgana lose her temper.

What was the point in having visions if they did nothing but offer vague warnings that made no sense?

Green fire? Her dead brother with some sort of weapon?

It was nothing more than gibberish.

"Your Majesty," Ash said in soft, fearful tones.

Whirling about she glared at him with impatience. "What?"

He licked his thick, pouty lips, looking as if it was taking all his courage not to toss himself through the window. There were few who would willingly linger when her powers began to fill the room.

"Perhaps we should leave here," he at last admitted, stumbling over his words. "If the seer speaks true . . ."

Morgana stepped toward her lover, her eyes narrowed in warning. "You would have me flee from a mere girl? A girl who has no idea of her own powers?"

The fairy wisely fell to his knees, his head bowed in respect. "She can't follow you to Avalon."

"I will not return to my prison," Morgana growled, her hair floating in the surge of power. "Not when I am so close to victory."

"But the seer . . ."

She reached down to grasp Ash's chin, jerking his head back to meet her lethal gaze.

"I allowed Modron and her pathetic visions to keep me imprisoned too long." She tightened her fingers until she threatened to crush Ash's bones. By her brother's rotten blood, she was tired of hiding within the mists of her island. She was a queen. A powerful leader who should be worshipped by demons and humans everywhere. To hell with prophecy, she would make her own fate. "Once Anna Randal is dead I will be free to spread my powers throughout the world. Never again will we be forced to hide in the shadows or to bow to those who are beneath us. It will at last be a world that worships the fairies."

Ash gave a low groan in pain. "But she spoke of Arthur. What if he still lives?"

"My brother is dead and in his grave," she hissed. "I should know, I buried him myself."

Something that might have been relief flashed through the blue eyes. "Then I must call for soldiers. You can't face her alone."

"Ah yes, my *soldiers*." Releasing her hold on the fairy's chin, Morgana turned to stalk across the cramped room. "They have proven so terribly useful, do you not think, Ash?"

"There have been . . . difficulties, my Queen."

With a swift motion, Morgana turned, her burst of power shattering the mirror that stood in the corner.

"So I am told with monotonous regularity," she said, her voice thick with disgust. How many fairies had she sent to capture Anna Randal only to be disappointed time after time? Clearly, she had been gone from the world too long. "It seems more likely that my beloved subjects have grown lax over the centuries. Or perhaps they have forgotten just how nasty my temper can be when I am disappointed."

Ash swayed and nearly tumbled backwards. "No, my Queen, we have not forgotten."

"Still, I think a reminder would not come amiss." She smiled, and Ash gave up his efforts and slumped sideways in a deep swoon. Moving forward, Morgana casually kicked his limp body into a distant corner before moving across the room to pull open the small, dark closet. A portion of her seething fury eased as she caught sight of the red-haired imp that hung by his neck from an exposed beam. Few things pleased her more than punishing a traitor, and Troy, Prince of Imps, had proven that he was a turncoat of the worst sort. For a moment she considered the notion of devoting a few hours to stripping the skin off the brawny imp, only to give a shake of her head. She was weary of sending out her incompetent, bumbling fairies to disappoint her over and over. It was time to take matters into her own hands. And this treacherous imp was the perfect means to accomplish her task.

Stepping forward, she chuckled as Troy's emerald eyes flashed with soul-deep fear.

"Well, well, Troy. It appears that you are to be given a chance to redeem yourself in the eyes of your queen." She reached up to place a hand on his chest, smiling as he screamed in pain. "If you don't want to spend the rest of eternity being my plaything I suggest you don't screw it up this time."

It was nearly two hours later when Anna and Cezar at last emerged from their underground room and made their way toward Viper's private study at the back of the large, but charmingly unpretentious, country house.

They had showered (a slow, hot, delicious shower) and changed into the clothes that Viper had sent to them, and since Cezar had earlier contacted his host and asked that he request Styx to meet him here, he knew they would impatiently be awaiting their arrival.

Still, he found his feet halting before he could reach the door to the study, as if they had acquired a mind of their own.

At his side, Anna turned to face him. "Is something wrong?"

"I wish . . ." His voice was thick, his body feeling stiff and awkward. *Dios.* He'd never felt fear such as this. Not even when he was wading through the bloodiest of battles. "I wish this was over and done with so we could just be together."

A sad smile touched her lips. "Yes."

On the point of reaching for her, Cezar was halted as the door was yanked open and Styx stepped into sight. As always, the looming Aztec looked ominous in his black leather and braided hair.

"Night is wasting, *amigo,*" the Anasso rasped. "We need to make our plans."

"We're coming," Cezar muttered, his narrowed gaze sending Styx retreating back to the study with a wry smile. Waiting until they were alone, he reached to take Anna's hand. He frowned as he realized it was even colder than his own. Quite a feat for a warm-blooded woman. "Ready, *querida?*"

She gave a short laugh. "Are you kidding?"

"Are you as ready as you will ever be?"

She sucked in a deep breath. "As long as you're at my side."

He squeezed her fingers. "Forever."

"Then let's do this."

Hand in hand they entered the study. Cezar instinctively sent a searching gaze around the room, noting the French doors set between the desk and long bookcases, and the window near the matching leather chairs. Only when he was confident there were no lurking fairies waiting to leap into the house did he turn his attention to the three vampires peering at something on the far wall.

Viper and Styx were easily recognizable, but it took a moment before he realized he knew the third vampire with his long blond braid and massive body.

Jagr.

"Dios," he breathed, shoving Anna behind his body as Styx hurriedly joined him near the door. "What's he doing here?"

"Who is it?" Anna demanded, smacking him in the middle of the back.

"Anna." Moving around Cezar, Styx offered a small bow of his head. "My wife has prepared dinner for you in the kitchen. She hopes that you will join her there."

Cezar turned to watch the conflicting emotions that flitted over his mate's expressive face. On one hand she understood the need to eat and keep up her strength; on the other she didn't want to be left out of the planning. With a smile he ran the back of his fingers down her cheek.

"You must eat, Anna. We will make no decisions without you."

Her gaze warned of dire retributions if he didn't keep his word before she grudgingly turned and headed back out the door.

Cezar couldn't deny a small flare of relief at her departure. He didn't want Anna anywhere near Jagr. Hell, he wasn't sure *he* wanted to be near Jagr.

Waiting until her slender form had disappeared down the hall, Cezar turned to stab his leader with an annoyed glare. "You haven't answered my question."

Styx pointed toward a map that had been pinned to the wall. "He possesses the most detailed maps of Illinois. Viper asked if we could borrow them."

"And he left his lair to bring them?" His attention returned to the large, feral vampire who was speaking softly with Viper. "Amazing."

"Not really." Styx's smile was cold. "I can be quite persuasive when I issue an invitation."

Persuasive? More like lethal.

"Are you sure it's safe?" he growled, still not pleased at having the vampire near Anna.

Styx shrugged. "He is . . . unstable and fiercely independent, but he knows better than to stir my anger."

Cezar smiled wryly. "Don't we all?"

Amusement briefly flickered through the dark golden eyes before the hard, aloof expression returned.

"How is Anna?"

"Scared."

"I meant, how did she receive the information that you mated her while she was unconscious?"

Cezar shoved a hand through his hair, which he'd left loose after his shower. Anna seemed to like running her fingers through it, and he liked letting her.

"Actually she received it better than I could ever have hoped," he muttered, still in awe at the memory of her ready acceptance of his bonding. He had spent hours preparing himself for her fury, even hatred. What he hadn't prepared himself for was her desire to complete the ceremony. *Dios*. He'd rather have taken a stroll through the sun than to deny her request. "Better than she should have."

Styx lifted his brows, easily sensing Cezar's raw flare of pain. "Tell me what troubles you."

"She desires to complete the ceremony," he admitted.

The dark eyes narrowed. "Should I offer my congratulations?"

Cezar briefly closed his eyes as his heart clenched with longing. "You were right before. We both know that Anna's future belongs to the Oracles."

"Perhaps . . ."

"No, Styx." Cezar gave a sharp shake of his head. "I will not allow myself to hope for the impossible."

Styx gave a small nod of understanding, knowing as well as Cezar that not even the most powerful vampire could fight the will of the Oracles.

Before he could offer his sympathies, Styx was jerking his head toward the door, sensing the approaching vampire servant before the door was pushed open.

Entering the room, DeAngelo bowed low at the sight of his king. "My lord."

"What is it?"

"An imp is at the door." The vampire grimaced. "He requested to speak with Conde Cezar."

Styx gave a hiss of annoyance. "Is it Troy?"

"That is the name he gave."

"Damn." Styx struggled against his dislike for the flamboyant imp. "Tell him to join us."

"He said that he has information that he will . . ." There was another grimace from DeAngelo. "Sell only to the Conde."

Styx growled low in his throat. "Troy needs to discover that vampires do not pay for information. I will deal with this."

"No." Cezar reached out to grasp Styx's arm. "If he does have information of Morgana I won't risk having him frightened away. You remain here and finish completing our plans. I will deal with Prince Troy."

A forbidding frown marred Styx's brow. "You should not go alone."

"You don't trust the imp?"

"I never trust those with fey blood." At Cezar's warning glance, Styx gave a laugh. "With the exception of your beautiful mate, of course."

"Of course." Cezar gave an impatient wave of his hand. He wanted to find out the information and then take a quick peek into the kitchen to make sure that Anna was eating as she should be and not brooding about the night ahead. "I think that I can deal with one imp."

Styx looked as if he wanted to argue, but at Cezar's stubborn expression he gave a grudging nod.

Wise vampire.

"As you wish."

Clapping his friend on the shoulder, Cezar allowed DeAngelo to lead him down the hall to the front of the house. Once again he was struck by the homey feel of the place. It had to be Shay's doing, he acknowledged wryly. Viper possessed an innate flamboyance that had made his various nightclubs a sensation throughout Chicago.

Halting in front of a closed door, the guard offered a bow before silently disappearing into the shadows.

Cezar paused for a moment, startled to discover his legs felt oddly weak. Damn. It had been too long since he'd last fed. Usually he was meticulous about his feedings. Being a pawn for the Oracles meant he never knew when he would be called to battle. Remaining at full strength was key to his survival.

Besides, if he were perfectly honest with himself, he hadn't wanted to drink the bottled blood. Not after tasting the sweetness of Anna's vein.

Which was not only foolish, it was dangerous.

For now, Anna was strictly off the menu.

Promising himself he would feed as soon as he was done with the imp, Cezar shoved open the door and stepped into the long, dark room that was nearly overflowing with Viper's vast collection of books.

He had no time to appreciate the thick leather tomes as he crossed toward the red-haired imp covered in a heavy black cloak, who was hovering near the window as if ready to bolt at the first sign of trouble.

Not an uncommon reaction. Most fey were uneasy entering the lair of a vampire, prince of imps or not.

Without bothering with preliminaries, Cezar halted directly before the imp. "You have information?"

A strange smile touched the long, pale face as Troy offered a stiff bow. "Conde."

Cezar struggled to contain his sorely tested patience. "What is your information?"

Straightening, Troy pressed a hand to his chest, a feverish glitter in his eyes as he studied Cezar with an unnerving intensity.

"First, I must know, did you mate the woman?"

Cezar's brows snapped together. "What?"

"Did you mate the woman?"

"What the hell business is it of yours?"

"That's the price for your information. Answer the question."

Cezar hissed, reminding himself that this imp had helped Anna to flee from Morgana's assassins. It was the only reason that the creature wasn't on the floor having the shit beat out of him.

"Yes."

"Then I have something for you." Troy took a step closer. "A gift."

Cezar's brows snapped together. Goddammit. He'd had enough of this. The imp would reveal his information or he would break the fool's neck.

"Damn your gift," he growled. "All I want . . ."

Moving with an unexpected swiftness, Troy reached out his hand, hidden beneath the folds of his cloak, revealing the silver collar and leash he held in his hands. Cezar attempted to leap backwards, but his utter astonishment, combined with his fading strength, proved to be his undoing.

Stumbling as Troy leapt toward him Cezar managed only one solid blow before he felt the burn of the silver encircling his throat.

"I'm sorry, vampire, but I have no choice," the imp muttered, his gaze wary as Cezar fell to his knees as the waves of shocking pain raced through him. "This has to end tonight."

Chapter 19

Anna was polishing off the last of her fettuccini when the first jolt of pain hit her.

It was so unexpected that she actually tumbled from her chair before she realized that it wasn't her own pain that she was feeling, but Cezar's.

In unison Shay and Darcy rushed to her side, their expressions concerned.

"Anna, what is it?" Darcy demanded.

"Cezar."

With a shake of her head, Anna ignored the pain that burned at her throat as she pushed herself to her feet. Dear God, Cezar was injured. She had to get to him. Now.

"Anna . . ."

Anna ignored the two women as she forced her shaky legs to carry her from the kitchen and back toward the study. Foolishly, a part of her tried to believe that what she was feeling must be some mistake. After all, this was a vampire stronghold and there had been no sounds of fighting. If someone had attacked there would be some sound of alarm, wouldn't there?

The thought floated through her mind at the same moment her legs broke into a panicked sprint. No amount of common sense was going to overcome the absolute certainty that Cezar was in trouble.

Reaching the study, she burst through the door, her frantic gaze skimming over the three hulking vampires who had all pulled out various lethal weapons at her noisy entrance.

"Where's Cezar?" she rasped.

Sliding the outrageously large sword back into its sheath, Styx crossed to stand before Anna, his expression hard with concern.

"Is something wrong, Anna?"

"Cezar." She had to suck in a deep breath. God, her throat hurt so bad, and the sense of Cezar that was tangled in her soul was getting more and more faint. "He's hurt. And I think he's being taken away."

"Damn." Taking Anna's hand he turned his head to bark over his shoulder. "Come with me."

With a sudden jerk on her arm, Anna found herself being hauled back down the hallway, Styx's long stride making her run for all she was worth to try to keep up. Not that she was complaining. The need to get to Cezar was a burning ache in the center of her heart.

There was a whisper of sound before a vampire guard appeared at Styx's side, falling easily into step with his master.

"My lord, is there trouble?"

"The imp—where is he?"

"In the library."

There wasn't another word spoken as they made their way to the front of the house. Nearing the door, Styx lifted his hand to burst it open so there was no pause as they all charged into the long, book-lined room.

The empty book-lined room.

Anna gave a low cry as she fell to her knees.

"He's gone."

"Damn that imp," Styx muttered. "I'm going to skin him alive and then shove his heart down his throat."

Anna struggled to think past the terror that clouded her mind. Dammit. Cezar needed her. She could be a babbling idiot later. For now she had to concentrate on finding her mate. Rising to her feet, she blinked back her scalding tears.

"What imp?" she demanded.

"Troy," Styx hissed, his attention turning toward the vampires gathered behind him. "I knew that son of a bitch couldn't be trusted."

"They can't have gone far," Viper said, his expression cold with fury. "We can catch him before he leaves the grounds."

The guard gave a shake of his head. "The imp came by car."

"It doesn't matter." Styx's smile was bone-chilling as he reached to grasp Anna's arm. With one motion, he shoved up the sleeve of her sweatshirt, revealing the tattoo that scrolled up her inner arm. "There's nowhere in the world they can take Cezar that we can't find him."

Cezar was astonishingly calm for a vampire being kidnapped.

He'd been an idiot to ignore Styx's warning about the imp, and an even greater fool to have met him while he was weakened. But now that he was a hostage, he was determined to ignore his blinding fury, and the searing pain of the thick silver collar that had been specifically crafted to imprison a vampire, and consider how best to turn this disaster to his advantage.

Retreating deep inside himself, he allowed Troy to believe he was unconscious as the treacherous imp sped along the dark highway, headed for Morgana's hidden lair.

His tactic gave him the opportunity to call upon his powers and begin to counter the burning pain of the silver. Few vampires possessed his tolerance for the deadly purity of the metal, and he was counting on the fact that Morgana would be assuming he was completely incapacitated by the collar.

It also gave him plenty of time to think.

There was no doubt that Troy was acting on orders from Morgana. He would never have pulled such a potentially lethal stunt unless he had no choice in the matter. Neither imps nor fairies were particularly courageous creatures, preferring to barter rather than battle.

Still, there had been something . . . off in the brief encounter. But what?

Certainly there had been a strange intensity about Troy that had nothing to do with fear. Almost as if he were willing Cezar to read his mind. And there had been his insistence to know if Cezar had mated Anna.

It took a while. Longer than it should have. But at last, his sluggish brain pinpointed the precise source of his suspicions.

Troy was taking Cezar to his queen, as commanded, but he knew he was also leaving a clear trail for Anna and his clan brothers to follow.

That's why he needed to know that Cezar had mated Anna. With the bond, Anna could follow him to the gates of freaking hell. And Styx would never allow her to come after him alone. The Anasso would insist on bringing the cavalry with him.

The wily imp couldn't fight the demented Morgana, but he was hoping like hell someone else could.

Of course, that didn't mean that Cezar didn't intend to beat the shit out of the demon the moment he was released from his chains. This dangerous stunt might be the perfect means of penetrating Morgana's lair, but no one was allowed to kidnap a vampire without some very painful punishment.

He indulged a few moments in imagining the various means of making an imp howl. There were a surprising number of them. Flaying, the rack, hot pokers. Then, with an inward shake of his head, he turned his thoughts to more important matters.

Any punishment of Troy would have to wait. And for now, he had no choice but to trust that his assessment was right and Troy wasn't willingly playing the queen's pawn. It was a risk, but at the moment he was a vampire between a rock and a hard place.

Allowing his essence to flow back through his body, Cezar swallowed a moan at the pain ravaging his throat and slit his eyes open to study the imp seated behind the wheel of the sports car.

Even in the thick darkness, he could make out the pale features that were strained with obvious fear. The imp was no happier than Cezar as they speeded toward Morgana.

"Why me?" he rasped softly.

Troy shrieked, and the car swerved off the highway before the imp jerked the wheel and sent them careening toward the guardrail on the opposite side.

"You crash this car and I'll rip your throat out," Cezar growled.

"Shit, vampire, I thought you were out," the imp muttered, managing to regain control of the car as he shot Cezar a terrified gaze. "How . . ."

"That doesn't matter." Cezar shifted on the seat until he was leaning his back against the door, his hands free to kill if the imp made one wrong move. Or maybe if he just pissed him off. "Tell me why Morgana sent you to capture me. It's Anna that she wants."

The car slowed and Cezar bared his fangs. Though the silver burning into his flesh might be a drain on his waning strength, there was nothing more dangerous in the world than a cornered vampire.

Troy swallowed the lump in his throat. "She'll never admit it, but she's genuinely afraid that the prophecy is true," he explained, his hands shaking so badly the car continued to weave on the empty highway. "When she at last confronts Anna, she wants to make sure she has an ace up her sleeve."

Cezar frowned. "I'm that ace?"

"Yes."

"Why?"

"She is able to sense that Anna cares for you." Troy swallowed another lump. "She believes that you are her Achilles' heel."

Shit.

Barely aware he was moving, Cezar smashed his fist into the dashboard, crumpling the steel supports.

He wanted to believe that Anna would never be foolish enough to risk her life to save his, that she understood he would never survive if anything happened to her. Unfortunately, he knew his mate too well to even go down that road.

As long as Morgana could use Cezar as her shield, Anna would never strike.

"I should kill you here and now," Cezar hissed, his savage fury filling the car.

"I had no choice, vampire," Troy insisted, one hand reaching to touch his chest, as if he were in pain. "Even if I'd been willing to sacrifice my life, which I assure you I wasn't, Morgana would just have sent another flunky to capture you. And at least with me you know that if the opportunity arises I will be the first in line to stick a knife in the bitch's back."

"And that's supposed to make me feel all warm and fuzzy inside?"

"No, but it is supposed to keep you from killing me before we reach the farmhouse."

Cezar gave a sharp crack of laughter, his fists itching to connect with that pale, perfect face. He'd be damned if he would lead Anna to her death. He'd kill Troy, and every other fey creature who tried to force him to become Morgana's bait.

"Obviously even unfounded hope springs eternal," he snarled.

Troy held the wheel with a death grip, his long, crimson hair floating as Cezar's power pulsed through the car.

"Listen to me, vampire. We can use this to our advantage," he urged, his eyes glowing like emeralds in the darkness. Obviously the fey was wise enough to understand he was a breath away from a bloody, messy death.

"What the hell are you babbling about? I'm not letting Anna anywhere near Morgana if the witch thinks to use me as her bargaining chip."

"Morgana will only *think* that you're her bargaining chip. After all, she'll be expecting you out cold and completely harmless." The imp shot a disgruntled glance in Cezar's direction. "As you should be."

Cezar smiled. It was a smile that made Troy shudder and hastily return his attention to the road.

"We all have our little talents," he said coldly.

Troy licked his lips. "Well, it's a talent you can use to your advantage if you'll just calm down and consider the possibilities."

"Troy, when I get desperate enough to need advice on battle strategy from an imp I'll throw myself in the sun."

"Just think about it, will you?" An edge entered the imp's voice. For all his fear, he was determined to have his say. "For the moment Morgana believes she has the upper hand and is arrogant enough to try to alter her fate. Hell, she's inviting the means to her own doom into her house. But the moment she realizes she might be in genuine danger, she will flee back to Avalon and out of your reach. Your mate will be forced to spend the rest of eternity looking over her shoulder for fear of an assassin."

Cezar stilled. Dammit. As much as it might gall him to admit it, the freaking imp did have a point.

He'd been so concerned with Morgana's relentless attacks on Anna that he hadn't actually considered the possibility that the aggravating bitch might retreat to her stronghold.

If she disappeared there would be no means to reach her, and as Troy pointed out, she could strike without warning whenever she wanted.

Anna would never be safe.

"Did you hear what . . ." Troy began, only to snap his lips shut as Cezar growled in warning.

"I heard," Cezar rasped, his mind struggling through his pain to sort out the various ways this night could play out.

"But . . ."

"Troy, shut your mouth before I rip out your tongue."

The imp heaved a deep sigh. "You know, vampires might be a bit more popular in the demon world if they weren't so surly all time. I mean, being gorgeous can only take you so far." A wicked smile touched his lips. "Okay, it can take you to my bed, but . . ."

Cezar battled back the lethal need to sink his fangs deep into the fey's throat. "Are you *trying* to get me to kill you?"

Troy's smile abruptly vanished. "It would be preferable to another round of Morgana's slap and tickle."

"What did she do to you?"

The imp shook his head as a shudder shook through his body. Whatever happened, it was still too raw to speak of.

"Conde Cezar, I have a request to make of you," he said instead, his expression suddenly grim with determination.

"What?"

"If I can't get out of there I'd rather you drain me than leave me with Morgana."

Cezar gave a slow nod. He better than anyone understood that there were many things in this world worse than death.

"Very well."

Anna kept her eyes closed as the Hummer raced down the dark highway. At her side Styx was behind the wheel with the terrifying Jagr seated in the back.

There was another Hummer behind them filled with Viper, Dante, Shay, Abby and Darcy. Anna had only been briefly aware of the low-pitched arguments that had erupted when the three women had insisted on being a part of the rescue mission. And then another argument when Styx had insisted Jagr join them.

She'd been far too anxious to chase after Cezar.

No, not anxious.

Overwhelmingly, chokingly desperate.

Every moment that passed was like a dagger being twisted through her heart and it was only the knowledge that she would need the help of Cezar's brothers that kept her from damning them all to hell and racing from the isolated house.

After what seemed to be an eternity they were at last on the road, using Anna's sense of Cezar to steer them out of the city and west through the flat fields and tiny towns that dotted the landscape.

Not that Anna's sense of urgency eased. Especially when her connection to Cezar became muted, as if their bond was weakening. Eventually the sense of him had returned along with the searing pain in her neck, but it had lasted only for a few minutes before it began to fade once again.

Anna didn't know what the odd sensations meant, but she didn't for a moment believe they could be good.

Clenching her hands so tightly that her nails dug holes into her palm, Anna turned her head to regard Styx with a wide gaze.

"He's stopped moving."

In the shadows of the car, the King of Vampires looked like some avenging god, all hard planes and coiled power. He was death, just waiting for the opportunity to deliver his gift. And in the back the golden-haired giant wasn't any more comforting. Jagr might possess the sort of savage beauty that would make any woman's heart leap in excitement, but there was no mistaking that frigid violence that crackled around him. He was a time bomb about to explode, and Anna didn't want to be anywhere near when it happened.

If she hadn't been terrified out of her mind for Cezar, she would never have been alone in a car with these two lethal demons.

"Good," Styx growled, the tiny medallions in his braided hair catching the moonlight as he shot her a dark glance. "How is he?"

"I don't know." Anna wrapped her arms around her chilled body, hating the aching void that filled her heart. "He's in pain, but he's distant from me again. As if there's some sort of shield around him."

Styx reached out to give her arm a brief pat. "He's protecting himself, Anna. A vampire has the ability to pull deep inside his own body. It will not only help him battle the pain, but it will convince others that he is not a threat."

"So he's . . . playing possum?" she demanded as she struggled to understand.

A grim smile touched Styx's lips. "Something like that."

Anna rubbed the goose bumps that prickled her arms. It was a relief to know that the muffled sensation wasn't a sign that Cezar was on the brink of death, or that another creature was capable of severing their bond.

Still, it was unnerving as hell.

"I wish he wouldn't," she muttered. "I need to feel him."

"We will get him back, Anna, that much I can promise you."

She sucked in a deep breath, sensing they were getting closer to Cezar with every passing mile.

"I still don't understand why Troy would kidnap Cezar. It makes no sense."

"It makes perfect sense," Jagr said from the backseat, his voice a low rumble.

Turning her head, Anna regarded the dangerous vampire with a hint of puzzlement. "Why?"

His smile was no more than the baring of his huge fangs.

"So long as Morgana holds the vampire captive she knows that none of you will risk his life, not even to save your own. She can lure you to her lair and kill you at her leisure."

Anna's breath caught in her throat. Oh . . . God. Of course Morgana would hide behind Cezar like the coward she was. Somehow she knew that Anna would offer her life to save the man she loved.

"Jagr," Styx rasped in warning.

The large vampire shrugged. "It is what I would do."

"You really need to work on those social skills of yours, brother," Styx muttered.

Jagr's expression hardened with fury. "I am not your brother."

Sensing that an ass-kicking was stirring, Anna hastily cleared her throat.

"No, Styx. I would rather know the truth." She touched Styx's hard arm, grimacing at the ripple of muscles that warned he was itching to hit something. Hard. "Do you think that's Morgana's plan?"

"Yes," he grudgingly agreed.

"So what do we do?"

"Obviously we walk straight into the trap," Jagr muttered.

There was a low growl as Styx's power filled the air, sending odd prickles over Anna's skin and making Jagr hiss in pain. Clearly whatever Styx was sending through the air was specifically directed toward a fellow vampire.

"Jagr, when I want your input I'll ask for it. Are we clear?"

Anna held her breath as a tense silence filled the Hummer, the sense of violence so tangible in the air she could almost taste it.

Oh . . . shit.

Preparing to slide off the seat and hide beneath the dashboard, Anna was spared such indignity when Jagr gave a low grunt, and with obvious anger forced himself to speak.

"Yes, my lord."

The prickling sensations ceased, and Anna managed to

suck in a deep breath. Holy . . . crap. That was waaaay too close for comfort.

Casting Styx a wary glance, Anna blinked at the man's smooth, aloof expression. There wasn't the faintest hint he'd been on the verge of committing murder.

"So," she said, more to break the uneasy silence than the need to speak, "do we have a plan?"

"We get Cezar, kill Morgana, and get the hell back to Chicago," Styx retorted, his voice clipped.

Anna grimaced. Not much of a plan.

"Okay."

Without warning the golden gaze swung in her direction, the hard features softening with a flare of compassion.

"Anna, if you'd rather wait in the car no one would think less of you."

Her mouth fell open at the mere suggestion that she would cower in the car when Cezar was in danger.

"No way," she barked, her eyes narrowing as Styx's lips parted. "No, Styx. Cezar's in trouble because of me. Besides, it's my duty to face Morgana. I'm the one in the prophecy. No one else can hurt her."

Styx's expression hardened. "You do know that Cezar will kill me if something happens to you?"

She might be all kinds of stupid, but she didn't even flinch beneath the hard glare.

"I might be Cezar's mate, but I still make my own decisions," she warned.

The vampire gave a short, humorless laugh. "That sounds remarkably familiar."

Anna's lips twitched at his reference to Darcy, but before she could respond she felt a tug deep inside her.

"Slow down," she commanded, pressing her hand to the window, as if it would help her connect to Cezar. "Take the next exit and turn right."

Without question Styx followed her directions, slowing the

car as she shut her eyes and concentrated on the muffled sense of her mate.

Styx slowed the car as they traveled farther from the highway and deeper into the isolated farmlands. Three more times they turned onto progressively smaller, less traveled roads until the way became nothing more than two ruts between fields.

"He's close," she whispered softly.

Without warning, the car came to a halt and Styx reached out to touch her arm.

"Anna?"

Keeping her eyes closed as she clung to that fragile sense of Cezar, Anna heaved an impatient sigh. Dammit, she couldn't bear anymore delays.

"What?"

"Anna, look at me," he commanded, his voice sharp enough that her eyes snapped open to meet his fierce, compelling gaze.

"Why have you stopped?" she demanded. "Cezar is . . ."

"Cezar is in danger, yes I know," he interrupted. "But Morgana is not his only risk at the moment."

Anna frowned, really not in the mood to consider yet another horror that might be lurking in the shadows.

A demented aunt with a God complex seemed like quite enough.

"I don't understand."

Styx's remote expression gave nothing away. "That is the problem. You are not a vampire."

Her raw nerves flared at his words. That was why he'd stopped? To point out that she wasn't a demon?

"That's hardly a news flash, Styx. Do you have a point?"

The gold eyes narrowed. "You are not a vampire, so you do not fully understand what it means to be mated."

"Styx, can't this wait until after we've rescued Cezar?"

"No, because I sense your desperation."

"She reeks of it," Jagr muttered from the backseat.

Anna shook her head in frustration, a hint of her power leaking out to swirl through the car, heating the air and stirring her hair. *What the hell was going on?*

"Would you rather I didn't give a damn what happens to him?" she rasped.

"It would be easier in some ways."

Anna sucked in a deep breath, struggling to control her straining powers. Was Styx trying to piss her off so she would be ready to explode once she was near Morgana?

If he was, it was working like a charm.

"Styx, just tell me why you're wasting precious time."

There was a brief pause, as if Styx were carefully considering his words.

"Cezar has taken you for his mate," he at last said. "If you die, he dies."

Anna froze in shock. "You mean . . . he'll actually die?"

"Not immediately. But yes." He gave a stiff dip of his head. "You have become his reason for living, Anna. Without you, he will lose any instinct to protect himself. In fact, he will seek out danger in the hopes that he will find an end to his suffering. Vampires rarely survive more than a few months after the death of their mate."

A cold chill clutched at her heart. Shit. Somehow Cezar failed to mention that little tidbit of info when he was telling her about the whole mate business.

"Why are you telling me this now?" she demanded, her voice barely more than a whisper.

"Because you are willing to sacrifice yourself to save him." He touched a cold finger to her pale cheek. "If you do, Anna Randal, you condemn Cezar to your own fate."

Chapter 20

The attic of the farmhouse was a filthy, cramped place that was barely fit for pathetic humans, let alone a powerful queen.

It was, however, a perfect location to keep an unconscious vampire hostage.

Ignoring the thick dust that marred the hem of her gossamer gown, Morgana studied the demon who hung from the rafters by the silver leash.

His rich, dark hair was disheveled to tumble around the elegant lines of his beautiful face, and since she had commanded Troy to strip him of his shirt, there was nothing to hide the chiseled perfection of his bronzed chest.

She could understand Anna Randal's fascination with the creature.

All vampires possessed a potent sensual appeal. They were predators who used sex to lure their prey. But this vampire . . .

He was perfectly formed to pleasure women.

And pleasure them well.

It was almost a pity she was going to have to kill him.

Shifting her attention from the unconscious vampire to the tall imp with his crimson mane of hair and wary expression, she allowed a cold smile to touch her lips.

"You have done well, Troy."

Kneeling, the imp lowered his head. "Thank you, my Queen. I live to serve."

Morgana's lips twisted as she moved forward to capture Troy's chin in a brutal grip. Yanking up his head she savored the stark fear that flared through the emerald eyes.

"Or you serve to live, eh my little traitor?"

"I have brought you the vampire," the imp rasped. "Surely I have proven my loyalty?"

Her anger whipped through the cramped space. She would not forget the imp's treachery. Anna might very well be dead now if the arrogant bastard hadn't whisked her away from the nightclub. But, she was wise enough to realize that for the moment Troy was a tool she could use to her advantage. He was the only one who could get into the vampire's lair. And now that she had so kindly reminded him of the pain she could inflict, he was the one creature she could be assured wouldn't disappoint her again.

Once she had finished this unpleasant business, she would consider whether to continue with the fun of tormenting him, or simply kill him and be done with it.

"I will decide when you've proven your loyalty, worm," she purred.

The imp shivered, but he never allowed his gaze to waver. Troy, Prince of Imps, possessed the sort of courage that was far too rare among the fey. Perhaps she should think about having his sperm frozen before killing him. With the right training his offspring might make suitable soldiers.

"Yes, my Queen," he murmured, his tone suitably respectful.

Releasing her hold on his chin, Morgana turned so she could study the beautiful vampire.

"You are certain he is secured?" she demanded.

"Of course." Rising warily to his feet, Troy pointed to the heavy collar around Cezar's neck. "The silver will keep him incapacitated so long as it touches his skin."

"And the fairies are in place?"

"They are hidden and await your word to slay the intruders."

Morgana closed her eyes as she allowed her senses to flow outward. "They are near. I can smell the stench of my brother's blood."

"Then I should go and make sure . . ."

Stepping to block the imp's hasty departure, Morgana pressed a finger to his chest, a smile twisting her lips as the imp screamed in pain.

"Oh no, Troy, I want you well away from my back while I'm finishing this unpleasant task," she drawled, flooding his body with a searing heat. "But know this—if you even try to slip away from me I'll rip your heart from your chest and eat it for dinner." She leaned close enough that their lips were touching in the mockery of a kiss. "Do we understand one another?"

Troy's ragged breath filled the room. "Perfectly."

"Good." Moving back, Morgana reached to grasp one of the numerous stakes that she had lined up on a decrepit chair. "Take this stake and place it against his heart. If he so much as twitches I want to know."

Still shaking with pain, the imp took the stake and pressed it against the vampire's chest.

"As you command, my Queen."

Confident that her trap was suitably baited and ready to snap shut on her prey, Morgana smoothed her hands over her glorious mane of hair and turned to make her way down the narrow flight of stairs.

Throughout the house, she could sense the fairies hidden among the shadows, all of them poised to protect her the moment she commanded. They might not love her, but they knew better than to fail her.

Unlike her ridiculous brother she understood the power of fear. Why would she waste her time groveling for the loyalty of her subjects when she could demand it instead?

At last reaching the ground floor, Morgana closed her eyes and reached out with her thoughts. She frowned as she sensed the various demons that were attempting to surround the farmhouse.

Vampires, of course. Those she had expected. But there was also a werewolf and a Shalott. Both rare creatures who were as dangerous as vampires in their own right.

No matter. She deliberately smoothed away the frown and dismissed the demons from her mind. They were clearly allies of the vampires. So long as she held Conde Cezar they wouldn't dare to harm her.

Just as Anna Randal wouldn't dare to harm her.

A faintly smug smile touched her lips as she felt her vulnerable young niece hesitate just outside the door.

At last.

After centuries of hiding in the mists and stalking her prey from the shadows, she was about to bring an end to her brother's line.

And then she would be free.

Free to rule as she had been meant to rule.

Reaching out her hand, she used her powers to wrench the door open, her smile widening at the faint gasp of surprise from the slender, honey-haired woman.

"Ah . . . my beautiful niece," she mocked. "Welcome to my home."

Something that might have been fear rippled over the delicate features before Anna Randal was squaring her shoulders and stepping over the threshold, closely shadowed by two powerful vampires.

Morgana briefly allowed her gaze to flick over the large, blond vampire. His icy fury filled the air with a dark hint of violence. A dangerous demon on the edge, but for the moment leashed by his fierce control. At his side the tall, dark Aztec was rigid with grim determination, his immense power coiled and ready to strike.

Morgana felt a tiny flare of surprise as she recognized that power. The Anasso, King of Vampires.

Obviously Conde Cezar had friends in high places.

The knowledge might have been unnerving if she didn't have the vampire chained upstairs with a stake to his heart.

Vampires were as ridiculously loyal as her brother had once been. They would readily give their lives for another.

Saps.

As if sensing her smug amusement, Anna Randal moved to stand directly before her, the hazel eyes flashing with anger.

"Where is he?"

Morgana flicked a brow upward at the sharp tone. "I know for certain you weren't raised by trolls, my sweet. Where are your manners?"

Anna's mouth fell open, as if outraged by Morgana's chastisement. "You slaughtered my family, stalked me like a psychopath, sent your minions to kill me, and kidnapped the man I love, and you want to lecture *me* on manners? That might be funny if it weren't so pathetic."

It was Morgana's turn to be shocked. No one spoke to her in such a manner.

No one.

"Pathetic? You loathsome little pest. I am your queen and you will give me the respect that I deserve," she hissed, stepping forward. She was going to teach the bitch to grovel before she killed her. "You will be on your knees when you speak to me."

Her hand reached out, but before she could grab Anna's hair and force her to her knees, the tip of a cold, steel blade pressed to her neck.

"Not a step closer," the dark vampire hissed, his eyes hard with warning.

Her hands clenched as she shifted her furious gaze to glare at the demon who dared to threaten her.

"Do you think I fear you, vampire?" she hissed.

"You should."

"Children." At her sharp command there was a rustle of sound as her fairies appeared from the shadows, their weapons lifted and pointed toward the intruders. "Each bow holds a wooden arrow. Not all of them will miss."

The vampire didn't even blink. "Perhaps not, but I'm betting I can cut off your head before one finally hits my heart."

There was another prick at her neck as the hulking blond vampire pressed his own sword to her neck.

"And if he doesn't, I will," he growled.

"Do you want to call my bluff?" the dark vampire demanded.

Morgana curled her lip at the display of testosterone. Men were always so eager to use brute force when cunning was more efficient.

Her foolish brother had been the same.

"I believe that my bluff is greater than your own," she drawled. "Unless the rumors of clan loyalty are grossly exaggerated. Your . . . brother is upstairs with a stake to his heart. One call from me and Conde Cezar is dust."

Anna's face paled as she reached out a hand to touch the vampire. "Styx. Jagr."

With a low growl the vampires lowered their swords, the king narrowing his gaze with a lethal hatred.

"What do you want?"

"What do I want?" Morgana laughed. "Everything, vampire. Everything that is owed to me."

"The only thing owed to you is a slow, painful death, Morgana," the vampire said coldly.

With a hiss, Morgana sent out her powers, throwing the vampire against the wall and pinning him there.

"It is Your Majesty to you," she hissed, increasing the pressure until the large body was bowed and writhing in pain.

"Morgana, stop it," Anna demanded, stepping between her and the vampire. The scent of figs spiced the air before Morgana was hit with a sharp, painful blast of heat. "I said . . . stop it," Anna gritted.

Her own power momentarily faltered, allowing the vampire to swiftly return to his protective position at Anna's side.

Morgana hid her unpleasant shock at the realization that the woman was capable of hurting her. Damn Arthur. Would her brother's potent blood never die? It should have been thinned to the point of nonexistence by now, but there was no mistaking the ease with which she had disrupted Morgana's own magic.

"Careful, Anna," she snapped. "Another stunt like that and your lover will be waiting for you in hell."

The woman tilted her chin, as if she didn't realize that Morgana could kill her with one blow.

"You obviously kidnapped Cezar to bring me here. I'm here now. Why don't you let Cezar and the others go?"

Morgana gave a sharp laugh. "Have I ever given you the least hint that I am stupid, Anna?" she mocked. "The vamps, as well as that werewolf and Shalott creeping around outside, stay to make sure you play nice."

"And what does *play nice* mean?" she demanded. "That I just stand here and let you kill me?"

Morgana slowly smiled. "Actually . . . yes. That's exactly what I mean."

The dark vampire growled deep in his throat. "Anna, don't even think about it. This is not what Cezar would want."

Morgana reached out to stroke a finger down Anna's soft cheek, her nail cutting a thin wound.

"Ah, but sweet Anna is willing to do anything, even sacrifice herself, to save her beloved, are you not?"

Anna jerked her head back, her hand lifting to wipe away the trail of blood.

"You know, Morgana, my grandfather warned me that you are an evil woman—I'm beginning to understand why he hated you so much."

A sharp chill pierced Morgana's heart. "What did you say?"

"Oh, didn't I mention my little visit with your brother?" Anna demanded sweetly.

"That's impossible."

"Why? Because you killed him?"

Morgana lifted her hand to strike the bitch where she stood. She had to be lying. Arthur was dead. Dead and buried. But her hand froze as she caught the sound of stirring fairies behind her.

She had been very careful to cultivate the legend that Arthur had died in battle once she realized that she was incapable of tarnishing the people's love for him. It was disgusting, the manner that they had worshipped the weak, stupid man.

To admit that she had been the cause of his death would cause nothing short of a mutiny.

She allowed her hand to continue forward, but rather than landing the lethal blow she longed to deliver, Morgana instead grasped Anna's arm in a biting grip.

"We will finish this in private," she rasped.

"Private?" The bitch had the nerve to meet her furious gaze without fear. "Do you have something to hide, Morgana? Don't your sycophants know what you did to your own brother?"

Morgana tightened her grip until the bone threatened to shatter. "Shut up."

The two vampires flowed forward, their swords lifted to strike. It was only Anna's sharp shake of her head that halted them.

"No, Styx. This is between me and my aunt." With an ease that should never have been possible, the honey-haired woman pulled from Morgana's grasp and regarded her with a hard expression. "You want private? That's fine with me."

In disbelief, Morgana watched as her niece walked calmly across the room and entered the dingy kitchen, her head held high and her back stiff. With no option, Morgana was forced to follow behind her, her fury a potent force that filled the house with a rush of prickling heat.

Once away from prying eyes, Morgana reached out to jerk Anna around to face her, her anger overcoming any fear of the woman's mysterious power.

"You worthless brat." She gave Anna a sharp shake, sadistically pleased when she felt the woman shudder in pain. "Do not ever turn your back to me. I am your queen."

Again Anna managed to wrestle from her grip, but not before Morgana had managed to leave a savage burn on her arm.

"You're a homicidal maniac," Anna hissed, lifting a hand to cover her ugly wound. "It's no wonder that your brother refuses to rest in his grave until you're dead."

With a sudden gesture Morgana sent Anna slamming into the wall. She was done screwing around. She wanted this woman dead. And she wanted her dead now.

"You know nothing of my brother," she mocked, her confidence returning as Anna swayed and leaned against the wall to keep her balance. Anna Randal might have the blood of ancients in her veins, but she was still a weak, easily shattered human. "This is nothing but a desperate trick to try to save your pathetic life."

Stiffening her knees, Anna reached in her pocket. Morgana smiled as she calmly smoothed the gossamer of her gown. If the stupid creature thought she could reveal some hidden weapon and frighten a powerful queen, she was about to learn a painful lesson.

"Really, then where do you suppose I got this?" Anna demanded, holding out her hand to reveal the perfect emerald glimmering against her palm.

Expecting a hexed knife, or even one of those charmed amulets that witches loved to flash around, Morgana's smug assurance cracked and shattered as she caught sight of the emerald that had once graced her brother's golden crown.

No. No, it couldn't be.

That gem had been buried with her brother, and despite her best efforts over the centuries to attempt to retrieve the powerful emerald, she had been continually blocked by Merlin's last and most potent spell.

Damn the wizard to hell.

If he hadn't managed to disappear Morgana would have dragged him to Avalon and devoted the centuries to teaching the bastard the true meaning of pain.

A tremor raced through her body as the energy of the jewel surged over her skin.

"How . . . ?"

As if taking courage from the emerald, Anna tilted her chin and stepped away from the wall.

"My grandfather gave it to me. He seemed to think that it might help me destroy you." She clenched her fingers around the stone. "What do you think? Shall, we give it a whirl?"

Morgana instinctively backed away. Until the spell was broken upon it, the emerald would respond only to her brother.

Or, obviously, to one of his blood.

"This is not . . . not possible."

Anna's lips twisted. "Over the past few days I've discovered that there are very few things that are impossible."

"He's dead," Morgana said, as much to convince herself as the annoying pest standing before her. "I watched him die."

"You betrayed him."

Morgana's lips curled at the accusation. Of course she had betrayed her brother. She was above the tedious morals that plagued the lesser beings. All that mattered was that she survived and that the world would bow before her.

"Arthur was a fool," she sneered, thrusting aside her brief unease. With or without the emerald, she still held the upper hand. So long as the vampire was chained in the attic this woman would do nothing. Nothing but die. "With me at his side he possessed the power to rule the world. No one could have challenged us. No one would have dared."

"Maybe he didn't want to rule the world," Anna countered.

Morgana laughed. Typical. There seemed to be some innate flaw in her brother's blood. An inability to see past the mundane humanity to the glory that was their birthright.

Fate had intended them to be above mortals. Above demons. Above all.

And yet, Arthur insisted on playing the role of the benevolent ruler, always determined to see that his shining vision of justice prevailed.

So weak. So ripe to fall into the hands of his enemies.

She had done him a favor by putting an end to his pathetic dreams.

If she hadn't, someone else would have.

"You rule or you follow or you die," she said coldly. "There are no other choices."

"Did you get that off a bumper sticker?"

Morgana narrowed her gaze at the flippant response. Enough of this foolishness. She wanted answers. "Tell me how you found that emerald."

"I told you."

"My brother's dead."

"He may be dead, but he has no intention of resting in peace. Not until he's had his revenge."

Morgana's gaze shifted to the emerald. She wanted to deny the bitch's claim. Arthur's powers were considerable, but not even he was above death.

Still, there was no denying the rare stone that glittered in the palm of Anna's hand. Or the fact that the girl couldn't possibly have acquired it without the assistance of her brother.

Somehow Arthur's shade had reached out to Anna.

"He has no powers." She lifted her hands, allowing her magic to swirl through the room, stirring the curtains and making the ugly framed pictures of roosters fall to the cracked linoleum floor. "He can't harm me."

Anna's hair tangled in the breeze, but her expression never faltered. "But I can."

"*Can* and *will* are two very different things, child." Morgana stepped forward. "You don't have the stomach to sacrifice your precious vampire to save yourself."

"Actually, dear Aunt, you've miscalculated." With an oddly haunted expression Anna shoved up the sleeve of her sweatshirt to reveal the unmistakable mark of a vampire. "Cezar has mated me, which means that if I die, he will die." Her eyes lifted to stab Morgana with a glare of pure determination. "Don't think for a moment I won't take you with us."

Chapter 21

Cezar awoke to a world filled with searing pain, and the annoying feeling of someone frantically slapping his cheek.

The ravaging pain he couldn't stop, but he'd be damned if he was going to be bitch-slapped while he was struggling to regain his wits.

With a swift motion he caught the pesky hand in a grip tight enough to make his assailant curse in pain.

"Shit, vampire, let go," the familiar voice of Troy muttered close to his ear.

Cautiously opening his eyes, Cezar glanced around to discover he was stretched on a filthy wood-planked floor with the prince leaning over him. Not the way any vampire liked to wake up.

"Back off," he growled, watching with a narrowed gaze as the imp sat back on his heels before loosening his grip.

"I didn't think you were ever going to wake," Troy groused, rubbing his bruised fingers.

Assured there were no prying eyes, Cezar forced himself to a sitting position, gritting his teeth against the wave of weakness that rolled through his body.

"I possess some resistance to silver, but I'm not impervious to it," he gritted. "How long have I been out?"

"Nearly an hour."

"An hour?" Hissing in anger, Cezar forced himself to his feet. He remembered being carried into the house by Troy and hearing the queen command that he be strung from the rafters. After that, everything was a searing blur. *"Dios."*

Rising, Troy dusted off his ridiculous spandex pants. "Don't get your panties in a twist. Your mate has only been here a short time."

Ignoring his companion, Cezar closed his eyes and reached out with his thoughts. He was briefly surprised by the sheer number of demons that filled the house. Not only Styx and Jagr, but nearly a dozen fairies. With a grimace, he shifted his attention to Anna, easily finding her just below him.

"She's with Morgana," he hissed, turning toward the narrow door across the dark attic. "I must go to her."

Ignoring his instinct for self-preservation, Troy moved to stand directly before Cezar.

"Hold on, chief. I didn't rescue your sorry hide to have you throw it away in some futile display of heroism."

Before the imp could so much as blink, Cezar had his hand wrapped around the fool's throat and was dangling him off the ground.

"Don't try to stand in my path, imp," he warned. "You won't like the results."

Troy's eyes bulged as he struggled against Cezar's hold, his complexion taking on a bluish tinge. "If you go charging down there Morgana will know that she no longer holds her threat over Anna. She will kill her before you can even get close."

"You expect me to hide up here while Anna is in danger?" Cezar rasped.

"Damn, vampire, unlike you I need air. Let go."

"I'm going to Anna."

"At least warn her that you're okay before you charge in there and start World War Three. She needs to know to protect herself."

Cezar grudgingly accepted that the imp did have a point. For the moment Morgana presumed that she held the advantage. As long as she continued to believe that, she would be willing to savor her defeat of Anna. She was too arrogant not to want to gloat.

However, the moment she actually feared that she might be in true danger . . .

"*Si*. You're right," he muttered, dropping the imp back to the floorboards. "I must think."

Troy managed to regain his feet, massaging his bruised neck. "Thank freaking God."

"Don't push me, imp," Cezar growled, closing his eyes and turning his thoughts to the vampires below.

"What are you doing?" Troy demanded.

"Making a call."

"You know it might be easier if you had a cell phone."

Cezar's hands twitched, but he managed to resist the urge to continue squeezing the life from the aggravating creature. Not out of any sense of compassion, but quite simply because he knew that Anna would not approve.

He was a mated vampire and the happiness of his female came before all other considerations.

"It would be easier if you would just shut up for a few minutes," he snapped.

"Fine." Troy made a sound of disgust. "This is the very last time I try to help vampires. Arrogant, cold bastards."

Wisely ignoring the imp, Cezar reached out to his Anasso, careful to keep his powers restrained. The longer Morgana believed he was still bound in silver and harmless, the better.

"Styx."

"Cezar, are you harmed?" The ancient vampire's voice echoed through his mind with a fierce concern.

"I'm recovering. Tell me what is happening."

"Jagr and I are downstairs surrounded by a bunch of very

nervous fairies with twitchy fingers. I don't think startling them would be a good idea at this point."

It was exactly what Cezar had been expecting. Morgana might be an arrogant bitch, but she wasn't stupid.

"What of Viper and Dante?"

"They are with Abby, Shay, and Darcy outside. They have the house surrounded, to make sure that no reinforcements can catch us unaware."

Cezar's lips unconsciously twitched. Styx might have been forced to take on the role of the Anasso, but he would always be a warrior at heart.

"I will try to reach Anna, although she's not accustomed to accepting my thoughts into her own. She may not understand that it is truly me and not an illusion."

"Anna Randal is remarkably intelligent, not to mention as stubborn as a werewolf, *amigo*," Styx assured him dryly. "She will not fail you."

No, she wouldn't.

She possessed enough heart and courage to make his blood run cold.

"That's not the question."

Sensing Cezar's frustration at his continual inability to keep Anna from harm, Styx filled Cezar's mind with a flood of stern disapproval.

"Cezar, you have sacrificed centuries for this woman. You are incapable of failing her." His voice echoed through Cezar, bringing a wry smile to his lips.

There was no point in arguing with the king. His loyalty was the stuff of legends. "After I contact Anna I will create a distraction," he said instead. "Can you disarm the fairies?"

There was no need to see Styx's expression to know he was outraged that Cezar would even ask such a question. "Are you trying to be amusing?"

"Just be ready."

"Always."

Pulling his thoughts from Styx, Cezar concentrated on his mate. On a distant level he was aware of the imp pacing the floor with a nervous step, and the stale dust that choked the air. He was even aware of the scent of the demons that patrolled the grounds outside. His attention, however, never wavered as he warily tapped into the thoughts of the woman he loved.

"Anna," he said softly.

Her shock was tangible as she struggled to understand what was happening. "Cezar?"

"Anna, don't speak aloud," he commanded, his body tight with fear that she might reveal his presence to Morgana. Anna was close, but still too far away to save if Morgana should strike out. "I can hear your thoughts."

There was a brief moment as Anna calmed her mind and body, the sweet smell of figs swirling through Cezar with a familiar warmth.

"Are you hurt? Morgana said . . ."

"I'm well," he hastily assured her. "What of you?"

"I'm fine."

Cezar greedily drank in the sense of Anna, a surge of anger racing through him as he felt the pain she tried to conceal.

"You've been injured."

"It's nothing."

His teeth snapped together in frustration, but unable to do anything to help ease her wounds, he reminded himself of the danger of wasting even a moment.

"You're with Morgana?"

"Yes."

"You must not allow her to suspect that I am conscious. Can you listen to me without revealing my presence to Morgana?"

"I'll try." Her courage wavered before she pulled it back around her like a well-worn cloak. "She said that she had you chained with a stake to your heart."

"Troy decided he didn't particularly care for the thought of being Morgana's whipping boy for the next few centuries," he assured her. "He's placed his bet on the fact that we can bring an end to her."

"Yeah, that's the same bet I placed."

His heart squeezed. *Dios.* He would find the means to save her. There was no other option.

"Just hold on, Anna, I'm on my way."

An astonishing blast of power rocked Cezar back on his heels as Anna reacted to his words.

"No, Cezar, get everyone out of here," she demanded. "I can deal with Morgana, but not if I'm worried about someone getting hurt."

He growled deep in his throat as he braced himself against her surge of energy. For all her raw power, he had had years to hone his skills.

"Don't even waste your time, Anna. None of us are leaving."

"Cezar . . ."

"Stall Morgana for as long as you can." He overrode her protest. "I'll be there."

Damn the pig-headed, unreasonable, insufferable . . . demon.

Anna fiercely attempted to reach out with her thoughts, but once again Cezar was capable of blocking her efforts.

When this was all said and done she intended to discover a means to break through that barrier. Her mate would learn a lesson in tossing her out in the midst of an argument.

Well, always assuming she lived that long.

A prospect that wasn't looking all that good as Morgana suddenly stepped forward and slapped her across the face.

"Don't you dare ignore me, you nasty rodent," she seethed, her fury a tangible force in the small kitchen. "When I'm about to kill someone I expect their full attention."

As the flare of pain rocked through her, Anna realized that she had missed most of the tantrum her aunt had been throwing. Obviously the queen knew enough of vampires to realize that holding Cezar wasn't quite the bargaining chip that she had hoped for. After all, if Anna died, the vampire would quickly follow her to the grave.

Trying to shake off the pain, Anna squared her shoulders and faced her furious relative with a grim determination. Dammit, time was running out.

Despite the pain and debilitating weakness that she could sense was plaguing Cezar, Anna didn't doubt for a minute that he was already rushing to the rescue like the Lone-freaking-Ranger. She had to end this before he got himself killed.

"Forgive me if I'm not nearly as impressed as you think I should be, but to be honest, after meeting my grandfather, I've come to realize that you're nothing more than a vain, pathetic wannabe." She forced a smile to her bruised lips. "Arthur was a true king. A man worthy to claim the title."

Morgana's hand lifted, but this time she didn't strike Anna. Instead her fingers circled Anna's neck and lifted her off the ground.

"If you are hoping to provoke me into making your death swift and painless, you're even more stupid than I thought," she mocked. "I intend to relish your screams of agony, sweet Anna. I intend to bathe in your blood and crush your heart in my bare hand."

"Lovely," Anna muttered, knowing she would be far more terrified if she hadn't been distracted by the sense of Cezar moving steadily closer. "Is this the part where I'm supposed to beg for mercy?"

The emerald eyes flashed with an inhuman fury as Morgana's fingers tightened on her throat.

"Oh, you will beg, Anna Randal," Morgana hissed, her fingers digging into Anna's throat with an agonizing force. "Before I am through with you . . ." The threatening words came to an abrupt halt as the overhead light in the kitchen flickered and then exploded with enough force to send a shower of glass slivers raining through the room. Both women froze for a heartbeat, then releasing her hold on Anna, Morgana spun on her heels to glare toward the empty doorway. "The vampire. He's been released."

Shit.

Dragging in a ragged breath, Anna battled the wave of darkness that threatened to consume her. She knew that she had to strike while Morgana was distracted. Before Cezar charged to his death.

Knowing that, however, and actually accomplishing the brave feat were two very different things.

Choking on blood and barely able to breathe, Anna clutched the emerald in her hand and closed her eyes as she attempted to call on the powers she had for so long considered a curse.

In this moment she didn't care if she was a freak. She didn't care if she couldn't control her powers and she brought the entire house down on their heads. After all, there was no one here who wouldn't survive.

All she cared about was distracting the woman before she could hurt Cezar.

She felt the familiar prickle race through her blood, the energy stirring her hair and heating her skin.

Unfortunately, Morgana wasn't a queen for nothing. The very moment that Anna began to focus her power the woman turned back and grabbed Anna's arm to shake her with a violent fury.

"Oh no you don't," she hissed. "Nothing is going to stop me from putting an end to you."

Her free hand lifted and she pointed toward the center of the room. Anna frowned as she watched a strange shimmer begin to glow in the darkness.

Anna's heart clenched with fear as the shimmer grew larger and a strange mist filled the center.

Holy crap. Was that a portal?

Oh, this wasn't good.

Not good at all.

"What are you doing?" she stupidly demanded.

Keeping her grim hold on Anna's arm, Morgana began dragging her toward the waiting mist.

"I'm taking you home, my sweet."

Waiting until the house was plunged into darkness, Cezar descended the stairs with one long leap. Landing at the bottom he was forced to crouch low as a hail of arrows flew over his head.

Damn fairies.

Why didn't they just get the hell out of the way so he could get to Anna?

"Styx," he bellowed, his gaze searching out the large vampire who already had his sword loose and was cutting a swath of carnage through the gathered fey. At his side Jagr was providing his own share to the death toll, his fluid motions a beautiful dance of death.

"Go to her, *amigo*," Styx growled. "We can handle a few fairies."

Cezar smiled wryly as he bolted toward the kitchen door. The fairies that hadn't been sliced in two were already fleeing in mindless panic. He was more in danger of being flattened in the stampede than shot.

Ignoring Troy, who ran at his side, Cezar reached the door and prepared to launch himself at Morgana.

Only there was no Morgana to launch himself at.

And no Anna.

Hissing in disbelief, he reached out with his mind, a stark fear piercing his heart as he found nothing but a yawning emptiness.

He stumbled to a halt, his gaze desperately searching the empty room even as logic told him that she was gone. Truly gone.

"Anna," he breathed, sinking to his knees as he reached out to touch the scorch marks that marred the linoleum floor.

"A portal," Troy muttered in disgust. "Morgana has taken her."

With a movement too swift to follow, Cezar had Troy pinned to the wall, his fangs close enough to rip out the imp's throat.

"Take me to her," he growled.

Troy had to swallow twice before he could find his voice. "I don't have that power."

"Damn you . . ."

"Cezar, no." Without warning Darcy was at his side, her hand lightly touching his arm. "He can lead us to her."

Troy winced beneath Cezar's painful grip, his eyes wide with fear. "Actually, I . . . can't."

Cezar hissed, his fingers tightening. "Can't or won't?"

"Can't," the imp managed to choke out. "She's returned to Avalon. No one can locate the Isle of Mists."

A red haze briefly clouded Cezar's eyes at the thought of Anna alone and helpless in the hands of Morgana. *Dios*. His mate might possess the power of the ancients, but she had no control. And even worse, her heart was far too tender. She would never be a cold-blooded killer, and if she hesitated even a moment . . .

Easily sensing that he was descending into a rage that could lead to a massacre of every fey creature in the state of Illinois and beyond, Darcy squeezed his arm with a painful grip.

"Don't do this to yourself, Cezar," she said sternly. "We'll get her back."

It was a struggle to pull himself back from the edge. He wanted to be bathed in blood, to purge himself of the aching void in the center of his chest.

Only the self-discipline forged by centuries of being imprisoned by the Oracles allowed him to fight through his bloodlust and calm his mind.

In this moment Anna needed his cold logic, not his mad-
dened battle skills.

He would get her back.

There was no alternative.

Spinning on his heel, he began pacing the kitchen floor, his
fury replaced by an icy determination.

At some point he realized that the tiny room had become
crowded with his clan brothers and their mates, but he ignored their concerned glances and whispered discussions of
what must be done next.

He had to find a means of finding an isle that had been
hidden for over a millennium. And he had to do it within the
next few moments.

Simple.

He circled the crowded room half a dozen more times
before he realized that it *was simple*.

Dios. He'd been so stupid.

With a swift step he once again had Troy pinned to the
wall. Ignoring the imp's yelp of pain he narrowed his eyes
with lethal intent.

"I know how to find her, and you're going to help me."

Landing face-first on the marble floor, Anna decided that she
seriously disliked portals. It was a stupid, painful way to travel.
Not just the whole ending up on her face part. Or the being
dropped into a strange place that might be half a world away. Or
even the scent of burnt linoleum that clung to her clothes.

It was the electricity that danced over her skin as if she
were in the midst of a storm and she was the lightning rod.

Jeez. No matter what the benefits of being able to pop from
one place to another, it wasn't worth the sensation that she
was being fried in the process.

Swallowing her groan, Anna managed to press herself to
her knees to study her surroundings.

Her brows lifted at the vast room with its marble columns, the rich tapestries, the towering glass rotunda, and the golden throne set on a dais.

Avalon.

It had to be.

Only Morgana le Fay would choose a palace that looked like it had been snatched from the Hollywood set of *Aladdin* and top it off with a throne that was so outrageous that any self-respecting monarch would shudder in horror.

Fear blasted through her, even as she told herself this was for the best. This was one place that Cezar couldn't follow. There would be no danger of him being killed as he sought to save her from the deranged queen.

She could concentrate completely on dealing with her dearest aunt once and for all.

Then again, she was all alone, a small voice whispered in the back of her mind. Completely and utterly alone with a powerful queen who wanted her dead.

Nice.

With a sense of dread, she at last allowed her gaze to search out Morgana among the shadows. A part of her had been braced for an attack from the moment the woman had hauled her out of the kitchen. Hell, she hadn't been entirely certain that she would even live to see the other side of the damn portal.

Now, as her senses slowly cleared, she began to wonder why she wasn't dead.

The answer came as her gaze at last landed on Morgana.

The queen was leaning against one of the fluted columns, her hand pressed to her stomach and her pale features oddly ashen. Despite her unearthly beauty that would never fade, she looked nearly as bad as Anna felt, as if creating the portal had somehow drained her.

Strike now, she told herself.

Strike while she's vulnerable.

Her fingers clenched around the emerald, but her powers

refused to rise. Not only refused to rise, but there wasn't so much as a tingle.

What the hell?

Desperately she forced herself to remember the endless attempts on her life, the brutal murder of the woman she had thought was her aunt, the dangers to Cezar, the tortured ghost of her grandfather.

Nothing.

Dammit. Had the trip through the portal somehow stolen her powers? Was there something about Avalon that was interfering?

Or could it be . . .

Cursing beneath her breath, Anna realized that it simply wasn't in her to kill the woman while she was weak and vulnerable. It wasn't compassion. Or at least, not entirely. It was more an absolute certainty that to kill the woman when she was incapable of defending herself would damage something inside her.

Morgana le Fay might deserve to rot in hell, but unless she forced Anna to kill her, Anna's powers refused to violate her basic nature.

Of course, on the bright side, the odds of Morgana *not* trying to kill her were slim to none. The trick was obviously to provoke her into making that attempt before she regained her full powers.

Yeah . . . that seemed like a great plan.

At last sensing Anna's narrowed gaze, Morgana abruptly pushed herself from the column and cloaked her weakness behind a disdainful sneer.

"Well, sweet Anna, we're at last alone. No one can find this isle." Her smile widened. "There will be no vampires riding to your rescue this time."

Pretending an indifference that she was far from feeling, Anna cast a casual glance around the nauseatingly ornate room.

"So, this is Avalon?" She returned her attention to Morgana, swallowing her revulsion at the malevolent hatred that shimmered in her aunt's gaze. "Love what you've done to the place."

The older woman hissed at Anna's flippant tone. "You cannot hide your fear behind your pathetic attempt at humor. I can smell it on you."

Anna shrugged. "Yeah, well, I have enough sense to be a little uneasy at being trapped on a hidden island with a certifiable lunatic who wants me dead." She deliberately paused, suppressing the horrid sensation that she was toying with a caged tiger. "Or at least you keep *claiming* you want me dead. I'm beginning to wonder if you're all talk and no action."

The mist swirling outside the glass rotunda darkened, as if reacting to Morgana's rising fury. Still, the woman made no effort to call on her powers.

"Are you in such a hurry to taste of death?" the queen demanded.

"There's no use putting off the inevitable, is there?"

The emerald eyes narrowed in annoyance. "Actually, Anna Randal, my first thought was to allow my minions to put an end to you. You didn't seem particularly worthy of bothering with, but after you were stupid enough to kill so many of my poor fairies I decided that I wanted to hear you beg before you died."

"And that's why I'm here?" Anna waved a hand around her golden prison. "Because you want to hear me beg?"

"Of course."

"You're lying."

The words had barely left her lips when Anna found herself being launched into one of the marble columns. She cracked her head, and briefly saw stars, but fortunately her ribs were intact and there didn't seem to be an inordinate number of internal injuries.

A sure sign that Morgana was still weak.

"That is but a taste of what I can do to you, worm," she warned. "You still think that I'm lying?"

Anna tugged her sweatshirt back into place, refusing to rub the rising lump on the back of her head.

"Oh, it's true that you tried to have your fairies kill me and when that didn't work you tried to do it yourself, but failed." She shrugged. "Actually you failed more than once. And now that you know that I have the emerald, I think you're scared. You aren't sure that you're powerful enough to put me in my grave."

Anna's taunt was nothing more than a means to annoy the woman, but surprisingly Morgana's gaze briefly shifted toward the gem clutched in Anna's hand, an unmistakable flare of craving darkening her eyes.

She wanted the emerald.

She wanted it desperately.

So why didn't she just take it?

Swiftly hiding her reaction behind a grating laugh, Morgana offhandedly waved her hand.

"Did my brother convince you that a mere bauble would actually harm me? How pathetically naïve you are," she mocked. "Did he happen to mention that he was wearing the emerald when he died? That the reason he had it in his possession is because he was buried with it?"

Anna narrowed her gaze. "If it's so worthless then why did you almost have a seizure when you saw it?" she demanded, instinct urging her to take a step forward with her hand outstretched. Astonishingly, Morgana shifted backward. The queen might long to possess the emerald, but for some reason she was frightened by it. "And why do you back away from it now?"

"It's revolting. The magic it holds is tainted."

Anna studied the magnificent jewel. "It doesn't feel tainted."

"And what would you know of ancient magic?" Morgana hissed, regaining her composure. "You are nothing more than a child who has foolishly convinced yourself that a bit of residual blood gives you true power."

Anna gave a short, humorless laugh. "Well, it's certainly true that I'm much younger than you, although I haven't considered myself a child for a number of years. Not since you murdered the woman I believed to be my aunt and forced me to live alone in the shadows."

Morgana frowned, as if surprised that Anna would even recall such a trivial event.

"That woman was nothing more than a pawn who was barely civil to you. You can't have mourned her loss."

"The two of you were the only relatives that I knew existed and, unlike you, I actually believe that means something," Anna gritted. "Especially now that I understand what it means to be a part of a family."

"You consider a clan of the walking dead as your family?" Morgana made a sound of disgust. "You are truly pathetic."

Without warning, Anna felt a surge of warmth flood her heart. It wasn't the strange heat of her elemental power, but it was power nonetheless. The power that Cezar had given to her when he had claimed her as his mate.

She would never again be alone.

Not even on this isolated isle. Cezar and his clan were with her.

And that knowledge gave her far more strength than any gem or ancient power.

Chapter 22

Tilting her chin, Anna wrapped herself in the unwavering comfort of Cezar's bond. This golden palace with the swirling mist and priceless works of art might be impressive, but it was nothing more than a cold, empty prison. Just as all the countless homes that Anna had inhabited over the centuries had been hallow shells.

Did Morgana realize her loss? Had she ever felt true emotions?

"You know, Morgana, as much as I might hate you and what you've done, I still pity you."

"Pity me?" Without warning, Morgana was moving forward, striking Anna across the face with enough force to split her lip. Obviously being pitied was more infuriating than being insulted. Go figure. "I have more than you could ever dream possible."

"You have nothing," Anna denied, determined to press the woman's temper. A fine notion, supposing her powers decided to make a timely return. If not . . . well, she was shit out of luck. "You have no one who loves you, no one who cares. You're completely alone and there's not a creature on this earth who would mourn if you died. Actually, I don't doubt that there would be a celebration on your grave. That's . . . just sad."

The next blow sent Anna to her knees. "Shut up," Morgana hissed.

Pain ricocheted through Anna's head, but along with it came the first stirring in her blood. Thank merciful heaven. She wasn't doomed to fighting the magical queen with nothing more than a chunk of emerald and her bare hands.

Sheer relief allowed her to climb to her feet.

Still, she didn't instantly strike out. The power was faint and elusive, as if stupidly hoping that it wouldn't need to be used.

Or perhaps it was her own conscience that was stupidly hoping.

In either case it was . . . yeah, stupid.

"It isn't too late, you know," she grudgingly muttered, wiping the blood from her lips. She had no idea if she was capable of besting Morgana even with her powers at full force, but her sense of fair play demanded that she at least try to convince the woman to avoid a bloody, lethal smack down.

"Too late?" Morgana sneered, her hand lifting to encircle Anna in bands of punishing air.

Anna groaned in pain, but refused to back down. "I assume that you're capable of changing if you really want to."

Morgana laughed in genuine amusement. "You mean that I could become a loving, benevolent queen who adores her subjects?"

The bands continued to slowly tighten, threatening to cut off Anna's air supply. Not to mention hurting like a bitch. "Something like that," she rasped.

Confident that she had Anna at her mercy, Morgana stepped forward and grasped her chin in a punishing grip. "And I suppose that would also include not killing you?"

"That would be first on the list," Anna rasped, her powers starting to pump full force as a blackness began to swirl through her oxygen-deprived mind. The choking bands wouldn't kill her, but they would make her pass out for a time.

Morgana narrowed her eyes. "Fool."

"No, simply a woman who understands that after two centuries of merely surviving, life is worth nothing without love in it. You might someday rule the world, but you will still be miserable."

The magnificent green eyes flashed, as if overwhelmed by the need to shut up Anna's soft words.

"Life is about power," she gritted, using her grip on Anna's face to bang her head into the column. "Who has it . . ." Bang, bang, bang. "Who doesn't."

Anna couldn't halt her cry of agony as her skull began to crack beneath the relentless pounding. She had to stop this. Now.

Unconsciously grasping the emerald tight in her hand, she forced her poor, abused mind to concentrate on the heat that bubbled in her blood.

For once the energy didn't just burst out of her in an uncontrollable flood. In fact, it didn't go anywhere. Instead, she felt herself sink into the golden waves that flowed through her body, like beautiful ribbons that sparkled with a brilliant glow.

Since the powers had first started to manifest themselves, she had hated them. No . . . she'd feared them. They marked her as even more different. Even more apart from the rest of the world.

Now she realized that the magic was a gift. It wasn't evil, just as it wasn't good. It just . . . was. An elemental force that was formed and directed by her own heart.

And it was that acceptance that offered her the control that had been so elusive.

Allowing the heat to pour upward, she focused on the bands that held her with a ruthless grip. In her mind she could picture them, as hard and thick as steel. They would be impossible to break with brute force, so instead she imagined her powers seeping deep inside them, the heat melting them until they became pliable.

Releasing her powers, she clenched her hands as Morgana continued with her assault, her blows becoming even more vicious as she sensed Anna's attempt to escape.

"No," Morgana hissed. "This time you die."

Anna gritted her teeth, battling the pain even as she sensed the bonds beginning to loosen.

"You're too weak to kill me, Morgana," she warned. "Stop this before I'm forced to hurt you."

"Hurt *me?*" Morgana gave a wild scream, her hand crushing the bones of Anna's chin. "I am a queen, a goddess. My powers are without end. You are nothing more than an abomination."

Not so many years ago, Anna might have agreed with her psycho aunt. She had felt like an abomination. But not anymore.

Now she realized that she was something special, something unique. Something worthy of being loved.

And that was everything.

"I'm Anna Randal, a woman who is intelligent, capable, and a damn fine lawyer," she said proudly, feeling the bonds slowly, but surely, loosening beneath her steady flow of energy. "I'm mate to Conde Cezar and distant granddaughter of King Arthur. And just as importantly, I'm the woman who is destined to kick your ass."

"Why you vain little bitch, I will . . ."

Sensing the bonds were fragile, Anna ignored Morgana's furious tirade, concentrating on one last surge of power. Her heart gave a leap of shock as she felt them shatter and fall away.

Before Morgana could react, Anna lifted her hand, grasping Morgana's wrist and with one fierce motion twisted it away from her face. The wrenching pain nearly sent her to her knees, but she refused to so much as blink as she glared into the murderous green eyes.

"Stop this now, Morgana," she said, her voice astonishingly

steady, although the words were slurred from her injured chin. "I won't tell you again."

Something that might have been genuine fear briefly flared through Morgana's gaze before she jerked her arm free and tossed her long mane of crimson hair. "You think I'm frightened just because my brother taught you a few tricks? It won't save you."

Anna smiled, not bothering to correct the impression that Arthur had taught her to use her powers. It was much better for Morgana to believe she had gained some training than to admit she was still fumbling and bumbling her way through it all.

"Actually, those tricks seem to be doing a fine job of saving me," she retorted, her hand lifting to touch her aching chin. It was healing, but that didn't mean that it didn't hurt. A lot. "And if you don't back off they're going to do a fine job of killing you."

Morgana's lips twisted, her hands pointed toward Anna as her hair floated in the rising breeze.

"Die."

Anna gasped and then braced herself against the sharp pellets of air that threatened to skewer her. Damn, she didn't know that you could turn air into bullets.

Not the most pleasant of surprises.

Jerking as a particularly vicious shard sliced open the skin of her stomach, Anna instinctively lifted the emerald that had begun to glow with a shimmering green light.

It was time for the gem to do what it was supposed to do.

Whatever the hell that was.

Still being peppered with the painful daggers of air, she ignored the urge to cower behind one of the marble columns and instead concentrated on the glow spreading from the gem. Surely Arthur wouldn't have called her to his grave to give her this if it didn't have some effect on Morgana?

For a time it did nothing but swirl about her. Pretty enough, but not exactly what she was hoping for. It was only when she was completely cloaked in the strange green flame that it stopped its swirling and thickened. Thickened enough that the agonizing attack was brought to an end.

Sucking in a deep breath, Anna leaned wearily against the column and studied the green glow. Through the flaming haze she could see Morgana, her arms outstretched as if she were still using her powers, but nothing passed through the fire.

In fact . . . narrowing her gaze, she reached out with her senses.

It was more than deflecting the powerful blows, she realized, although she didn't know how. It was absorbing them.

Okay. This was a good thing. A really, really good thing.

Unfortunately, she didn't really know how to use the weapon beyond protecting herself.

Straightening from the column, she took a cautious step forward. The glow followed her, keeping her protected even as Morgana screamed in fury and hurled what looked to be a fireball directly at her.

She took another step and another, ignoring Morgana's shrieks and even the distant knowledge that the palace was beginning to shake with the force of the queen's power. Overhead the glass dome shattered, littering the room with deadly shards, but neither woman took her eyes off the other as the lethal battle of wills persisted without pause.

Lost in her anger, it took Morgana some time to at last realize that her desperate strikes weren't harming Anna. It wasn't until Anna was standing almost directly in front of her that she dropped her hands and took a step backward.

Or at least she *attempted* to take a step backward.

The green eyes widened as she was snapped forward, presumably by the force of the emerald.

"What are you doing?" the queen demanded, an unmistakable fear threaded through her voice. "Stop this."

Anna managed a wry smile through her lingering pain. "You want me to stop so you can kill me?"

"I will kill you either way, but it's up to you whether it's fast or painfully slow."

The brave words echoed through the crumbling chamber, but they rang empty as Morgana was jerked closer to the pulsing emerald glow.

Anna's eyes widened as she realized that the emerald had gone from absorbing Morgana's power to actually trying to absorb the woman behind the powers.

Was that possible?

Even in the wacky world of demons it seemed . . . bizarre.

Not at all sure what was coming next, Anna took a step back, needing a moment to consider the implications. It was a moment that was to be denied her as Morgana gave a low cry and tried to grab a nearby column as she skidded across the marble floor in Anna's wake.

Holy crap.

Anna glanced down at the emerald that had started to pulse in her hand, the green glow darkening and spreading as if it scented its prey.

And that prey was Morgana le Fay.

Coming to a sharp halt, Anna could do nothing but watch as Morgana was hauled ever closer to the strange flames that surrounded her.

"No," Morgana rasped, arching her back as if she could somehow avoid the encroaching shimmer. "What do you want? Gold? Power? To sit at my side and rule?"

Now she wanted to bargain?

Anna gave a sad shake of her head. She didn't know what the hell was going on with the emerald, but whatever it was, it was now out of her control.

"I told you what I wanted, but you refused to listen," she muttered, her stomach twisting with a strange sense of resignation. "You just had to keep pushing me until it came to this."

"Fine, I'll push you no more," the woman promised with more desperation than sincerity. "You set me free and I will never trouble you again."

Anna rolled her eyes. For God's sake, did the woman think she was completely brain-dead? Even assuming she could set Morgana free, she knew beyond a shadow of a doubt that her homicidal aunt would strike without blinking an eye.

A promise from the Queen of Fairies wasn't actually something she could take to the bank.

Gritting her teeth, she tried to ignore the steady pulse of the gem. Ugh. It felt as if . . . as if Morgana's very essence was being absorbed into the stone.

Damn.

Her grandfather had promised the stone would help direct her powers. He hadn't said anything about sucking Morgana into it.

Obviously the emerald's power came something as a surprise to Morgana as well. Her expression was contorted as she wrapped her arms around herself, once again calling on her powers as if they might save her from the inevitable.

"Damn you, Anna Randal," she screeched, her eyes glittering with a feral hatred. "You can't best me. It isn't possible. I'm your queen."

"You're not my queen," Anna muttered, resisting the urge to close her eyes. If she had to be the one responsible for killing Morgana le Fay, then by God, she would have to be the one to witness the tragedy. "Never my queen."

"You're wrong," Morgana hissed. "I'm destined to rule the world."

Anna grimaced as the green glow crawled relentlessly up Morgana's arms and the overly proud woman fell to her knees. Around her the room continued to shake beneath Morgana's power, pieces of marble and gold flying through the air.

"Yeah, not so much," she breathed.

A disturbing cry was wrenched from Morgana's lips as she became consumed in the green fire.

"Modron. Where is my seer?" Morgana wailed, giving a confused shake of her head. "I need her. I need . . ."

A wave of regret crashed through Anna as Morgana was completely swallowed by the power of the emerald. It wasn't that she didn't accept that this was the only possible choice. Morgana le Fay was not only determined to kill her, but she was a megalomaniac who wouldn't be satisfied until she had the entire world bowing at her feet. But, that didn't mean Anna could take pleasure in her horrid punishment.

The flickering flames were beginning to thicken, obscuring the kneeling woman in a thick cloak of green.

For a moment the awful wailing continued, then there was an explosion of green fire and Anna screamed as she was thrown across the vast room and crashed into the golden throne.

The various demons and others who crowded into the cramped kitchen froze in wary unease as Cezar hauled Troy against the wall. No doubt they expected him to rip out the throat of the imp who had, after all, taken him hostage. Cezar, however, was not nearly as furious with Troy as he was with himself.

How the hell had he forgotten for even a moment that he had given his ring to Anna for her to wear around her throat? *Dios*, he must be losing his mind. The ancient ring might not claim the same magic as her emerald, but it possessed the one thing he needed to find her.

He ignored their questioning glances as he glared into the imp's wide eyes. "You're going to take me to Anna," he growled.

Troy swallowed the lump in his throat. "I told you it's not possible."

"Can you make a portal or not?"

"Of course I can make a portal. I am fey."

"Then do it."

Troy rolled his eyes. "I have to know where I'm going and no one, *no one*, knows where Avalon is located. Only Morgana can create a portal there."

Cezar couldn't allow the thought of Anna alone on the isle with Morgana to enter his mind. He was too close to the edge. Suddenly Styx was at his side, his hand landing on Cezar's shoulder to keep him steady.

"You can use a person to anchor your portal," he said to Troy, his voice edged with his barely contained fury.

"I may be the Prince of Imps, but I don't have the sort of power to latch on to a woman I've met on two occasions, through the protective mists that surround the isle," Troy retorted, his expression hardening with impatience. "It's like randomly dialing numbers on the telephone in the hope you hit the person you want to talk to. I don't have enough of her essence to call her to my mind."

"You won't have to. You can dial my number."

Troy blinked, and then blinked again. "Forgive me, Conde, but I don't think it's going to be a lot of help if I make a portal leading to you."

"No." Cezar gave the imp a small shake. It was that or choke him. "Anna is not only my mate, but she was wearing my ring. A ring that has been an intimate part of me for the past five centuries. You search for an echo of me and you will find her."

A silence filled the room as Troy considered his words. "I suppose it might work," he at last conceded.

"It will work," Cezar said grimly, not willing to allow any doubt that he would soon have Anna in his arms. "Now do it."

Troy frowned, a hint of reluctance flashing through his eyes. "Before I do this, I want your promise that you will protect me from the queen. Morgana's not particularly happy with me right now and . . ."

Cezar growled low in his throat. "Troy, you test my patience."

"Fine," Troy huffed. "Release me and I'll make your damn portal."

Stepping back, Cezar kept a close watch on the imp as he smoothed his long mane of crimson hair before moving to the small clearing in the center of the kitchen. At Cezar's side, Styx snorted in disgust as Troy held out his slender hands, waving them in a fluttering motion, as if searching for the best location for his portal. Like one spot on the cracked, filthy linoleum was better than another.

Ridiculous poof.

Impatiently awaiting the portal to appear, Cezar was caught off-guard when Troy abruptly reached back and grasped his wrist in a tight grip.

"Careful, imp," he hissed.

"The more strongly I have the sense of you, the easier it will be to locate Anna," Troy retorted, his eyes trained straight ahead. "Besides, a vampire can't travel through a magical source unless he is connected to a fey. You're nothing more than a passenger on this ride."

Styx abruptly moved to Cezar's side, growling deep in his throat. "Cezar, take care. I do not trust this fey. It could be a trap."

"Don't worry, Styx." With a swift movement he turned his hand, taking command of the imp's grip with a painful squeeze. "Troy knows what will happen if he disappoints me."

Giving a squawk of pain, Troy glared at Cezar over his shoulder. "I really, really hate vampires."

"Not as much as you're going to if you fail me," Cezar warned.

Muttering under his breath, Troy lifted his free hand and the shimmer of a portal began to form. Instinctively the vampires backed away, their distaste for magic clearly etched on their faces.

Cezar didn't so much as flinch. It was going to take a hell of a lot more than magic to keep him away from Anna.

Coiled and prepared to strike, Cezar waited as Troy closed his eyes and did whatever it was the fey did to reach out and sense others. His muscles were trembling by the time Troy sucked in a sharp breath and stiffened in fear.

"Damn my luck," he muttered. "I found her."

Cezar didn't allow himself to feel relief. Not yet. Not until Anna was away from Avalon and Morgana was dead. "Let's go."

Troy hesitated for a heartbeat before he muttered another foul curse and stepped into the portal, dragging Cezar in his wake.

In the blink of an eye the kitchen dissolved, to be replaced by an impenetrable blackness. He'd heard that most portal travelers saw flashing lights and experienced electrical charges that pulsed over their skin but as a vampire he could sense nothing. That didn't mean he enjoyed the trip. Actually he'd rather have his fangs pulled than plunge himself in the middle of so much magic.

Keeping a crushing grip on Troy, Cezar closed his mind to the disturbing mode of transportation and instead concentrated on his bond with Anna. *Soon*, he soothed his ravaged nerves. Soon he would be at her side and he would destroy anyone or anything that was trying to harm her.

In the end it was soon, although it seemed like an eternity. Troy led him out of the portal and into a vast, marble room that was in the process of falling in on their heads.

"Shit," Troy breathed as he was hit by a flying piece of marble. "This doesn't look right."

Cezar ignored the debris that battered his body, his senses leaping with stark relief at the unmistakable sense of Anna.

"She's here." He swiftly scanned the room, seeking his mate among the piles of rubble. *"Anna!"* he shouted, moving forward without concern for the dangers that might be hidden. He would deal with anything that sought to keep him from his woman.

"Damn, it looks like World War Three just arrived," Troy

muttered, grimacing at the layer of powdered marble that was coating his spandex pants. He cowardly remained close to the portal he had left open for a quick escape. "Where's Morgana?"

Ignoring the pest, Cezar stiffened in fear as he caught sight of the slender body lying in a broken heap near the ornate throne.

"Anna," he rasped, flowing swiftly to her side and bending next to her. With exquisite care he gathered her off the floor and held her tightly cradled against his chest. His heart twisted with pain. She was alive, but she was gravely wounded.

Clearly sensing his presence, Anna struggled to lift her lashes and regarded him in dazed confusion.

"Cezar? Is that really you?" she whispered.

He bent his head to press his lips to her forehead. "*Si*. It's really me," he assured her softly, a sharp fear piercing his heart as he felt her violent tremble. Damn, she must be convulsing. Pulling back, he regarded her with a concern that rapidly shifted to disbelief. *Dios*. Was she laughing? "What's so funny?" he demanded.

Her smile lingered despite the tears that were streaming down her filthy face. "I saw the portal and I thought . . ."

"What? What did you think?"

"'Beam me up, Scotty.'"

Chapter 23

Anna was vaguely aware of Cezar holding her tight as he spoke in a low, rough voice to someone else in the room. His touch seeped into her aching body, easing the agonizing pain that still wracked her. Even more, it battled back the lingering memory of Morgana's screams that continued to echo in her ears.

But the weakness that she had ignored for too long held her in its grip and, snuggling against Cezar's welcome strength, she allowed herself to sink into her weariness, trusting that Cezar would keep her safe.

It was done. Over.

Surely she had earned a few minutes of rest?

She stirred briefly as she felt the unpleasant prickles of a portal surround her. It was hard to ignore the sensation of lightning dancing over her skin. But still held tightly in Cezar's arms, she didn't attempt to fight the clinging darkness.

There was something waiting for her there.

She had sensed the presence from the moment the explosion had consumed Morgana and tossed her across the room. It had whispered in the back of her mind, although it seemed to realize she couldn't respond so long as she was alone and defenseless in Avalon.

Now that Cezar was carrying her to safety, however, the voice became more insistent, pulling her deeper and deeper into the dark void.

Trusting completely in her mate's ability to fight off any danger, Anna allowed herself to be swept through the strange swirl of black mist, not at all surprised when she found herself standing in the ruined castle on the cliff. Her family seemed to have missed that whole concept of picking up a telephone and politely inviting someone to visit. They seemed to prefer the snatching-a-person-from-wherever-they-might-be-and-forcing-them-to-appear route.

As before, she could hear the crash of waves from below and smell the faint hint of sage that filled the motionless air. Reaching out, Anna allowed her hand to touch the nearest wall, her fingertips registering the rough dampness of the ancient stone.

It was so astonishingly real.

With a shake of her head, Anna slowly turned, her heart clenching with bittersweet happiness at the sight of the large wolf stepping through the arched doorway. Okay, maybe she was pathetic to find pleasure in visiting with her long dead grandfather. But by God, she'd spent two hundred years desperately alone. She was going to enjoy her time with Arthur, ghost or not.

Well, she was going to enjoy her time with Arthur just as soon as she got a few answers, she decided, as the strange mist swirled about the wolf and it shifted to the form of a large man in heavy armor.

It was impossible to determine his features, but in her mind she sensed the strong, craggy face and green eyes that held a mixture of fondness and ancient regret.

"Anna," he intoned with a formal dip of his head that held an unspoken respect.

Lifting her chin, Anna extended her hand that held the glowing emerald.

"Tell me what I've done," she demanded without preamble.

She sensed his bewilderment. "Done?"

"Is Morgana dead?"

The mist stirred, the air suddenly cold enough to make Anna shiver.

"No, she is very much alive."

Anna grimaced. Deep in her heart that was precisely what she had feared.

"My God." She barely resisted the urge to toss the emerald on the dirt floor. "Then she's trapped in there?"

"Her spirit is now contained within the gem."

Anna didn't miss the dark satisfaction in his voice. Obviously Arthur wasn't quite as queasy as she was at the thought of trapping a living being in a chunk of stone.

Of course, he'd had a lot of centuries to wait for this day. That might warp anyone's sense of compassion.

"Is she in pain?" Anna demanded.

There was an impression of an indifferent shrug. "Only the pain of her frustration. In spirit form she has no mortal discomforts."

"Can she escape?"

"Only if you decide to release her."

Jeez. Like she didn't feel bad enough. Now she had to live with the knowledge that every day that passed she was responsible for holding the woman captive.

"Great," she muttered.

"You would prefer that Morgana was dead?"

"I don't know." Anna gave a restless shrug. "It just seems such an awful fate."

"It is a fate far more kind than that Morgana le Fay offered to her many victims," Arthur growled. "She was fortunate that it was you who was destined to be her final judge."

Anna shuddered as she remembered Morgana's shrieks as she was pulled into the power of the emerald. The woman probably didn't consider herself rolling in good fortune.

At the moment, however, there didn't seem much purpose

in debating the matter, and instead Anna turned her thoughts to the question that had nagged at her since her confrontation with Morgana.

"Why me?" she demanded.

"I may be old by most standards, Anna, but not even I can explain the fickleness of fate."

She made an impatient sound. "No, I mean, why didn't *you* use the emerald all those years ago? You could have saved . . ."

Her words broke off at the flare of pain that raced through her at the thought of her family being senselessly slaughtered. How different it would have been if Morgana had been locked away and unable to destroy those who might have loved her.

The mist darkened and the sensation of ancient grief rolled over her.

"I mourn their loss as much as you, perhaps even more," Arthur said, his voice low and raw with pain. "I felt each death as it occurred, like a dagger through my heart. It is a burden I must carry."

Anna blinked back the hot tears that filled her eyes. "Then why?" she breathed. "Why didn't you destroy her?"

The mist moved forward, bringing with it the sensation of calloused fingers closing around her hand that held the emerald.

"I was not as strong as you, Anna."

She frowned at the whispered words. Even in mist form she could sense the stunning energy that swirled through Arthur.

"I don't believe that."

"I do not speak of my powers. They were considerable." She sensed him give a rueful shake of his head. "Perhaps too considerable, since in my arrogance I began to believe I was beyond harm, despite Morgana's endless treachery. But my heart was filled with anger. When I attempted to use the emerald it was out of my burning need for revenge, not justice. Too late I have realized that it was your refusal to allow anger or bitterness to rule your heart that allowed you to gain mastery over the stone."

Anna slowly considered his confession. A part of her couldn't deny a sense of relief that this man hadn't willingly allowed their family to be destroyed, while another regretted the fate that had forced her into confronting the evil woman.

At last she heaved a rueful sigh. She'd done what had to be done.

Nothing could change that.

"What am I supposed to do with the emerald now?" she demanded.

"I will hold it for safekeeping."

She lifted her brows. She wasn't sure she wanted to know what devious games this man intended to play with his sister.

"Is that wise?"

He gave a shake of his head. "I am at last at peace, Anna. I have no need to seek further revenge. And in truth I believe it will be best if the fey world realizes that the emerald is beyond their reach." She could sense his deep concern. "They are capricious and unpredictable, but they could be dangerous if they believed the vampires were holding their queen captive."

Anna couldn't argue his logic. If she were the one holding the emerald, the fairies might very well presume that her bond with Cezar would mean that their queen was at the mercy of the vampires. The last thing she wanted was some sort of demon war.

Besides, she was freaking sick and tired of being ambushed by one creature after another.

Releasing her hold on the stone, she allowed the spirit to take the emerald from her hand. There was a brief flutter of the mist and the emerald, along with Morgana, disappeared.

Anna breathed a renegade sigh of relief.

She wouldn't be sorry if she never had to see that damn emerald again.

Cowardly, but true.

"Those fairies wouldn't be so eager to rescue her if they knew the truth," she said, recalling the fairies that had filled the farmhouse. "They don't know that Morgana was responsible for your death."

"No." The mist darkened, a haunting sadness filling the ruined castle. "Someday the story will be told, but not now."

Anna slowly nodded. She had hoped that she would discover the truth of her grandfather's past, but she understood that there were some things too painful to speak out loud, as if the words themselves could rip open scars best left undisturbed.

"I . . ." Her words of comfort were cut off as the image of Cezar's anxious face seared through her mind, a near painful compulsion to reach out to him clenching her heart.

"Anna, what is it?"

"It's Cezar. I must go."

"You are so eager to return to your vampire?" her grandfather's spirit demanded.

She lifted a hand to rub her aching head. "He's upset."

A soft laugh filled the air. "There might have been a day when I would have been angered at the thought of my granddaughter mating with a vampire, but now I feel nothing but relief he will always be near to protect you."

Anna dropped her hand to regard him with a warning frown. "I'm not bad at protecting myself, thank you very much."

"My beloved Anna." The misty fingers trailed over her cheek in a fond caress. "You are so much more than I ever dreamed possible."

She felt a sudden twinge of fear. There was something in the smoky voice that sounded very much like good-bye.

"Will we ever speak again?"

He paused, almost as if listening to a voice only he could hear.

"Once your fate has been decided," he at last said. "Until then I am not allowed to interfere."

"Oh, no." Anna gave a sharp shake of her head. "I'm done with fate. All I want is a nice, peaceful life with the vampire I love."

"I fear that destiny is not yet finished with you," he warned in a rueful voice. "Now go to your vampire. I'm not of this world and even I can hear his anguish."

Anna felt herself beginning to fade from the castle and, with a wistful smile, she watched as her grandfather shifted back to the shape of a wolf.

She didn't care what destiny might want from her.

She'd done her duty and she intended to reap her rewards.

In the arms of her vampire.

Cezar kneeled beside the large bed in Styx's mansion with his hands threaded through Anna's lush hair. At his side, Levet studied the unconscious woman, his delicate wings twitching with unease as he attempted to inch away from the frigid waves of desperation that were pouring off Cezar.

Smart gargoyle.

His inability to rouse Anna had pressed his temper to a lethal edge and he was itching to kill something or someone to ease his frustration. Unfortunately, for the moment he needed the gargoyle's ability to sense magic. Which meant he could do nothing more than glare at the creature with an icy fury.

"Well?" he snarled, making Levet jump with a nervous squeak.

The gargoyle cleared his throat and struggled to find his voice. "She seems . . . healthy enough."

Cezar muttered a foul curse, his hand running a tender path down Anna's cheek, lingering on the healing wounds that marred her perfect skin. He could tell she was healthy. She wouldn't be healing with such speed if she weren't.

What he needed to know was why she wouldn't wake despite being far away from the crumbling Avalon.

"Then why is she still unconscious?" he gritted. "Is it magic? Did Morgana put a spell on her?"

Levet wrinkled his snout, the gray eyes troubled. "There is something that feels fey, but the scent is . . ."

Cezar hissed at the gargoyle's uncertainty. "Curse your hide, the scent is what?"

"Sage."

"What does that mean?"

"I truly don't know."

"Then who would?" he snapped, furious that he had wasted his time with the impotent demon.

Wisely taking several steps from the furious vampire, Levet was still struggling for an answer when Anna abruptly stirred beneath Cezar's fingers.

"Cezar?" she murmured softly.

A savage relief jolted through him as he lowered his head and touched his lips to the pulse beating at her temple.

"Anna," he husked, allowing the scent of honeyed figs to sink deep inside him. "Anna, what is it?"

She forced open her heavy lashes to reveal a rueful amusement glittering in the hazel eyes.

"Leave poor Levet alone."

There was the sound of flapping wings, and then without warning, Levet landed in the middle of the bed, a smug expression on his ugly face.

"Oui." He reached out a stunted arm to pat Anna on top of her head, blowing a raspberry in Cezar's direction. "Leave poor Levet alone."

"Don't press your luck, gargoyle," Cezar growled, never taking his gaze from Anna's pale face. *Dios.* He would happily kneel here for an eternity just to be near this woman.

"Ha. You are the one pressing your luck, vampire," Levet retorted, his courage miraculously returning now that he was hovering behind Anna. "You should have seen him, Anna. There I was sitting in the kitchen, enjoying a delectable roasted pig, a pig I might add that I was forced to hunt and kill all on my own, not to mention roast, and then this demented vampire comes charging in, demanding that I drop everything to . . ." His words broke off as the lamps in the room began to glow and then flicker before the bulbs burst in a shower of glass. With remarkable speed the gargoyle was flying toward the door. "Fine, I'm going, I'm going."

Waiting until the door slammed shut behind the fleeing demon, Cezar regarded his mate with a stern expression. "Don't you dare smile, Anna Randal. Someday I'm going to do the world a favor and have that pest stuffed and mounted."

Her hand lifted to run her fingers through his hair, the simple caress enough to send a blaze of heat through his body. Of course, just the thought of Anna was enough to send a blaze of heat through his body.

He'd been blazing for her for two centuries.

"I don't believe you for a minute, Conde Cezar," she said, her voice low and filled with an unmistakable invitation. "I think you have a lot more bark than bite."

His fangs lengthened, his erection so hard that he was relieved he was wearing nothing more than a pair of silk boxers.

"Dios," he groaned, "don't say such things."

Pressing herself higher on the pillows, Anna allowed a wicked smile to curve her lips.

"Why not?"

His gaze instinctively lowered to drink in the beauty of her breasts, barely covered by the lacy white bra. When he'd taken off the sweatshirt and jeans earlier it had merely been to make her more comfortable. Now he silently applauded his decision for an entirely different reason.

"Because it makes me desire to do things that you are in no condition to enjoy."

Her fingers tightened in his hair, relentlessly pulling him forward. "I think I should be allowed to decide what I do or don't want to enjoy," she husked.

"Anna," Cezar protested, even as he readily allowed himself to be pulled onto the bed beside her.

The hazel eyes darkened, revealing a vulnerability that revved his protective instincts into overdrive.

"Just hold me, Cezar," she said softly. "Hold me close."

With a swift motion he had her wrapped in his arms, her head tucked beneath his chin.

"Always." He buried his face in the satin of her honey hair, reveling in her heat as it soaked into his chilled body. "Ah, *querida*, I have felt more terror in the past few hours than I felt in the past five centuries combined. You are turning me into a very old vampire."

She burrowed even closer, her hands smoothing over his chest in a comforting motion.

"No more. Morgana is gone."

"Bueno," he growled with relish. "I regret you were the one forced to kill the evil bitch, but I'm not sorry she's dead."

"She's not dead. At least, not exactly."

Cezar stiffened, his brows snapping together at the mere thought that Morgana might still be plotting to harm his mate.

"Not exactly?"

With obvious reluctance, Anna revealed what had occurred after being pulled into the portal with Morgana. Cezar didn't need to be a vampire to know that she was deliberately skimming over the more terrifying details and downplaying her own role in capturing one of the most powerful women in the demon world.

Now didn't seem the best time, however, to press her for details. Not when she was still battered and bruised from her battle. Instead he ran a comforting hand down her back as his lips touched the tender skin of her temple.

"So her spirit is trapped in the emerald that is now being held by Arthur?" he murmured, unable to disguise his dark satisfaction. The thought of Morgana being trapped for an eternity was even better than a swift death.

"Yes."

"A fitting end."

Anna shuddered. "I suppose."

Shifting on the bed, Cezar put a finger beneath her chin and tilted her head up to meet his fierce gaze.

"Don't feel sympathy for the woman," he commanded. He wasn't about to allow Anna to drown in a guilt that she hadn't earned. "She would have happily slaughtered us all."

"I know." She grimaced. "I still wish . . ."

"What?"

"That it could have been different." She gave a restless shrug. "That *she* had been different. I've longed for a family for so many years and now when I finally find them they are either a raving lunatic or a ghost. Talk about dysfunctional."

A slow smile curved Cezar's lips. Despite the faint sadness in her voice, he sensed that she was beginning to make peace with her past.

"You're wrong, *querida*."

Her brows lifted. "I am?"

With a fluid movement, Cezar turned onto his back, tugging her warm, delicious body on top of him.

"Your family is a mate who will love you for all eternity; a vampire clan who will protect you with their very lives; a werewolf, a Shalott, and a goddess who adore you; and a very annoying gargoyle," he murmured as he buried his face in the curve of her neck.

With a soft chuckle she shed the lingering regrets and regarded him with a wicked smile that made his hard body jerk in response.

"Now that *is* dysfunctional," she murmured, straddling his aching erection as she bent down to brush her lips over his. "And wonderful. So very wonderful."

The groan was wrenched from his throat as Cezar tried to think past the raw surge of need. "*Querida*, as much as I'm enjoying the feel of you in my arms, I beg you to hold still," he rasped. "I may be a vampire, but merely having you near is enough to shatter any restraint I might possess. I've hungered for you for too long."

Her mouth wreaked havoc as it traveled the line of his jaw, pausing to give his chin a sharp nip. Cezar muttered a curse as his body jerked and threatened to go up in flames.

"Who said I wanted you to be restrained?" she husked.

His fingers gripped her hips, a pained moan rumbling in his throat.

"Anna, you need to rest."

His words of sanity were stolen as Anna gave a low growl and covered his lips with a kiss that sent jagged bolts of lightning through his body.

"What I need is you, Conde Cezar," she muttered against his mouth, rocking her hips forward. "Just you."

Cezar grimly held on to the last strand of sanity. "You've been injured . . ."

The strand snapped as she trailed her tongue down the curve of his neck, sprinkling hot, mind-numbing kisses over his chest. *Dios*. Vampires might possess the sort of self control that others might envy, but not even they were a match for a determined mate.

Especially not a mate bent on seduction.

The fingers that had been attempting to halt the sweet movements of her hips now trailed up the creamy skin of her back, swiftly dealing with the clasp of her bra, tugging the lacy garment away.

She shivered at his light touch, but she never faltered in her determined attack on his senses. Using her tongue and teeth she nibbled toward a hardened nipple, lavishing it with loving care before moving to the other and offering the same exquisite attention.

Cezar's teeth clenched as his body bowed in sharp, brutal need.

"Ah . . . *querida*," he groaned, drowning in her honeyed scent and the feel of her tongue as it trailed a searing path along the edge of his boxers. So close. So agonizingly close. "Your touch is magic."

She chuckled as she nibbled the tip of him through the fine silk of his boxers. Cezar gave a low shout, his hands dropping from her body to grab at the cover beneath him. He was terrified he would bruise her tender skin.

Enjoying her power over him way too much, Anna took her time as she slid the boxers down his body. Even then she remained kneeling above him, drinking in the sight of his hard, straining erection with a smile teasing at her lips.

"Oh, you haven't seen anything yet."

Cezar's hands lifted. He was going to yank her downward and put an end to his torment. He needed to be inside her. Deep inside. But before he could do more than grasp her waist she was bending downward and . . . blessed saints, she was taking him into her mouth.

His eyes slid shut as his ragged moan filled the air.

Who knew that torture could feel so damn good?

Chapter 24

Over the next three days, Anna discovered the true pleasure of being a vampire's mate. Never in her long existence had she been so pampered, so loved, so happy.

And it was more than just Cezar's tender attentions, although they were enough to fill the heart of the most demanding woman. What female in her right mind wouldn't adore having a mouthwatering, drop-dead gorgeous man indulging her every whim? It was the stuff of fantasy.

But there were also days spent shopping with Abby and Shay and Darcy, along with evenings surrounded by Viper's clan, who readily treated her as one of their own.

This is what it was to have a family.

It was . . . astonishing.

Of course, for all her happiness, Anna knew that there was still something troubling Cezar.

He might be a master at hiding his emotions, but she was his mate. There was no way he could disguise his aching pain when he denied himself the temptation of her blood. Or the brooding fear she could occasionally sense deep in his heart.

That vague, annoying destiny that everyone and their freaking dog seemed to know about, except her.

Perhaps foolishly, Anna refused to dwell on the future.

If she had learned anything over the years, it was that these moments of contentment were all too rare. And all too fleeting.

She intended to enjoy this time while she could.

A wise choice as it turned out.

Snuggled in Cezar's arms in one of Viper's countless bedrooms, Anna was deeply asleep when a sudden explosion of light had her sitting upright, her powers already filling the air with a hot, threatening prickle.

Half expecting a horde of ravaging fairies, she was startled to discover a . . . well, she wasn't exactly sure what it was.

The creature looked human. Actually she looked like a little girl, her short stature and slender body covered by a white robe. But there was nothing human about the strange oblong eyes that were solid black, or the ancient wisdom that was etched on the delicate features.

Oh, and then there were the sharp, pointed teeth.

Yikes.

Obviously sensing Anna's power, the intruder held up a gnarled hand in a gesture of peace.

"I am no enemy, Anna Randal," she said, her voice low and strangely hypnotic.

Unnerved by the unexpected appearance of the woman, not to mention the fact that Cezar had yet to stir next to her, Anna tugged the covers up to her chin.

"Holy crap. Doesn't anyone know how to knock in the demon world?" she muttered.

The tiny head dipped, the long gray braid slipping over her shoulder and nearly brushing the ground.

"Forgive me. It was not my intent to frighten you."

Not her intent? Then maybe she shouldn't be popping into private bedrooms, Anna silently acknowledged, smart enough to keep the thought to herself. She was learning that size had no bearing on how much power a demon might possess.

"Who are you?"

Straightening, the demon regarded her with those strange, unblinking eyes.

"I am Siljar." Her head tilted to one side. "No, I have no relationship to Morgana or the fairies, nor did I bring harm to your vampire."

Anna's breath caught in her throat as the woman answered the questions that burned through her mind.

"How did you . . ."

"I am capable of reading your thoughts," the woman interrupted.

"Oh."

Sensing her discomfort, the woman shrugged. "Yes, it is quite disconcerting for those not accustomed to my talent."

It was more than disconcerting, but Anna had greater things to worry about than what random thoughts the woman might be reading.

"What have you done to Cezar?" she demanded, her gaze shifting to the unconscious vampire at her side.

"He merely sleeps," she soothed. "I assure you, he is not harmed."

Returning her attention to Siljar, Anna reached out to place a hand on Cezar's arm. Sleeping or not, he provided her comfort just by being near.

"Is that your doing?"

"Yes."

Anna swallowed an impatient curse. She just wanted to be left alone with the man she loved.

Was that too much to ask?

"What do you want?"

The woman pressed her hands together in an oddly formal motion. "Anna Randal, you are summoned to appear before the Commission."

She was going to be hauled before the all powerful Oracles?

Shit.

"Why?" she rasped.

"All your questions will be answered in time. For now you must come with me."

Anna pressed against the headboard, her hand ridiculously clutching at Cezar. This was bad. This was really bad.

"Maybe I don't want to be summoned," she breathed, her heart lodged in her throat.

The oblong eyes held a cold, ruthless glitter. "That is not an option, Anna Randal."

"I'm not a demon. What authority does the Commission have over me?"

Moving toward the bed, Siljar reached out her hand toward Anna. "The first thing you must learn is that an Oracle is to be obeyed, not questioned."

"No," Anna whispered, but there was no avoiding the fingers that grasped her wrist.

At first she felt nothing more than the painful grip of the woman's hand. The gnarled fingers dug into her skin, too strong for such a tiny creature, and just a breath from cracking the bones of her wrist. Then slowly a cold chill spread over her skin. It wasn't the weird prickles of a portal, but something similar. Her lips parted in a scream in the same moment that there was a brilliant flash of light that scorched her entire body.

Anna wasn't certain if she had passed out, but when she opened her eyes she discovered that she was standing in a dark, dank cave wearing nothing more than Cezar's T-shirt, which she had pulled on before falling asleep. At her side the tiny demon was regarding her with that unblinking gaze.

"Good . . . God," Anna breathed, a combination of fear and fury beating through her body. Dammit, she'd been kidnapped with annoying regularity over the past week. There surely had to be some law against it. "What the hell did you do?"

Siljar shrugged as she headed toward one of the numerous tunnels. "I brought you to the Commission."

For a stubborn heartbeat, Anna remained planted in the

middle of the cave. She wasn't some stray dog to be plucked from the street and expected to follow behind her new owner with pathetic gratitude.

On the other hand, she wasn't overly eager to be left alone in the dark cave.

If the great and mighty Commission was near, then there were bound to be all sorts of nasty things guarding them. Things that Anna didn't want to meet without some sort of protection.

Muttering a few of the French curses she had picked up from Levet, Anna scurried after the retreating form of Siljar.

"That wasn't a portal," she accused, wincing as she stubbed her toe on an unseen rock. Jeez, would it have hurt to have poofed her here with shoes and a few more clothes on?

"My powers allow for teleportation," the demon said, her hand lifting to light the narrow tunnel with a soft glow.

"You could at least warn a person before you do something like that," Anna muttered.

Ignoring her, the demon turned into a tunnel that was not only wider, but decorated with heavy tapestries on the dirt walls and a long crimson rug on the floor.

Thankfully there were also a number of torches that offered far more light than the strange glow the demon had conjured.

"This way," Siljar commanded, walking down the tunnel briskly.

"What is this place?" Anna demanded. "It doesn't look like something the Commission would call home."

Siljar clicked her tongue. "You are a female with an annoying number of questions."

"Hey, I've just been zapped from my bed by a demon I don't know. I think it's understandable I'd have a few questions."

"This is the lair of the previous Anasso. It is south of Chicago by human standards and near what they have named the Mississippi river." The tiny head cocked to the side before the woman came to an abrupt halt. "You fear for your vampire—why?"

Anna jerked to a halt. She didn't like the fact that the demon could read her mind, but maybe it was better this way. She wasn't sure she would have otherwise had the nerve to confront the powerful demon.

"From what I've heard, you haven't treated Cezar very well over the past few centuries," she said, her expression tight with disapproval. "I can't help but wonder if you took me from him as some sort of punishment."

A hint of puzzlement touched the delicate face. "It was not our intent to punish the vampire. Or at least, not entirely. I suppose there were those on the Commission who took exception to his drinking of your blood, but he was made our servant to ensure he fulfilled the destiny that was given him."

Anna frowned in confusion. Why the hell would they care if Cezar took her blood?

"And has he fulfilled it?" she demanded, not bothering to hide her anger.

"You are alive, are you not?"

"Me?" Her anger tumbled away as a rising horror replaced it. "That was his destiny? To keep me alive?"

"It was foreseen that he would have a pivotal role to play in your survival."

"My God." Anna pressed a hand to her suddenly aching heart. Cezar had endured years of being the Commission's personal slave because of her? Holy crap. "It's my fault that you held him captive for two centuries?"

"I do not believe he begrudges those years," Siljar said, without a hint of remorse. "Indeed, he seems quite pleased with his fate."

Anna sucked in a deep breath. There was no point in ranting and raving at this . . . creature. Obviously the Oracles were firm believers in "the end justified the means."

Instead she made a silent, solemn promise to do everything possible to make sure that Cezar never had cause to regret the sacrifices he'd been forced to make for her.

"Then I'm not here because of Cezar?" she demanded.

"No."

"Is it Morgana?"

"No."

Okay. This was getting her precisely nowhere.

"Do I at least get some sort of lawyer?"

Something that might have been amusement flashed in the black eyes. "You are not here to be judged, Anna Randal."

"Then why am I here?"

With a formal gesture, Siljar pointed toward the opening that loomed just down the tunnel.

"Step into the cavern and all will be explained."

Not at all satisfied with the vague promise, Anna abruptly threw her arms up as there was a brilliant flash of light and the demon just . . . disappeared.

"Great. Just freaking great," she muttered, blinking the pain from her eyes and turning toward the opening of the cavern. The fear that had clutched her since the arrival of the demon in her bedroom remained, but along with it was a rising sense of resignation. Deep in her heart she knew that this was the secret destiny that Cezar had kept hidden from her. That even if she turned and ran from these tunnels she would only be returned. There was no avoiding what was waiting for her in the darkness, so why the hell not just get it over with?

Squaring her shoulders, Anna allowed the always tangible sense of Cezar to fill her mind. He might be miles away, but the sensation of him flooded through her with a comforting force. Her thinly stretched courage returned, as if Cezar were standing at her side, and with an unconscious tilt of her chin she forced herself to walk forward.

If this was to be her fate, then she would meet it with her head high.

At least physically speaking.

Stepping into the inky darkness she sensed a vast opening

with a high ceiling that made the slightest noise echo eerily through the silence.

She stopped not far from the entrance, unable to see a damn thing. She wasn't overly anxious to make her entrance by tripping over something and landing flat on her face.

"Hello?" she called out, unable to hide the impatience in her voice.

Without a breath of sound a torch set in the center of the stone floor flared to life, revealing a small wooden chair.

"Anna Randal," a deep male voice echoed through the cavern. "Sit. We offer you welcome."

She hesitated only a moment before moving to settle on the seat. Despite the fact that she could make out only shadowed forms seated at what appeared to be a long table on a dais, she was acutely aware that she was wearing nothing more than a T-shirt, and her hair hung in tangles.

She could actually *feel* the weight of their gazes on her.

"Thank you," she muttered, a shiver wracking her chilled body.

"Do not fear, we mean you no harm," a softer voice soothed. A voice that held the faint hiss of a snake. Yikes.

Suddenly relieved that she couldn't actually make out more than their outlines, Anna sucked in a deep breath.

"Then why am I here?"

"You know who we are?" the male voice demanded.

"I suppose you must be the Oracles, although I don't really know what all that entails."

"We are the justice of the demon world," a new, guttural voice proclaimed. "It is our duty to ensure that the ancient laws are obeyed and to arbitrate disagreements between the species. We punish those who threaten our world and offer answers for those who seek our wisdom."

"We are the protection of the demon world." The hissing woman continued the strange litany. "With our powers we hold the veils between dimensions and help to shroud our people from the sight of the humans who infect this world."

"We are the compassion of the demon world." This time it was Siljar who spoke. "We provide sanctuary for those in need. We protect those who cannot protect themselves."

It was an unfamiliar female voice who spoke the last words of the recitation. "We are the future and the past of the demon world. With the gift of foresight we steer the paths of those who have been revealed to alter our history. We preserve our traditions for those to come."

Okay.

It sounded as if they had rehearsed that impressive little spiel more than once.

It didn't, however, answer her question.

"Yes, well, that's all very interesting, but I'm still not sure what it has to do with me," she said.

"We have been watching you for some time, Anna Randal," the guttural voice informed her.

"Watching me? Why?"

"It is foreseen that you are to become an Oracle."

The breath was wrenched from her lungs as if she'd taken a blow.

Actually, it was worse than a blow, she acknowledged, as numb disbelief flooded her body and threatened to shut down her brain. She'd taken enough hits over the years to shrug most of them aside.

But to be told, out of the freaking blue, that she was destined to become some omnipotent being that was in charge of the entire demon world . . . well, that wasn't something anyone was going to shrug off.

She gave a shake of her head. The Commission didn't seem the sort to use nefarious ploys to trick people. And certainly they didn't seem the sort to play practical jokes. She'd bet her last dime they didn't even know what the hell a joke was.

On the other hand, she couldn't believe for a minute that

they were actually serious. It was insane to believe she was in any way Oracle material.

The demons would laugh themselves sick.

Christ, she would laugh herself sick.

"No." She swallowed the lump in her throat. "Oh no. There has to be a mistake."

"We do not make mistakes," the hissing woman said, her voice cold.

Anna's brows snapped together. Obviously people skills weren't a necessary requirement to be on the Commission.

"There has to be a first time for everything," she said tightly. "There's no way in hell that I'm an Oracle."

There was a brief stir in the air, as if she'd managed to shock the ancient demons.

"Why are you so certain?" Siljar at last demanded.

She resisted the urge to roll her eyes. Dammit, what was going on? No one could believe that she was suited to such an important position. Not even remotely.

"In the first place I'm not a demon," she pointed out, her hands clenched tightly in her lap.

"Neither are you human," a deep male voice retorted. "Your blood is that of the ancients."

"I don't even know what that means."

"Your powers are elemental, the most pure of all powers," the same demon answered. "They draw upon the energy of the nature that surrounds you without the corruption of lesser magic."

They sounded great. A pity they only worked when they wanted to.

"They're also unpredictable, randomly destructive, and occasionally missing in action."

Siljar, or at least Anna assumed it was Siljar, gave a soft laugh. "You are very, very young, Anna Randal. With time you will learn control."

"Even if by some miracle I do, they will never compare to the sort of power that the rest of you obviously possess."

There was a deep, rumbling sigh. The sort of sigh that was usually reserved for annoying children.

"You are mistaken," the gravelly male voice informed her, "but it does not matter. It is not your powers that mark you as an Oracle."

"Then what does?"

"Your heart."

Anna gave a choked cough, that numb disbelief threatening to return. She didn't know squat about these Oracles, but they didn't strike her as being touchy-feely types. More the do-as-we-say-or-we'll-rip-your-throat-out types.

For God's sake, they held Cezar captive for two centuries just because they had a vision he might keep her alive.

"If you truly know my heart then you must realize I can't play hardball with the rest of you. It's just not who I am."

She thought she heard a muttered agreement from more than one of the Oracles, but it was Siljar's comforting voice that floated through the shadows.

"You have proven a rare ability to fight for justice, even when you knew it was hopeless, even when you knew that all of your efforts would lead to nothing more than disappointment."

She stiffened in surprise, disturbed by the thought that these demons had been watching her for so many years. Maybe from her very birth.

"You mean my career as a lawyer?"

"It was more than a career, was it not?"

She thought back to her years battling for those who had no voice. Those who were oppressed. Those who were taken advantage of simply because they were too old, too poor, or too frightened to fight back.

It had been more than a career.

It had been a foundation that had given her life meaning.

"I suppose."

"And the manner in which you confronted Morgana reveals you are capable of overcoming your human emotions and battling an enemy without the desire to punish your opponent," a deep male voice boomed.

Anna shuddered. Her fight with Morgana had been a nasty necessity that would give her nightmares for centuries to come, not a job reference.

"I trapped her in a chunk of stone."

"Yes," the hissing woman murmured. "Quite amusing."

Right.

Enough was enough.

With a surge of emotion, Anna rose to her feet and glared at the shrouded forms.

"This is crazy." She shook her head. "There have to be thousands of demons who would make far better Oracles than I ever would. I barely even know about your world."

"You are young and immature, it is true," the gravelly voice agreed. "But in a few centuries you will be suitably trained to take your place among us."

"Why not just take someone who's ready now?"

"We do not choose Oracles, they are foretold by prophecy. We have known for some time that if you managed to survive Morgana you were destined to join us."

"Did it occur to you that I might have a better chance of surviving Morgana if you'd helped?"

"But we did," Siljar reminded her. "We gave you the vampire."

The tangled emotions oddly eased at the mere mention of Cezar. For all the trials and uncertainty she had endured over the years, not to mention the annoying attempts on her life, she wouldn't change one damn thing.

Not when it had brought her an extraordinary man who would love her for the rest of eternity.

"Yes, I suppose you did, although I don't think he'd appreciate it being put in those terms." With a smile, Anna slowly lowered herself to her knees and bowed her head. "Thank you. I doubt that it was your intention, but you've given me more than I ever dreamed possible."

There was no missing the stir of astonishment that rippled through the air. Obviously the demons expected this response at the offer of becoming an Oracle, not at the mention of Cezar.

"You speak of the vampire?" the hissing woman demanded.

"I speak of Cezar." Her head lifted with a flare of pride. "My mate."

There were several low growls and mutterings at her words, as if the announcement of Cezar being her mate wasn't overly popular.

Too damn bad.

"An . . . unfortunate decision by the vampire," a new, ominous voice rasped. "Not the first I might add. He is lucky that he is not to be punished again."

"Punished?" Anna scrambled back to her feet. By God, she wasn't going to stand aside and let Cezar ever be hurt again. She didn't care who the hell these demons thought they were, she would battle them to the death. "For what? Protecting me against my demented aunt? Caring enough to save my life? It's certainly more than anyone else has ever done for me."

"She is right, the vampire did what was necessary." Siljar overrode the mutterings, her voice holding a rich command that filled the vast cavern. "He has served his purpose."

"Perhaps, but he will be a blessed nuisance for the rest of eternity. You know how vampires are when they're mated," a demon groused.

"True," another agreed. "He will be forever hovering around the female. He will have to be restrained when the Commission is in private session."

Her eyes narrowed. She'd been kidnapped from her bed, forced to meet the mystical, powerful Commission in nothing more than a T-shirt, and bluntly informed that she was supposed to become an Oracle rather than enjoy a peaceful future with Cezar. She was in no mood to listen to them speak about the man she loved as if he were no more than a pesky bug they wanted to squash.

"The female has a name, and I haven't said that I even want to be on the Commission," she gritted.

There was a collective gasp, the shock a tangible force in the air. Clearly they expected potential Oracles to leap with joy at the thought of joining their exclusive ranks.

"Anna Randal, you do not understand the honor that has been given you," the gravelly voice chastised with obvious annoyance. "There has never been an Oracle who has turned away the opportunity to serve upon the Commission. Indeed, there is none who would not be eager to fulfill such a destiny."

Anna shrugged. "Then you shouldn't have any trouble finding someone to take my place."

There was more muttering, most of it in a language she thankfully didn't understand. She didn't think they were saying anything nice.

At last it was Siljar who attempted to ease the rising tension. "That is not how it is done, Anna. We do not simply *find* someone. The Oracle is prophesized. It could be several millenniums before another is shown to us."

Millenniums?

Good grief.

They seriously needed to consider a new method of choosing their Oracles.

What if one of them died? Or wanted to retire? Or preferred to spend the next few centuries tucked in bed with a delicious vampire?

Oh . . . yes. A few centuries alone with Cezar were exactly what she wanted.

"Look, I don't know what cosmic joke made you believe that I should be an Oracle, but I don't want the job," she said, her voice clear and determined.

This time there was no muttering, no foreign curses. Instead a thunderous silence filled the cavern. A silence that was far more terrifying than their earlier annoyance.

Anna swallowed a lump that felt the size of Gibraltar as she waited for the looming shit to hit the fan.

Okay, that wasn't probably the smartest thing she'd ever done. Even an idiot realized that denying a request from a powerful assembly of demons needed to be done with a bit of tact. Where the hell was her law training when she needed it?

Of course, it might be better to simply have her cards on the table, she tried to reassure herself. If they were going to kill her for her refusal then she'd just as soon have it over and done with swiftly.

When the silence at last was broken, however, it wasn't with a lightning bolt or earthquake. Instead it was Siljar's soft question.

"What do you want?"

Anna licked her dry lips. She would try to be more diplomatic, but she wouldn't lie. This was too important.

"I want to complete the mating ceremony with Cezar and live in peace with his clan," she said, her voice thick with the need that burned in her heart. "That's all."

"A moment," Siljar demanded.

The darkness deepened around the forms until they were lost in shadows. It was almost as if they had placed a tangible cloak over themselves, shutting her out as effectively as if they'd slammed a door in her face.

Realizing her knees were shaking, Anna abruptly dropped back in her seat and sucked in several deep breaths. She wanted to believe this was all some horrible nightmare. That she would awaken to discover she was safely tucked in Cezar's arms with nothing to worry about but whether to enjoy a private dinner with her mate or a few hours with her newfound friends. But the damp chill of the cave and smoke of the torch were all too real.

And downright uncomfortable.

Concentrating on her powers, Anna was able to warm her skin and send the smoke toward the back of the cave, but there was nothing to combat the hardness of the wooden chair or the queasy ball of nerves in the pit of her stomach.

Those she endured, for what seemed like hours, although it was probably no more than twenty or thirty minutes.

At last the darkness thinned so that Anna could determine the vague outline of the Commission and she slowly rose to her feet. It seemed a good idea to be ready for a hasty exit if things went to hell.

"We agree," Siljar said.

Anna blinked in shock. She'd expected a thunderous lecture on duty, or bitter recriminations, or bolts of deadly lightning.

She hadn't expected this mild capitulation.

It made her wonder when the ax was going to fall.

"What did you say?"

"You shall be allowed to keep your mate."

"Are you serious?"

"Yes," Siljar agreed. "And as a concession to your extreme youth we will not require you to commence your duties as an Oracle for the next century."

It was one of those deals that sounded too good to be true. With a frown she struggled to peer through the murky darkness.

"And at the end of that century?"

"You will take your place on the Commission."

"Does that mean giving up Cezar?"

"Once mated it is impossible to break the bonds," the hissing woman retorted in annoyance.

Obviously not everyone was happy with the Commission's decision.

Anna refused to be intimidated. Stupid, but there it was.

"As you know, I'm a lawyer. I'd rather have everything spelled out in black and white," she stubbornly said. "If I take my place as an Oracle, will Cezar be at my side?"

Chapter 25

Cezar knew the minute he woke from his magically induced sleep that the Commission had come to take Anna.

There could be no other explanation. Viper's defenses were impenetrable to all but the most powerful of demons. And, of course, there was the fact that whoever had entered the bedroom had managed to do so without him being aware of their presence.

Besides, the lingering scent of Siljar still hung heavy in the air.

Leaping from the bed, Cezar's first thought had been to rush to the distant caves and physically fight his way to Anna's side. He'd be damned if she was forced to face the Commission alone.

Then sanity had made an unwelcome intrusion as he yanked on the black jeans that Anna always preferred, and a plain T-shirt.

He could easily make his way to the caves hidden beside the Mississippi river, but for all his power he couldn't possibly hope to enter them without the permission of the Oracles.

Even worse, his impulsive attempt might very well endanger Anna.

They might be the leaders of the demon world but they could be as petty and vindictive as a clutch of harpies. They wouldn't hesitate to punish his mate for his own sins.

Besides, he'd known this day was coming.

He'd known it for two long centuries.

He just hadn't expected it to come mere days after making Anna his mate.

Plagued by a sorrow that pulsed through his body, Cezar paced the bedroom that he shared with Anna, soaking in her lingering scent and stroking his fingers over the few possessions she had scattered around the room. A jagged pain constricted his heart as he touched the hairbrush that he had used only a few hours ago to brush her thick, honey hair. He could still feel the rich satin texture beneath his fingers and smell the intoxicating scent of figs that had filled the air.

Dios. The bulbs in the room exploded as his power swirled through the room.

How was he expected to live without her?

She was his life. His sole purpose to exist.

Without her . . .

A sharp knock on the door interrupted his agonizing thoughts, although it brought no relief to his pain. He could sense Styx standing in the hallway and as much as he respected his Anasso, at the moment he was no more than an unwelcome intrusion.

"Not now," he called out, his voice raw with emotion.

In answer the door was thrust open, nearly coming off its hinges as Styx stormed into the room, his massive form covered from head to toe in black leather, his expression revealing that he wasn't going to take *no* for an answer.

Cezar gritted his teeth. Damn Viper. It had to be the clan chief who had sensed Cezar's stark pain and sent for the leader.

That all-seeing golden gaze swept over the glass littering the carpet before landing on Cezar's tense form.

"Come with me," he commanded.

Cezar shoved his fingers through his tangled hair, struggling to contain the power that still swirled through the air.

"I'm not really in the mood for company, Styx."

Styx folded his arms over his massive chest. "You would rather be pacing a hole in Viper's rather expensive carpet?"

"I'd rather be in my bed with my mate," Cezar snapped.

"There is no point in wishing for the impossible." Styx narrowed his gaze. "And even less point in locking yourself in this room and brooding. Let's go."

Cezar gritted his teeth. He wanted to tell the older vampire to go to hell. The last thing he wanted was to leave this room and pretend as if his life wasn't crashing down around him.

Unfortunately, Styx wasn't just another vampire. He was the Anasso and he possessed the power to force the cooperation of others.

Including Cezar.

"If you insist." With a stiff bow of his head, Cezar forced his feet forward, passing by the older vampire and stepping into the hallway. "But if you tell me that everything is going to be fine, I swear I'll throw you out the nearest window."

Joining him in the hall, Styx pointed toward the back stairs that led to Viper's private tunnels. For a time they walked in silence, the vampire guards that filled the house disappearing into the shadows at the approach of the two powerful demons.

As they reached the stairs, Cezar felt the heavy weight of Styx's gaze on his tight expression.

"The Oracles will not harm her, you know," he said softly.

He didn't ask how Styx had known why he was so disturbed. They'd both known that this day would come sooner or later.

Cezar hissed as he thought of his sweet, tenderhearted mate in the hands of the Commission. They would be ruthless to get what they wanted. And what they wanted was Anna to take her place as an Oracle.

They might not physically harm her, but they might very well crush her spirit if they thought it necessary.

"I pray you're right," he rasped. "But even assuming that Anna's transition to the Commission is without complications, they will never return her. She's lost to me."

"I claim no knowledge of the Commission's inner workings, but surely Anna will have some say in her future?"

Cezar stiffened at the soft question. No. He wouldn't allow the dangerous hope to settle in his mind. It would only drive him mad.

"She's an Oracle." He closed his eyes as he forced the words past his clenched teeth. "It was the reason she was born."

Without warning, Styx grasped his shoulder in a tight grip. "Destiny is not always etched in stone, *amigo.*"

Cezar opened his eyes as he glanced toward his friend. "What's that supposed to mean?"

"I once believed that fate could not be altered. *Should* not be altered," Styx said, a rueful smile touching his lips. "And I was prepared to sacrifice all that I held dear to battle those who would dare to change the future. I was a fool."

Cezar nearly stumbled as they reached the wide opening at the bottom of the stairs. Forcing Styx to admit that he might be wrong was like trying to force an imp to confess where he'd hidden his gold.

"Good God, I never thought to hear those words from your lips, my lord."

Styx laughed as he led them down a wide tunnel. "Enjoy them while you can. They will never leave my lips again."

They continued through the thick darkness and Cezar found his renegade thoughts dwelling on his companion's words.

"So you no longer believe in destiny?" The words were out before he could stop them.

Styx halted before a large wooden door, his expression somber as he studied Cezar's haunted expression.

"I believe that destiny, good or bad, is crafted by our own hands."

"It was foreseen that Anna is to become an Oracle," Cezar muttered. "That's a destiny that I can't craft away."

"Have faith in your woman, Cezar," Styx said gently.

"My faith in Anna is beyond question," he growled.

"Then that's all you need."

With his cryptic assurance offered, Styx reached to push open the door and with a mere thought ignited the numerous torches that were set in the walls of the large room. With a sweep of his arm he gestured Cezar forward.

Cezar's brows lifted as he stepped through the doorway. A mere glance was enough to confirm they were in Viper's private armory. And that there were enough ancient and modern weapons in the glass cases to take over a third world country.

Viper's rare collection was whispered of, but rarely seen. Little wonder. There were demons that would stop at nothing to get their hands on such a lethal arsenal.

"What are we doing here?" Cezar demanded as Styx crossed the floor to retrieve two long swords from a nearby case.

Styx turned and tossed one of the swords in Cezar's direction. "It's been some time since I've had an opportunity to spar with a worthy opponent."

Catching the sword by the delicately carved hilt, Cezar absently tested the weight and balance of the weapon. It was, of course, perfectly crafted and fit his hand as if it had been forged for him. Viper would never have anything but the best.

He glanced toward Styx, who was eyeing him with an expectant expression. Maybe a few hours of testing his skill with a master was precisely what he needed. It would be hard to brood with a very large vampire swinging a sword at his head.

Pretending to study his sword, Cezar casually settled his weight on the balls of his feet and bent his knees to a fighting stance.

"It won't be much of a competition," he warned. "I'm no match for you even when I'm not distracted."

"Ah no." Styx gave a shake of his head, his lips twisted in a wry smile. "Others might be fooled by your pretense of ineptitude, Conde Cezar, but I am not one of them. I have battled at your side and know just how lethal you are with a sword in hand."

Cezar barely had time to react before Styx was flowing forward in a flurry of lethal steel and fangs.

Anna decided that teleportation was only marginally better than traveling through a portal. Sure, there was no lightning crawling over her skin, but to compensate there was the feeling that her stomach was being turned inside out and her retinas being seared by the violent flashes of light.

It was the sort of thing to make any sane woman appreciate public transportation.

Of course, on the plus side she did arrive back at Viper's country estate just after midnight. She would endure a lot more than a twisted stomach and spots before her eyes to ease the aching sadness she could sense from her mate.

Politely thanking Siljar for the quick trip home, Anna waited for the demon to disappear in a flash of light before going in search of Cezar.

To avoid any unnecessary unpleasantness, Anna had requested that they be popped into the beautiful conservatory rather than the bedroom. The last thing she'd wanted was for Cezar to attack the Oracle and be toasted before Anna could stop him.

Now she closed her eyes and allowed the sensation of him to flow through her body. She felt a flicker of surprise as she realized that he wasn't in the main house, but somewhere in the vast connection of tunnels that ran throughout the estate.

There was a brief hesitation as she debated between returning to the bedroom to change into something halfway decent and the burning need to be with Cezar.

The burning need won out as she left the conservatory and made her way to the door that led to the tunnels. The half-dozen vampires and demons that were spread throughout the house had seen a hell of a lot more than bare legs over the past few centuries.

Relieved to discover the hidden door already opened, Anna made her way down the steep staircase, her pace slowing as she was forced to stumble blindly through the pitch black that shrouded the tunnels. Someday she intended to convince the demon world that not everyone possessed the vision of a freaking owl.

Would a night-light kill them?

It was the sound of faint grunts and the unmistakable clang of steel swords being struck together that led her down one of the larger tunnels. She might have been worried if it weren't for the complete lack of fear she sensed from Cezar.

Bitter sadness, anger, a frustrated need to vent the emotions that threatened to overwhelm him, but no fear.

Biting her lip against the raw pain she could feel pulsing through him, Anna hurried toward the open door that thankfully had a soft glow of light spilling through it. Stepping through the opening, Anna halted at the sight of Cezar and Styx flowing across the bare floor, their swords moving so swiftly she could barely follow the motions.

For a moment she watched the lethal dance with breathless fascination. Good God, she'd never seen anything quite so beautiful. Despite Styx's size advantage, Cezar possessed a superior speed that allowed him to avoid the savage swing of the massive blade, sliding past the blows and delivering a few of his own.

They were master predators, she silently accepted. Deadly, exquisite creatures who ruled the night.

With a shake of her head she took a step forward. As much as she was enjoying the show, she didn't want Cezar to suddenly realize that she was near and lose his concentration. It was obvious that it took his full attention to keep Styx from doing serious damage.

"Is this a private battle or can anyone join in?" she demanded softly.

As one the vampires halted their swinging swords and whirled to face her. Styx merely narrowed his gaze, but with a low growl Cezar launched himself across the floor and pulled her into his arms.

"Anna." He crushed her against his chest for several long moments before pulling back to run trembling hands over her rumpled, half-naked body. "*Dios*. Are you okay? Did they hurt you?"

"I'm fine." When it was clear that her words hadn't penetrated the fear clouding his mind, Anna reached up to frame his face with her hands. "Cezar, listen to me. I'm fine."

"I thought . . ." With a shudder he buried his face in the curve of her neck.

Anna allowed her gaze to lift to meet Styx's steady regard, surprised by the softening of his stark bronzed features.

"Is there anything you need, Anna?"

She smiled as she wrapped her arms around Cezar and allowed his sandalwood scent to explode through her senses.

"Not now."

"Then I will be upstairs with Viper." With a formal bow of his head the vampire moved toward the door, halting for a moment to lay a light hand on Cezar's shoulder. "Fate is in your hands, *amigo*. You have only to grasp it."

Waiting until Styx was gone, Anna shifted her hand to run her fingers through his tangled hair.

"Should I ask?" she teased.

Nuzzling several desperate kisses along the line of her throat, Cezar reluctantly pulled back to study her flushed features with a wary gaze.

"Anna, do the Oracles know you're here?" he demanded.

She leaned forward to kiss the tip of his nose. "Not only do they know, but it was Siljar who was kind enough to use her powers to return me." She grimaced. "Not my favorite mode of transportation, but at least it's fast."

The dark brows snapped together at the mention of the powerful demon. "Did they tell you why they summoned you?"

"Unfortunately." She arched a chiding brow. "You could have at least warned me that I was supposed to join the damn Commission. I don't like surprises. Or at least, not that sort of surprise."

His beautiful features tightened. "It was forbidden."

"Typical." She rolled her eyes. "You know, they might be all-powerful but they're way too fond of playing cloak-and-dagger games. Not everything has to be some mysterious secret. And don't get me started on their manners. I intend to make some changes now that I'm an Oracle."

Cezar stilled, his dark eyes smoldering with a fierce, aching regret. "You've already taken your place on the Commission?"

Her breath caught as his grief slammed into her with the force of a speeding truck. Dear God. She knew that he would be upset by her promotion to the Commission, but this wrenching sadness nearly sent her to her knees.

"Officially I'm a member, but unofficially my duties won't begin for a while," she told him softly.

He shuddered with longing as she stroked her fingers through his hair.

"How long is a while?" he rasped, his eyes darkening with something other than pain.

"Oh . . . a century or so."

He hissed in sharp surprise. "What?"

"Well, I'm very young, you know."

"Anna, you're making me crazy," he growled. "Will you just tell me what happened?"

Not about to torment a dangerous vampire when he was so obviously suffering, Anna swiftly related her encounter with the Oracles, skimming over the attempts to browbeat her and emphasizing their grudging agreement that they wouldn't interfere in her mating with Cezar.

Not that she needed to bother.

Cezar had spent two centuries bound to the ruthless Commission. Which explained his horrified expression by the time she was done.

"Dios." She was once again hauled against his chest, his arms so tight she had to struggle to breathe. "Only you would dare to barter with the Commission. Do you know what they could have done to you?"

Anna smiled as she snuggled her face against his shoulder. This was it. What she'd waited her entire life to feel.

"Nothing that would be any worse than being forced to give you up," she said, so softly only a vampire could hear her words. "They could threaten and bluster all they wanted, but there was no way in hell that I was giving in. We're in this together or they can find a new Oracle."

"Querida." Turning his head, Cezar pressed his lips to the sensitive hollow behind her ear.

Anna allowed a low moan of pleasure to escape her parted lips. Her fingers tightened in the lush black hair in silent encouragement.

"Of course, I haven't asked you yet how you feel about being stuck with an Oracle," she said, struggling to concentrate on their unfinished conversation. A task that would be considerably easier if he wasn't kissing a delicious path down the line of her jaw. "You could walk away and never have to deal with the Commission again. That's got to be tempting after the way they treated you over the past few centuries."

Pressing a rough, hungry kiss to her lips, Cezar pulled back to regard her with a burning gaze.

"I would live in the pits of hell if that was the only way I could be with you, Anna Randal. You are mine."

She gave a tug on his hair. "Not exactly. At least not yet. You still have to make an honest woman of me."

"Anna . . ."

She slapped her hand over his mouth. She knew that tone. It meant he was going to say something she didn't like.

"No. If you tell me there's still some mysterious destiny I've yet to fulfill I'll pick up that sword you dropped and stick it through your heart."

She felt his lips curve into a smile as he spoke against her palm. "That won't kill me, you know."

Dropping her hand she gave him the evil eye. "Maybe not, but it'll hurt like a bitch."

"There's that." His amusement faded as he ran a tender hand up the curve of her back. "I just want you to be certain, *querida*. There's no going back once the ceremony is completed."

Anna lifted herself to her toes, pressing her lips to his with all the love that flowed through her heart.

"Conde Cezar, there was no going back from the moment I followed you through that London townhouse and was hauled into the bedroom by a wickedly beautiful vampire," she whispered against his lips.

A groan was wrenched from his throat. "Wickedly beautiful?"

"Absolutely."

With one smooth motion Cezar had swept her off her feet and cradled her against his chest as he headed for the door.

A sinful smile touched his lips as he held her gaze with a dark intensity.

"I like the wicked part."

Anna looped her arms around his neck, her heart racing with the excitement this man would always inspire.

"I'm kind of fond of it myself."

Epilogue

Two months later

The exclusive nightclub near Lake Michigan was filled to the rafters with a combination of vampires, demons, and at least one goddess enjoying a performance by the rare dew fairies, who fluttered on delicate wings in a complicated dance.

Viper's newest establishment was a beautiful testament to refined elegance that catered to a more sophisticated clientele than many of his others. There were no open orgies, no blood battles, no public feedings. Instead there were elegantly attired guests who were seated at small tables and bathed in light from the massive chandeliers.

All very chichi.

Or at least it was all very chichi until Jagr stormed through the doors.

The mere sight of the vampire's massive body covered in a leather duster that went down to his ankles, his pale blond hair tightly braided to reveal his stark, frigid expression, was enough to make several lesser demons hide beneath their tables. There were even a few vampires who swiftly moved to the darker shadows.

Jagr ignored them all.

He didn't give a damn about the crowd who had forgotten about the dew fairies and instead watched his long-legged stride toward the back of the room. In truth, he didn't give a damn about anything.

All he wanted was to be done with this obligation and return to the silence of his lair.

Damn Styx.

The ancient vampire had known that only a royal command could force him to enter a crowded nightclub. Jagr made no secret of his disdain for the companionship of others.

Which begged the question of why the Anasso would choose such a setting to meet.

In a mood foul enough to fill the vast club with an icy chill, Jagr ignored the two Ravens who stood on sentry duty near the back office, and lifting his hand allowed his power to blow the heavy oak door off its hinges.

The looming Ravens growled in warning, dropping their heavy capes, which hid the numerous swords, daggers, and guns attached to various parts of their bodies.

Jagr's step never faltered. Styx wouldn't let his pet vampires hurt an invited guest. At least not until he had what he needed from Jagr.

And even if Styx didn't call off the dogs . . . well hell, he'd been waiting centuries to be taken out in battle. It was a warrior's destiny.

There was a low murmur from inside the room and the two Ravens grudgingly allowed him to pass with nothing more painful than a heated glare.

Stepping over the shattered door, Jagr paused to cast a wary glance about the ice-blue and ivory room. As expected, Styx was consuming more than his fair share of space behind a heavy walnut desk, his bronzed features unreadable, with Viper standing at his shoulder.

"Jagr." Styx leaned back in the leather chair, his fingers steepled beneath his chin. "Thank you for coming so promptly."

Jagr narrowed his frigid gaze. "Did I have a choice?"

"Careful, Jagr," Viper warned. "This is your Anasso."

Jagr curled his lips, but he was wise enough to keep his angry words to himself. Even presuming he could match Styx's renowned power, he would be dead before ever leaving the club if he challenged the Anasso.

"What do you want?" he growled.

"I have a task for you."

Jagr clenched his teeth. For the past century he'd managed to keep himself hidden among his vast collection of books, never bothering others and expecting the same in return. Since he'd been foolish enough to allow Cezar to enter his lair it seemed he couldn't get rid of the damn vampire clan.

"What sort of task?" he demanded, his tone making it clear he didn't appreciate playing the role of toady.

Styx smiled as he waved a slender hand toward a nearby sofa. It was a smile that sent a chill of alarm down Jagr's spine.

"Have a seat, my friend," the Anasso drawled. "This might take awhile."

Please turn the page for an exciting sneak peek of
DARKNESS UNLEASHED,
the next installment in the Guardians of Eternity series,
now on sale!

Prologue

Jagr knew he was creating panic in Viper's exclusive night-club. The elegant establishment with its crystal chandeliers and red velvet upholstery catered to the more civilized members of the demon world. Jagr was anything but civilized.

He was a six-foot-three vampire who had once been a Visigoth chief. But it wasn't his pale gold hair that had been braided to fall nearly to his waist, or the ice-blue eyes that missed nothing, that sent creatures with any claim to intelligence scurrying from his path. It wasn't even the leather duster that flared about his hard body.

No, it was the cold perfection of his stark features and the hint of feral fury that smoldered about him.

Three hundred years of relentless torture had stripped away any hint of civility.

Ignoring the assorted demons that tumbled over chairs and tables in an effort to avoid his long strides, Jagr concentrated on the two Ravens guarding the door to the back office. The hushed air of sophistication was giving him a rash.

He was a vampire who preferred the solitude of his lair hidden beneath the streets of Chicago, surrounded by his vast library, secure in the knowledge that not a human, beast, or demon possessed the ability to enter.

Not that he was the total recluse that his vampire brothers assumed.

No matter how powerful or skilled or intelligent he might be, he understood that his survival depended on understanding the ever-changing technology of the modern world. And beyond that was the necessity of being able to blend in with society.

Even a recluse had to feed.

Tucked in the very back of his lair was a plasma TV with every channel known to humankind, and the sort of nondescript clothing that allowed him to cruise through the seedier neighborhoods without causing a riot.

The most lethal hunters knew how to camouflage when on the prowl.

But this place . . .

He'd rather be staked than mince and prance around like a jackass.

Damn Styx. The ancient vampire had known that only a royal command could force him to enter a crowded nightclub. Jagr made no secret of his disdain for the companionship of others.

Which begged the question of why the Anasso would choose such a setting to meet.

In a mood foul enough to fill the vast club with an icy chill, Jagr ignored the two Ravens who stood on sentry duty near the back office, and, lifting his hand, allowed his power to blow the heavy oak door off its hinges.

The looming Ravens growled in warning, dropping their heavy capes, which hid the numerous swords, daggers, and guns attached to various parts of their bodies.

Jagr's step never faltered. Styx wouldn't let his pet vampires hurt an invited guest. At least not until he had what he needed from Jagr.

And even if Styx didn't call off the dogs . . . well hell,

he'd been waiting centuries to be taken out in battle. It was a warrior's destiny.

There was a low murmur from inside the room and the two Ravens grudgingly allowed him to pass with nothing more painful than a heated glare.

Stepping over the shattered door, Jagr paused to cast a wary glance about the pale-blue and ivory room. As expected, Styx (a towering Aztec who was the current king of vampires) was consuming more than his fair share of space behind a heavy walnut desk, his bronzed features unreadable. Viper (clan chief of Chicago, who, with his silver hair and dark eyes, looked more like an angel than a lethal warrior) stood at his shoulder.

"Jagr." Styx leaned back in the leather chair, his fingers steepled beneath his chin. "Thank you for coming so promptly."

Jagr narrowed his frigid gaze. "Did I have a choice?"

"Careful, Jagr," Viper warned. "This is your Anasso."

Jagr curled his lips, but he was wise enough to keep his angry words to himself. Even presuming he could match Styx's renowned power, he would be dead before ever leaving the club if he challenged the Anasso.

"What do you want?" he growled.

"I have a task for you."

Jagr clenched his teeth. For the past century he'd managed to keep away from the clan who called him brother, never bothering others and expecting the same in return. Since he'd been foolish enough to allow Cezar to enter his lair, it seemed he couldn't get rid of the damn vampires.

"What sort of task?" he demanded, his tone making it clear he didn't appreciate playing the role of toady.

Styx smiled as he waved a slender hand toward a nearby sofa. It was a smile that sent a chill of alarm down Jagr's spine.

"Have a seat, my friend," the Anasso drawled. "This might take a while."

For an insane moment, Jagr considered refusing the order. Before being turned into a vampire, he had been a leader of thousands. While he had no memory of those days, he had retained all his arrogance. Not to mention his issue with authority.

Thankfully he had also kept the larger portion of his intelligence.

"Very well, Anasso, I have rushed to obey your royal command." He lowered his hard bulk onto a delicate brocade sofa, inwardly swearing to kill the designer if it broke. "What do you demand of your dutiful subject?"

Viper growled deep in his throat, the air tingling with his power. Jagr never blinked, although his muscles coiled in preparation.

"Perhaps you should see to your guests, Viper," Styx smoothly commanded. "Jagr's . . . dramatic entrance has disrupted your charming entertainment and attracted more attention than I desire."

"I will not be far." Viper flashed Jagr a warning glare before disappearing through the busted door.

"Is he auditioning for a place among your Ravens?" Jagr mocked.

Pinpricks of pain bit into his skin as Styx released a small thread of his power.

"So long as you remain in Chicago, Viper is your clan chief. Do not make the mistake of forgetting his position."

Jagr shrugged. He wasn't indifferent to the debt and loyalty owed to Viper. The truth was, he was in a pissy mood, and being stuck in the chichi nightclub, where there wasn't a damned thing to kill beyond a bunch of dew fairies, wasn't helping.

"I can hardly forget when I am forever being commanded

to involve myself in affairs that do not concern me and more importantly do not interest me."

"What *does* interest you, Jagr?" He held Styx's searching gaze with a flat stare. At the last the king grimaced. "Like it or not, you offered your sword when Viper accepted you into his clan."

He didn't like it, but he couldn't argue. Being taken into a clan was the only means of survival among the vampires. "What would you have of me?"

Styx rose to his feet to round the desk, perching on a corner. The wood groaned beneath the considerable weight, but didn't crack. Jagr could only assume Viper had all the furniture reinforced.

Smart vampire.

"What do you know of my mate?" Styx abruptly demanded.

Jagr stilled. "Is this a trap?"

A wry smile touched the Anasso's mouth. "I'm not a subtle vampire, Jagr. Unlike the previous Anasso, I have no talent for manipulating and deceiving others. If there comes a day when I feel the need to challenge you, it will be done face-to-face."

"Then why are you asking me about your mate?"

"When I first met Darcy she knew nothing of her heritage. She had been fostered by humans from the time she was a babe, and it wasn't until Salvatore Giuliani, the current king of the Weres, arrived in Chicago that we discovered she was a pureblood who had been genetically altered."

Jagr flicked a brow upward. That was a little tidbit that the king had kept secret.

"Genetically altered?"

"The Weres are increasingly desperate to produce healthy offspring. The pureblood females have lost their ability to control their shifts during the full moon, which makes it all but impossible to carry a litter to full term. The Weres altered Darcy and her sisters so they would be incapable of shifting."

Jagr folded his arms over his chest. He didn't give a damn about the worthless dogs. "I presume you will tell me why you have summoned me, before the sun rises?"

Styx narrowed his golden eyes. "That entirely depends on your cooperation, my brother. I can make this meeting last as long as I desire."

Jagr's lips twitched. The one thing he respected was power. "Please continue."

"Darcy's mother gave birth to a litter of four daughters, all genetically altered and all stolen from the Weres shortly after their births."

"Why were they stolen?"

"That remains a mystery Salvatore has never fully explained." There was an edge in the Anasso's voice that warned he wasn't pleased by the lack of information. "What we do know is that one of Darcy's sisters was discovered in St. Louis being held captive by an imp named Culligan."

"He's fortunate that she's incapable of shifting. A pureblood could rip out the throat of an imp."

"From what Salvatore could discover, the imp managed to get his hands on Regan when she was just a child and kept her locked in a cage coated with silver. That is, when he wasn't torturing her for a quick buck."

Torture.

The Dutch masterpieces hanging on the walls crashed to the floor at Jagr's flare of fury.

"Do you wish the Were rescued?"

Styx grimaced. "Salvatore already freed her from Culligan, although the damned imp managed to slip away before Salvatore could eat him for dinner."

Jagr's brief flare of hope that the night wasn't a total waste was brought to a sharp end. Slaughtering bastards who tormented the weak was one of his few pleasures.

"If the woman was rescued then why do you need me?"

Styx straightened, his bulk consuming a considerable amount of the office space.

"Salvatore's only interest in Regan was installing her as his queen and primary breeder. He is determined to secure his power base by providing a mate who is capable of restoring the purebloods' dwindling population. Unfortunately, once he freed Regan he discovered she was infertile."

"So she was of no use."

"Precisely." The towering Aztec was careful to keep his composure, but even an idiot could sense he wouldn't mind making a snack of the Were king. "That is why he contacted Darcy. He intended to send Regan to Chicago so she could be under my protection until he established her in the local Were pack."

"And?"

"And she managed to escape while he was conferring with the pack master."

Jagr grunted in disgust. "This Salvatore is pathetically inefficient. First he allows the imp to escape and then the woman. It's little wonder the Weres are declining in number."

"Let us hope you are more efficient."

Jagr rose to his feet, his expression cold. "Me?"

"Darcy is concerned for her sister. I want her found and brought to Chicago."

"The woman has made it fairly obvious she doesn't want to come."

"Then it will be your job to convince her."

Jagr narrowed his gaze. He wasn't a damned Mary Poppins. Hell, he would eat Mary Poppins for breakfast.

"Why me?"

"I've already sent several of my best trackers to St. Louis, but you're my finest warrior. If Regan has managed to run into trouble you will be needed to help rescue her."

There were no doubt things worse than chasing after a

genetically altered Were who clearly didn't want to be found, but he couldn't think of one off the top of his head.

In the outer room the sound of a string quartet resumed, along with the soft "ohhs" and "ahhs" of the audience as the dew fairies resumed their delicate dance. Jagr could suddenly think of one thing worse than chasing the Were.

Remaining trapped in this hellhole.

"Why should I do this?" he rasped.

"Because what makes Darcy happy makes me happy." Styx moved until they were nose to nose, his power digging into Jagr's flesh. "Clear enough?"

"Painfully clear."

"Good." Styx stepped back and released his power. Slipping his hand beneath his leather coat he pulled out a cell phone and tossed it to Jagr. "Here. The phone has the numbers of the brothers who are searching for Regan as well as contacts in St. Louis. It also has my private line. Contact me when you find Regan."

Jagr pocketed the phone and headed for the door. There was no point in arguing. Styx was struggling to force the vampires out of their barbaric past, but it wasn't a freaking democracy.

Not even close.

"I will leave within the hour."

"Jagr."

Halting at the door, Jagr turned with a searing fury. "What?"

Styx didn't so much as flinch. "Do not forget for one moment that Regan is precious cargo. If I discover you have left so much as a bruise on her pretty skin you won't be pleased with the consequences."

"So I'm to track down a rabid Were who doesn't want to be found and haul her to Chicago without leaving a mark?"

"Obviously the rumors of your extraordinary intelligence were not exaggerated, my brother."

With a hiss, Jagr turned and stormed through the shattered opening. "I'm not your brother."

Viper monitored Jagr's furious exit with a wary gaze. Actually it hadn't gone as bad as he had feared. No death or mutilation. Not even a maiming.

Always a plus.

Still, he knew Jagr too well. Of all his clansmen, he had always known that the ancient Visigoth was the most feral. Understandable after what he'd endured, but no less dangerous. He was beginning to regret having brought the tortured vampire to Styx's attention.

Slipping past the seated demons who were once again enthralled with the dew fairies, Viper returned to the office, finding Styx staring out the window. "I have a bad feeling about this," he muttered, his gaze taking in his priceless paintings, shattered on the floor.

Styx turned, his arms folded over his chest. "A premonition? Shall I contact the Commission and inform them they have a potential Oracle?"

Viper arched a warning brow. "Only if you want me to lock you in a cell with Levet for the next century."

Styx gave a sharp bark of laughter. "A nice bluff, but Levet has decided that he is the only one capable of tracking Darcy's missing sister. He left for St. Louis as soon as Salvatore informed me that Regan had slipped from his grasp."

"Perfect, now we have two loose cannons charging about Missouri. I'm not sure the natives will survive."

"You believe Jagr is a loose cannon?"

Viper grimaced, recalling the night that Jagr had appeared at his lair requesting asylum. He had encountered any number of lethal demons, most of whom wanted nothing more than to kill him. He'd never, however, until that night, looked into the eyes of another and seen only death.

"I think beneath all that grim control he's a step from slipping into madness."

"And yet you allowed him to become a clansman."

Viper shrugged. "When he petitioned, my first inclination was to refuse. I could sense he was not only dangerously close to the edge, but that he's powerful and aggressive enough to challenge me as clan chief. He's by nature a leader, not a follower."

"So why allow him into Chicago?"

"Because he swore an oath to disappear into his lair and not offer any trouble."

"And?" Styx prodded.

"And I knew he wouldn't survive if he were without the protection of a clan," Viper grudgingly admitted. "We both know that despite your attempts to civilize the vampires, some habits are too deeply ingrained to be easily changed. A rogue vampire with that much power would be seen as a threat to any chief. He would be destroyed."

"So you took mercy."

Viper frowned. He didn't like being thought of as anything but a ruthless bastard. He hadn't become clan chief because of any Dr. Phil sensitivity bullshit. He was leader because the other vampires were scared he'd rip out their undead hearts.

"Not mercy—it was a calculated decision," he growled. "I knew if the need ever arose he would prove an invaluable ally. Of course, I assumed that I would need him as a warrior, not as a babysitter for a young, vulnerable Were. I'm not entirely comfortable sending him on such a mission."

Styx grasped the medallion that always hung about his neck, revealing he was not nearly as confident in his decision as he would have Viper believe.

"I need Regan found, and Jagr has the intelligence and skills that are best suited to track her and keep her safe. And he possesses an even more important quality."

"It can't be his sparking personality."

"No, it's his intimate knowledge of the anguish Regan has suffered." Styx regarded him with a somber expression. "He, better than any of us, will understand what Regan needs now that she has been freed from her tormentor."

More by Bestselling Author

Lori Foster

Romantic Suspense from
Lisa Jackson